INNOCENCE ROAD

TITLES BY LAURA GRIFFIN

STAND-ALONE NOVELS

Far Gone
Last Seen Alone
Vanishing Hour

The Last Close Call
Innocence Road

THE TEXAS MURDER FILES SERIES

Hidden
Flight
Midnight Dunes

Deep Tide
Liar's Point

THE TRACERS SERIES

Untraceable
Unspeakable
Unstoppable
Unforgivable
Snapped
Twisted
Scorched

Exposed
Beyond Limits
Shadow Fall
Deep Dark
At Close Range
Touch of Red
Stone Cold Heart

THE WOLFE SECURITY SERIES

Desperate Girls

Her Deadly Secrets

THE ALPHA CREW SERIES

At the Edge
Edge of Surrender
Cover of Night

Total Control
Alpha Crew: The Mission Begins

THE GLASS SISTERS SERIES

Thread of Fear

Whisper of Warning

THE BORDERLINE SERIES

One Last Breath

One Wrong Step

THE MORENO & HART MYSTERIES, WITH ALLISON BRENNAN

Crash and Burn
Hit and Run

Frosted
Lost and Found

INNOCENCE ROAD

LAURA GRIFFIN

BERKLEY
New York

BERKLEY
An imprint of Penguin Random House LLC
1745 Broadway, New York, NY 10019
penguinrandomhouse.com

Copyright © 2025 by Laura Griffin
Penguin Random House values and supports copyright. Copyright fuels creativity, encourages diverse voices, promotes free speech, and creates a vibrant culture. Thank you for buying an authorized edition of this book and for complying with copyright laws by not reproducing, scanning, or distributing any part of it in any form without permission. You are supporting writers and allowing Penguin Random House to continue to publish books for every reader. Please note that no part of this book may be used or reproduced in any manner for the purpose of training artificial intelligence technologies or systems.

BERKLEY and the BERKLEY & B colophon are registered trademarks of
Penguin Random House LLC.

Library of Congress Cataloging-in-Publication Data
Names: Griffin, Laura, 1973– author.
Title: Innocence road / Laura Griffin.
Description: First edition. | New York: Berkley, 2025.
Identifiers: LCCN 2025016184 (print) | LCCN 2025016185 (ebook) |
ISBN 9780593819319 (hardback) | ISBN 9780593819326 (ebook)
Subjects: LCGFT: Detective and mystery fiction. | Novels.
Classification: LCC PS3607.R54838 I56 2025 (print) |
LCC PS3607.R54838 (ebook) | DDC 813/.6—dc23/eng/20250509
LC record available at https://lccn.loc.gov/2025016184
LC ebook record available at https://lccn.loc.gov/2025016185

Printed in the United States of America
1st Printing

The authorized representative in the EU for product safety and compliance is Penguin Random House Ireland, Morrison Chambers, 32 Nassau Street, Dublin D02 YH68, Ireland, https://eu-contact.penguin.ie.

For Megan and Emily

INNOCENCE ROAD

ONE

Most of all she regretted the drink.

Sour tequila clogged her throat as she stumbled through the desert. The rocks were sharp under her feet, but she kept going, moving through the darkness with her cell phone gripped in her hand.

Something sliced her thigh, and she tripped to the ground. An agave? She scrambled up, clutching the phone like a lifeline. She checked the screen. Still no signal.

Somewhere behind her, an engine groaned. He was getting closer. Glancing over her shoulder, she saw twin white beams bobbing in the distance.

She ran through the blackness, knowing that at any second she could fall off a cliff. How could it be so dark out here? She kept going, ignoring the cramp in her side as her lungs started to burn. Spears of yucca stabbed at her, but she ignored those, too. She had to hide, to make herself invisible. If she could just flatten herself into the ground.

She thought of Jordan's worried face. *Are you sure?*

I'm fine. Really.

Headlights found her, and the world lit up white. Panic took hold, and her breath came in shallow gasps. No escape now. Still she plowed through the brush until her heart wanted to burst.

Then the roar filled her ears. Right on top of her, nowhere left to run. She hunched her shoulders and braced for impact, but the truck veered wide and skidded to a stop.

Everything went still. She didn't move, didn't breathe.

A spotlight hit her face. She blinked at the brightness as fear sucked the air from her lungs. She couldn't see him—only the blinding beam and the glint off the gun barrel.

"You shouldn't have done that." His voice was low and tight. But *calm*.

Jordan was right. He really was crazy.

"Please," she squeaked. "I'm sorry."

No response. Just a soft *click* as he cocked the gun.

TWO

The day Leanne Everhart's life changed forever, she'd been cleaning out the garage.

Not that you could tell. After an hour of heaving paint cans and rearranging junk, she had barely cleared space enough to walk, much less set up a home gym. She was surveying her lack of progress when the call came, and she jumped into her truck without even bothering to lock up. Five minutes later, she pulled off the highway and rolled to a stop behind a patrol car.

Will Akers, twenty-four. Six weeks on the job. Relief filled his young face as she slid from her Chevy and slammed the door. The rookie walked over. His boots were dusty and his desert brown uniform fit snugly over the Kevlar vest.

He gave a crisp nod. "Ma'am."

She managed not to flinch. "What happened?"

"I was getting coffee at around oh ten hundred—"

"Where?"

"The Texaco." He glanced over his shoulder at the dinged white Volkswagen parked ahead of him on the shoulder. "This lady runs in. Said she saw my car and starts telling me how she found this girl. So I called it in and followed her out here."

A woman got out of the VW. Tall, thin. Curly brown hair

twisted up in a knot. She fisted a hand on her hip and shot them a hostile look.

Leanne glanced at Will. "Where exactly?"

"Over there. Right by that bridge."

Leanne turned toward the parched patch of desert, empty for miles except for this narrow highway and a lonely stretch of train tracks. The routes paralleled each other to the east side of town before diverging at the water tower.

A wind whipped up, and Leanne pulled the sides of her flannel shirt together. In jeans and worn sneakers, she was dressed for swatting cobwebs and hosing down rat crap. With her hair yanked back in a messy ponytail, she hardly looked like a senior detective.

Will was watching her now, probably thinking the same thing.

"It's Patty Paulson," she told him.

"What?"

"The lady. That's Patty Paulson. She's an Angel."

He looked blank.

"The Desert Angels," she said. "You know, with the jugs of water."

Leanne glanced at the railroad tracks as dread filled her stomach. Then she studied Will's face. Beads of sweat slid from his temples, and the armpits of his uniform were soaked through, despite the cold.

"You call Izzy?" she asked.

"I haven't—"

"Call her," she said, giving him something easy. "And tape off this perimeter. We need fifty yards in every direction. I've got extra tape in my truck, if you need it."

She set off through the scraggly plants. Her shirt snagged on an ocotillo, and she yanked it free. As she neared the train tracks, her gut tightened. The "bridge" Will had mentioned was really just a few feet of tracks spanning a rocky culvert that today—like most days—was dry as a bone.

Leanne scanned the area, noting the marks in the dirt left by Will's department-issue all-terrain boots. Bits of trash fluttered in the breeze—scraps of plastic that to the untrained eye might look like flowers or butterflies. She paused at a set of tire marks. Deep impressions, wide wheelbase. Pulling out her phone, she snapped a photo before carefully approaching the culvert.

The dark rectangle of shade was a stark contrast to the sun-baked earth. Leanne crouched and took a moment to let her eyes adjust. The smell hit her, rank and pungent, and she was transported back to a sterile autopsy suite with a cohort of green-faced cadets about to lose their breakfast on the tile floor.

Flies buzzed around her head. Clamping a hand over her nose and mouth, Leanne waited for the form to emerge from the shadows.

She noticed the shoulder first—a round protrusion. Then the neck, the chin. As the image came together, Leanne's breath whooshed out.

She was small. Almost childlike.

Leanne scooted closer, startling a beetle that scuttled behind a rock. She searched the ground for more insects. Blinking into the shadows, she made out the bare, splayed legs, the thin arm bent backward at an impossible angle. She forced herself to look at the face—a distorted mask that had once been a person. The side of the skull was crushed, and shards of bone peeked through strands of dark hair. The place where the nose should have been was all torn up, probably from scavengers.

Fighting nausea, Leanne shifted focus to the body, clothed in only a T-shirt that had once been white but was now a dusty gray. She tried to make out the wording across the front, but the fabric was ripped.

Like the arm, the hand was bent at a weird angle, and the skin of the wrist had been gnawed on by something.

Leanne stood up. Shuddering, she glanced at the sky, where a pair of buzzards circled. Back at the highway, Will was rolling out yellow crime scene tape as Patty Paulson looked on and the occasional big-rig truck blew past without slowing.

Leanne looked at the body again, studied the maimed face. A faint ringing sound filled her ears. *This is you. It's yours. No going back now.*

She realized her phone was chiming. She dug it from her pocket and checked the screen.

"Everhart."

"You there yet?" the chief asked.

"I'm here." She turned north, so their conversation would be lost on the wind.

"What do we got?"

She took a deep breath. "Young female. Teens to twenties, I'd say."

"Dehydration?"

"No."

Jim McBride muttered a curse. "How long?"

"No idea." She glanced at the buzzards. "A day? Maybe two?"

"Call Isabella," he told her. "Do it direct, no radio."

"We did."

"Get her to photograph everything."

"Roger that." Something blue glinted from an ocotillo branch. Leanne stepped closer to take a look. "There are some tire marks here. I'd like to get a CSI down from county to make a cast."

No response.

Leanne knelt beside the branch. A scrap of blue duct tape was caught on the spines. She glanced around, wishing she had some evidence markers. She stood and waved at Will, but he was busy cordoning off the scene with the yellow spool.

"Chief?"

"It'll take hours to get them there," McBride told her. "There's a jackknifed eighteen-wheeler near Alpine. Everyone's busy."

"Well, you'll see when you get here. I think—"

"Have Isabella get a photo," he said. "And I want you and Akers to do a grid search. I'll send Cooper and Rodriguez out, too. Comb the entire area. Get everything, even if it looks like garbage. Collect whatever you can, and we'll go from there."

"Yes, sir."

"Any press yet?"

"Press? No." The town of Madrone wasn't exactly a sizzling-hot media market. "Nobody but us and the witness who called it in, Patty Paulson."

"Christ."

Leanne didn't comment. The Desert Angels were a thorn in the chief's side for multiple reasons, including that the organization had been founded by his sister-in-law.

"Sir, about the tire marks, I really think—"

"Not happening. We don't have time to wait on county. The ME's people are almost there. Collect what you can and then clear the scene."

Leanne gritted her teeth. Without help from the county crime lab, they had only a part-time CSI who moonlighted as a nature photographer. Izzy was good, but she could only handle so much, and this was a major crime scene.

"Okay, I just texted Cooper, and he's on his way," McBride said. "You guys get that grid search done and get back here. We're having a shit morning, and it's about to get worse, so don't talk to reporters. About anything, understood?"

"I got it."

"No press whatsoever."

"I understand."

The ringing was back in her ears, only louder now. *This is what you wanted.*

"I'm making you the lead on this, Everhart. You got that?"

"Yes, sir."

"This one's all you."

THREE

Madrone was the sort of place where everyone knew everything about everyone, for better or for worse. People looked after one another's homes. Their kids. Their wandering dogs. People waved at intersections and drove through town without using a turn signal, because what was the point if everyone knew where you were going? Having grown up in Madrone, Leanne was accustomed to the inherent intrusiveness of life in a small town. She hadn't minded so much as a kid, but eight years in Dallas had shown her the allure of privacy and the life-altering freedom of being able to shop for groceries without someone peering over your shoulder.

"Thanks, Bip." Leanne collected her sixteen-ounce coffee as Bernhard Nielson, aka Bip, slid two packets of sugar across the counter.

"I heard about the gal out by the tracks." Bip watched her closely from underneath fuzzy gray eyebrows. "Migrant?"

"We're investigating."

"Coyotes?"

"We're investigating."

One of the eyebrows lifted, a giant caterpillar arching its back. "Say hi to Mel for me." She turned and left the store before Bip could squeeze in any more questions. Nestling her coffee in the cup holder, she pulled out of the parking lot and dialed Josh Cooper.

"Where are you?" she asked when the detective picked up.

"The station. I just pulled in and—"

"Is Izzy there?"

"I thought she was with you. Aren't you still at the scene?"

"I had to run up to county and drop off something. I thought she'd be there by now."

"It's just me and Rodriguez. Akers is back on patrol, and the chief is in his office with the door closed."

Leanne slurped the coffee, scalding the roof of her mouth.

"Crap!"

"What?"

"Nothing. Hey, if you see Izzy, could you tell her not to go anywhere? I'm on my way," she said.

"Roger that."

Leanne tapped the brakes at an intersection, scanning the sidewalks along Main Street. The cafés and shops were busier than usual as stragglers wrapped up their weekends before heading back to Austin and Santa Fe in their fancy SUVs. January was high season for Big Bend National Park, and Madrone had seen a boom in tourism in recent years as they diverted some of the visitors bound for Marfa and Alpine on their way to the park. Madrone was an up-and-coming travel destination, but it hadn't quite found its groove yet. It didn't have Alpine's university or Marfa's art-scene vibe. But the town's railroad museum, coupled with its quaint adobe bungalows, gave Madrone a burgeoning charm of its own. Plus, the craggy red canyons nearby had attracted some of the artists and nature lovers who'd been priced out of Marfa as rents skyrocketed.

Leanne slammed on the brakes as a cyclist cut her off. Yet another thing they'd managed to steal from Marfa—an abundance of mountain bikers who took over their roads every weekend.

It wasn't only tourists in town today. Two men in slacks and dress shirts stood in front of the chamber of commerce. And the woman in line behind Leanne at the gas station had been wearing a black pantsuit and full makeup. Reporters, all of them—she would bet her badge on it.

As Leanne pulled into the police station parking lot, her stomach started to churn, and not because she was on her third cup of coffee. She grabbed her cardboard cup, along with a thick brown accordion file, and headed for the low brick building that housed the Madrone Police Department.

The station house was the same chilly temperature as outside. Leanne made eye contact with Nadine, who was on the phone in her usual weekday spot even though it was three o'clock on a Sunday. Her extra-tall blond hair told Leanne the receptionist had come here straight from church.

"He in?" Leanne asked.

Nadine covered the phone with her hand. "He's looking for you. He's in a meeting, though." She craned her neck to peer through the plexiglass window that divided the reception room from the bullpen. "Door's closed, so you'd better wait."

"Thanks. Heater out again?"

"You betcha."

Nadine returned to her phone call, and Leanne noticed the stack of pink message slips at her elbow. She pushed through the door to the bullpen.

The department's newest detective, Mark Rodriguez, sat pecking away at his computer, no doubt typing the first of many reports that would result from this morning's discovery. Leanne wended her way through the sea of cubicles and dropped her accordion file on her desk, which was already piled with paperwork.

She'd planned to spend part of her Monday catching up, but that wouldn't be happening now.

"Leanne."

She turned to see Josh coming at her like a missile. "Hey, Coop. What's up?"

He stopped in front of her and glared down, hands on hips. Like her, he was in flannel and jeans today, but he wore shit-kickers, too, and she figured he'd been helping his dad around the ranch when he got this morning's call.

"You seen the chief?" he asked.

"No. Why?"

Josh glanced over her head at Chief McBride's closed office door. "He's in there with Novak."

She took a moment to digest that. "As in the district attorney?"

"Yep."

She looked at the door again, which normally stood open. The chief talking to the DA this early in the investigation was a surprisingly good sign. She'd felt like he was blowing her off earlier when he hadn't bothered to come to the crime scene, but maybe she'd misread things.

"Something's up," Josh said. "They've been in there almost an hour."

Leanne spied a New York Yankees cap peeking up from a cubicle.

"Izzy's here?"

Josh followed her gaze. "Yeah, she just got in."

Leanne cut through the bullpen to one of the unassigned computers, where Izzy and other part-timers worked.

"Hey."

The CSI glanced up. Chunks of purple hair stuck out from beneath her baseball cap, and her cheeks were sunburned. Leanne had offered her sunblock back at the scene, but she'd been too intent on her work to take any.

"I'm just getting started." Izzy pivoted the screen, and Leanne saw that she was uploading more than three hundred images. "I'm about halfway through. Everything's high-res, so it takes a while."

Leanne leaned closer to study the thumbnail images as they appeared. "You got the hands, right?"

"I got everything."

Her tone caught Leanne's attention. Izzy's brown eyes looked somber. She was in her first year as a CSI—a job she'd trained for after realizing that her passion for nature photography wasn't enough to pay the bills. Izzy had a degree from NYU and, like Leanne, had spent her early twenties as far away as she could get from her sleepy hometown. But—also like Leanne—circumstances had pulled her back.

Izzy's forensic photography work showed promise, but at the moment she looked shell-shocked. A violent death scene would do that. Leanne had wrestled with thoughts of quitting after her first homicide, but she'd stuck it out and learned to compartmentalize. She hoped to hell Izzy wasn't thinking of leaving. The department desperately needed her.

Izzy turned to the computer. "Some of these shots are . . . pretty disturbing."

"I know."

Izzy shook her head. "What is it about the hand, exactly?"

"There was some kind of mark on the wrist. I couldn't really see in the shadows of the culvert, but I thought maybe a tattoo?" Leanne leaned closer to the screen as Izzy tapped open a photo. "I'm talking to the nearby sheriff's offices, trying to run down MP files."

A close-up shot of the victim's wrist filled the screen, and once again the angle of the hand gave Leanne a jolt. Had the killer snapped the victim's wrist? Was it a defensive injury? Leanne had been thinking about that wrist all day, and she hoped the victim had put up a fight.

"MP files?"

She looked at Izzy. "Missing person cases. So far, no matches, but a tattoo might help."

Izzy enlarged the image and tipped her head to the side. "I don't know. It's pretty hard to tell with all the skin damage. You'll have to talk to the medical examiner."

"Everhart."

Leanne glanced up. The chief stood in the door to his office, motioning her over. She crossed the bullpen.

Jim McBride was fifty-eight, bald, and had the heavyset build of a man who'd spent the past four decades ignoring medical advice. He liked fried food and bourbon and kept a carton of cigarettes in his desk because his wife threw out his packs whenever she found them at home.

"You clear the scene?" he asked.

"Yes, sir."

McBride ushered her into his office, where Trey Novak sat in one of two visitors' chairs. The signature gray Stetson that the Chisos County DA wore for his campaign posters sat brim up on his lap.

"Leanne," he said with a nod.

She nodded back. "Hello."

McBride closed the door behind her, and her sense of foreboding ratcheted up. The last time she'd had a closed-door meeting with the chief, he'd informed her that her brother had been arrested, this time in Alpine.

The chief sat on the edge of his desk and looked her over, making her wish she'd taken the time to go home and change clothes instead of buying coffee.

"Tell me about the crime scene," he said.

God, where to start?

"Well." She took a deep breath. "The victim's face was smashed in. She had multiple broken bones. Given the state of her clothes, I'd say sexual assault is a strong possibility."

"Hispanic?" the DA asked.

"That's undetermined. The body was in rough shape."

Novak and McBride traded looks.

"We found tire tracks, as I mentioned," she continued. "Also, a scrap of duct tape near the body. I've reached out to the sheriff's offices in the tri-county area, and so far, no MP report that matches. I'm working on a more detailed description, so—"

"What about debris?" the chief asked. "Trash? Clothing? Water jugs?"

"We collected some empty water bottles and soda cans. Plus, some food wrappers, that sort of thing."

"And the carpet?"

"Sir?"

"Carpet squares." McBride grabbed the cell phone off his desk and held it up. "Akers sent me pictures. He said you found two at the scene?"

"That's correct."

Shoes taped with carpet squares were sometimes used by coyotes to hide their tracks from border agents as they took people across the desert.

"So, sounds like she was a migrant, likely killed by her trafficker," the chief said.

"I don't know that we can jump to that yet, sir."

"No? The water bottles, the food trash, the carpet squares. Seems pretty evident what happened."

"Well, the carpet pieces were recovered a good ways from the body. About forty yards, I'd say?" She glanced at Novak. "It's not clear they're connected to whatever happened to this woman. And they could have been out there a while. I'd want to hear from the ME about time of death."

McBride nodded. "Right. We will. Anyway, there's something else I need to talk to you about."

The knot in Leanne's stomach tightened. Something besides the hours-old homicide case that he'd just put her in charge of? What could possibly take priority over that?

She glanced at Novak, but his handsome face gave nothing away.

"I got a call from Judge Hausmann early this morning," the chief said.

Hausmann. Hausmann. Leanne scrambled to place the name but drew a blank.

"Sean Moriarty is out of prison."

That name she knew, and it hit her like a slap.

"Sean Moriarty is . . ." She leaned forward as her brain raced to catch up. Had he escaped?

"Got out yesterday after a special hearing," the chief continued. "He's a free man."

Sean Moriarty was in a maximum-security prison in Huntsville serving life without parole. Or he had been.

"But . . . how?" was all she could say.

"New evidence emerged." This from Novak. "His conviction was set aside."

Leanne blinked at the DA. She'd heard something about Sean Moriarty's case a few months ago. But she'd dismissed it. He had made appeals before, and everything had failed. She'd never thought anything would go anywhere.

"What new evidence?" Leanne's palms felt sweaty, and her voice sounded strange. "Like, you mean DNA?"

McBride shook his head. She looked at Novak, the lawyer, who seemed to have a command of the details.

"His new attorney claims it was a coerced confession. Among other issues."

She stared at the DA. A coerced confession would implicate

the entire Madrone Police Department. Every badge in Chisos County had worked that case, including her father.

"That's impossible," she blurted.

"That's reality," Novak said. "It's a done deal. And the blowback's already started, so we need to make a plan to handle it."

She looked at her boss. Jim McBride had been a senior detective when eighteen-year-old Hannah Rawls was killed. The local teen's murder had hit like an earthquake, and their town had been dealing with the aftershocks ever since.

Leanne's mind reeled. She itched to get out her phone and call . . . who? Her mother? Her brother? Given her mom's connections, she probably already knew by now. Any news about Sean Moriarty would spread like a brushfire.

"This is a shock to all of us," the chief said. "Especially the Rawls family. We need you to go talk to them."

She gaped at him. "Me?"

"You're good with people. It's one reason we hired you."

You're female, he meant.

Ever since she'd transferred here from Dallas PD, Leanne had been given way more than her share of touchy-feely assignments. Counseling victims. Interviewing female witnesses. Talking to grieving families. It had been that way in Dallas, too.

Typically, Leanne took the assignments in stride, or at least without complaint. Jim McBride wasn't known for his tact. Leanne wasn't any kind of expert at handling families in crisis, but she was better than the chief. Still, the thought of talking to Hannah's parents made her queasy.

"I really don't think they want to talk to any of us," she told the chief. "Least of all me."

"We need to get ahead of this," Novak said. "That's just basic PR."

PR. Right. Leave it to the elected official to be focused on damage control.

"I've got enough shit right now with all these reporters flapping around like vultures," the chief said. "They're ringing my phone off the hook. Some of the nearby ones are already in town. By tomorrow we'll have them in from Dallas and Houston. They're hunting for quotes and interviews, getting everyone stirred up. And not to mention the fucking lawsuit we'll probably be hit with the minute some slimy lawyer gets hold of this. Forget that this department's damn near broke—we'll never hear the end of it."

"It would be good if you'd go talk to the family," Novak told her. "Calm everyone down. This is a public relations nightmare, and it's best we get out in front of it."

Sure. Like getting out in front of a freight train.

If Sean Moriarty had any kind of case that his confession had been coerced—and presumably he did, or how could he have gotten his conviction overturned?—then there would no doubt be lawyers lining up to sue. Didn't matter that they were a pint-size police department and had practically no budget. The Hannah Rawls murder trial had been big news back in the day. Some lawyer would probably take the case purely for publicity.

Sean Moriarty is a free man.

Leanne stood up. She had to get some air.

"We need you to step up for us," the chief said. "Go talk to the Rawls family."

"And tell them what, exactly?"

"Tell them we have their back. Whatever this is, we'll get to the bottom of it. The case against Moriarty was airtight. We put thousands of man-hours into it. The son of a bitch can sue us, but he won't have a leg to stand on."

Leanne glanced at the DA, who didn't look nearly as convinced. Novak was early forties, if Leanne remembered right. He would have been at the start of his law career when Moriarty's case went to trial. He might not even have been living in the county back then, and he probably had no idea how the murder had rocked their entire town.

Sean Moriarty is a free man.

"Go talk to Trish and Rocky for us," McBride said. "I'm sure all this comes as a blow. Let them know this community is behind them."

Leanne nodded. As if she had a choice.

"And the ME?" she asked.

McBride just looked at her.

"Our homicide case?"

"I'll call over there, see about when the autopsy's scheduled for," the chief said. "Of all the shitty times to have a body turn up. We're crawling with reporters."

"They're distracted with the Moriarty thing," Novak said.

McBride walked over and opened the door, effectively dismissing her.

"Sean Moriarty out of prison." The chief shook his head. "I'm sure as hell glad your dad's not alive to see this."

Leanne halted in the doorway. It was a callous comment, even for him.

The chief ushered her out. "Thanks for stepping up."

Izzy splashed water on her face and looked in the mirror. She just needed to get through the next hour. The next thirty minutes, even. Then she could go home and unravel.

She cupped her hand under the faucet and slurped some water. It was warm and metallic tasting, but she gulped it down to soothe her dry throat. She braced her hands on the sink and closed her eyes. Images of that face came back, and her lunch wanted to come up again.

The bathroom door opened, and she straightened.

"Hey, you all right?" Leanne looked at her in the mirror.

"I'm fine, just . . . a little dehydrated, I think."

Leanne stepped closer, studying Izzy's face with those sharp green eyes that caught every detail. "Want me to get you a Gatorade?"

"I'm good. I've got one at my desk." Izzy grabbed her baseball cap off the sink and settled it on her head.

"Thanks for your work today," Leanne said. "I know it was tough out there."

"I'm fine."

Leanne watched her eyes, probably well aware that she was lying. The woman was a detective. She'd probably picked up on the fact that Izzy wasn't fine at all. She was barely holding it together, and it wasn't just because of the maimed woman she'd just photographed. She looked at Leanne and felt the urge to open up. But letting Leanne Everhart into her problems would only make things worse.

"Death scenes take some getting used to," Leanne said.

"I'm okay." Izzy scooted past her. "Anyway, I need to go finish up."

"Wait."

She stopped, and Leanne looked worried again.

"You sure you're all right?"

"Absolutely."

"You need any help, let me know, okay?"

Izzy nodded. "Of course."

FOUR

The Triple R Ranch was a shadow of its former self, but you wouldn't know it at first glance. The wrought iron arch over the gate was decorated with the ranch's iconic brand—a capital *R* surrounded by a horseshoe. According to local lore, the horseshoe was an allusion to Orville "Lucky" Rawls, who had won the ranch in a poker game back in 1925.

Unfortunately for the Rawls clan, their luck had peaked a century ago. Like so many ranching families, they had been pummeled in recent decades. A combination of drought, business consolidation, and fluctuating cattle prices had left them struggling to get by. The worst luck of all was that, unlike some of their neighbors up near Midland, the Rawls family's swath of land had missed out on the petroleum reserves that had enabled other operations to stay afloat and, in some cases, make an obscene profit. After the most recent drought, the Triple R had sold off half its herd. The land had come next, and now the original twenty thousand acres at the foothills of the Davis Mountains had been whittled down to less than half that.

Still, it was beautiful.

The late-day sun painted the cliffs rose gold as Leanne followed the curved dirt road to the sprawling hacienda. Flanked by live oaks and perched on a hill overlooking a garden of yucca and agave, the house could have been a poster for the mythical ranching culture of West Texas. Four generations had once occupied the home. But since the family had begun taking hunting leases for out-of-towners, the hacienda had been converted to a swank guest lodge outfitted with top-of-the-line smokers and big-screen TVs. Leanne hadn't seen the renovated interior firsthand, but like everyone else in town, she'd looked up the website.

Leanne curved around the lodge and pulled up to a more modest wooden structure that had once been a bunkhouse. She parked beside the black Jeep Wrangler belonging to Trish Rawls. Rocky's silver pickup was nowhere in sight, and Leanne figured the dusty white dually either belonged to Jake Rawls or one of the ranch hands.

She slid from her pickup and wiped her palms on her freshly washed jeans before smoothing her blouse. She'd gone home and dressed up for this, like she would for any visit with a bereaved family. Sixteen years had passed, but the parents of Hannah Rawls were caught in a grief without end.

Leanne glanced around as she approached the house. She'd been here once before, maybe age six or seven? It was back in the heyday when the Rawls family had thrown lavish Fourth of July picnics. At this particular party, they'd had a mariachi band, homemade ice cream, and big silver horse troughs filled with cold beer and soft drinks, free for the taking. Leanne remembered the overflowing picnic tables and trays of mini sausages with American-flag toothpicks sticking up from each one.

Those were the days when her dad had been moving up the ranks in county politics, possibly with an eye toward running for sheriff. Her dad was well-known in law enforcement circles, and back then Rocky Rawls had been an ally of her father, maybe even a friend.

But Hannah's death had turned everything on its head.

The slats creaked under Leanne's ankle boots as she mounted the stairs to the wraparound porch. A wooden swing swayed in the cold breeze. A pair of plastic clogs caked with something—cow manure, from the smell of it—sat abandoned by the welcome mat.

In the center of the door was a heavy knocker made from a horseshoe, and beside the door was a Google doorbell. Leanne eyed them both, debating, and then opted for technology. Within seconds of her ringing the bell, the door swung open.

A young girl stared up at her. She wore purple glasses and a pink leotard with a glittery star on the front. With her blond ringlets and doe eyes, she looked amazingly like Hannah Rawls as a child.

She had to be Jake's daughter. Emily? Amanda?

"You must be Amelia," Leanne said.

She looked patiently up at her visitor. "Yes?"

"I'm here to see your grandmother. Is she in?"

Amelia nudged the glasses up the bridge of her nose. "She's in the greenhouse. You can go around back if you want."

"Thank you." Leanne smiled and turned to go. She felt the girl's gaze follow her as she tromped down the steps and around the house.

Leanne passed a tangle of pipes and irrigation tubes on her way to the glass door. The greenhouse was a serious operation, and Trish sold her peppers and heirloom tomatoes to grocery stores throughout the area. Delivering produce was one of the few errands that kept her in touch with townspeople. The family's lavish barbecues—like so many other traditions—had come to an abrupt end the summer Hannah was killed.

Leanne knocked lightly before walking in. In contrast to the chilly outdoors, the greenhouse felt like a balmy seventy degrees.

Across the rows of leafy plants, she spotted Trish Rawls. She wore a plaid flannel shirt over black leggings, and her once-brown hair was streaked with gray.

Trish looked up, a pair of shears in her gloved hand. She wiped her brow with her sleeve.

"I was wondering when y'all would show up."

Leanne approached her and gave a nod. "Mrs. Rawls."

She fisted her hand on her hip. "Don't know why I expected Jim. That man never did have any balls."

Leanne stopped in front of her. "So . . . I take it you heard about Sean Moriarty?"

She flinched at the name—just slightly, but Leanne caught it. "I did."

She turned her back on Leanne and walked toward a big metal sink at the end of the row. Leanne followed and stood there as Trish rinsed her shears.

"I'm sure it must have been a shock," Leanne said to her back. "We wanted to see if there was anything we could do for you or your family."

She whirled around, her blue eyes flashing. "Like what? Reopen the case?"

Leanne groped for something to say. She'd known this conversation wouldn't go well, and she wished she'd had more time to prepare.

"He got his conviction thrown out," Trish said. "He had to have something." She tossed her shears into a bucket beside the sink. "Something more than a fancy lawyer."

Leanne resisted the urge to shift on her feet. "I don't know all the details yet. But despite this development, the chief believes the core case against Moriarty is airtight."

Trish glared. Leanne remained still. Tension crackled between them, and Leanne found herself in a staring contest.

"Grandma?"

They turned to see Amelia standing at the side door.

"What is it, hon?"

The girl cast a wary look from Leanne to her grandmother. "Can I have my iPad now?"

"No, you may not. There's a jug of tea in the kitchen. Take it out to your daddy and Grandpop. Then you may have your iPad."

Amelia slipped out, letting the door slap shut behind her.

Leanne turned to Trish again. Her cheeks were gaunt, and her sunbrowned skin was wrinkled well beyond her fifty-nine years.

"You know." She tugged off her gloves, one finger at a time. "My husband has sources. Rocky knows every last thing there is to know about the case." She dropped the gloves into the bucket with the shears. "He read every report."

Leanne watched her eyes. The implication was that Trish had not. And Leanne didn't blame her. She had never read the Hannah Rawls case file, but she had heard enough to know that the paperwork—particularly the autopsy report—would have been horrific.

Leanne cleared her throat. "On behalf of the department, I would like you to know that if there is anything we can do for your family—"

"I hear he's coming back," Trish cut in.

Who? Leanne almost said.

"Where did you hear that?" she asked instead.

"I have sources, too." Trish looked out the window and sighed quietly. "I haven't told Rocky and Jake that, though."

The anger seemed to have left her, and she looked deflated now, staring through the glass at the dusty landscape.

Leanne watched her, unsure what to say. She was pretty sure Madrone, Texas, was the very last place Sean Moriarty would come within hours of gaining his freedom. But she didn't want to make phony reassurances.

Trish turned to Leanne, her expression sharp again. "I

appreciate the house call, but tell Jim he can save his sympathy. We don't want it."

"I understand."

Trish lifted an eyebrow, and Leanne turned to go. She'd known this visit would be a waste of time.

"There is one thing you can do for me."

She turned around, and Trish folded her arms over her chest.

"When you see Sean Moriarty, you tell him to steer clear of my husband if he values his life."

Leanne shook her head. "A threat like that . . . is not something you should say in front of a police officer."

"That's not a threat. It's a fact," Trish said. "If Rocky sees that man, he'll break his neck."

FIVE

Leanne sped down the highway as the last glimmer of daylight faded over the mountains.

"What's this shit about the autopsy being at noon?"

Josh sighed on the other end of the phone. "No idea. All I heard is that it's tomorrow."

"It should have been tomorrow morning at the latest. What else have they got going? This is clearly a homicide."

"I don't know. Maybe they're backed up," Josh said. "Listen, about that tire cast you made. I hear it's a no-go."

"Says who?"

"McBride."

When the chief had refused to call a CSI down from county, Leanne had hauled the evidence kit from the back of her truck and made the plaster cast herself.

"He wouldn't let me send it in, says we don't have the budget," Josh told her. "So, it's still sitting here."

"Where are you?"

"The evidence room."

She pictured him in the windowless storage room where they kept evidence dating back to the 1980s. At least he was working late, which was more than she could say for anyone else.

Anger simmered inside her. If a rancher's daughter had been found dead on the side of the road, McBride would have every sworn officer working round the clock.

"He's blowing me off, Coop. Has been since this morning."

"Yeah, well. He's a little distracted. Besides Sean Moriarty, he's dealing with the jackknifed truck thing."

"Why? That's all the way in Alpine."

"Yeah, but one of the injured motorists is from here. Frank Murcheson's nephew. You know Scott?"

"He graduated ahead of me," she said.

"Well, he was in town visiting family, and he was involved in the collision. Now he's in the ICU."

Leanne hadn't heard that. She chalked it up to her being tasked with visiting the Rawls' place when she should have been focused on her homicide case.

Her head throbbed, and she glanced at the clock. Almost seven, and she hadn't eaten anything since the chocolate Pop-Tart she'd had for breakfast.

"I'm heading out," Josh said. "Are you going to the autopsy?"

"Of course."

He didn't offer to join her, and she didn't ask. They didn't both need to be there, and he'd already put in a full Sunday.

"Thanks for the update," she said. "Let's catch up tomorrow."

"Sounds good."

She tossed her phone on the passenger seat as she passed the Texaco where Will Akers had stopped for coffee and gotten word of the body. Less than a mile down the highway was a low-slung building with a neon blue sign out front. On impulse, Leanne pulled in.

She didn't see Duncan Harper's black pickup, but most of the bar's parking was around back. Plus, it was a Sunday during football season, so her odds were good. Leanne swung into a space and cut the engine, then flipped down the mirror. Her eyes looked bloodshot, and her long hair was a stringy mess because she'd been out in the wind earlier. She gave it a quick finger-combing that didn't really help.

Giving up on her looks, she got out and crossed the lot, skimming the rows of cars and luxury trucks with out-of-state plates. More tourists—and a watering hole once known for five-dollar pitchers now sold imported beer and top-shelf cocktails.

Someone exited the bar, and a noisy guitar riff burst out. Leanne sidestepped a pair of laughing young women in miniskirts and heels. She watched for a moment to see if they were steady on their feet before yanking open the door and going inside.

The Javelina was packed tonight. A glance at the TVs above the bar explained why. The Cowboys were playing the Packers, and it was tied. A cacophony of sportscasters and rock music filled the air as Leanne squeezed her way through the crush of warm bodies surrounding the bar.

"Katie."

The bartender glanced up. She had long blond braids and wore her year-round uniform—a white tank top and push-up bra.

"Is Duncan here?" Leanne asked over the din.

"He was." She poured foam off a pint and glanced over her shoulder. "I haven't seen him in a while. Maybe check the back?"

Leanne wove her way through the crowd to the back room, where the three pool tables were occupied. One of the games was all women. The other two were mixed, but no sign of Duncan or any of his friends.

"Well, if it isn't little Miss Everhart."

She turned to see Liam Moriarty eyeing her from the corner. He sauntered over, pool cue in hand. Leanne cast a wary glance around but didn't see Sean.

Liam stopped in front of her and rapped the butt of his cue on the floor. "Looking for someone?"

"Nope."

He stared down at her. She lifted her chin and stared right back. Liam wore a chambray work shirt and jeans. He smelled like sweat, and the dirt-filled creases around his eyes suggested he'd come here straight from a job. Last she'd heard, he worked in the oil fields near Odessa. He didn't live in town anymore—none of the Moriartys did—so what had brought him here tonight?

Liam wobbled his cue back and forth so that it almost grazed her breast. Leanne held her ground.

"You heard about Sean." He leaned his free hand against the wall, boxing her in. "He's out now."

"I'm aware."

He leaned closer, and she got a blast of beer breath. "Good thing your dad's rotting in hell already. Saves my brother the trouble."

She didn't respond, and the side of his mouth curved up.

"Your mom's still alive, though." His smirk became a grin. "She still working on her back to pay for your brother's meth habit?"

"You know something, Liam? You reek."

She moved to duck under his arm, and he blocked her with the stick. She grabbed it and jabbed the toe of his boot.

"Fucking bitch," he growled, grabbing it back.

"Hey, hey, hey. Whoa."

Someone pulled Liam away and took the pool cue from him. Justin Carr.

"Let's relax, okay?" Justin glanced at Leanne, then turned to glare at his friend. "Come on, man. What are you doing?"

Everyone in the room was watching them now. Scowling, Liam yanked the pool cue from Justin and walked off. Leanne's heart rate came down as he returned to his game.

Justin looked at her. "You all right?"

"Of course."

He frowned down at her. At six-two, he was nearly a foot taller than she was. She stared up at him, refusing to be intimidated by his muscular build or the disapproving look in his brown eyes. As a seasoned river guide, Justin was accustomed to settling drunken disputes around the campfire.

He rested his hands on his lean hips, and butterflies filled her stomach, but she kept her face carefully blank. Justin was one of the few men from her past who actually seemed more attractive, not less, since she'd moved back home.

Not that she would ever let him know that.

"Come on, Leanne."

She drew back. "Come on, what?"

"You've got a lot of nerve approaching him right now."

Her cheeks warmed with a combination of anger and embarrassment. "Mind your own business, Justin."

"I'm just saying. Give him some space, tonight of all nights. Don't you think you owe him that much?"

"I don't *owe* him anything."

Justin shook his head.

"Not to mention, he's an asshole," she added.

He stepped closer, and she felt his disapproval to the soles of her feet.

"Well, can you blame him? Your dad ruined his brother's life."

Leanne surveyed the glowing white tents as she neared her driveway. Of Desert Star's fifteen campsites, twelve were occupied, judging from the cars. It was a busy Sunday, even for the high season.

Leanne passed a low adobe bungalow decorated with swags of twinkle lights. Pots of bougainvillea lined the path, and a rope of dried chili peppers hung beside the door. Unlike her neighbor's house, Leanne's adobe cottage was dark and uninviting. Her only decoration consisted of a concrete birdbath that had been dry for months.

Leanne parked in the driveway and spied a small blue cooler by the front door. She scooped it up on her way inside the drafty house. After setting it on the table, she switched on the heating unit, which rattled and creaked before emitting a puff of air.

Her phone chimed, and she checked the screen. Michelle.

"Hey, thanks for dinner," Leanne said.

"Sure thing. We had extra."

Leanne opened the cooler, and the oniony scent of barbecue wafted out. She picked up a warm, foil-wrapped bundle.

"Any problems tonight?" Leanne asked.

"Nope. We're almost full, but it's been pretty quiet."

Quiet was good. Leanne didn't enjoy getting up in the middle of the night to deal with unruly tourists—drunk, high, or otherwise. She got enough of that in her day job.

Michelle owned the Desert Star Campground, and she and Leanne had an informal arrangement. In exchange for the occasional meal delivery, Leanne helped keep an eye on things when she happened to be home.

"This smells amazing," Leanne said now, unwrapping the sandwich. "Pulled chicken?"

"Carnitas."

She chomped into the warm bun stuffed with spicy meat. She closed her eyes and moaned.

"Oh my God."

"Thanks," Michelle said. "Hey, one thing. The lady in Nine told me that she came back from a hike, and now she thinks her laptop is missing."

"She thinks?"

"She's not sure. Says she may have left it at her office in Houston. But she wanted me to know just in case something turns up. Super annoying, I know."

"Does she want to file a report or not?"

"For now, no. She's going to ask someone to check if it's at her office, then get back to me tomorrow."

Leanne grabbed a bottle of water from the fridge.

"So, is it true they found a body out by the tracks?" Michelle asked.

"It is."

"God, that's awful. Was it an accident?'

"I can't talk about it."

"That means no." Michelle sighed. "I'm sorry. You must have had a long day. I'll let you go."

"Thanks."

"Forget about the lady in Nine. If she wants to report it, I'll send her to the station. I'm guessing you'll be up early?"

"Yup."

"Night, then."

Leanne stood at her kitchen sink, staring out the window as she savored the last few sticky bites of meat. Several tents went dark as people called it a night.

The Desert Star "Campground" was really a misnomer. Michelle's glamping operation consisted of fifteen canvas-sided huts elevated off the ground on wooden platforms. The units came equipped with hot showers, toilets, electricity, and phone chargers. For these people, roughing it meant walking fifty yards to a giant yurt, where they could purchase lattes and breakfast tacos, along with a rotating dinner menu that inclued craft beer and wine pairings.

The central yurt went dark as Michelle shut down for the night. Leanne continued to stare out her window, swigging water as she watched her friend's black silhouette tromp across the grounds to her house.

A clattering noise outside caught her attention. She walked to the back door and switched on the porch light, but nothing happened. The bulb was out. Leanne stepped onto the concrete patio and looked out. She and Michelle were at the rear of the twenty-acre property, backing up to what had once been a working ranch but was now a dusty wedge of land dotted with sotol and prickly pear. A steep mesa rose in the distance, a black line against the purplish night sky.

Unlike Michelle's carefully cultivated yard, Leanne's consisted of a couple of weedy beds. The previous tenant had left behind a plastic chaise lounge, and Leanne sometimes used it on the rare occasions when she allowed herself to sit under the stars and think. But those nights were few and far between, especially since the tourist season had ramped up.

Leanne eyed the row of tents in the distance. All but three were dark now, including Nine. She pulled the door shut behind her and ventured out into the campground, surveying the barbed-wire fence as she went. The fence had gaps in places, and it wasn't much of a deterrent for trespassers of the animal or human variety. Michelle had signs posted all over about locking cars and securing valuables, but people were careless on vacation, and electronics had a way of disappearing.

Snick.

Leanne whirled around. A shadow moved in the brush. She took the mini Maglite from her pocket. Aiming it at the noise, she illuminated a spiny hechtia.

Snick.

Turning, she scanned the ground. An armadillo darted behind a cactus.

She switched off her light and traipsed back to the house. When she reached the doorstep, her path was blocked by a skinny white cat.

"Hey, Gus."

He blinked up at her. One of his ears was torn, which gave him an advantage when begging for handouts.

"Don't give me that look. You ate already." She opened the door and waited for him to go inside. He belonged to Michelle, but he slept wherever he could find the warmest bed. He sniffed the air for a moment before sashaying off into the yard.

Leanne gazed out at the darkened landscape. The throbbing at the base of her head was back again, stronger now. Her muscles felt heavy, but she knew she wouldn't sleep. She'd be up roaming. Or worse, staring at the ceiling, thinking of the crushed skull and mutilated face. That was someone's daughter, someone's child, left out there to rot and get feasted on by scavengers.

This one's all you.

Leanne looked up at the sky and felt a pang so strong it took her breath away. Her eyes burned. If only her dad were here to talk it through.

She stopped the thoughts before they could spiral. It didn't matter.

And anyway, if her dad were here, she wouldn't be. His death had sucked her back home. That and her dysfunctional family. But her dad's death was the catalyst, the thing that had thrown everything into chaos, and sometimes she resented him so much it was a white-hot coal in the center of her chest.

She closed her eyes and took a deep breath. She needed a shower and a good night's sleep. She needed a drink, too, but she knew that wouldn't help.

She looked at her phone as the craving set in. It slid into her mind and made its way down, prickling nerve endings along the way. It had been twenty-nine days, almost a month. Her thumb started to move, scrolling, scrolling.

This won't help, either.

Her brain knew that, but her fingers didn't. She tapped out a message.

> RU up?

She stared down at the screen, waiting.

"Come on," she murmured.

A gray bubble popped up, and she held her breath. Then a word appeared.

> Yes.

Her breath whooshed out. A heady combination of relief and excitement filled her, and her pulse started to thrum.

> I'm working though.

Leanne blinked down at the words. For the second time tonight, she felt a flush of embarrassment. She squeezed her eyes closed. Twenty-nine days, blown. Some New Year's resolution that was.

She tapped out another message and pocketed her phone. Then she went inside her house and locked the door.

"I got her."

Silence.

"You there?" Max held his phone in his hand, waiting for a response. In the background he heard highway noise, and he pictured his boss at a motel somewhere, probably trying to get laid.

"Yeah, copy," he finally responded. "Is she alone?"

"Yes."

Max stared at the little adobe house and waited. Patience was both a skill and a weapon, one that he'd honed to a sharp edge over the years. But right now patience was a challenge, even for him.

A light went on at the side of the house. The bathroom. It had a pocket door leading to the bedroom in back, the one where she slept. The front bedroom was full of moving boxes.

"She's getting ready for bed," Max said.

"Wait until tomorrow."

"You sure? I can—"

"Not tonight. Wait."

Max gritted his teeth. Tonight was better. She was alone, and he was ready. They had a limited window, and it was closing.

"Tomorrow, Max. You copy? We can't afford to get this wrong."

SIX

The train blew through nightly with a piercing horn that rattled windows and set the coyotes howling throughout the canyon.

The humans slept through it. Or at least, the locals did. Tourists who stayed near the railroad tracks were likely to bolt upright in bed and curse the noise. Leanne was immune to it, and even after years away, the sound of more than six thousand tons of metal and freight roaring through town at two thirty A.M. didn't cost her a wink of sleep.

With the exception of last night.

Leanne leaned against the door of her unmarked police unit, swigging coffee as she stared at the train tracks. The crime scene had been cleared yesterday, but she could still see the tire marks from the half dozen emergency vehicles that had converged on the culvert. And then there were the countless other tracks that had come later, as word spread about the body and people gave in to the morbid impulse to come see for themselves.

"Any update on those printouts?" Leanne asked Izzy over the phone.

"I left everything on your desk."

"Everything?"

"Yep. I left a batch for the chief, too, but he wasn't in yet. Where are you?"

Leanne checked her watch. "On my way to the autopsy."

Izzy made a low grunt, which Leanne took to mean she didn't want to trade places.

"Good luck. I hope you get what you need," Izzy said.

"Thanks. And for the printouts, too. Makes life easier."

"No problem. Let me know if there's anything more I can do."

Leanne ended the call and trekked over to the train tracks. Yesterday, the tire marks had made her jump to the conclusion that the victim had been driven out here and either killed on the spot or killed beforehand and dumped near the culvert. But last night, for the first time since Leanne could remember, she'd been jarred awake by the train. She'd lain there in bed, picturing the crime scene as her brain sparked with a new possibility.

The victim could have been thrown from the train. In the middle of the night, no witnesses. On the outskirts of town, where no one would see or hear or smell, except for the scavengers. Clearly, the body had been mutilated. Maybe it had been dragged, too, and ended up in that culvert because of animal activity.

From the killer's perspective, it wasn't a bad plan. If, as everyone seemed to assume, the victim *had* been a migrant, maybe she'd been hitching a ride on that train when someone killed her, and maybe that person threw her off under cover of darkness, leaving the body, and any evidence that was on it, to decompose in the desert.

The idea of this young woman being heaved from a train barreling through town was no less horrible than the victim being murdered in town and then dumped by the tracks. It was horrible no matter what. *Disturbing*, as Izzy had said. But the two scenarios were very different in terms of how Leanne needed to investigate.

Gravel crunched behind her, and she turned around to see a familiar Volkswagen rolling to a stop on the shoulder. Patty Paulson got out. Her curly hair was up again, and today she wore a blue Desert Angels T-shirt.

Leanne returned to her car as Patty walked over and peeled off her sunglasses.

"It's good to see you back," Patty said.

"I'm just going over some things."

"No, I mean back home. I figured you were gone for good once Dallas got its claws in you."

There was an edge in her voice. Plenty of locals resented that Leanne had moved to a big city, and they weren't shy about letting her know it.

Patty looked out at the culvert where she'd found the body while leaving jugs at a water station.

"She's not the first." Patty nodded at the tracks. "There have been others."

"Others who?"

"Who knows? Girls raped and beaten to death, left out here to rot. They don't wear name tags."

"How do you know?"

"You hear things." Patty leveled a look at her. "Do your job, Leanne. Don't let him intimidate you."

A chill swept over her. She was talking about the chief.

"He's a bully," Patty said. "Always has been."

Leanne didn't disagree. But she wasn't about to bad-mouth her boss to someone. Especially not his sister-in-law, who considered it her Christian duty to help stave off death and dehydration in the desert.

The chief saw *his* duty very differently.

Patty slid on her sunglasses and tromped back to her car. A

knot formed in Leanne's stomach as she watched her drive away. She took one last look at the culvert before sliding behind the wheel and pulling onto the highway.

She's not the first.

Leanne knew that. People died out here all the time.

But this time was different. Leanne had felt it since she first saw that crime scene—something called to her about it. She hadn't pinpointed it yet, but she *would*. Despite whatever Patty thought, Leanne wasn't intimidated by the chief. But she wasn't careless, either, and she had to be strategic. Underneath McBride's good-old-boy persona, he was smart. And he knew how to work the system to get things done, so she needed him as an ally.

Leanne ran through what she had and didn't have as she drove to Chisos.

One, still no missing person report that matched the victim, not in Chisos County or any others nearby. Two, no clear tattoos or identifying marks, but Leanne was hoping the ME would find something at the autopsy. Three, the question of sexual assault. The ME could probably make a preliminary determination during the exam and maybe even recover a DNA sample.

By the time Leanne reached Chisos, she had her questions ready and prioritized. She swung into the county justice complex and found an empty space at the back of the lot. They were busy, even for a Monday, and Leanne waited behind two people at the reception desk before signing in and collecting a visitor's badge.

"Third door on the right," the receptionist said with a smile. She was a new hire and had no idea who anyone was. "Then it's down the hall and around to the left."

"Thanks," Leanne said, clipping the badge to her jacket.

As opposed to yesterday, Leanne was in her usual cold-weather detective uniform—a button-down shirt, jeans, and a black leather jacket that concealed her holster. She walked down the long white corridor, which smelled of industrial cleaning solution. The third door on the right swung open as she reached it.

"Hey." Leanne pulled back, startled. "What are you doing here?"

Mark Rodriguez stepped into the hallway. "What do you mean?"

"I didn't know you were coming."

His black eyebrows tipped up. "Well, yeah. I mean, the chief said—"

"McBride sent you?" Her gaze sharpened. "Why? I told him I'd cover it."

The junior detective flushed, clearly uncomfortable. "Well, he told me to be here, so I figured you were busy." He tucked his hands into his pockets. "Anyway, I didn't mind."

Leanne blinked at him. "You *didn't* mind? You mean, it's already happened?"

"Uh . . . yeah. He started at nine." Rodriguez looked down at his watch. "It took about three hours."

"Son of a bitch." Leanne turned away, pulling her phone from her pocket.

"Is there something—"

"Forget it," she said over her shoulder. "I'll take it up with the chief."

She stalked over to the water fountain alcove. She waited through four rings, but the call went to voicemail. She tried the main line.

"Madrone Police Department. How may—"

"Nadine, it's Leanne. Is the chief in?"

"No, you just missed him. He said he'd be out most of the afternoon."

She bit back a curse.

"You want to leave a message?"

"No. Thanks. I'll catch up with him later."

Leanne hung up and closed her eyes. She took a deep breath. Then she turned back toward the hallway where Rodriguez was still standing.

"I didn't mean to step on toes," he said. "But the chief said you were busy, so—"

"Thank you. Not your fault. Is Korbin still back there?"

"I don't know."

Leanne strode past him and pushed through the door. She passed several offices, glancing in windows as she went. As she reached the door to the ME's office, she spied a short man in blue scrubs rounding the corner.

"Doctor?" She jogged after him. He wore a red do-rag on his otherwise bald head, and she knew it was him. "Dr. Korbin?"

He turned around, his hand on the door to the men's room.

"Sorry to bother you, but—"

"Something you need, Detective?"

"Yes." She glanced at the door. "But it can wait."

"What is it?"

She cleared her throat. "I'm the lead investigator on the Jane Doe case. The victim you just examined? I was told the autopsy was scheduled for noon."

"I moved it." He folded his arms over his chest. "At the request of your department."

"I wasn't informed. I had planned to be there."

A toilet flushed, and she glanced around, wishing they weren't having this conversation outside the bathroom.

"I really need—"

The door opened, interrupting her plea. Leanne stepped out of the way as a sheriff's deputy squeezed between them.

"Come with me," Korbin said.

She followed the pathologist down the hall and through a set of double glass doors into a waiting area furnished with gray plastic chairs. He led her into a narrow conference room with a table in the center.

"Have a seat."

"Thank you."

Leanne sat down as he left the room. She checked her phone to see if she'd missed a call from McBride or anyone else. Nothing. Her last text was an exchange with Izzy about the crime scene photographs.

Leanne pictured Izzy's blanched face when she'd bumped into her in the bathroom yesterday. She hoped Izzy wasn't second-guessing her career choice. Besides Nadine at reception, Leanne and Izzy were the only women at MPD. And Leanne was the sole woman with a badge, which meant that she was constantly on a mission to prove herself.

Despite having a solid reputation with her department in Dallas, Leanne had no illusions about how she'd landed this job. McBride would have preferred someone who wasn't a literal lightweight, someone who looked the part of a take-no-shit border cop. But pressure to hire at least a token female, plus the weight of her father's legacy, had forced the chief's hand. If not for those two factors, though, Leanne had no doubt McBride would have hired a man.

But whatever. She didn't like to dwell on how she'd gotten here or the weight of her dad's reputation around this town. She wanted to focus on her job and let her work speak for itself.

"Water?"

She glanced up as Korbin returned. His do-rag was gone, and now he had a pair of reading glasses perched on his bald head. He set a water bottle down in front of her and took the chair at the head of the table.

"There was a mix-up with the time. I—"

He held up a hand. "I've only got ten minutes. What are your questions?" He set down a water bottle for himself and opened a manila folder.

"First off, any ID?"

"No. We collected prints, so we'll see if anything comes back."

Leanne took a notepad from her jacket pocket and started writing.

"Manner of death, homicide—as you're obviously aware." He settled the reading glasses on the end of his nose and peered down at the file. "Cause of death, asphyxiation due to manual strangulation."

Her gaze snapped up. "What? I thought—"

"The head trauma occurred postmortem." He nodded down at the paperwork. "And it was extensive. However, she was strangled first. The hyoid was fractured, and I found signs of petechial hemorrhaging."

Leanne made notes in her pad.

"As for other injuries . . ." He skimmed the paper, which showed a black-and-white diagram of a female body with handwritten notes along the sides—presumably made by Korbin's assistant as he conducted the exam. "Fractured right parietal." He glanced up. "The side of her skull was smashed with a heavy object."

"Okay." She jotted it down. "A rock, maybe?"

"I don't think so. I would expect to see grit or dust in the wound. No, this was something smooth, possibly the butt of a pistol. She was bludgeoned after death, in other words."

She stared at him, absorbing the violence of it.

"The same object, in my opinion, was used to inflict additional damage to the torso. Although it's hard to say for sure due to the postmortem animal activity."

Leanne took a deep breath and looked down at her notes.

"Any idea how long she'd been out there?"

"About thirty-six hours. Maybe more."

"So . . . if she was found at ten yesterday morning, we can assume—"

"We can *estimate*," he corrected, "that she had been dead for about a day and a half."

"So, she was killed Friday night."

"Most likely, yes. Postmortem interval is not an exact science."

"Do you have anything to indicate where she was killed?" Leanne asked. "I mean, was it maybe in a car, and she was dumped there? Or maybe she was killed on a train and thrown off? Her body was recovered right by the railroad tracks."

Korbin was shaking his head. "She had abrasions on the heels of both feet, and there was dirt in the wounds. I believe her body was dragged at least a short distance to the place where it was found." He flipped a page in the file. "And finally, a fractured scaphoid." He glanced up. "Her wrist was broken."

"Would that have been a defensive injury?"

"Possibly. Also, multiple abrasions suggest sexual assault. We'll know more when the rape kit comes back."

Leanne took a deep breath. "All right. What about age?"

"Based on the X-rays? I'd say late teens. Early twenties, at the most."

Leanne watched Korbin, trying to read his eyes. He looked haggard, and she didn't know whether it was because of the autopsy he'd just performed or because the last decade as a medical examiner in a border region was taking its toll.

Leanne glanced down at her notepad. She needed his insights now, not next week or next month, when his final report would be ready. Korbin was a busy man and hard to pin down—which was precisely why she had wanted to be present at the autopsy. She still couldn't believe she'd missed it.

"Is there anything else that might help us?" She glanced up. "Maybe a scar, or tattoo, or some other distinguishing mark?"

"She appears to be Hispanic, if that helps. Also, she had a small tattoo on her right wrist."

For the first time all day, Leanne felt a twinge of relief. "A tattoo of what?"

"A butterfly." He shuffled through the file and pulled out a Polaroid. The picture showed a close-up of skin, some of which was ragged and blackened. "The animal activity makes it difficult to see the design, but it's easier with our overhead light."

He slid the Polaroid toward her, and Leanne's chest squeezed. It was a small tattoo, only black ink. There was something so sad, and personal, about the simple feminine design on that torn flesh.

Shitty time to have a body turn up. We're crawling with reporters.

Leanne clenched her teeth. It was beyond callous. McBride made everything about him, as though this young victim had picked an inconvenient week to be strangled.

"You can have that snapshot. My assistant took two." The pathologist checked his watch and closed the folder. "Any other details you need will be in my report."

"Thank you," she said. "I really appreciate this."

"No problem." He pushed back his chair. "Oh, one last thing. The bone."

"What bone?"

"A fragment of bone was recovered at the scene. It looked to me like a deer femur or maybe a small cow. I sent it to the university to be sure. The anthropologist there can confirm. In any event, this victim's legs were intact, so it wasn't associated with her remains."

Leanne made a note in her pad as the doctor stood up.

"Hopefully, the tattoo will help you get an ID." He checked his watch again. "The sooner we have somewhere to release the body, the better. We're short on storage space here, as I'm sure you know."

He turned to leave, and she jumped up.

"One more thing, Doctor. Her clothes? I'm guessing you had them sent to the lab, with the rape kit?"

"My assistant is packing everything up now." He reached for the door. "Exam Room Two. You may be able to catch her if you hurry."

SEVEN

The onslaught had started.

A row of white vans occupied the metered spaces in front of the police station. A pair of television reporters stood at opposite sides of the building talking to cameras, likely recording clips for the five-o'clock news. Leanne recognized the blonde she'd seen at the gas station yesterday, but the other reporter was new. Was she from Austin or Dallas, maybe? Leanne didn't want to get close enough to find out, so she drove around to the back and parked between the dumpsters and the jail entrance. She tapped in her four-digit door code and hurried down the dim hallway, which smelled of vomit and disinfectant.

The booking desk was empty. Same for the his-and-hers jail cells. Leanne passed the break room, ignoring her growling stomach as she made a beeline for the bullpen. She'd skipped breakfast because of the autopsy, and she hadn't had time for lunch. Looking over the sea of cubicles, she saw that McBride's office door was closed again.

She crossed the room and tapped her knuckles on the door. After waiting a few seconds, she leaned her head in. The room was empty, the desk cleared of paperwork. The lingering cigarette smell told her he'd been in at some point in the past few hours.

She closed the door and glanced through the window at the reception room. Nadine was on the phone, and Leanne recognized the reporter with his mop of white hair camped out on the sofa with a laptop perched on his knees. Marty Krause with the *Madrone Sentinel*. He was pecking away at his computer and looked like he was in no hurry to leave—at least not without a quote.

"Hey, Leanne."

She turned to see Mark Rodriguez walking toward her holding a Dairy Queen bag that smelled of warm French fries.

"Hey, you know where the chief is?" she asked.

"No idea. I just got here."

Leanne wended her way back to her desk, where she found a thick manila file folder with her name on a yellow sticky note. She grabbed the folder and darted a glance at the reporter. He hadn't noticed her yet, but Leanne ducked into a conference room just to be safe. She dropped into a chair and began combing through photographs, starting with the wrist picture, which Izzy had thoughtfully placed at the top of the stack.

Leanne dug her phone from her jacket pocket and called her.

"Did you get the file?" Izzy asked.

"I did, thanks. Turns out it's a tattoo of a butterfly," Leanne said. "The ME confirmed it."

"That's good news, right? Any ID yet?"

"No." She flipped through the pictures, trying not to focus on the grisly images as she made her way through the stack. "He also mentioned something about a bone fragment?"

"The deer bone, yeah. I got a picture of it."

"How do you know it's a deer bone?"

"That's what Josh thought it was. He does a lot of hunting, so I figured he'd know."

"Where was this, exactly? I didn't see it."

Leanne paused on a photo of what resembled a broken stick bleached white by the sun. The bone fragment was partly covered by weeds, and Izzy had placed a metal ruler beside it to provide scale.

"This was the far northwest corner of the crime scene," Izzy said. "Over near where we found the empty water jug?"

"I'm looking at the photo now."

"Josh collected it," Izzy went on. "He turned it over to the ME's people, I think. Hey, by the way, is Chief McBride there? I had something to ask him earlier, but he wasn't in."

Leanne glanced at his closed office door again. "No. I haven't seen him all day. Listen, let me let you go. Thanks for the printouts."

"No problem."

Leanne disconnected and called Josh. He answered on the first ring.

"How was the autopsy?" he asked.

"I don't know. I missed it."

"What? Why?"

"McBride sent Rodriguez instead."

"Why didn't—"

"Where are you?" she cut in.

"At the courthouse. I'm supposed to testify this afternoon about that drug bust near Quicksilver Road."

"Have you seen the chief today?"

"No. Why?"

"I need to talk to him about that tire tread I made a cast of. The ME confirmed the victim was *dragged* to that dump site, not thrown from the train."

"Okay. So?"

"So that means we need to track down the vehicle that took her out there. The tire tread could be our best lead."

"I wouldn't hold your breath on that," Josh said. "He's focused on the Moriarty thing. I hear he and Novak are putting together a press conference."

"Why? McBride hates press conferences."

"Why do you think? The shit's hitting the fan. Reporters are coming in from all over the state. They're camped out around the courthouse. We've got a lot to answer for."

"But Novak wasn't even the DA back then. He was fresh out of law school," Leanne said. "And McBride wasn't the chief."

"Yeah, well, he was there. So was your dad," Josh added, as though she needed the reminder. "These reporters are going to want something, and we can't just ignore them. It's a hot story—innocent man gets out of prison and all that."

"That's bullshit, and you know it. Sean Moriarty *confessed*. And her blood was in his car! It's an airtight case."

"That's not what his lawyer said."

Tendrils of fear unfurled inside her. "Where did you see his lawyer?"

"He was on freaking CNN. I'm telling you, Leanne, this thing's blowing up."

"But—"

"Look, I can't get into this now. They're about to call me into court. We'll talk later, okay?"

She got off the phone, fuming.

A hot story.

What about the homicide victim from *yesterday*? Sean Moriarty's trial was fifteen years ago. Of course, in that case the victim was a white girl, so the story would live in infamy, and every reporter in the state wanted a piece of it.

"Hey, I didn't know you were here."

She turned around. Nadine stood in the doorway.

"I snuck in the back," Leanne said.

"Did you get my message? McBride wants an all-hands meeting at four."

"Four today?" Leanne checked her phone. "That's in half an hour. And I need to go to the crime lab before close of business."

Nadine shook her head. "Sorry, but he said no exceptions. Four o'clock sharp, all hands."

EIGHT

Leanne's headlights swept over the limestone ranch house as she curved up the driveway. A light was on in the TV room, and she pictured Boone asleep in his leather recliner. She parked behind his silver Cadillac Escalade and took out her phone.

I'm here, she texted. U home?

She stared down at the screen, but her brother didn't answer. Sighing, she slid from her truck and closed the door with a quiet *click*. The front yard was dark, and the whisper of wind through the oak trees was the only sound.

Walking up the driveway, Leanne passed the limestone guest cottage, which sat empty much of the time. She went around the side of the detached three-car garage and stood on an overturned flowerpot to slide her hand along the top of the doorframe until she found the key. She unlocked the door, then stepped inside and paused for a moment in the cold darkness before turning on the light.

Three spotlights shone down, illuminating her stepfather's pride and joy. In bay one was a 1921 Rolls-Royce Silver Ghost, a near-perfect replica of the one used in *Giant*, which had been filmed down the road near Marfa. In the middle bay was a painstakingly restored 1938 Ford pickup. Bay three held a much more modern vehicle—a Ford F-350 capable of pulling a loaded horse trailer.

The horses were her mom's pride and joy. Her two chestnut mares occupied the stables behind the house, where they were showered with attention daily. Regina Everhart often said that she liked horses more than people, and anyone who knew her understood that she wasn't joking.

Leanne glanced around the garage. The gleaming epoxy floor was cleaner than the one in her kitchen. She slid between the Rolls-Royce and the antique pickup, careful not to scratch the paint with the zipper of her leather jacket.

At the back of the garage was a wooden ladder. Leanne maneuvered it beneath the door to the attic, then climbed the creaky steps and pushed open the hatch. The door stuck, so she gave it a hard shove, and it flopped onto the attic floor with a *whack*.

Dust filled her lungs, making her squint and cough. When the tickle was gone, she groped around for the light switch.

A bare bulb came on, lighting up a space with a plywood floor. Irritation surged through her. A six-thousand-square-foot ranch house, and all her dad's belongings had been relegated to a musty attic not big enough to stand in.

Leanne hitched herself into the cramped space. She grabbed a rafter to pull herself up and stood hunched beneath the sloped ceiling. The tips of roofing nails glinted through the decking, and she ducked lower as she sidestepped boxes of vinyl records and bins of fishing tackle.

Swatting at cobwebs, she approached a row of cardboard boxes, all labeled with her mother's loopy handwriting. Leanne remembered loading the cartons into her mom's car, with the help of some of her dad's friends, on the day her childhood house was sold. It had been two years ago this February, barely two months after Leanne's father was killed in a drunk driving accident. A week after selling the house, her mother married Boone Sullivan.

Even for people who knew about Regina and Boone's affair, it was a shockingly short timeline. For Leanne, it was the blink of an eye.

It was hard not to feel bitter about the marriage, although Leanne tried. Before her mom became Regina Everhart, she'd made a name for herself as Regina Mays, a three-time barrel racing champion. She was a rodeo queen, a local legend, a consummate performer. How hard would it have been for her to play the role of the grieving widow for one short year? Or even six months?

Leanne crouched beside the first box and tipped her head to the side to read her mother's writing. According to the labels, the first two boxes contained tax files. She lifted the lid off the third box. Several folded copies of the *Madrone Sentinel* sat on top. Leanne knew the headlines without even having to look, and she moved the papers aside. Stacks of yellow legal pads stared up at her.

Her dad's notes.

Not his notes from official police interviews—those were preserved with case files and other reports. These notepads contained her dad's to-do lists, which he always kept close at hand. The yellow pads floated between the kitchen table and his truck, and sometimes his workbench in the garage, where he would jot down to-dos that came to him while he was sanding wood or staining a piece of furniture.

So much had been trashed in the move, and Leanne hadn't known whether the lists had made the cut. To see that they had brought a wave of relief. The legal pads were bound by big rubber bands, four and five to a batch. Leanne lifted out the first stack, glimpsing the date at the upper right corner.

She unbundled a notepad, and a sense of calm settled over her as she flipped through page after page of her dad's familiar handwriting. The lists were like a journal of sorts, and if you could decipher the messy script and cryptic abbreviations, they provided insight into her father's life.

Tues 9:30, crime lab—Wayne?
17:00—follo w/ E.M.
Wed. 8:30—MPD mt
14:00 depo @ courthouse—Gonzales
Call R.

Was "R" a reference to her mother? Or was it a professional phone call, something to do with a case he was working on? A case, most likely. Leanne couldn't imagine her father making a note to call his wife in the middle of the afternoon.

Leanne flipped through the pages, skimming through the hours, days, and weeks that made up her dad's life. So much was recorded. So much was not. Page after page devoted to meetings and phone calls and places he intended to be. But not a single line referenced a trip to the liquor store or a detour by Paco's Pub on the way home from work.

She reached the end of the first legal pad and set it aside. Sifting through the bundles, she found a pad from the year Hannah Rawls was murdered.

The year that changed everything.

July Fourth, a normal day, according to the list. Her dad noted a staff meeting, some phone calls, something about the fire department—likely related to the fireworks display scheduled for that night.

July fifth, nothing.

July sixth, nothing.

July seventh, nothing.

Those days were a frantic blur, but even all these years later, the details were engraved on Leanne's brain. She'd been fifteen that summer and had just started her first real job working the concession window at the town pool. Fourth of July had been packed until dusk, and she'd come straight home from work and crashed, only to be awakened at three in the morning when someone showed up at the house looking for her father. Leanne remembered her dad putting on his boots and leaving. She remembered the steady stream of cops tromping through their back door for days, and the endless pots of coffee her mom kept brewing in the kitchen. She remembered the TV reporters, the press conferences, the pleas for help from the public. After three and a half days of searching, aided by law enforcement agencies from far and wide, the search came to an end when Hannah's body was found at the bottom of an abandoned well. She'd been beaten and strangled.

The day after Hannah's body was discovered, Lee Everhart's notes resumed.

> 7:00 ME, mt w/ Syd
> 11:30 Sher. Off.—all hands
> 13:00 presser?
> Follo w/ ME—prelim rp?
> Call crime lab—tox screen,
> Vic clothing—white powder?
> 15:00 MPD—all hands
> 16:30—presser—dress unif

The note about the press conference preceded a list of phone calls that went on for two pages, followed by several weeks' worth of detailed to-do lists. Paper-clipped to the final yellow page was a business card for Dark Sky Gallery. The address was in Marfa, but Leanne had never heard of the place. Not that she knew much about the Marfa art scene, but she'd at least been to a few galleries. She unclipped the card and flipped it over. A seven-digit number was written on the back.

"What on *earth*?"

She jumped at her mother's voice.

"Is that you, Leanne?"

"It's me."

The ladder creaked as her mom mounted the rungs and poked her head through the hatch. She wore a black silk robe, as though she was getting ready for bed. But her auburn hair was done, and her ruby red lipstick told Leanne she'd been out earlier that evening.

"What in *heaven's* name are you doing up here?"

"Just looking through some stuff. I'm coming down." Leanne stashed the legal pad in the box and replaced the lid.

"You damn near scared me to death! I thought you were a prowler."

"I'm coming down now."

In the light of the bare bulb, her mother's makeup looked garish. She shook her head and stepped down the ladder. Leanne followed, switching off the light as she went.

Then they were standing in the garage, surrounded by Boone's expensive toys.

"What on earth are you doing rooting around the attic like a racoon? That's a good way to get shot."

"Since when do you shoot raccoons?" Leanne brushed the dust off her shoulders.

"I thought you were a burglar." Her mom planted a hand on her hip, and her shiny red fingernails put Leanne's filed-down nubs to shame.

"You're all dressed up," Leanne said. "Where'd you go tonight?"

Her mom ignored the question, still searching Leanne's eyes for clues. But the last thing Leanne planned to do was bring her mother into her secret investigation.

"We had a committee dinner."

That would be the Rodeo Committee, which Regina co-chaired. Outside of riding, it was her favorite activity.

"You never answered my question," her mom said. "What were you doing up there?"

"Just looking through some paperwork."

"The Moriarty case?"

Leanne didn't respond.

"Not you, too." She rolled her eyes. "What is everyone's fixation on that damn girl? She's been dead sixteen years."

"*Mom.*"

"Well, it's all anyone can talk about! They've got it on CNN, for God's sake."

"It's a high-profile case. People are interested." Now she sounded like the DA.

Her mom shook her head. "Hasn't Sean Moriarty destroyed enough lives? That case drove your father to distraction. He was obsessed. Sean Moriarty ruined our marriage."

Leanne turned away. "Right."

"What? He did!"

"You don't think you and Boone had something to do with it?"

Her mom drew back, clearly offended. The affair was no secret, but they didn't talk about it openly.

Her mom took a deep breath and settled her fists on her hips. Her chest was flushed now, and she seemed to be making an effort to calm down. She was on blood pressure medication, and Leanne felt a wave of guilt.

"Have you seen Ben this week?" her mom asked, changing the subject.

"No. Have you?"

Her tense expression answered Leanne's question.

"He hasn't been home in six days." Her mom nodded in the direction of the empty guesthouse. "I think he's with that girl, Diandra."

Diandra was her brother's sometimes-girlfriend, who—lucky for Ben—had supposedly kicked her drug addiction. Unlucky for Ben, she'd replaced it with alcohol. Leanne's mom believed she was a bad influence on Ben, and Leanne concurred.

It was one of the few topics they could agree on.

"I'll call him." Leanne didn't have the heart to mention that she'd texted him three times today and gotten no response.

"You want to try him tonight?"

"It's almost midnight, Mom. He's probably asleep at her place."

At her mother's worried expression, she felt another wave of guilt.

You need to look out for your brother. His damn head's in the clouds.

How many times had her dad said that? The words lived in her brain, no matter how often she reminded herself that Ben was an adult, free to screw up his life however he wanted. He wasn't her responsibility, but for as long as she could remember, her dad had told her otherwise, and even now, he was telling her from the grave.

"I need to go." Leanne moved for the door. "I've got a big day tomorrow."

"Not the Moriarty case, I hope."

"This is something else."

"The girl at the train tracks?"

"Yeah."

"I heard about that."

Leanne reached for the door. "Don't worry about Ben. I'm sure he's fine."

Her mom sighed. "Bullshit, Leanne. You're sure of no such thing."

NINE

The white adobe building looked like nothing from the street. In keeping with Marfa minimalism, you had to venture inside to see what attracted visitors from as far away as New York.

Frigid air greeted Leanne as she stepped through the door. She tucked her hands into the pockets of her leather jacket, feeling out of her element as she glanced around the gallery. Glass light fixtures suspended by gleaming silver chains hung down from the ceiling, illuminating a trio of sculptures in the center of the room. Leanne crossed the concrete floor to the first piece, trying to make sense of the mishmash of crumpled tin and copper wires. She'd taken an art class in college, but the slide carousels filled with Renaissance churches hadn't given her much of a guide for appreciating modern sculpture.

Leanne eyed the security camera staring down at her from the ceiling. Instrumental music drifted from the back of the gallery, indicating someone was here, but the gallery staff was evidently fine to leave customers alone with the merchandise.

She approached an enormous floor-to-ceiling photograph depicting a starry sky above a canyon. The silhouetted rock formations looked familiar, and a glance at the nameplate confirmed her take: *Milky Way Above Big Bend*. The photographer was listed as Zach Olmstead.

Muffled voices emanated from a corridor, but still no one came out, and she moved to the next colossal photograph—a black mountain set against an indigo sky with chartreuse green swirls. Like the neighboring piece, it was attributed to Zach Olmstead, but Leanne was certain the photograph wasn't taken in Texas. The third photo in the series showed another familiar rock formation, this one in the Australian Outback. *Uluru at Night*, read the caption.

The far wall contained another series of photographs, also taken at night. Leanne wandered over for a closer look. She recognized more views of Big Bend, as well as the McDonald Observatory in nearby Jeff Davis County.

"Good morning."

Leanne turned around, unsettled that she hadn't heard anyone approach. The woman behind her was tall and model thin, with straight blond hair that hung to her waist. She wore a white cashmere dress and slouchy suede boots.

Leanne nodded. "Good morning."

"How may I help you today?"

The woman had an accent, maybe Scandinavian.

"Are you the manager here?"

She smiled indulgently. "I'm Freya, his assistant. Would you like to speak to Zach?"

"I would, thanks."

"He's in back unboxing a new shipment. One moment, please."

She walked off, her shiny blond tresses fluttering behind, and Leanne stared after her. Living in Dallas, Leanne had become accustomed to seeing women who looked like they'd just stepped off a runway. Living in Madrone, not so much. But Marfa, Texas, was a whole different world and had much more of a fashion scene.

Leanne resumed her perusal of the gallery, making a full circle and arriving back at the Milky Way photograph as she heard footsteps on the concrete that were decidedly masculine. She turned around.

"Zach Olmstead." He stepped forward and thrust out a hand. He wore all black, from his Hugo Boss polo to his shiny leather shoes. With his thick dark hair and deeply tanned skin, he was the visual opposite of his flaxen-haired assistant. Yin versus yang.

His handshake was firm and confident.

"I'm Detective Everhart with Madrone PD."

An eyebrow arched. "The police. Wow." His smile became a smirk. "To what do I owe the pleasure?"

People had all sorts of reactions when Leanne showed up unannounced. The most common one was wary. In south Dallas, she might get a demand for a warrant or a door slammed in her face. Madrone was more low-key—maybe a suspicious eye peering through the gap in the door. Sometimes she got simple curiosity.

What she didn't usually get was lighthearted banter.

"I was just looking at the photographs here." She turned to face them. "Are all these yours?"

"Not all. I have a few guest exhibitors."

"Locals?"

"Some."

"And do you own the gallery?"

"I do." He stepped closer and folded his arms over his muscular chest. "Have you been in before?"

"I haven't."

"You'll recognize this subject, I'm sure." He nodded at the Big Bend piece.

"Santa Elena Canyon."

"You've been out there, I take it. Do you like to camp?"

"No." She nodded at the neighboring photograph. "And these are the northern lights?"

"Aurora australis." He smiled. "Same thing, different hemisphere. This one was taken in Argentina."

"I see." Leanne glanced around. "Looks like you travel a lot."

"Wherever the work takes me. These are part of my running series on dark sky destinations. We're one of the few."

"We?"

"Here in the Davis Mountains. We're leading the way in astrotourism and combatting light trespass."

"Interesting."

He smiled. "You look skeptical."

"I would think the two would work against each other."

"Not at all." He eased closer, warming up to the topic. "We're one of the foremost dark sky reserves in the world. And the lack of light pollution here allows for some dramatic visual effects from a photography perspective."

"So I see."

He smiled again. "So, tell me, Detective. What can I do for you today? I'm sure you didn't drive all the way from Madrone to discuss photography."

She nodded, once again struck by how comfortable he seemed talking to a cop at his place of business. Most people would have become antsy with the small talk and gotten defensive by now.

"I came across this card in a file." She pulled the business card from her pocket.

Now he looked genuinely intrigued. "Well, that's a blast from the past. We changed our logo ten years ago."

"You were the owner here then, too?"

"I was. I've been out here eighteen years."

"And before that?"

He gave a shrug, and for the first time, she caught a hint of discomfort. "Before that, I moved around."

"Are you from West Texas originally?"

"Originally? I'm from Florida." He sighed. "At some point, are you planning to tell me what this is about?"

"Just doing some background research." She gave a shrug and mirrored his easygoing stance. "Do you remember being contacted by a Madrone detective at any point with regard to a missing teenager? Her name was—"

"Hannah Rawls. Of course I know who she was. That was all over the news." His brow furrowed. "And it's back in the news *now*, if I'm not mistaken."

"So, you remember talking to a detective at the time?"

"No. I said I remembered the case. I don't recall talking to a detective about anything."

She watched his eyes for signs of evasiveness. The words "I don't recall" were a red flag. On the other hand, this would have been sixteen years ago, so maybe he truly didn't remember. Maybe Leanne's father had stopped by here to ask about something, possibly about someone Zach Olmstead knew or something he may have seen, and the interaction was so minor he didn't even recall it.

Or maybe her dad hadn't spoken to this man at all—merely stopped in and picked up a business card. Why, though?

And why was Zach Olmstead's former home phone number—a now defunct landline—written on the back of this business card? Clearly, her dad had taken the time during the extremely hectic days after Hannah Rawls's murder to make the forty-minute drive to Marfa. The same drive she had just made.

He had to have had a reason.

Zach Olmstead was watching her with whiskey brown eyes that held a mix of interest and curiosity.

And something else. Uneasiness.

She smiled. "Well, I appreciate your time today."

A slow smile spread across his face. "That's all? Really?"

"Really."

He shook his head. "All right, then."

"I'll let you get back to your work. Thanks again for the information."

"Anytime, Detective."

Leanne squinted up at the sun as she left the gallery. She unhooked her aviators from her shirtfront and slid them on. After glancing up and down Highland Street, she headed north, following the vague recollection of a tucked-away burrito shop. She passed a pair of boutiques showcasing designer boots and cowboy hats. Similar shops were popping up in Madrone now, too, selling western-themed housewares and obscenely priced candles with names like "junipine" and "tooled leather." Moving past the display windows, she replayed her conversation with Zach Olmstead.

He was smooth. And—she had to admit—extremely nice-looking. But nothing about his *GQ* looks or his glib answers made her think that she'd accomplished anything at all this morning other than wasting her time.

Her phone chimed and she pulled it from her pocket.

"Everhart."

"Where the heck are you?"

It was Josh.

"Investigating. Where are you?"

She pictured him holding his phone, gritting his teeth at her nonanswer.

"I'm on my way to a domestic in Canyon Glen."

Canyon Glen was a trailer park on the west side of town where some of their frequent flyers resided.

"Skip Sanders?" she ventured.

"You guessed it. It's your turn, but you're MIA so they tossed it to me."

"Sorry," she said. "I told Nadine I'd be out this morning. I'm in Presidio County running an errand, and then I'm making the rounds, checking on MP reports."

"Hey, heads up, Novak is here again, and the word is they're planning another press briefing sometime this afternoon."

So, maybe she hadn't wasted her time coming here. Looked like she had a reprieve from today's photo op.

Leanne spied a yellow café awning and sped up her pace.

"Leanne?"

"I'll be sorry to miss that."

"Uh-huh."

The awning turned out to be a coffee shop, and she glanced around, trying to remember where she'd seen the burrito place. She spotted a chalkboard sign at the end of an alley, and a line of people waiting.

"Thanks for covering Canyon Glen," she said. "I'll catch the next one."

"I'm holding you to it."

"Really, I promise."

Leanne ended the call as she neared the line of people. She halted in her tracks when she realized they weren't waiting in line for food. She glanced around for the chalkboard, but it was blocked now.

A murmur rose from the crowd, drawing her closer. People spoke in hushed voices, and Leanne's radar went up. Was someone injured? She hustled past the line of people and came to a small courtyard surrounded by a low stone wall. At the back of the courtyard was a pink adobe house.

Leanne turned to the white-haired woman standing beside the gate. "What's everyone doing?"

The woman said something in Spanish and nodded toward the side of the courtyard. On the wall of the building was a mural of the Virgin Mary. She was depicted in a sky-blue cape adorned with pink stars, an oval of lilies surrounding her. Her hands were folded in prayer, and she gazed down at the people in the courtyard.

Some knelt at the Virgin's feet. Others stood with their eyes closed, holding rosary beads. Something about their quiet reverence made Leanne stop to watch. Her gaze fell on a woman standing near the door to the house. She was short and round, and her dark brown eyes were fixed firmly on Leanne.

"Señora." The woman stepped forward, gesturing toward the house. "Come in."

Leanne glanced around, thinking she was talking to someone else.

The woman nodded. "Come. Please."

Leanne hesitated. Then she stepped toward her.

"You are a police officer?" The woman pointed at the badge clipped to Leanne's belt, partly hidden by her jacket.

"I am, yes."

The intensity in her eyes put a knot of dread in Leanne's gut. She'd seen this look before.

"I was just walking by, and I saw the crowd," Leanne said. "What's everyone doing here?"

"They've come to visit the Virgin."

Leanne glanced at the mural again, then back at the woman. "Do they pay you?"

She smiled. "Some leave offerings."

"Offerings?"

"Candles, fruit, money. We give it to the church."

The cynic in Leanne took that with a grain of salt.

"I am Alma."

The woman offered a hand, and Leanne took it. Her soft, two-handed grip felt like warm bread dough.

"I'm Leanne Everhart. I was just happening by—"

"It is okay." She nodded. "Many people come by chance. The Lord brings them here."

More like a burrito craving.

Leanne turned to look at the pilgrims shuffling through the courtyard in a slow-moving line. It was a mix of women and men, old and middle-aged, speaking English and Spanish in low voices. Some reached out to touch the mural as they neared it. A row of bricks at the base of the painting was covered with coins and votive candles.

"Come in."

She looked at Alma. This detour was the very last thing she had time for today. But the quiet plea in the woman's eyes made Leanne follow her inside.

TEN

The house was small and warm and smelled of garlic. Alma led her down a narrow hallway crowded with bicycles and strollers. In the kitchen, a young woman stood at the stove, stirring something in a soup pot as a baby in a high chair bounced and gurgled.

Alma ushered Leanne into a living room dominated by a worn beige sectional and a green recliner. The carpet was littered with toys, and in the corner was a round adobe fireplace filled with candles and religious statues. The mantel above had more candles and had been made into an altar of sorts with a woman's photo at the center.

"My daughter. Marisol."

Leanne looked at Alma and then approached the mantel.

On closer inspection, the person in the framed photograph wasn't a woman—she looked barely sixteen. The girl had dark hair and luminous brown eyes, and she wore a purple sweater in what was clearly a school portrait taken in front of the usual blue backdrop.

Leanne's stomach tensed as she studied the photo. The girl wore black eyeliner but no lipstick or jewelry, not even the arc of earrings that seemed to be a rite of passage for teenage girls. Her white smile was somehow more perfect because of a slightly crooked incisor.

Leanne looked at Alma, who was watching her. "Marisol is . . . ?"

"Missing."

Missing, not dead.

"Tell me what happened."

Alma stepped closer, her brow furrowing as she gazed at her daughter's face.

"She went to a party with her friends in Fort Stockton. One of those parking lot parties? This was behind a warehouse there, where no one could see the cars." Alma paused, and Leanne knew what was coming. "They were drinking, you know. Her friends came home, all in different cars. But Marisol didn't."

Leanne watched her pinched expression. The deep creases in her face showed the extended agony of waiting.

Leanne cleared her throat. "How long ago?"

Alma pulled her gaze away from her daughter's picture. "Six years."

ELEVEN

Leanne spotted Duncan's pickup and whipped into the parking lot before she could talk herself out of it. She found a space in front, not far from the door. Easy in, easy out.

She checked her reflection in the mirror and tucked some loose strands into her ponytail. Not that it mattered. Her beauty regimen consisted of moisturizing her skin against the dry desert air and keeping her hair pulled back so it didn't look like a tumbleweed by the end of the day. Anything beyond that was a waste of time.

As she clicked her key fob and headed for the entrance, she noticed a black Jeep Cherokee turning into the lot. Dark tinted windows, chrome rims. She could have sworn she'd seen the same Cherokee this morning in Marfa when she was leaving the gallery. Coincidence? Maybe. The SUV pulled around to the back, and she didn't get a look at the driver.

Leanne pulled open the heavy wooden door and stepped inside. The Javelina Cantina was full, but not nearly as packed as Sunday. No football tonight. The TVs were playing a Rangers game, but it was a rerun from their last trip to the World Series.

Leanne scanned the room and spotted Justin Carr at the dart

board with some of his river guide friends. No Liam Moriarty this time.

Duncan occupied a stool at the far end of the bar, and he was alone, which was sure to be temporary. Leanne swooped in before anyone could beat her to it.

"Hey."

He looked up from the phone in his hand. "Hi."

"Boozing it up on a Tuesday night?"

"I just got here."

He looked her over as she hitched herself onto the stool beside him. She hadn't been home since work, and she felt grubby. He, on the other hand, looked like he was dressed for a night out in his snakeskin cowboy boots and a blue flannel shirt that matched his eyes.

Like Leanne, Duncan had started his law enforcement career in Dallas. Unlike Leanne, he had moved out here as part of his strategic plan. He'd joined the Chisos County Sheriff's Office to jump-start his career and rise through the ranks more quickly than he would have been able to in a huge department like Dallas. Leanne liked to give him crap about his urban roots, but she secretly admired him. He was more open-minded than most of the people out here, more amenable to change and willing to embrace new technology. So many cops she worked with were mired in the past.

"Saw you on TV yesterday," he said with a sly smile. "You clean up nice, Everhart."

"Ha."

"What? You don't like being used as a prop for the DA's reelection campaign?"

"Where were you guys? I thought the sheriff never missed a chance to get in front of a camera."

"Don't think we were invited," he said. "Novak doesn't like to share the spotlight."

Katie walked over and slid a pint in front of Duncan. "Get you a beer?" she asked Leanne.

"I don't know." She nodded at Duncan's glass. "What's that?"

"Black IPA," he said.

Leanne made a face.

"It's pretty hoppy. You'll like it."

"Your Dallas is showing." She looked at Katie. "I'll have a Bud Light."

"You got it."

She sashayed off, and Leanne turned to Duncan.

"I need a favor from you."

He lifted an eyebrow.

"Not that kind of favor. It's about my case."

He picked up his beer. "Yeah, I heard you're leading up the train tracks homicide."

"That's what they're calling it?"

"I don't know that they're calling it anything. I just heard the vic was found on the outskirts of town by the tracks."

"She was." Leanne took out her phone and clicked open a photograph. "We recovered some tire marks out there. You still have that friend at the state crime lab? The tire expert? I was hoping you could run this by him."

One of the many things she liked about Duncan was that he kept up with people and had contacts everywhere. Leanne was allergic to schmoozing.

Duncan pulled her phone closer and examined the picture. "Not bad. There's a lot of good detail here. Did you take this?"

"Izzy Huerta did, our part-time CSI," she told him. "I made a plaster cast of this, too, but McBride doesn't want to send it in. Thinks it's a waste of money."

Duncan studied the photo and pursed his lips. "He's probably right."

She bristled. "Yeah, I mean, why waste valuable resources on mundane crimes like rape and murder when we could be chasing down car thieves?"

Duncan shot her a look. "Don't get your back up. I'm just pointing out, tire tread is class evidence. Best case, even if you ID it, all you'll know is that it was made by some tire that's on probably thousands of vehicles in the tri-county area. Waste of funds." He passed the phone back and picked up his beer. "Why don't you go for the jugular and push your chief to send in some DNA evidence? Do you have any?"

Frustration welled in her chest. "The ME collected a rape kit, but you know how that goes. It'll be freaking Christmas before we get anything back. I figured your guy would be faster. And even if all we manage to do is narrow it down to a list of possible vehicles, that's progress."

Katie was back with a beer. Leanne picked up the glass and took a cold, bitter sip.

"So, will you talk to your guy for me?" she asked.

"Maybe. Sometimes he won't answer when he knows I'm hitting him up for a favor."

"Well, could you at least try?" She leaned forward so he'd have to look her in the eye. "I'm out on a limb here, and McBride's being his usual self."

"I'll try. Shoot me that photo."

"Try" was better than "maybe." She took another sip and slid the glass away.

He was watching her now with those ocean blue eyes.

When it came to work, she and Duncan had a lot in common. They'd been through the same training academy and knew some of the same people in Dallas. But Duncan wasn't from here originally, and he stood out. It wasn't just his looks; it was the way he talked, the way he carried himself, his whole approach to everything, including his job. He had a degree in forensics, which made him an expert on topics Leanne had only vaguely heard about. Duncan was smart, super analytical, and a thorough investigator.

In some ways, he reminded her of her dad.

"I have another question for you," she said.

"I don't have any ins with the state lab when it comes to rape kits, if that's what you're thinking."

"This is something else. Do you remember an MP case from a while back? Marisol Cruz? This would have been six years ago."

"That's before my time."

"I know. I just thought you might have heard something."

"Before your time, too." He frowned. "Missing high school girl, right? She went to a keg party in Alpine and never came home?"

"Fort Stockton, but yeah, that's the case. You heard about it?"

He tipped his head to the side. "I think so. Why?"

"I met her mother today."

Duncan shook his head.

"What?"

"Six years, Leanne."

"I know. But she's still holding out hope. What did you hear about it?"

"Not a lot. I thought they'd pegged her for a runaway? She had an older boyfriend or something, and everyone figured she took off with him."

"Not everyone. Her mom believes she was kidnapped."

"Maybe she was. Like I said, older boyfriend."

Duncan watched her, and the look on his face telegraphed what he was thinking. The likely outcomes for a missing person case that had been cold for six years were not good. Alma Cruz's best hope was that her daughter had gone somewhere—either willingly or unwillingly—with a man she knew. If she'd been taken by a stranger, the odds of her being found alive at this point were depressingly low.

Katie was back with a smile. "Y'all want another round?"

"I'm good," Duncan said.

"Me, too."

Katie dropped off a glass with their tab and walked away. Leanne glanced at Duncan, and he was watching her now with a look she recognized.

"Sorry about the other night," he said.

She bristled again for an entirely different reason.

"It's cool."

"I was working. I'm still on that ICE op."

For the past three months, Duncan had been part of a joint task force trying to roll up a human-trafficking ring operating in the region. ICE was officially calling the shots, but several local sheriff's offices were providing extra boots on the ground.

"This is my first night off in weeks," Duncan said. "They keep roping me in."

"Forget it."

Her stomach filled with nerves, as it always did when he talked to her in that low voice. Maybe she shouldn't have pulled in here when she spotted his truck. It would have been smarter to have this conversation over the phone. But she had a bad track record of doing anything smart when it came to him.

He kept watching her, and she wasn't able to tell what he was thinking now. She couldn't remember the last time they'd had a drink alone together and not as part of some off-duty cop group.

His phone vibrated on the bar, breaking the spell. He flipped it over and muttered a curse.

"I have to go in."

She was already getting out her wallet. "That's your office?"

"My task force lead."

"How's the op going?" She put some cash on the bar.

"You know how it is." He took out his wallet. "It's pretty

much whack-a-mole. But it's been going a little better lately. We've got some new surveillance tools."

"The Trojan horse thing."

He frowned. "Where did you hear that?"

She shrugged. "Around."

According to rumors, the feds had managed to get hold of a few key cell phones and install some new spyware that enabled them to eavesdrop on several criminal networks.

Duncan gave her a look of disapproval. "You shouldn't talk about that."

"I'm not. I'm talking to *you*."

"I'm serious, Leanne."

"I know."

He continued to frown as she slid off her stool and zipped her jacket. She walked to the door, and they stepped outside together.

The temperature had dropped, and it felt like a thousand cold pinpricks on her face. She glanced up at the sky, the rare *dark sky* that was the subject of Zach Olmstead's artwork. She thought of the Virgin Mary mural and the pink adobe house. What a long, strange day it had been.

She turned to Duncan.

"Let me know about—"

"I will." He stared down at her, and the moment stretched out.

"What?"

"Nothing."

He headed off toward his truck, clicking his key fob as he went.

Leanne slid into her pickup and watched him in her rearview. She waited until his taillights were tiny dots of red. Then she pulled onto the highway and buzzed her windows down, letting the wind whip through the cab until her cheeks went numb. She neared the sign for Desert Star Campground and glanced at the side mirror.

The Cherokee was back. It was way behind her, but she recognized the headlights.

"Son of a bitch."

The Desert Star sign drew nearer. Instead of slowing, she hit the gas.

"Come on," she muttered. "Let's see what you got."

Max stared at the empty highway.

"I lost her," he said over the phone.

"You what?"

"She's gone."

"I thought you said you had her."

"I did." He looked left and right into the empty desert. There wasn't a house in sight, never mind a pair of red taillights.

"Listen. Get a bead on her, ASAP."

"I will," Max said.

"Execute the assignment, or I'll find someone who will."

"Got it," Max said, but the line was already dead.

He tossed his phone on the seat beside him.

He didn't have time for this. He stomped on the gas, squinting at the sign in the distance as he raced down the highway. Madrone, five miles. Fort Stockton, fifty.

Headlights lit up his rearview. He twisted to look over his shoulder. A truck loomed behind him, blue and red grill lights.

"No fucking way."

Max checked the speedometer. Eighty in a seventy.

The headlights zoomed closer.

He put on his turn signal and tapped the brake. The truck behind him slowed. He pulled onto the shoulder and rolled to a stop.

He watched with amazement as Leanne Everhart slid from the pickup and approached him, her slender body silhouetted in the headlights.

She flashed her badge and rested her hand on his roof as he lowered the window.

"License and insurance."

"I wasn't—"

"License and insurance." She shined a flashlight in his face.

Squinting at the glare, Max pulled his wallet from his pocket and fished out the driver's license. He handed it over, then reached for the glove compartment. The Maglite beam followed his hands as he rummaged through it.

"This your vehicle, Mr. Scott?" She handed back the driver's license.

He passed her the insurance paperwork, and the flashlight beam shifted to the clipped papers.

"You've been following me for two days," she stated.

"I wasn't—"

"Why?"

Max cursed inwardly. Then he reached for the laminated card stashed in his cup holder.

"I'm with the *Dallas Morning News*," he said, handing her the press pass.

The beam shifted to his face again.

"I've been trying to reach you since Sunday," he said. "I wanted to talk to you about an interview."

Silence.

He squinted into the glare. "Hey, do you mind—"

"Yes, I do mind. An interview about *what*?"

She leaned closer. The blinding light made it impossible for him to make out her expression, but the tone of her voice told him she was not happy.

"You're Lee Everhart's daughter, correct?"

No response.

"And you're with Madrone Police Department now, where your father spent his career, right?"

Hostility radiated from her. But still no response.

"We're doing a feature on the Sean Moriarty case, and we want to talk to you about—"

"No."

"—your father's legacy—"

"No." She shoved the press pass at him. "I don't give press interviews. Talk to our PIO."

He stared up at her. She'd lowered the flashlight now, and he could make out her face enough to see the fierce scowl.

Did she believe him or not? Unclear. But they both knew the Madrone Police Department didn't have a public information officer. So maybe she thought he was full of shit.

"We're doing an in-depth story about Sean Moriarty's exoneration, whether you talk to us or not," he said.

"Listen up." She rested her forearm on the roof and leaned closer. "If I see you on my six again, you will be sorry."

"You can't—"

"Are we clear?"

"Sure, whatever. But our coverage will detail your father's role in Sean Moriarty's wrongful conviction. Things will go better for you if you work with us, not against us."

She scoffed. "Are you *threatening* me?"

"No."

"I repeat: I do not give press interviews."

"Suit yourself."

"I will." She stepped back. "I advise you to go back to Dallas, Mr. Scott. And if I catch you tailing me again, you're going to find yourself in handcuffs."

TWELVE

Izzy chewed on her lip as she stared at the photograph.

She'd missed it.

Five hours at that hellhole crime scene, and she'd missed a crucial piece of evidence. She clicked into another shot and zoomed in on her screen, hoping for a better result, but the oblong impression in the dirt was slightly cut off.

"*Damn* it."

She toggled back to the original photo and sighed.

"What's that?"

She jumped, startled, as Leanne stepped into the cubicle and leaned down to look at the computer screen.

Izzy's shoulders tensed. She'd wasn't ready to talk about this yet. But she recognized the look on Leanne's face. She'd never let it go. When something caught her attention, the detective was like a dog with a bone.

Izzy cleared her throat. "This is from Sunday's crime scene by the railroad tracks."

"I can see that." Leanne nodded at the screen. "Is that a shoeprint?"

"Maybe. I mean, *yes*, it's a shoe impression. The question is, is it usable?" Izzy turned to the computer and zoomed in on the corner of the image that showed a faint impression in the dirt.

She looked back at Leanne. "So, the thing is, I didn't see this at the time. I was photographing the cigarette here." She pointed at the flattened cigarette butt that was the actual subject of the photograph. "We collected this as evidence, along with all the other trash inside the crime scene perimeter. The water bottles, the soda cans, the carpet squares. I photographed everything before we picked it up."

Leanne nodded. "I remember. Zoom me out. Where was this, exactly?"

Izzy clicked open another picture that gave a wider view of the area. "This is about ten yards west of the body. It's a pretty faint impression. I didn't even see it originally when I was taking a shot of the cigarette. But when I was combing back through these photos, looking for anything we might have missed, I thought I noticed something. So, I increased the contrast, and there it is."

"Can you increase the contrast more?" Leanne asked.

"It's maxed out."

The detective leaned closer, and Izzy watched her study the photograph. Near the shoeprint was a red Tecate can bleached pink by the sun.

"Well, this probably isn't clear enough to pin down a specific shoe type," Leanne said. "I mean, it's a wavy pattern—"

"Herringbone."

"What?"

"The pattern on the sole is called 'herringbone.'" Izzy nodded at the image. "And it's *not* consistent with the all-terrain boots worn by me or any of the first responders—I already checked. Those all have heavy-duty treads. And the woman who found the body was wearing Nike running shoes. This is more of a casual, all-purpose shoe. Like maybe a lace-up sneaker."

"Okay."

"But you're right—the detail probably isn't clear enough to pin down what type exactly. If I had noticed it at the time, I could have taken a better photograph using an oblique light source to pump up the detail. That's on me. I missed it."

"Well, don't beat yourself up," Leanne said. "It was a big crime scene. And there was a lot going on. You were focused primarily on the body."

Her words didn't lessen Izzy's guilt.

"The good news," Izzy said, "is that I *did* include my metal ruler in the frame for scale. With some research, I may be able to tell you the shoe size of whoever left this print."

"Seriously? That could be useful."

"I know."

Leanne glanced around the empty bullpen and then perched on the corner of Izzy's desk.

"There's something else I wanted to ask you," Leanne said. "About your other job."

That caught her attention. "Yeah?"

"I know you exhibit some of your nature photographs at different art galleries."

"Well, I've got some pieces at *a* gallery. And a piece on display at the chamber of commerce building."

"Wow."

"Not really 'wow.' I mean, every amateur photographer in town has their stuff there. Mark Gaffney, Justin Carr, Alex Contreras. Even Nadine has a piece on display there." She glanced around to make sure the receptionist wasn't walking by.

Leanne frowned. "Mark Gaffney. Why do I recognize that name?"

"He teaches yearbook at the high school." He had been Izzy's very first mentor. "My point is the chamber of commerce exhibits work from local hobbyists. Having your stuff there isn't exactly hitting it big."

"You said you have stuff at a gallery, too. Which one is it?"

"It's in Marfa. The West Tex Art Co-op? It's on Highland Street right down from the theater."

"Have you heard of Dark Sky Gallery?" Leanne asked.

"Uh, yeah."

"You ever exhibited there?"

"No way."

"Why not?"

Izzy smiled. "They're really exclusive. They show artists from New York and Los Angeles. Have you ever been in there?"

"Yeah. Yesterday, as a matter of fact." Leanne folded her arms over her chest. "I met the manager, Zach Olmstead. He runs the place and shows a lot of his work there, too. You know him?"

"No. I've heard of him, sure. But I've never met him or anything."

"What do you hear about him?"

Izzy studied Leanne's green eyes, trying to read her expression. These definitely weren't casual questions. What was she up to?

"Well . . . I have a friend who went out with him. She's a textile artist in Marfa. She met him at some museum party there."

"What did she say about him?"

"Not a lot. They only went out a couple times, and then it ended, I think. Why?"

Leanne shrugged. "Just asking around. He seemed a little high on himself when I talked to him. Just wanted to see what his reputation is."

"I'm probably not the one to ask," Izzy said. "His gallery is pretty famous. They don't exactly carry my work."

"They could, though. They exhibit local artists, too."

"Yes, well. Some places say that, but it's for PR. A lot of places only show big-name photographers whose work commands a higher price. Most of the galleries in Marfa won't even look at locals."

"You should try," Leanne said. "Your work is impressive. I've seen it. And you have a degree from NYU. You can compete with anyone."

Izzy glanced around uncomfortably. She wasn't used to talking about her art in the middle of the police station.

Leanne's phone chimed, and she pulled it from her jacket pocket.

"Everhart."

She listened intently, and Izzy could tell it was something important.

Leanne twisted around to look at the clock on the wall. "Okay, got it. I'm on my way."

The skull stared out at her from the glass case, two hollow orbits that gave Leanne the creeps whenever she passed through here. The cranium was yellowed and old, with zigzag fissures along the sides, and it felt strange to think about how it once was part of a living, breathing person.

"It's been a while."

Leanne turned around as Jen Sayers breezed into the lobby. The forensic anthropologist wore a white lab coat and jeans, and her auburn hair was pulled back in a bun.

Leanne walked over. "Thanks for meeting."

"No problem." Jen nodded toward the glass case containing an array of skulls, including a cow and a bighorn sheep. "I see you've met Herman."

"He has a name?"

"My students named him after Herman Munster. Here, come on back."

As they crossed the lobby of the science building, Leanne looked Jen over. Freckles covered the bridge of her nose, and she'd gotten some sun recently.

"You been at the beach?"

Jen rolled her eyes. "I wish. I was on a dig in Guatemala over the holidays with some grad students."

Dr. Jennifer Sayers wore multiple hats. She taught forensic anthropology at the university in Alpine and also consulted for law enforcement agencies whenever the need arose, so she got pulled in on all sorts of cases, from fires to drownings. When bones of unknown origin turned up in the region, they typically ended up in her laboratory.

Jen pushed through a door marked STAFF ONLY. The air was chilly, and Leanne tucked her hands into her pockets as she followed the anthropologist down a long corridor with checkered linoleum flooring. They reached another closed door, and Jen used her badge to swipe open the lock.

They stepped into a spacious laboratory with a stainless steel table at the center. Hoses and equipment hung down from the ceiling, and long metal sinks lined the walls. This room was even colder, and the air smelled faintly of bleach.

"Through here," Jen said, ushering her past the exam table, which thankfully was empty at the moment.

Leanne had never been in the adjacent room before. It was small and cramped, filled with floor-to-ceiling shelves containing bones of all shapes and sizes. Along the side of the room was a tall slate counter with a pair of microscopes on it.

"Whoa. That's a lot of bones," Leanne said, walking over to one of the shelves. Atop a paper shelf liner was a row of long white bones arranged from smallest to largest. "Are these human?"

"No," Jen said, pulling on a pair of latex gloves. "That's the point, actually. This is our reference collection. You're looking at femurs from a variety of species."

Leanne walked over to the longest bone.

"This looks like a mastodon."

"Good guess," Jen said. "That's an elephant femur."

"Where's it from?"

"A zoo in Houston. We get bones from all over. There's a kangaroo in there somewhere. An anthropologist friend of mine in Tasmania sent it. Besides skulls, we like to collect femurs because they're useful for determining size, age, all sorts of characteristics."

Jen slid something from a manila envelope, and Leanne stepped up to the counter. She recognized the bone from Izzy's crime scene photo as Jen placed it on a piece of butcher paper.

"Here we are." She reached up and switched on an exam light, then adjusted the metal arm so that the light shone down on the specimen. "The bone from your crime scene."

Leanne caught the shift in Jen's tone as she rotated the bone beneath the light.

"To get straight to the point, this bone is, in fact, human."

"Everyone thought it was from a deer," Leanne said. "You're certain?"

"One hundred percent. Microscopic examination reveals a scattered osteon pattern. Also notable—it's a femur, the longest and strongest bone in the human body. Thus, they tend to be well-preserved."

"How old?" Leanne asked.

"Hard to say. It's not ancient, I can tell you that. I'd say this bone has been out there exposed to the elements for at least a few years." She held the bone by the tip and rolled it over. "You see these scratches here? Those are from teeth and claws. The skeleton was likely scattered by animals. Coyotes would be my guess."

"No, I mean how old is the person? Or how old *were* they?" Leanne asked. "Is there any way to tell?"

"Yes. Although, it would be useful to have more than one bone to look at. But, by examining the epiphysis here"—she pointed to the rounded end—"I can estimate that this is from someone in their late teens."

Leanne stared down at the bone. Another young person.

"Is there any way to know the gender?" Leanne asked.

"You mean sex. Gender is a social construct. And, yes, there is, but it requires further analysis. Given that we only have a partial bone to work with, versus a full skeleton, I'll need to extract DNA." Jen stepped back. "That takes time, and I was under the impression you were in a hurry to get my findings. This was discovered at a homicide scene, correct?"

"That's right. One of our officers came across this when we were collecting evidence near the body."

"The train tracks girl?"

Leanne nodded.

"Do you know that victim's postmortem interval?"

"The ME estimates a day and a half between the murder and when the body was found."

Jen pursed her lips. "Any ID yet?"

"We're working on it."

Leanne looked down at the bone fragment and shook her head.

"Damn. What are the odds of two sets of human remains being found in the exact same place in that vast swath of desert?"

"Given the proximity to the highway? It's not that surprising," Jen said. "And it's more than two."

Leanne frowned. "What do you mean?"

"Off the top of my head I can think of four other instances of bones found along that same stretch of highway between Fort Stockton and Marfa."

"*Human* bones?"

"Those are just the ones I've personally examined."

"When?"

"Over the years. I've been here almost a decade now. The first set came during my second winter. Some hunter pulled over to take a leak and his dog sniffed out the remains. They were pretty much skeletonized at that point."

Leanne stared at her, trying to get her mind around it.

"Any IDs?"

Jen shook her head. "Three of the sets of remains were female. The fourth—hard to tell. All I got in was a jawbone. That was three years ago over in western Chisos County, near the county line."

That would have been the sheriff's jurisdiction.

"Any clothes or personal items?" Leanne asked.

"What you'd expect for a body left exposed to the elements. Some tattered clothing, scraps of fabric. And—notably—some bits of duct tape."

"Duct tape," Leanne repeated. "That suggests—"

"A criminal element. Yes, I know. These weren't migrants passing through the desert who died of dehydration, if that's what you're thinking. No, at least three of these four victims showed obvious signs of violence."

"Specifically?"

"Fractured skulls and ribs. Another thing that stood out to me? In one of the cases, there was a chunk of hair missing."

"Hair," Leanne repeated.

"Hair is fairly durable compared to soft tissue. Stands up to the elements remarkably well. Despite the dried, desiccated state of the remains, the hair was pretty much intact, but—as I said—it looked like someone had cut a chunk out. Like maybe for a trophy or a souvenir?"

"That's . . ." Leanne searched for a word.

"Fucked up. I agree." Jen leaned back against the counter. "You know, the first set of remains was recovered near Madrone. I submitted a report to you guys, but as far as I know, nothing ever came of it."

Leanne's chest tightened with frustration.

"Guess your chief chalked it up to transients passing through," Jen added.

Which was code for illegal immigrants. Who—in McBride's mind—got what they deserved when they embarked on a journey across the border.

"*Four* unidentified bodies," Leanne said. "All along that same highway?"

"Six if you count these recent two." She nodded at the splintered femur under the spotlight.

Patty Paulson's words echoed through her head. *She's not the first.*

"I don't know why I never heard of these cases," Leanne said.

"Oh, come on." Jen tipped her head to the side. "Yeah, you do. Not everyone who goes missing is from some connected family that's willing to raise hell over it. And anyway, murdered women aren't good for tourism. Some of the cops around here would just as soon look the other way."

"That's outrageous," Leanne said.

Jen crossed her arms. "Doesn't mean it doesn't happen."

THIRTEEN

The chief intercepted her as soon as she walked into the bullpen. "Good. You're here." He jerked his head toward his door. "Come into my office."

Leanne glanced across the cubicles. Josh was on the phone, and several uniforms sat at computers, pecking away at their keyboards. No one looked in her direction, but she could tell everyone was listening.

She followed the chief into his office, where Trey Novak occupied a visitor's chair, his cowboy hat in his lap again. Standing beside the door was Phil Mowry, president of the Madrone Chamber of Commerce. He nodded at Leanne on his way out.

"Miss Everhart."

"Hello."

McBride ushered her in and closed the door. "Have a seat," he said.

Leanne's shoulders tensed as she took the empty seat. She desperately needed to talk to the chief this afternoon, but she hadn't planned on doing so in front of an audience.

"I just got a call from a TV producer in Houston." McBride leaned back in his chair. "They want to interview you."

She frowned. "Who does?"

"One of the news stations there. They're looking into the Hannah Rawls case, and they found out we have a detective who's the daughter of one of the original investigators." He paused. "They want to do a feature about you, talk about you going into law enforcement, following in your dad's footsteps and all that. It's a human-interest piece."

She crossed her arms. "How original."

It sounded remarkably similar to what the Dallas reporter supposedly wanted. She had no doubt that his real objective was to dig up some exclusive dirt about her department.

"We think you should do it," Novak said.

She blinked. "Excuse me?"

"It could be good for us," the chief said.

"How?"

"We've been dragged in the press for four days," McBride said. "All this talk about a wrongful conviction, police misconduct. This could soften our image some. You know, humanize us. Put a face on the department."

"And on the Hannah Rawls investigation," Novak added.

"There already *is* a face on the investigation. Hannah's face." Leanne looked from Novak to the chief.

"You know how the media is," Novak went on. "Everything's black-and-white with them. Good guys versus bad guys. A human-interest story could change the narrative."

"Right now, we're the bad guys," McBride said. "And it's about to get worse. It's only a matter of time before we get slapped with a lawsuit."

Novak checked his watch, then stood up and settled his cowboy hat on his head. "I'm surprised it hasn't happened already. Sean Moriarty is lawyer shopping—that's my bet." He nodded at the chief. "Talk to you later." Then he nodded at Leanne. "Detective."

The district attorney walked out, pulling the door shut behind him.

Leanne looked at McBride, and his calm expression gave her a twinge of panic. Was this what Phil Mowry had been here to talk about? Using Leanne to clean up the town's image so they wouldn't take an economic hit from bad publicity?

"Sir, you don't really think this is a good idea, do you?"

He patted his shirt pockets and glanced around the room. "It could be."

"But—"

"We haven't decided yet." He yanked open a drawer and rummaged through it, probably looking for cigarettes.

"I don't have time to sit for media interviews," she said. "I'm focused on our new homicide, plus a regular caseload of domestics and property crimes."

He tossed an empty pack on the desk and muttered a curse.

"Speaking of which," she said, changing the subject, "I was just at the university meeting with Jen Sayers."

McBride hummed the empty pack into the trash. "Who?"

"Dr. Jennifer Sayers, the forensic anthropologist. Turns out, the bone fragment recovered from our crime scene is human. And you know what else? She tells me *six* different sets of unidentified human remains—including our case from Sunday—have been recovered near Highway 67 between Fort Stockton and Marfa over the past nine years."

The chief frowned. "What's your point?"

"The point is . . . it could be a pattern. Someone could be murdering people and dumping them near the highway."

"The desert's a cruel place."

Leanne stared at him. Annoyance bubbled up as he turned to his file cabinet and fished out a pack of smokes.

"I'm not talking about people out there dying of heatstroke," she said. "I'm talking about violent deaths. Murders. People who have had their skulls bashed in."

He lit a cigarette and took a long drag.

"Six known bodies along the same route," she reiterated. "It could be the work of one person, Chief."

He leaned back in his chair, blowing out a stream of smoke. "Are you talking about a serial killer?"

"Yes."

He squinted at her through the haze. "Everhart . . . exactly how long have you been working here?"

She tried to keep her voice even. "Two years in March. Sir."

"I've been here twenty-four years." He grabbed a Coke can from the trash bin and ashed his cigarette into it. "In all those years, you know how many times this department's been sued? None. Not once. And now it's about to happen." He leveled a look at her. "I need you to be a team player right now."

"How do you mean?"

"For starters, don't drum up any talk of a serial killer," he said. "We need to focus on the problem at hand."

"They could be related."

His face reddened. He took another drag, and she stifled a cough.

"Related to what? You mean Hannah Rawls?"

"Yes. Four of the unidentified victims are female, and the other two are undetermined," she said. "And when you look at the location where Hannah's body was discovered—"

"We already know who killed Hannah. Because the motherfucker confessed in that interview room right over there."

"He also managed to convince a judge that his confession was coerced—"

The chief held up a hand as his face turned red as a tomato. "Stop. Just stop right there. Those un-IDed bones you're talking about? I've heard about those cases. And I guarantee you every last one of them were transients coming through here who got mixed up with a criminal element and got themselves killed."

"They got themselves bludgeoned, too? Because the forensic anthropologist determined that's what happened to at least three of them, the same as Hannah Rawls. Maybe Hannah was mixed up with a criminal element. My dad's case notes mention white powder on her clothing. Maybe she was into drugs."

McBride went quiet and tapped his cigarette, and she couldn't tell whether he was done talking or just building a head of steam.

"You want to talk about criminals? Let's talk about Sean Moriarty," he said. "He had crack cocaine in his possession at the time of his arrest. And he also *confessed* to the murder."

"Under duress, he claims."

"You bet your ass he was under duress! He was looking at the death penalty. That doesn't mean he's innocent. He had the victim's blood in his goddamn car. It was a rock-solid case." McBride leaned back in his chair. "Your father's not here to defend his work, so the rest of us have to."

The comment landed like a dart to her chest, and she knew it was meant to. It was his way of getting her to stop talking.

He poked the butt of his cigarette into the soda can.

"Listen up, Everhart. Get that case cleared and don't get distracted. It's not a pattern. You got me? We have reporters crawling all over, and we don't need them sniffing out some new story about a serial killer. Jesus." He rubbed his hand over his shaved head. "That's the last thing we need."

Leanne watched him, simmering with frustration. She'd come in today hoping to convince him to let her expand her investigation, and now he wanted her to wind it down. She needed to get out of here before things got any worse. Or before he circled back to the interview request.

She stood up. "I'd better get to work, then." She reached for the door.

"Hey, since you brought it up—have you read through the Hannah Rawls case file?"

The question surprised her.

"Not completely."

"Well, I have. I know it backward and forward. So did your dad." His gaze narrowed. "And let me tell you something. You do this job long enough, you'll realize everything isn't always black-and-white. It's gray."

She started to respond, then bit her tongue.

"And *two* things can be true at once," he said. "Sean Moriarty could have made that confession under duress. And the lying son of a bitch is guilty as hell."

FOURTEEN

Leanne raced down the trail, dodging branches and scrub trees. The uphill hurt—a 20 percent incline over 2.3 miles—but the downhill was harder, requiring total concentration.

She regulated her breathing as she navigated the rocky terrain while moving at top speed. This was the most difficult section. Her legs felt like Jell-O, and one careless step could result in a wipeout. She liked the challenge, though, because it made her feel invigorated.

The trail at Mesa Rosada used to be a breeze. The summer before entering the police academy, she'd worked up to doing it twice a day, along with push-ups, sit-ups, and enough pull-ups to make her arms quiver. She'd been manic about physical conditioning back then. The pull-ups were the worst—she'd never had much upper-body strength—but she'd done them anyway, along with countless trail runs, propelled by a burning desire not to be shown up by her male counterparts. Her determination not to embarrass herself had been her rocket fuel.

Leanne had worked her ass off that summer. She'd dropped weight and gotten in shape, and she'd managed to stay that way up until a year ago. The moment she hit thirty, everything changed. It was like her metabolism somehow knew she was sensitive about the milestone and suddenly decided to take a nosedive. The abrupt change had caught her off guard, and she didn't like that.

As a teenager, Leanne hadn't spent much time considering what life would look like in her thirties. Whatever vague idea she'd had, had been of something else, though. Maybe a partner by this point. Maybe a place of her own in a big city. Definitely a better car, not a battered Chevy pickup with a hundred thousand miles on it. And she absolutely hadn't planned to still be in Madrone—a town where dating apps were pointless because the pool of people was so tiny—living in a rental house with a stray cat for an occasional bedmate.

Never get too confident, her dad used to say. *Life has a way of knocking you on your ass.*

Of course, she hadn't listened. She *had* gotten too confident. Putting Madrone in her rearview mirror had made her feel a little too pleased with herself, maybe even smug.

The last two years had taught her that her dad was right. And the biggest irony? His death was the thing that had knocked her flat.

Leanne passed a mile marker and took her gaze off the trail for a moment to check the stopwatch on her phone. Despite a two-week gap since her last workout, she was making good time. She rounded another switchback.

I'm sure as hell glad your dad's not alive to see this.

Anger festered inside her as Jim McBride's words came back. It was a feeling that hit her with increasing frequency these days.

Leanne had discovered that Grief, Year Two, was very different from Grief, Year One. That first year, especially in the early months, people took pains not to say her father's name—as if the mere mention of him would remind her of a crushing loss she might otherwise forget. That whole first year she'd found people's avoidance of saying his name to be hurtful, even insulting. But Year Two was different. Now she didn't care what people did or didn't say about him. She'd gotten used to not caring.

With the odd exception of Jim McBride. Whenever he said anything about her father, she felt the overwhelming urge to smack him in the face. She thought of their meeting today, and his cavalier responses. The man infuriated her, and Trish Rawls was right about him never having any balls.

Leanne rounded another switchback. Her toe caught a rock, and she pitched forward, catching herself on a cedar tree right beside the drop-off. She stopped to get her breath and looked out from the cliff.

The valley stretched out before her, vast and empty. A two-lane highway bisected the arid land, and in the far distance, she could see the snowy white peak of the Desert Star yurt. The late-day sun cast a golden glow over the canyon, making the shadows long, and she took a moment to take it all in. Leanne understood the severe, untamed beauty of her desert birthplace. But she also knew the ugly side—the racism, the poverty, and the constant threat of violence in a region crisscrossed by coyotes and drug traffickers and vigilantes set on frontier justice.

She stepped back to the trail and focused on her run. Her quads burned, and she had a cramp in her side, but the thought of water spurred her on. Rounding the last switchback, she spied her Chevy at the trailhead, alongside a familiar black pickup.

"Crap," she muttered.

She picked up her pace for the final stretch and tried not to look like she was on the verge of collapse.

Duncan watched her from behind his mirrored Ray-Bans.

"Hey," she said, approaching him.

The left side of his mouth ticked up. "How far'd you go?"

"The loop."

"Nice."

She stopped beside him, taking care to position herself downwind.

"I haven't been out here in months." He peeled off his sunglasses and looked her up and down.

"What are you doing here?" she asked.

"I saw your truck from the highway. I was planning to call you later."

She waited. She wasn't about to assume it would have been a social call.

"I got in touch with my friend Jackson."

"Jackson's your tire expert." She pulled a key from her zipper pouch and clicked open her locks.

"Yeah, Brett Jackson, with the state lab in Austin. He agreed to take a look at that tire tread. I sent him your photo this afternoon."

She grabbed her water bottle from inside. "Thanks." She unscrewed the cap and took a swig.

"I told him it was a homicide case and that I need it soon. He owes me a favor, so it shouldn't take too long."

"I appreciate it." She searched Duncan's eyes. Where was this sudden cooperation coming from? "Thanks for calling in a favor for me."

He stepped closer. "What's wrong? You look pissed."

"I'm not."

"You are. I can tell."

It irked her that Duncan could read her so easily when most of the time his emotions were a black box. She took another swig of water.

"McBride is—" She wanted to launch into a rant about him, but she didn't want to seem like she couldn't handle a tough boss. "He's on a tear this week."

"Because of the Moriarty thing?"

"Probably."

He tipped his head to the side. "What's the story there, anyway?"

"Don't you watch the news?"

"I want to know from you. Your dad was on the case, right?"

"Yeah."

"So, you remember it?"

She wiped her brow with her forearm and looked away. "Everyone remembers it."

She felt him watching her, waiting for more. Naturally he was curious, being a cop. But it was hard to describe to someone who wasn't from here what an impact the case had. One minute they were this sleepy little town, and the next they'd been hit by a meteor.

"My dad headed up the case." She looked at Duncan. "Him and McBride. They were smack in the middle of it."

"And Novak?"

She shook her head. "He wasn't here yet. This was Ron Hausmann. He's a judge now." She took a swig of water and tried to compose her thoughts.

"You know the Rawls family?" she asked.

"I haven't met them. I've driven past their place."

"Well, their daughter's murder was the biggest law enforcement thing that ever happened here. It shook everyone up. Nothing has been the same since."

"Why?"

She looked at Duncan's calm blue eyes. It was such a basic question, and she wasn't sure she knew the answer, just that there was a *before* and an *after*.

"I guess... it shattered illusions for people? Idyllic small town and all that?" She shook her head. The concept probably sounded ridiculous to someone who'd grown up in a large metroplex where murders happened all the time. "I mean, this teenage girl goes missing, and then there's a frantic search, cops in from everywhere, people on horseback, search dogs. This place was a circus. Then finally they found her, and it was as bad as your worst nightmare. She was stuffed in an old well. She'd been strangled and beaten. Then the real trouble started."

"You mean the investigation?" he asked.

"For weeks, they didn't have a clue, and there was all this finger-pointing. It was a drug cartel that got her, a long-haul trucker, a coyote. And then they arrested someone *from* here. Sean Moriarty."

"Were they a couple?"

"They didn't run in the same circles, but it came out that she'd been seeing him on the sly, knowing her parents wouldn't approve. And that's when the rifts happened. Everyone's toxic biases came out."

He frowned. "Biases how? Moriarty's white."

"Yeah, but I mean, there's different types of white around here. There's rancher white and tourist white. There's oil field white. Sean's family was dirt-poor, and he'd been in trouble all his life, so people were pretty quick to believe he'd done it. Plus, he confessed, so . . ." She looked away again. This was the part she didn't want to talk about with Duncan. The part where her dad's work was now being called into question, along with his integrity. She knew what people were saying, even though they weren't saying it to her face.

"As damning as it was, though, the confession wasn't the only evidence they had at trial," she said. "Moriarty lied to investigators multiple times about his interactions with Hannah on July Fourth, the night she disappeared."

"So, their relationship came out, I take it?"

She nodded. "Her friends tipped off police. They questioned Sean, and he denied even seeing Hannah that night. But several witnesses saw them in the parking lot of the Dairy Queen, where people were hanging out after the fireworks. Hannah had been standing beside Sean's car and talking to him through the window. When they confronted him, Sean admitted that he'd talked to her in the parking lot but said that was it."

"Let me guess. That was a lie, too."

She nodded. "Turned out, they hadn't just talked, they'd argued. Then he took off and she stayed behind with friends. Police later turned up video footage from a gas station that showed Sean driving back past the Dairy Queen around the same time Hannah was last seen. So police asked if she'd gotten into his car, and of course, he denied it. But when confronted with *another* contradictory witness, he admitted giving her a ride."

"So . . . that makes him the last known person to have seen her alive?"

"Exactly. He claimed they had 'stuff to work out' and he offered to drive her home so they could talk in private. He initially claimed he dropped her off along the highway near her family's ranch because she didn't want her parents to see his truck pull in. Said she wanted to walk. It wasn't until police got a search warrant and found her blood in his front seat that he finally broke down and admitted killing her. They got the confession on videotape."

Moriarty's court-appointed defense attorney made several attempts to get the confession thrown out, but those attempts failed. The video made it in, and jurors watched as a mumbling, sometimes tearful, Sean Moriarty recounted to detectives—including Leanne's father—how he'd offered Hannah a ride home, but then taken her to an isolated road to have sex, and when she'd refused him, he'd killed her and dumped her body in a well.

"The blood evidence might have been enough to convict him, but the confession made it a slam dunk," Leanne said. "The jury only took four hours to find him guilty."

"I'm surprised he didn't end up on death row."

"He could have," she said. "His age and lack of previous felonies helped him out there. I'm sure his race helped, too."

At the time, Leanne had naively thought the tensions in town would go away when the trial ended. But the aftermath turned out to be almost as contentious as the trial itself. People who had been divided about the case against Sean Moriarty were equally divided about his sentence. To some, he embodied the very reason capital punishment existed. To others, he was a troubled young man who had made terrible mistakes but deserved mercy.

Leanne didn't know where Hannah's parents stood. But based on what Trish Rawls had said the other day, she figured they were in the no-mercy group.

"Anyway, now he's out of prison and the whole thing is upside down." She rubbed the sweat off her forehead again. "So, McBride's freaking out every minute and saying how we might get sued."

"You will."

"I know that."

She looked at Duncan, challenging him to say something along the lines of *well, at least your dad's not here to see his biggest case unravel*. But he simply returned her stare with a cool, steady look.

She finished off her water. "So, long story short, the chief is being a prick, and today we butted heads. Again."

"Why this time?"

She sighed. "You know Jen Sayers?"

"The forensic anthropologist."

"Yeah. She informed me of five additional cases of un-IDed bones in this area that could possibly be related to my Jane Doe."

His eyebrows arched.

"I want to expand my investigation, and McBride wants me to wrap it up," she said.

"What are you going to do?"

"I don't know."

He smiled slightly. "So, you came here to pound out a few miles and devise a way to go around him."

She didn't respond.

He laughed and shook his head.

"I'm glad you think this is funny."

"I think *you're* funny."

A phone chimed softly. It took her a moment to realize it was hers. She pulled it from her pouch and checked the screen. Josh.

"Everhart."

"Canyon Glen again," Josh said. "Looks like you're up."

Leanne wasn't on call, but she'd made him a promise.

"Send me the address," she said.

"I just did."

She hung up as a text landed on her phone.

Duncan pulled his keys from his pocket.

"I have to go," she said.

"I know."

He rounded the front of his truck and looked at her over the roof. "Call me next time you come out here. We'll run it together."

"I'll smoke you," she told him.

"We'll see."

Izzy gave herself a pep talk as she stared at the building from her car.

Her meeting started in two minutes.

She didn't have time for nerves. Or doubts. Or the sudden wave of panic that made her feel like she was going to throw up before she even walked in there.

She flipped the visor down and checked her reflection. Maybe she'd overdone the eyeliner. Not maybe. She definitely had. She didn't usually wear makeup, but she wanted to look put together—not like someone who'd spent the afternoon on the side of the highway in a fluorescent yellow vest photographing skid marks on the pavement.

Not that she hated her job. Some days she even liked it. But documenting traffic accidents was not what she'd had in mind when she accepted a scholarship to NYU and went off to pursue her dream of becoming a professional photographer. She'd come back home for a good reason. But her mom's cancer was in remission, and she no longer needed Izzy to shuttle her back and forth to doctor appointments on a regular basis. Izzy had no more excuses, and she was running out of time to get her life back on track.

She carefully applied lipstick, then flipped up the visor. No more stalling.

She grabbed her portfolio from the passenger seat and got out of her car. She'd dragged out her knockoff Fendi boots for this, and as she strode up the sidewalk, she tried not to catch a heel on the pavement and do a face-plant in front of the window.

It was six o'clock sharp, but the door was unlocked.

She stepped into the gallery and was confronted by a wall of cold air. The enormous photographs on display immediately caught her attention. She'd seen them on the website, but nothing compared to viewing them in person and being dwarfed by their scale. She approached the one closest to the reception desk.

"You must be Isabella."

She turned around, and nerves flitted through her stomach as Zach Olmstead crossed the gallery. He wore black slacks and an espresso-colored sweater that matched his eyes.

"Hello." She shook his outstretched hand. "I'm here to meet with Freya?"

He smiled, and she understood why her friend Aspen had slept with him on the first date.

"She had to step out. But come on." He nodded toward the back of the gallery. "We can get started without her."

Izzy followed him behind a matte black wall with a pair of photographs mounted on it. Behind the partition was a glass conference table surrounded by chairs.

"Freya tells me you went to NYU," he said.

"That's right."

"I see you brought some work. Let's have a look." He nodded at her portfolio, and she hesitated for a split second before unzipping it and sliding out the first of ten pieces.

Ten should be plenty, Freya had told her when Izzy had asked how many to bring. So of course, she'd spent an hour stressing over which ones to choose.

Izzy placed the photographs on the table. Zach arranged them into two straight rows as she held her breath.

"Ah. Moab." He picked up the one on the end, an eight-by-ten of a vibrant orange canyon set against an azure sky. "I was out there in September."

He studied her photograph with a furrowed brow, then set it down. "Digital?"

"That one, yes. I do both, though. I prefer my analog camera for black-and-white shots."

"So do I." He picked up a photo of a towering rock formation. "Arches National Park?"

"Canyonlands."

He stepped over to the final of the ten pieces, a crooked Joshua tree silhouetted against a dusky sky. Izzy had saved this photo for last. It was one of the ones she'd sent to Freya that helped land her this interview.

His eyebrow lifted as he touched the corner. "This is good."

"Thank you."

He looked at her. "You ever work at night?"

"Not a lot, actually." She cleared her throat. "I've been focused on color contrasts."

He stepped back from the table and studied the array of photos.

Years and years of work condensed into a handful of eight-by-ten images. Compared to the gigantic pieces a few feet away, hers felt small and amateurish.

"Well, Freya was right." He looked at her. "She usually is."

It sounded like a compliment, and Izzy's stomach did a somersault. She sensed she'd passed some sort of test.

He stepped closer, and she caught a whiff of expensive cologne. "I'm a member of the Presidio Arts Council. We're putting together an exhibit at the observatory—*Lone Star Nights*, we're calling it." He gave a crooked smile. "I didn't come up with the name. At any rate, we're looking to highlight local artists. Do you live in the county?"

"I'm in Madrone."

"Close enough." He tilted his head and looked at the Joshua tree picture again.

"When is the exhibit?" she asked.

"April. That gives you some time."

"So . . . since you're partnering with the observatory, I assume the focus is constellations?"

"Anything after dark would work. As you can see, we take our night sky seriously." He smiled again. "Why don't you take a crack at it, see what you come up with?"

"I will."

He checked his Rolex, and she took that as a cue that she'd used up her time. She collected her prints off the table and felt his gaze on her as she slid them into her portfolio.

"Have you been out to the observatory?" he asked.

She didn't want to mention her middle school field trip, which would only remind him that she'd grown up in a town that didn't even have a movie theater.

"It's been a few years," she said.

"I should take you to one of their star parties sometime."

The nerves were back again. There was something in his tone, and she remembered Aspen telling her that with Zach Olmstead, everything was transactional.

He stepped over to a shelf and plucked a business card from a silver holder. He wrote something on it and returned to the table.

"My number's on the back there. Are you interested in the show?"

Was she interested? There was a certain ick factor to the way he said it. But she'd made it this far, and she was determined to see it through.

He held out the card. "I'd love to see you submit something."

"Yes, absolutely." She took the card from him. "I'm definitely interested."

It was after nine by the time Leanne wrapped up for the day and pulled the report off the printer. She skimmed the first page as she walked across the bullpen.

"How was Canyon Glen?"

She glanced up to see Josh. He wore a button-down shirt and slacks and had a computer bag slung over his shoulder.

"Fine," she said.

"Sanders again?"

"It was the neighbors this time. The husband came home drunk, and the wife poured out a case of his beer in the street. They got into it, and someone called it in."

"Thanks for taking it," he said. "I had a dinner thing."

"No problem."

A date, probably. She'd heard that Josh had been out with Nadine's daughter Selma a few times, and Nadine had mentioned that Selma had a birthday this week. Based on Josh's attire, she guessed they'd been to Cattleman's Steakhouse, the only place in town worth dressing up for. She also guessed it hadn't gone that well or he wouldn't be stopping by the office afterward.

Leanne was curious, but she didn't ask. Prying was a two-way street, and she hated when people quizzed her about her personal life at work. She went to great lengths to keep her private life private, which was hard to do when her father had worked in the very same department her entire childhood.

Josh nodded at the report in her hands. "A little light reading?"

She glanced down at her stack of papers. An autopsy photo was peeking out.

"The Jane Doe report. Korbin just sent it."

"Wow."

"I know, right? I couldn't believe it." It was a fast turnaround, and she appreciated that he'd picked up on her urgency.

"Let me know if there's anything new in there," Josh said, eyeing the report with a look that told her he didn't intend to read it unless he absolutely had to.

"Will do. See you tomorrow."

She swung by her desk and added the paperwork to her overstuffed accordion file, then grabbed her keys. Her phone chimed as she stepped out of the station house into the chilly night air.

"Hi, Mom."

"Have you heard from Ben?" she asked without preamble.

"No."

Leanne slid into her truck and checked the clock. She'd left her brother a message this morning and another two hours ago.

"I tried him earlier, but he didn't pick up." Leanne chucked her file into the passenger seat. "Has he been home?"

"No."

It was a loaded *no*, and she knew there was more to the story.

"He was supposed to have a drug test today, but I think he missed it."

"Shit."

"Can you try him again?"

Leanne sighed. "Yeah."

A sour ball filled her stomach as she pulled out of the parking lot. Ben couldn't afford to miss another drug test. She'd used up all her favors with his probation officer.

"He's probably with that Diandra again."

That Diandra.

"Maybe he's with Alan," Leanne said, naming the only one of her brother's friends who wasn't a complete burnout.

"Alan moved."

"He did?"

"He lives in El Paso now. He has a real job, like most people."

Leanne scanned the streets for her brother's dinged blue Kia as she made her way through town. She tapped her brakes in front of Shooters but didn't see his car in the lot. Diandra didn't have her own car, which was one of the reasons she'd attached herself to Ben like a lamprey.

"Will you call him, Leanne? He'll pick up for you."

"No, he won't."

"He might."

She sighed. "I'll try. But don't stay up worrying. He's probably just hanging out somewhere."

"That's exactly what I'm worried about. Listen, there's something else."

Leanne heard the rattle of ice cubes and pictured her mom with her highball glass in hand.

"Sean Moriarty was here today."

Leanne's blood went cold. "Where?"

"Here."

"He was at your *house*?"

"He was at the ranch. Same thing. He followed me home from my bridge club meeting."

She gripped the steering wheel. "Are you sure it was him?"

"I'm not blind, Leanne. I know what the man looks like."

"You haven't seen him in years, though."

"He was in his brother's truck. And no, it wasn't his brother. It was Sean Moriarty. I'd know him anywhere. He looks the same as he always did, only without the long hair."

Leanne checked her rearview mirror. She glanced around, now looking for Liam Moriarty's silver pickup. Ever since her run-in with him at the bar, she'd been checking up on the Moriarty family. Liam had a short rap sheet, but nothing compared to his older brother.

"How did you get rid of him?" Leanne asked.

"I didn't. He stopped when I drove through the gate. He pulled off the road and watched me drive in."

"Did you tell Boone?"

"No. It would only rile him up."

Leanne gritted her teeth. "Well, what do you think he wanted?"

"To scare me. What else?" More ice cubes rattling. "He likes to intimidate people. I just wanted you to know in case . . ." She trailed off.

"In case what? Did he threaten you?"

"I didn't talk to him," she said. "But I thought I should tell you, and now I have. End of conversation. Call your brother for me, all right? I'm going to bed."

"Wait, Mom. Mom? Lock your doors," Leanne said, but she'd already hung up.

FIFTEEN

The autopsy photos were spread out across the table like a gruesome memory game. Leanne was a visual person, which was both a blessing and a curse. Seeing details up close would sometimes spark a new direction in her investigation. The downside was that staring at death pictures for hours on end was guaranteed to give her insomnia.

Leanne closed her eyes and pinched the bridge of her nose. She'd been sifting through paperwork for hours and still had more to go. After a hectic morning, she'd slipped away from the station house and driven to the university to pay another visit to Jen Sayers. She wanted more information about the cold cases. Now Leanne was holed up in the reading room of the science library, where she was isolated from interruptions and better able to concentrate on the reports that she needed to analyze. Buried somewhere in the thick stack of papers might be an overlooked clue that could provide a fresh lead. Leanne was determined to find it.

Downing her last sip of lukewarm coffee from the student center, she returned her attention to her primary case, focusing on the part of the Jane Doe autopsy report where Dr. Korbin described the victim's injuries.

Right hand: fractured scaphoid, fractured trapezium. Fractured fifth proximal phalanx.

Leanne had consulted her phone to translate all the jargon. The victim had a broken wrist and broken pinkie, along with a torn fingernail, all on her right hand. That sounded like she'd put up a fight.

The torn fingernail was potentially explosive. DNA was the gold standard in terms of identifying a perpetrator. If the victim had scratched her attacker during a struggle, maybe his DNA had ended up under her fingernail, which would be analyzed as part of the rape kit.

When the rape kit got analyzed, which could take months. It might not get looked at until investigators zeroed in on a suspect and attempted to link him to the crime.

Investigators. Right.

Leanne was pretty much flying solo at this point. And despite her best efforts, she still hadn't been able to identify the victim yet. Zeroing in on a suspect seemed like a distant fantasy.

The sticky scrap of duct tape found near the body could be a source of DNA, too, but getting that tested presented a whole different challenge. Because the tape had been found on the bushes near the body, and not on the body itself, it was considered part of the crime scene, and not something the ME handled. Leanne would have to get McBride's approval to send it in separately, and he'd made it clear he wasn't keen to waste valuable resources on a Jane Doe.

Leanne flipped to the ME's diagram—a simple line drawing surrounded by notes that had probably been dictated by Korbin and jotted down by his assistant during the exam. Since Leanne had missed the autopsy—*thanks again, Chief*—she could only speculate as to how it all played out.

Fractured hyoid. The words were scribbled in the margin, with a line pointing to the victim's neck.

Leanne was familiar with the injury, which occurred in many strangulation deaths.

Fractured right parietal was written beside the skull.

ZMC fracture.

Fractured mandible.

Korbin had said these injuries happened postmortem. So, the perpetrator had choked this woman to death and then beaten her. What kind of person strangles the life out of someone and then lets loose on the corpse? That was some kind of rage. Some kind of . . . next-level crazy, really.

Leanne slid the autopsy report aside and pulled her legal pad closer. Like her dad, she had a fondness for notepads, and writing down her thoughts helped her to clarify them. She reread her notes and then examined the map she'd printed out of the tri-county area, complete with X's showing where bodies had been recovered. The X's were scattered up and down the highway between Fort Stockton and Marfa.

Four sets of remains, all recovered along the same stretch of highway, as Jen had said. And that wasn't even counting the stray jawbone or the femur.

It wasn't only the location that was interesting. Leanne shifted focus to the stack of reports Jen had submitted to various law enforcement agencies in the region.

The similarities were jarring.

All of the intact skeletal remains showed injuries remarkably similar to Leanne's current homicide. Fractured skulls. Fractured wrists. Broken fingers. Two victims had a broken hyoid bone, indicating they'd been strangled. Two sets of remains included duct tape. In one case a strip was wrapped around the victim's head. In another case, a strip was tangled in her hair.

Leanne flipped a page and skimmed through her detailed notes. Beating, strangulation, duct tape. An MO was starting to emerge, and it was hideous.

"You're here late."

She glanced up to see Jen in the doorway. The white lab coat was gone now, and she had a set of keys in her hand.

Leanne checked her phone. It was after five, and she'd been in here almost four hours.

"Damn, I lost track of time," Leanne said.

"You're in the zone." Jen looked at the photographs lined up on the table, and her expression turned worried. "You doing okay?"

"Yeah. It's just . . . a lot."

"I know." She gave a sympathetic smile. "Don't stay too long. It helps to get a break."

After she was gone, Leanne checked the time again and decided on a deadline. One more hour, and then she was calling it a day. She'd been so absorbed with this homicide, she'd started to neglect the rest of her workload, and it wouldn't be long before McBride took notice.

She slid aside the legal pad and shuffled through the stack of reports from Jen until she found the one about the jawbone. This report was the shortest because the lone mandible had yielded little information.

Leanne scanned the summary, focusing on the bone's location in western Chisos County near the county line. Like one of the other sets of remains, the jawbone had been discovered by a hunter. Unfortunately, instead of leaving the bone where he found it, he'd collected it and taken it to the sheriff's office himself.

The original police report was attached, and Leanne thumbed through it. There wasn't much there beyond the hunter's account of finding the bone when he'd pulled off the highway to relieve himself and him saying he was pretty sure the bone wasn't human, but that he'd decided to turn it over to the sheriff's office "just to be sure." The police report was dated the day after the finding, which further compromised the chain of custody. Leanne figured the hunter had been drinking leading up to his discovery and didn't want to talk to police until he'd had a chance to sober up. The one bit of good news was that the report included GPS coordinates of the bone's location.

Leanne entered the coordinates into her phone, and a pin appeared on her mapping app.

Her pulse quickened. She zoomed in on the pin. The jawbone was found on the north side of Long Canyon Road, less than a mile away from the juncture of Long Canyon Road and Highway 67.

The location fit.

Leanne stared at the map, and the silence of the reading room closed in on her. What had been a shadowy feeling for the last few days was now as bright and clear as the West Texas sky.

Jane Doe was part of a pattern.

She was part of a string of murders that no one had solved, or even tried to, really. And why hadn't they? Leanne had a creeping suspicion it was because no one cared.

Since the moment she had pulled up to that crime scene and spotted Will Akers looking pale and shaken, Leanne had been dogged by a feeling of dread. From an investigative standpoint, everything about this case was terrible. They were dealing with an outdoor scene that was exposed to the elements. The victim had no ID on her. Her description didn't match any missing person report Leanne had been able to dig up, so five days into the investigation, the victim was still anonymous. Given those factors, the probability of solving this case was low. Barring a surprise lead, such as an eyewitness coming forward, the Jane Doe murder was exactly the sort of crime that was likely to slip through the cracks and remain forever unsolved. Leanne wasn't naive; she knew this. And she could admit—if only to herself—that part of her longed to drop the case like a hot potato.

But another part of her was furious. This was her jurisdiction, her *home*. How dare someone commit murder here and think they could get away with it?

The question answered itself. Someone dared to do it because they had done it before. They had gotten away with it for years. Who was stopping them from doing it again?

Outrage festered inside her as she stared down at the map. Now that the pattern had emerged, it was like one of those Magic Eye pictures. She couldn't *unsee* it. These crimes were connected, and they were dealing with a repeat offender who was getting bolder and bolder as he committed crimes with impunity. He had to be stopped.

As she studied the map, something inside her shifted. Regardless of the odds, or the chief's resistance to approving the resources she needed, or the jurisdictional issues she was up against, Leanne was all in. These were her cases to solve, and there was no going back now.

She read the report again, looking for any more details that might help her, but that was it. Maybe she could track down this hunter and interview him. Or talk to the deputy who'd taken the report. She scanned the page for names and found one she recognized right there at the bottom.

"No freaking way."

SIXTEEN

Leanne pulled up to the little brick house and strode to the front door. The porch light was on, but no TV. She cupped her hands and peered through the window, but the blinds were closed tight, and she couldn't see inside.

Headlights swept across the yard, and the garage door opened. She whirled around, shielding her eyes from the glare as a pickup rumbled up the driveway.

Leanne walked over and waited as Duncan eased into the garage. He took his time getting out.

"Where have you been?" she asked.

He walked back to the tailgate. "Take a guess."

He wore a dusty black T-shirt and black tactical pants. He reached into the back and grabbed a flak jacket and duffel bag. He'd obviously been on an op, but that did nothing to calm her temper.

"I left you two messages."

He slung the duffel over his shoulder. "I had my phone off."

He crossed the empty half of the garage.

Well, not completely empty. There was no vehicle parked there, and he'd converted the space into a home gym that had made Leanne green with envy the moment she'd seen it. She did her workouts in the blazing sun.

He dropped his gear onto the rubber mat and sank onto the weight bench.

"What's up?" He pulled off his sweaty T-shirt and flung it to the floor in front of a stacking washer-dryer.

"Why didn't you tell me you were the primary on the un-IDed remains from Chisos County?"

He looked up at her. "Come again?"

"The jawbone, Duncan. Long Canyon Road."

Recognition sparked. "The deer hunter?"

"Yes! I spent an entire afternoon combing through reports, looking for connections to my case, only to find out *you* were the primary investigator. What the hell? Why didn't you tell me?"

He leaned over and unlaced his boots. "I didn't realize that's what you were talking about when you told me about un-IDed bodies. Anyway, there's not much to tell."

"What do you mean?"

He tossed a dirt-caked boot into the corner. "The guy who found the jawbone brought it in himself. Fucked up the chain of custody. He'd been drinking all day with his buddies, couldn't even say for sure where he found it." He pulled off his other boot and tossed it away. Then he stood up.

"Where'd you get GPS coordinates for the police report?" she asked.

"That's an approximation. I drove out to this location he described and took them down." He rested his hands on his hips. "How do you know this is related to your homicide case?"

"Isn't it obvious? The *human* jawbone was found near where Long Canyon Road intersects with Highway 67 on the western side of the county. Even if it's an approximation, that location makes it part of the pattern." She crossed her arms. "*Six* unidentified victims dumped near a ninety-mile stretch of highway in the last ten years. Four of those are definitely female, and the other two might be. And those are just the ones we know about. Did you guys search for the rest of the remains?"

"We did a canvass."

"I mean seriously search, with a cadaver dog."

"No."

"Why not?"

"I suggested it, and it went nowhere. Just like if you suggested it to McBride."

Frustration flashed through her because he was right. Given the number of deaths in the desert, her department didn't have the resources to track down every last bone. The closest canine search team was based in El Paso.

Leanne turned away and pressed her fingertips to her temples. This case kept snowballing, and instead of more support, she was getting pressure to wind it down.

"Hey."

She turned back to Duncan.

"You really believe it's connected." It was a statement, not a question.

She took a deep breath. "I spent my day buried in forensic anthropology reports. The MO is the same. Duct tape, strangling, crushed skulls. And the locations where the bodies are being dumped—"

"You sound like it's an ongoing thing." His brow furrowed as he stepped closer. "You realize what you're saying, don't you?"

"Yes."

She was saying they were dealing with a serial killer.

"McBride won't touch it," she said.

His eyebrows tipped up. "You ran this by him?"

"I started to, but he shut me down."

"Lemme guess. He's distracted by the Moriarty case."

"Our last high-profile homicide is exploding in our faces right now," she said. "He's not exactly looking for more stuff to investigate. He's already made it clear he's unwilling to spend any resources on this. Not to mention, there are reporters everywhere and our department is under a microscope."

Duncan was watching her now with a wary look, probably because he knew what was coming.

She cleared her throat. "So, I was thinking."

"No."

"Just hear me out. We found some duct tape near the culvert where my Jane Doe was recovered."

He turned around, shaking his head.

"There was duct tape with two of the other bodies that Jen Sayers handled. That's not a coincidence—that's an MO."

He scoffed. "Yeah, because duct tape is so hard to come by."

"One of those cases was in Chisos County, too. You could submit the evidence on behalf of the sheriff's office, along with mine—"

"Leanne—"

"Just listen. You could submit it as part of following up on your cold case investigation of the unidentified jawbone."

"There *is* no cold case investigation. I'm up to my neck in active investigations." He waved an arm at his gear strewn across the floor. "Not to mention the task force that has me on call twenty-four/seven."

"You don't have to do anything—just send in the duct tape. If anything comes of it, I'll handle the follow up."

"Bullshit. If anything comes of it, we'll both be in the middle of a shitstorm."

"Okay, but if anything *does* come of it, that means my theory is right and someone is out here murdering people and getting away with it."

She stared up at him, waiting for him to agree.

He closed his eyes and rubbed his face with his dirty hands. "I swear to God, Leanne—"

"Please? This is the last favor."

He dropped his hands and laughed. "Right."

"I mean it."

"Look at you." He shook his head. "You can't even say that with a straight face."

By the time Leanne made it home, the yurt was dark and the campground was quiet. What few weekday tourists Michelle had this evening had apparently turned in early and were tucked under their feather duvets for the night.

Leanne pulled into the driveway and eyed her front door as her stomach grumbled. No Igloo cooler or skinny cat to welcome her home this time.

She let herself into the house and dropped a plastic bag of gas station groceries on the counter. It was cold again, so she switched on the heater and stripped off her clothes as she made her way to the bedroom. She tossed her jacket on the bed, then added her holster and gun to the pile, followed by her T-shirt and bra. After a few minutes standing under a warm shower spray, she pulled on a tank top and sweatpants and padded barefoot into the kitchen.

Her phone was nearly dead, and she plugged it into the charger before getting out the burrito she'd bought for dinner. She popped it into the microwave and watched it spin on the turntable, where—despite her appetite—it looked even less appetizing than it had under the convenience store heat lamp.

Leanne grabbed a water bottle from her fridge and twisted the cap, then stared out the window.

Something looked off outside, but she couldn't place it. She turned off the light above the stove and scanned the darkened landscape beyond her yard. A nearly full moon shone down over the canyon, and she heard the stuttering *hoo-hoo-hoo* of the great horned owl that lived nearby. She studied the rocks and scrub trees. On a distant ridge, the light of a campfire flickered, but other than that everything looked normal.

Except . . .

She realized what was bugging her as the microwave dinged. The backyard was too dark. She padded into the bedroom and grabbed a pack of lightbulbs from the top of the closet. Dragging her stepladder outside, she positioned it under the porch light and climbed up to change the bulb.

She twisted it, and the light went on.

"What the . . . ?"

She turned it the other way, and it went off again. She twisted it back on, then climbed down and set the pack of bulbs on the ladder, staring at the fixture as gnats started to swarm.

Who had loosened the bulb? She couldn't remember when she first noticed it being out. Several nights ago, at least.

A scratching noise made her turn around, and she looked out at the dark yard.

A man stood up from the lounge chair. Leanne reached for her service weapon, but it was under a pile of clothes in her bedroom.

The shadowy figure stepped forward, and some primal corner of her brain sent a warning before her conscious brain caught up.

Sean Moriarty.

Her hands curled into fists as he emerged from the darkness.

"What are you doing here?" she demanded.

He stepped into the glow of the porch light, and her heart skittered. Her mother was right—he looked the same. But different, too, in ways that mattered.

He had the same tall, broad-shouldered build that she remembered from high school. But the muscles that had once been swollen from football practice and steroids were now lean and sinewy. He wore a gray T-shirt over stiff new jeans. His head was shaved, and the porch light glinted off his pale scalp.

Most men around here, from cowboys to border cops, had skin that was tan and leathery from the sun. Sean Moriarty's skin had the pasty look of someone who had spent years under fluorescent prison lighting.

"What are you doing here?" she repeated.

He lifted a shoulder. "It's a free country."

The word *free* was loaded with accusation.

He swaggered forward and rested his hands on his hips—the same hands that had once plucked fifty-yard passes out of the sky like magic. Now his knuckles were covered in prison ink.

He nodded at the fixture above her head. "Your light was out. I been waiting in the dark."

"This is private property. You need to leave."

He pulled a toothpick from his pocket and slid it between his lips. "I will."

"Boone Sullivan's ranch is, too. Same for the Triple R. I advise you to stay away from there. Someone might mistake you for a prowler."

He smiled slightly, but it didn't reach his eyes. They were flat and gray.

He stepped closer, and she caught a whiff of cigarettes. His gaze raked over her, lingering on her thin white top.

"You look good, Leanne. All grown up."

She stared at him, refusing to be cowed or even blink.

He pulled the toothpick out and looked at it. On his right forearm was a faded viper, and seeing her high school mascot with all the prison tattoos put a pinch in her chest.

"Know something I learned in Huntsville?"

She crossed her arms.

"Patience," he said. "I've had fifteen years to think about all the people who wronged me. It's a long list, and your dad's at the top. You're on it, too."

She scoffed. "Me? You don't even know me."

"That's where you're wrong."

He smiled again, and she felt the chill in her bones.

"Don't worry, Leanne. You'll get what's coming."

He moved forward, and she flinched. Still smiling, he stepped around her and walked to the side of her house, then disappeared around the corner.

Leanne stared after him, replaying his words and wishing she'd responded with something stronger. *This is private property.* What the hell was that? Her cheeks flushed.

Somewhere in the distance, an engine started. It sounded like a truck, low and throaty, and she stood there listening until it faded away.

SEVENTEEN

Leanne struggled to focus on her job while her mind kept replaying her encounter with Sean Moriarty. Everything about it put her on edge, and she'd come to agree with her mom—his following her home was an intimidation tactic. He wanted her to know that he was there watching and that he was close.

Her phone buzzed from the cup holder of the SUV she'd borrowed from the motor pool. She glanced at the screen. Josh.

"Where are you today?" he asked.

"Getting my nails done."

"What?"

"I'm on my way in. What's going on?"

"Some lady's here looking for you. She's been here since I got back from lunch."

Lunch. Another thing she didn't have time for today.

Leanne scanned the streets around the station house, but if there were any reporters in the area, they were keeping a low profile.

"What does she want?" Leanne asked him.

"I don't know. I think she's from Marfa. It's something about her daughter. I tried to talk to her, but she wants to see you."

"I'm on my way in. I'll be there in five."

Leanne pulled into the parking lot and whipped into a space near the back door. She clicked the locks with a *chirp* and strode up the sidewalk to the back door, still on the lookout for Max Scott or any other pushy reporters. Marty Krause with the *Sentinel* had left her a message this morning, and she was dodging calls from three separate news outlets now.

The bullpen was crowded, even for a Friday. She spied Josh at his desk, and he made eye contact as she wove through the cubicles. As she neared the glass partition, Leanne saw Alma Cruz in the waiting room. She sat on a plastic chair, her hands folded in her lap and a black purse at her feet. She wore a long skirt and heels, like she might be headed to church.

Leanne stepped through the door, and Nadine spotted her and nodded toward the waiting area. Alma Cruz was already on her feet.

Leanne forced a smile. "Mrs. Cruz. How are you?"

The woman cast a wary glance at Nadine, who'd no doubt been playing gatekeeper, probably trying to get her to share whatever she needed with a uniform instead of holding out for a detective. Nadine knew how understaffed they were and made it part of her mission to protect their time.

Alma stepped forward. "I wanted to talk to you. Do you have a moment?"

"I do." She glanced at Nadine. "Is the conference room open?"

She shook her head. "Try Interview Two."

Leanne ushered Alma into the bullpen and led her past a row of cubicles to the first open door.

"Have a seat." Leanne gestured to a gray plastic chair identical to the one she'd just been sitting in. "Can I get you anything? Water? Coffee?"

"No, thank you."

Leanne closed the door, hoping to head off questions from nosy coworkers. She took a seat opposite Alma and looked at her across the faux-wood table. Alma's hair was in the same loose bun as last time, and she wore a necklace with a gold Madonna pendant that resembled the mural outside her house.

"What brings you in?" Leanne asked, although she had a hunch that she knew.

"It's about Marisol."

Leanne nodded.

"I saw on the news . . . about the body that was found?" Alma bit her lip, her eyes filled with a mix of fear and hope.

"Your daughter's description doesn't match the remains we recovered," Leanne said.

"Are you sure?"

"Yes. I investigated the possibility."

It was one of the first things Leanne had done after returning from Marfa. The timing seemed unlikely, but there was always the chance that Alma's missing daughter had been alive until recently.

"You are sure?" Alma asked again.

Leanne nodded. "In this case, the victim is five foot one. According to the report on file with Presidio County, your daughter is five-five." Leanne paused. "Is that correct?"

Alma nodded and closed her eyes.

Leanne's stomach tensed as she watched the woman stare down at her lap. Her pain filled the little room, crowding the space like an extra presence.

"Mrs. Cruz, I'm glad you came in today. I had planned to call you."

She looked up.

"Marisol is your biological daughter, correct? She isn't adopted?"

"She's mine."

"Has anyone asked you or your family to provide a DNA sample? I didn't see anything about that in the file."

She shook her head.

Frustration welled in Leanne's chest. This should have been done six years ago.

"Would that help?" Alma asked.

"It would, yes. That would allow us to create a record for Marisol in a nationwide database of people whose families are searching for them. It's a very useful tool."

She took a deep breath. "All right."

Leanne pulled a spiral notepad from the pocket of her jacket. Then she took out her phone and looked up the contact info for the detective assigned to Marisol's case.

"Have you met Detective Orozco? He's with the sheriff's office?"

She shook her head, and Leanne felt a fresh wave of frustration.

"The person who originally worked on your daughter's case— Detective Hastings?—he left the department last year. There's someone new now." Leanne tore off the slip of paper. "You can make arrangements with him to give a DNA sample." She slid the paper across the table. "I'll reach out to him today and let him know to expect you."

Alma folded the paper and tucked it into her purse. By her solemn expression, Leanne could tell she knew exactly what a DNA match would mean.

She slid her chair back. "Thank you."

"One more thing."

Her dark brows arched.

"As you've searched for Marisol, have you met anyone else, maybe in your community or a neighboring community, who is looking for a missing daughter?" Leanne paused. "Sometimes people don't feel comfortable filing a report."

Alma nodded. She understood what Leanne was getting at. Some people took pains to avoid police even when they needed them most. The undercurrent of distrust went back decades, and the influx of wealthy urbanites into Marfa and Madrone had only made things worse. The privilege gap kept getting wider.

"No one like Marisol, no," Alma said. "I don't know anyone whose daughter just"—she waved at the air—"disappeared without a word. I know a few other mothers whose *hijas* are older, and they left with a boyfriend." She shook her head. "Marisol wouldn't do that."

Leanne watched her, looking for signs of ambivalence. Parents were not always the most reliable authority on what their teenage children would or wouldn't do.

"I know what you're thinking." Alma stood up. "But I know my daughter."

EIGHTEEN

The suspect hadn't invited her inside yet. But he hadn't slammed the door in her face, either, so Leanne pressed on.

"This would have been Wednesday night around eleven thirty," she said.

"Nope."

Twenty-six-year-old Bryce Biswell slouched against the doorframe, faking nonchalance and giving smug, one-word answers to all her questions. He got under Leanne's skin, and not just because he had a rap sheet that included burglary and criminal damage to property stemming from an incident when he took a hammer to his ex-girlfriend's windshield.

"Now, see, here's the thing, Bryce. We have a witness who saw two men loading electric bikes into a trailer right there behind Big Sky Sports. And you fit the description of one of those men to a T. Fact, the witness is one hundred percent sure it was you."

He lifted a shoulder. "Nope."

"How do you explain this person's account?"

"Mistaken identity, I guess."

Leanne watched his eyes for signs of agitation. He had a decent poker face. Fortunately, in addition to an eyewitness, Leanne had footage from a security cam across the street from the bike place.

Also fortunately, Bryce Biswell was not the sharpest tool in the shed.

And speaking of sheds...

"That your storage unit?" Leanne nodded at the small metal building beside Biswell's mobile home. The shed was surrounded by weeds and had a rusty padlock on the door.

He leaned out and glanced at it. "Yeah."

"Mind if I look inside?"

He frowned. The question was so bold, he seemed to be at a loss for words.

Biswell rubbed his goatee. "Well. I reckon you'd need a warrant for that."

"Technically, you're right," she said. "But that's a pretty big hassle, to be honest. Are you sure you don't want to just open it up, let me have a quick look, and we can put this thing to rest? Otherwise, I'll have to go write something up and make another trip out."

He shook his head. "Sorry. No can do."

"Fine. Have it your way." She took out a business card and handed it over. "If you hear anything about who might have taken those bikes, give us a call."

Now he looked amused. "Sure will."

Leanne tromped back to her unmarked patrol car and slid behind the wheel. Biswell stood on his doorstep as she did a three-point turn. She watched him recede in her rearview mirror and then texted Josh.

I'm done.

Leanne pulled out of Canyon Glen and hung a right into the adjacent neighborhood. She drove down the dead-end street that backed up to an asphalt basketball court that would be empty until the elementary school let out at 3:50. From her vantage point, she had a view of Biswell's door and the metal carport beside his home.

She cut the engine and settled in to wait. Biswell's trailer was at the end of a long row of homes that ranged in appearance. Some had flowerpots and yard ornaments while others had sagging gutters and blistered paint. Despite the run-down condition of many of the places, this neighborhood had become more popular as vacation rentals took over a bigger share of their housing stock and locals were forced out of homes they'd lived in for decades.

Once upon a time Madrone's poorest neighborhoods had been made up of tiny adobe houses with dirt floors. But now some of those same homes were being renovated and sold for eye-popping sums to owners who let them sit empty much of the year or rented them to tourists for hundreds a night. Marfa was full of such bungalows, and the gentrification was making its way here now, too.

Leanne's gaze settled on a gray double-wide trailer that had once been the home of Sean Moriarty. Patrick Moriarty had raised his three sons there after his wife left when the boys were in elementary school. Sean's dad had worked as a wrangler at the sprawling Miller Ranch north of town. When Sean was arrested for murder, that job evaporated as area families took sides in the case, with most people lining up with the Rawlses. Around the time of the trial, Patrick Moriarty moved to Fort Stockton and took a job at a tractor supply store. Last Leanne heard, Liam and his younger brother were working for an oil company.

She studied the trailer, with its patchy roof and torn screens. As kids, Leanne and Ben had been warned to stay away from the Moriarty brothers, who were known to run wild, with no supervision. Sean in particular had a reputation as a troublemaker that Leanne had found both frightening and fascinating. Besides breaking into cars and vandalizing school property, Sean had a propensity for getting into fights and picking on kids half his size—which was big, as Sean had hit a growth spurt early. The summer after his freshman year, one of the coaches took note of Sean's height and recruited him into the football program, where for the next three years he found an outlet for some of his aggression. Sean proved to be a natural athlete and worked his way from a second-string cornerback to starting wide receiver by his junior year. His senior year, he and Jake Rawls led their team to the regional championship.

Sean's talent on the field made the Moriartys more socially acceptable—but only to a point. People would talk to Patrick Moriarty in the stands on Friday nights, but that didn't mean they wanted his son dating their daughters. Being from a prominent family, Hannah Rawls was way out of Sean's league. But Hannah had a rebellious streak, which was probably why she started seeing Sean after her older brother went off to college.

During the dark days following Hannah's disappearance, a half dozen different law enforcement agencies had converged on Madrone to help with the search. Leanne remembered all the talk about "pulling together" and "taking care of our own" and someone coining the term "Madrone Strong." At the time, she'd felt a sense of pride in her town, amid all the chaos.

Leanne studied the dilapidated trailer and tried to imagine the three big Moriarty boys growing up there. She wasn't fifteen anymore, and she looked at Madrone through a different lens now, the lens of someone who'd been a cop for almost a decade. She had spent a lot of time thinking about Patrick Moriarty, a mean drunk who didn't mind smacking his sons around. People talked about it as though it was one of those unpleasant facts of life, like tornadoes or hailstorms, something people didn't much like but were powerless to change.

Would things be different for everyone—especially the Rawls family—if someone with a badge had done something differently back then? Could Leanne's father have done something? Why had everyone in her supposedly tight-knit hometown looked the other way as three young boys suffered through a crappy situation? Despite his volatile track record and violent temper, Sean Moriarty was a kid from this community, same as Hannah Rawls.

I've had fifteen years to think about all the people who wronged me.

Leanne pictured Sean's dead gray eyes as he'd said those words.

What did he mean, exactly, by being "wronged"?

Lee Everhart had plenty of failings. Leanne knew them better than almost anyone. But she also knew he had a moral compass. It was part of who he was, part of his very *being*. She couldn't accept the idea that he had coerced a confession from a nineteen-year-old suspect.

Movement down the street caught her attention. She snatched up her phone.

He's leaving, she texted Josh.

Seconds later, her phone chimed.

"Which car?" Josh asked.

"Don't know yet. He's locking his house." Leanne watched Biswell fumbling with his keys. "I think it's the minivan."

"Why?"

"I don't know," she said. "I've got a feeling about it."

Leanne held her breath, waiting to see which of the two vehicles under the carport Biswell would choose. His girlfriend's gray minivan had a registration sticker that was three months expired. But if he chose his white Honda, they were shit out of luck today.

The taillights on the minivan flashed as Biswell clicked open the locks.

"It's the van."

"You sure?" Josh sounded as amped up as she was.

"He's pulling out now. Get in position."

"Roger that."

She clicked off as Biswell drove away in his girlfriend's vehicle. He was about to be pulled over for an expired sticker and—Leanne would bet her right arm—arrested for possession of stolen property. The storage shed question had been a decoy, and if Leanne's legwork proved accurate, the stolen bikes were stashed in the back of that van.

She left her surveillance spot and retraced her route through the neighborhood, feeling good about her job for the first time in days. As she neared a stop sign, she spotted a blue Kia in her rearview mirror.

She slammed on the brakes and grabbed her phone.

> You got this? I need to handle something.

Josh texted back, I'm good.

She shifted into reverse and gunned it until she was even with the dinged blue car. She whipped into the driveway of the house where it was parked, a 1970s bungalow with a flat roof and peeling paint. She strode up the sidewalk and rapped on the door. Nobody answered, but she heard music inside. She rapped again.

The door swung open. Roland Rivas stood there in faded jeans. No shirt, no shoes, but he had a green bandana wrapped around his head. Roland was a talented bass player and a suspected drug dealer. Leanne had had her doubts about the drug part until now.

"Where's Ben?" she asked.

He took a drag from a cigarette. Then he opened the door wider and stepped back.

NINETEEN

She entered the room and paused to let her eyes adjust to the dim lighting. The shag carpet and furniture were as old as the house. Given the brick fireplace and Coke-bottle windows, a clever decorator might have been able to pull off a mid-century modern theme, but in the absence of any TLC, the place was a dump. Beer cans littered the floor, and fast-food bags blanketed the coffee table, along with red Solo cups that doubled as ashtrays. Through the breakfast room window, Leanne spied some people in chairs on the patio.

She crossed the living room, ignoring the blank stares from a pair of glassy-eyed women lounging on the floor. She paused at the back door to look at her brother. He slouched in a plastic deck chair with a cigarette dangling between his fingertips.

Leanne's heart squeezed. She hadn't seen Ben since Thanksgiving, when they'd gotten into a fight before the turkey even came out of the oven. He'd left Boone's house in a huff, which had put Leanne at the top of her mother's shit list for weeks. She didn't really blame her mom. Leanne had purposely picked the fight with Ben after he'd borrowed money to fix a flat tire so he could drive to work—which had been a lie. In reality, he'd given the money to Diandra for God only knew what.

After the Thanksgiving dinner fiasco, Leanne had signed up to work Christmas, the least desirable shift of the year. She didn't want to be around her brother or her mother and sure as hell not Boone.

Leanne opened the back door, and all three men turned around.

"Hey! Officer." One of them grinned and waved.

She looked straight at Ben. "Can you talk?"

He glared at her a moment, then flicked his cigarette away and stood up. She led him around the side of the house where a rusty Buick was up on cinder blocks.

Ben wore a loose T-shirt that made his bony shoulders look like a clothes hanger. The left half of his face was burned, as though he'd passed out in the sun somewhere.

"What is it, Lee? I'm busy."

She took a deep breath. "Mom said you missed your drug test."

"I didn't." He crossed his arms. "Anything else?"

She stared at him, gauging his truthfulness. Years of interrogations by their detective father had made them both skilled liars.

"Where have you been?" she asked. "I left you a bunch of messages."

"I went camping."

Her bullshit meter fired to life. Ben had hated camping ever since their dad had forced him to do Boy Scouts and dragged the family on trips where they ate charred eggs and slept on the ground. Their father had wanted Ben to follow in his footsteps and become an Eagle Scout, but Ben wasn't interested.

"I went by the motel, and they said you quit," she told him.

"So?"

"So, what are you going to do for work?"

He slipped his hands into his front pockets, hunching his shoulders up around his ears. "I don't know. I'm looking."

"You should have looked before you quit. That was a good job."

His eyes sparked. "That job fucking sucked. Changing sheets

and cleaning up puke and condoms? You wouldn't have lasted two minutes."

Leanne gritted her teeth. As a rookie in Dallas, she'd been in more squalid apartments than her brother could imagine and done plenty of shit work. But Ben didn't know that aspect of her life, and she was losing control of this conversation.

"They're hiring at the campground," she said. "I can talk to Michelle."

"I'm done being a janitor."

"She needs a handyman. You still have Dad's toolbox, don't you?"

His eyes turned somber. Ben had spent countless hours in their dad's workshop as a kid, and he had a knack for carpentry. Was it a guilt trip? Yes. After bailing him out of jail twice and taking him to rehab, she wasn't above manipulating his grief to help get him back on track.

You need to look out for your brother.

Her dad's voice came back, and with it a sharp pang. She'd been trying to look out for Ben her whole life—even more so now that her dad was gone—but everything seemed to backfire.

"I can tell her you're interested," she said.

"I'm not." He looked over his shoulder at his friends. When he looked back the spark of resentment had returned to his eyes. "I don't need you to get me a job. And I sure as shit don't need you babysitting me."

She recognized the stubborn set of his jaw. This conversation was over, and the more she pushed the more he'd pull away.

"Fine." She shrugged.

"Fine."

"I'll remind you of that next time you hit me up for money."

Leanne slipped into the evidence room and took a moment to get her bearings. The space was dim and quiet and smelled of musty paper. It reminded her of the ghostly top floor of her college library, but instead of endless shelves of books, the room contained endless shelves of cardboard boxes filled with evidence and case files.

Not everything fit neatly into a box, though, and along the far wall was a floor-to-ceiling steel cage for storing oversize items: a rusty wheelbarrow, a cattle brand, a double-bladed paddle that had once been used to bludgeon someone. Leanne walked past the cage, eyeing the large gray safe in the corner. The three-by-three-foot cube had been ripped out of a nearby home after a couple was hog-tied and robbed at gunpoint by a gang of masked intruders. The safe was later recovered at a crack house and still had black smudges on it from where CSIs had lifted fingerprints, including one that belonged to the couple's teenage son.

Leanne walked past the shelves. Empty spaces outlined in dust showed where boxes had once been. A year ago, the department had started digitizing paper files. The process was a time-consuming slog, and anything that went farther back than ten years had yet to be touched. Leanne went row by row, perusing the shelves and reading labels until she found the shelf she needed.

The Hannah Rawls case file comprised four bankers boxes that occupied the bottom level of a metal shelving unit. Of the four total boxes, only one was there now. The others, presumably, were in the hands of the DA, who would have had to provide copies of much of the material to Sean Moriarty's attorney during discovery.

Leanne glanced over her shoulder at the door, which she'd left ajar so as not to arouse suspicion. As a detective, she had access to this room, but if someone came in and saw her rummaging through the Rawls case, they might have a few questions.

Leanne crouched down in front of the one remaining box, which was labeled with a case number. She lifted the dusty lid and was relieved to immediately see the item she was after, the murder book. In the Hannah Rawls case—the most extensive investigation in department history—the murder book was actually three separate binders, each marked with a roman numeral. Leanne tugged out the binder marked "I."

The murder book was meant to be a summary, so investigators could locate key facts of the case without having to comb through dozens and sometimes hundreds of individual folders. At the front of the binder was a table of contents, followed by material from the investigation's early days. Leanne scanned the sections, which included police interviews and transcripts of 911 calls. Tucked behind a batch of clear sleeves containing key crime scene photos was a section marked "Autopsy." Behind that were more police interviews, along with follow-up reports, all labeled and categorized.

A sour ball formed in Leanne's stomach as she recognized her father's handwriting on many of the police forms. His fingerprints were, quite literally, all over this investigation.

I've had fifteen years to think about all the people who wronged me.

She pictured Sean Moriarty's flat gray eyes again. She didn't like that he'd shown up at her house. She liked even less that his first stop had been her mother's. It was a bold move for someone fresh out of prison. To Leanne, it signaled a don't-give-a-fuck attitude that she found unnerving.

Shoving aside thoughts of Sean Moriarty, Leanne thumbed through the entire binder. Then she clicked open the rings and removed several reports. She took them to the bullpen, which was nearly empty right now because it was after five. A lone patrol officer sat in a cubicle, and Leanne traded nods with him on the way to the copier. She fed the reports into the machine in one big stack.

"Leanne."

She whirled around. Nadine stood behind her in a green barn jacket, a set of car keys in her hand.

"You're back?" Nadine asked. "I thought you left already."

"Just finishing up." The machine behind her spit out pages, and Leanne resisted the urge to move sideways to block the view.

"That lady who was here earlier? She called while you were out," Nadine said. "I left a note on your desk."

"I saw it, thanks. I called her back."

Nadine tipped her head to the side. "She's the one whose daughter ran off a while back?"

"Her daughter's missing, yes."

"What's it been now?"

"Six years."

"Lord." Nadine shook her head. "That's awful. I can't even imagine."

The copier made a loud chirp, and Leanne's heart lurched.

"Here." Nadine stepped forward as Leanne reached for the paper drawer.

"I can—"

"You have to feed it just right." Nadine set her keys down and jerked open the drawer. She grabbed a chunk of printer paper from the shelf and slid it into the tray, then gave the drawer a little shake before slamming it shut. "There."

"Thanks."

Nadine grabbed her keys and her gaze landed on the stack of printouts. Leanne held her breath. She didn't want to lie to Nadine, but she didn't want to explain herself, either. Nadine was friendly with everyone, but her first loyalty was to her boss.

Nadine lifted an eyebrow and looked at her. "Don't stay too late."

"I won't."

"You know how the chief is about overtime."

TWENTY

Izzy didn't have it yet.

She'd been trying for hours, and she still didn't have the shot. Setting down her tripod, she knelt to tie her hiking boot. The last thing she needed was to trip and break an ankle, which would make it nearly impossible to work.

She stood and zipped her jacket, surveying the canyon as the wind whipped against her cheeks. Daylight was fading, and the temperature was dropping fast. Five hours out here, and she was no closer to accomplishing her goal than she had been when she'd decided to spend one of her precious days off scouring the area for the perfect shot that would impress Zach Olmstead. She'd been out here a few weeks ago with a different camera, mainly playing around with contrasts. But this time was different because she had a specific mission. She was determined to come away with *at least one damn photograph* that she could add to her portfolio. So far, she had shots of the canyon floor, along with dozens of La Ventana, the rock window that was one of the most famous landmarks in the area. But every tourist who hiked through here posted the same picture on social media, and she wanted something original.

Izzy pulled the water bottle from her pack and took a long

swig. Despite the cold, she'd worked up a sweat hiking from the rim of the canyon all the way down to Gold Springs Creek and back up again, and she was losing fluids. She remembered her boyfriend's worried look this morning when she'd told him where she was going.

Hydrate, he'd said. *And watch out for mountain lions.*

Izzy took another sip and tucked the bottle into her backpack. She debated getting out her headlamp, but she still had a few minutes of light left, and anyway, she was almost there. She swung the tripod onto her shoulder and continued up the trail.

It didn't used to be this hard.

Or maybe it did, but she hadn't minded because back then everything was shiny and new. Things seemed different ever since she'd moved back home. She couldn't remember the last time she'd felt that giddy excitement of capturing the perfect shot. Years ago, she had felt it a lot. But that was before she had taken her most special hobby, the *one* thing she'd ever really been good at, and tried to turn it into a paycheck. Izzy had once been convinced that she had what it took to make it as a professional photographer. But that was after she'd managed to escape Madrone and the world still felt brimming with possibilities. That was before fate reached out and yanked her back here.

She trudged up the path, straining to see as the dusky purple shadows started closing in on her. It was time to get serious. She envisioned the trail in her mind and thought about potential night shots she could get along the ridge between here and the trailhead. Because the Dark Sky Gallery owner was all about nighttime photography. What was it he'd told her?

We take our night sky seriously.

She adjusted her camera on its strap and checked the settings. The camera was new—or new to her, at least—but that wasn't the problem. She'd been using Nikons ever since high school, when her yearbook teacher had put a D600 in her hands and assigned her to take pictures of the homecoming parade. Soon, Izzy was shooting pep rallies and Friday night football games and school fundraisers. Mr. Gaffney took her under his wing that fall and spent time with her in the darkroom, showing her how to use an analog camera and develop film to achieve different effects. Not long after that, Izzy discovered nature photography, and that was when she truly got hooked.

Izzy picked her way up the rocky trail, which, ironically, was the same place she'd come to create the portfolio that she'd sent to NYU. That portfolio had included sandstone bluffs and towering hoodoos and giant yuccas with sword-shaped leaves. She had often wondered what it was about those pictures that convinced the admissions officers to give her the chance of a lifetime. To a committee of urbanites, her arid landscapes and weird rock formations must have looked like something from another planet.

She still didn't know why they'd picked her. She hadn't gone to a top-tier high school or taken art lessons her whole life or won loads of awards. Izzy had spent her entire first year there feeling self-conscious about her roots, determined to hide the fact that she'd never been to a real concert and the only things to do in her hometown were parking lot parties and midnight trips to Stop-N-Go. It wasn't until year two, when everyone moved past the "where are you from?" phase, that Izzy started to let her guard down and ease into her program. Even after that, though—and even to this day—she still sometimes felt like an imposter.

Izzy moved through the brush, taking care not to snag her clothes on the ocotillo and catclaw that jutted into her path. A noise made her freeze.

Holding her breath, she tried to listen.

She heard it again—the soft, tambourine-like hiss of a rattlesnake. Adrenaline surged through her. She glanced around the trail, but the sound faded before she could place it. It was almost dark, and she could barely see out here. Which was the point, really. She had hoped to cap off her expedition with some dusk and nighttime shots. But when she'd packed her gear for this, she'd been thinking about cold and dehydration, not nocturnal predators. She had a tube of pepper spray, but she'd left it in her car at the trailhead.

Izzy swung the tripod off her shoulder. Striding up the path, she whisked it back and forth like a machete. Not that it would help if a diamondback struck from the shadows. But she at least felt like she was doing something. Her thighs burned as she powered up the trail. She reached the crest and was greeted by a gust of cold air. Shivering, she looked ahead and spotted the wooden sign for Gold Springs Trailhead.

She turned to face the overlook. A juniper skeleton on a rocky ledge caught her eye. The tree's black form was silhouetted against the purple sky.

Her pulse quickened. *This* was her shot.

She looked past the juniper to the valley below. She'd seen this view before, but only in the daylight when the highway was visible, and she hadn't liked the way the man-made asphalt road intruded on the landscape. Everything looked different now with the moon rising over the mountains.

Screw rattlesnakes. She wanted this shot.

Izzy snapped open her tripod, attached her camera, and peered through the viewfinder.

A pair of headlights moved along the highway, and she waited for them to disappear around a bend.

"Come on, come on."

When the headlights were gone, she got ready to take the shot. But something felt off.

Zoom with your feet.

The words of her yearbook teacher came back to her. Mark Gaffney had drilled into her the importance of not being lazy when it came to composition. She picked up her tripod and moved it closer, allowing the curvy branches to fill up the space.

It was back again—that bright, bubbly feeling of composing *just the right shot*. This was the photograph that was going to land her an exhibit with Zach Olmstead. She could feel it.

She adjusted the lens.

Perfect.

She stepped back to make sure. Another step, and her heel caught on something. She tripped backward, flinging her arms out to catch herself as she landed on her butt.

Fire shot up her arm.

She snatched her hand back, but the fire burned hotter.

"Omigod omigod omigod."

It felt like she'd grabbed a fistful of razor blades. She unzipped her backpack and rummaged for her flashlight. Switching it on, she aimed it at the ground.

A devil's head cactus. She'd planted her hand smack in the middle of the sharp white needles.

Izzy swept the flashlight over the area and saw something pale and smooth on the ground. She leaned closer.

"What . . . ?"

Recognition dawned.

Izzy crab-walked backward as a scream tore from her throat. She scrambled to her feet and ran.

TWENTY-ONE

Leanne surveyed the murder book pages spread across her kitchen table. She'd sorted them into stacks labeled with orange sticky notes. Sliding aside the pile marked "Police Reports," she turned her attention to the pile marked "Autopsy."

Autopsy photos were never easy to look at, but there was a particular horror in seeing a person you'd known in life laid out on the table and cut open like a science experiment. Leanne sped through the grisly photographs of Hannah Rawls until she reached the ME's diagram, which was easier to stomach. Like the Jane Doe autopsy, this report included a black-and-white line drawing of a generic female form surrounded by handwritten notes made during the procedure. The words scrawled by the neck instantly caught Leanne's attention.

Fractured hyoid.

Leanne knew Hannah had been strangled, but she hadn't known that particular detail until tonight. She jotted a note on her legal pad and tapped her pencil on the page.

Gus jumped onto the table and nudged her arm.

"You ate already." She scratched his neck, and he collapsed on top of her papers, arching his back and purring. She gave him a few more scratches before sliding him off the reports. "Here, scoot."

Leanne flipped past the diagram to the typewritten detail about Hannah's injuries. *Fractured right parietal. Fractured scaphoid. Fractured fourth proximal phalanx, right hand.*

She read through the full description. Then she read through it again. Based on the hand and wrist injuries, it looked like Hannah had tried to fend off her attacker. She imagined Rocky Rawls combing through this same report. Had he come to the same conclusion? And if he had, did knowing that his daughter fought for her life give him any kind of comfort?

Or did it instill in him a bone-deep rage?

Trish Rawls had said her husband went through all the reports, and Leanne shuddered to think of it. No amount of medical jargon could ease the shock of viewing these photos and reading the details of his daughter's death.

In the days after Hannah's murder, the department had been under immense pressure to make an arrest. Had that pressure made Lee Everhart bend his own strict moral code? Leanne had always looked up to her dad. To this day, his directive to look out for Ben had reshaped her life, driving her back to Madrone. But she wasn't blind to the stress he must have been under right after the murder when the whole town was up in arms. Everyone's fear and grief translated into demands for police to lock in on a suspect. Hannah's parents were definitely part of the pressure campaign. Rocky Rawls had a powerful personality and liked to throw his weight around, even before his daughter's killing.

She flipped back to the diagram as the ME's words percolated in her brain.

Fractured hyoid.

Fractured right parietal.

Fractured scaphoid...

She thumbed through Hannah's crime scene photos again but saw no sign of any duct tape collected on the body or anywhere nearby. She flipped to an autopsy photo and zeroed in on Hannah's long blond hair. It didn't look as though a chunk of hair had been cut off, and there was no mention of anything like that in the description.

The idea that Hannah Rawls might be connected to the unidentified bodies was starting to feel like a stretch. Yes, Hannah had been strangled and beaten. And, yes, the abandoned well where her body was found was not far away from Highway 67 and the other human remains. But aside from those factors, the cases felt very different.

To start with, Hannah Rawls was reported missing mere hours after she didn't come home for her midnight curfew. Her disappearance launched an intensive search that brought in law enforcement agencies from across the region. It also launched a media circus that turned out to be a preview of the sensational trial to come.

By contrast, the other cases received little attention—almost none at all. Leanne had been a detective here for nearly two years, and she'd never even heard of these cold cases until Jen Sayers tipped her off. It wasn't like the un-IDed bones were being talked about around the watercooler. Days and months and even years after discovery, the remains still weren't identified. That fact alone ratcheted up the difficulty factor. How could investigators develop a theory of the crime—or a motive or a suspect—if they didn't even know who the victims were and what they might have in common? Without IDs, it was nearly impossible to determine how the killer and the victims crossed paths.

Gus arched his back again, and Leanne stroked his chin. Then she took a last sip of the Dr Pepper Slurpee she'd bought on the way home from work. Once again, she'd stopped at the gas station for dinner—another calorie bomb she'd have to run off on the trail.

Sighing, she flipped back to the autopsy report. Was she making her life difficult? Definitely. Maybe she should give up on this theory and be the "team player" that her chief wanted her to be. But she couldn't shake the nagging feeling that she was missing something important.

She studied the diagram again and then skimmed through the pathologist's notes about Hannah Rawls.

Fractured hyoid.

Fractured right parietal.

Leanne fixed her gaze on her kitchen window as the ME's words swirled through her brain.

A chill snaked down her spine. She reached under the table for the thick brown accordion file at her feet and pulled out the Jane Doe autopsy report. Flipping through the pages, she located Korbin's detailed notes.

Fractured hyoid.

Fractured right parietal.

Fractured scaphoid . . .

Leanne gazed at the kitchen window again, visualizing the attacks as an idea took shape. The victims would have been on their backs struggling. Their worst injuries were on their faces and chests. Their attacker would have been on top, pinning them down.

Korbin's words about the bludgeoning came back to her. *This was something smooth, possibly the butt of a pistol.*

She looked down at his diagram and reread the notes in the margins. *Fractured right parietal.*

In the cold cases, and the Jane Doe case, *and* the Hannah Rawls case, the right side of the victim's skull was bashed in.

She pounded her fist on the table. "Son of a bitch! You're left-handed."

Gus jumped away, and Leanne stared down at the diagram as the implications sank in. Roughly 10 percent of people were left-handed. This was an important discovery, potentially game-changing.

But would McBride agree?

Something clattered outside.

She jumped up and went to the window. Switching off the light above the sink, she looked out at the yard. The area behind the house was still and quiet, the lounge chair empty.

But she hadn't imagined it. She'd definitely heard something.

Leanne grabbed her service weapon off the kitchen counter as a sharp knock sounded at her front door. She crossed the living room and peered through the peephole.

Max Scott stood on her doorstep. He wore jeans and a sweatshirt and had his hands tucked into his pockets. He glanced over his shoulder at her truck in the driveway and knocked again.

How the hell had he found her address? He must have followed her home, which irked her, and not only because he knew where she lived now.

How had she not noticed a tail? Being observant was a point of pride for her.

She tucked her pistol into the back of her jeans and yanked open the door.

"Hi." He made a cringey attempt at a smile. "I saw that you're home, so . . ."

"I thought you went back to Dallas."

"Nope. Still here."

"What do you want?"

"Mind if I come in?"

"Yes."

He sighed. "All right. I wanted to run something by you. Call it a quid pro quo."

She didn't respond.

"That's like a trade."

"I know what a quid pro quo is. The answer is no." She started to close the door, and he edged forward.

"Touch my door, and you'll regret it."

He stepped back. "Sorry. My bad." He heaved a sigh. "Would you hear me out? I want to offer you a trade. You give me an exclusive interview."

"In exchange for what?"

"In exchange, we give *you* a heads-up about the exposé we're running."

She pursed her lips.

"I'm not interested in whatever you're running," she said.

"That's where you're wrong. You'll be interested in this, I guarantee it. The topic is some very prominent people in Chisos County."

Leanne stared at him. Her wheels were turning now, but she wasn't about to tell him that.

Her phone chimed in the kitchen. She glanced over her shoulder, then back at the reporter on her doorstep.

He grinned. "You're interested, I can tell."

"I told you before, I don't give interviews."

"But—"

"Talk to our PIO."

She closed the door and locked it.

Her phone chimed again as she strode into the kitchen. Grabbing it off the table, she checked the screen.

Big Bend Outfitters.

She connected the call.

"Everhart."

"Um, hi." The woman's voice sounded timid. "Is this Detective Leanne Everhart?"

"Yes."

"I'm Terry Ryan, with Big Bend Outfitters. Izzy Huerta asked me to call you?"

Leanne's heart skittered. "What's wrong?"

"Izzy needs you to come out here. It's an emergency."

TWENTY-TWO

Leanne sped down the highway, searching for the sign. She passed the turnoff for Long Canyon Road. The highway curved, and the wooden sign for Big Bend Outfitters loomed ahead.

Leanne slammed on the brakes and hung a left. She bumped along the pitted dirt road as a log cabin came into view. A light shone from the porch, but the parking area was empty except for an old white pickup and a dusty black Jeep. Off to the side was a boat trailer stacked with three long river rafts.

Leanne parked beside the Jeep and tromped up the wooden steps to the cabin, where bundles of firewood lined the porch. Ignoring the SORRY WE'RE CLOSED sign, she yanked open the door.

The woman seated behind the cash register looked up.

"Are you Terry?"

She slid from her stool, setting her phone face down on the counter. "That's me."

The clerk wore a green T-shirt with the rafting company's logo on the front, and her long red hair was pulled back in a braid.

"I'm Detective Everhart."

"You're with the sheriff's office?"

Leanne flashed her badge. "Madrone PD." She glanced around the shop. Boxes of T-shirts sat in the middle of the floor beside piles of hangers, as if the clerk had been putting out inventory when she got interrupted.

"Where is Izzy?" Leanne asked.

"She just left. Someone came to get her."

"Who?"

"I think one of the sheriff's people? I'm not sure where they went."

"I can take you."

Leanne turned around as Justin Carr stepped through the door. The river guide wore brown cargo pants and a long-sleeved T-shirt with the Big Bend Outfitters logo on it.

"They wanted to talk to her out at the scene," Justin said. "Want me to show you?"

"Yes."

Leanne followed him out of the cabin and down the steps as he glanced over his shoulder. "Izzy called you?"

"Terry did. She told me Izzy's phone was out of juice."

He led her to the pickup loaded with oars and propane tanks.

Leanne slid inside the cab. "Where's this place, exactly?" she asked as Justin hitched himself behind the wheel.

"Near the trailhead. Terry didn't tell you?"

"She didn't explain anything. All she said was Izzy found a body and wanted me to meet her here ASAP."

They bounced over ruts in the road as they made their way back to the highway.

"Do you know what happened?" she asked.

"Only what she told me. I was running a load of propane down to the park when I saw—"

"Which park?"

"Big Bend. Our main location." He pulled onto the highway, and soon they were speeding south. "I passed the sign for Gold

Springs Nature Preserve, and I saw this woman on the side of the road, waving me down. I didn't realize it was Izzy until I pulled over. She said her phone was dead and she needed to call 911."

"Did you see the crime scene?" Leanne asked.

"No."

"Who called it in?"

"Izzy used my phone. Soon as she got off, she threw up all over her shoes. She was shaking pretty bad, and her hand was bleeding. I think she was in shock, so I took her back here to use our first-aid kit."

Leanne looked ahead at the highway. She checked her phone. Nothing yet. But given that Terry had been on her cell phone a minute ago, Leanne guessed it wouldn't be long before word got out.

She muttered a curse and raked her hand through her hair.

"You all right?" Justin asked.

"Yeah," she said, even though she wasn't at all. She looked at him. "What are the odds this stays quiet until tomorrow?"

"Zero." He glanced at her. "People are already talking."

By "people," she assumed he meant river guides and park rangers. Word traveled fast around here, and it was probably only a matter of time before the media got wind of it and showed up.

Leanne sighed. "Crap."

"Sorry. Not my fault, though," he said. "I didn't tell anyone, and I don't think Izzy would. Maybe the sheriff's people did?"

"Doesn't matter. It was bound to get out."

The sign for Gold Springs Nature Preserve appeared ahead. Justin slowed down and pulled onto the road leading to the trailhead. The narrow road curved, and a line of emergency vehicles came into view—two sheriff's cruisers, an ambulance, a red pickup from Chisos County Fire and Rescue.

Leanne recognized the black pickup parked beside the ambulance as Justin pulled in behind one of the sheriff's cruisers.

She pushed open her door. "Thanks for the ride."

"Sure."

She got out and tried to get the lay of the land. No red-and-blue emergency lights, luckily, but someone had set up a big white spotlight near the trailhead, which was sure to attract attention. She scanned the people milling around, mostly sheriff's deputies and a couple of guys from the fire department.

Duncan caught her eye from across the lot. He said something to a uniformed deputy and then broke away to meet her on the edge of the parking area.

"Where's Izzy?" she asked.

"Giving a statement." He nodded toward a white sheriff's SUV near the trail sign. Leanne didn't see Izzy but assumed she was seated in the vehicle being interviewed by someone.

"Why didn't you call me?" she asked Duncan. He was dressed in his typical jeans and navy blue sheriff's office polo, his badge and gun on his hip.

"I just got here two minutes ago."

"What happened?"

"From what I hear, Izzy was out hiking, and she came across a body."

"Female?"

Duncan nodded.

"You see it?"

He nodded again.

"Sounds like you've been here more than two minutes."

He rested his hands on his hips. "Leanne—"

"Forget it." She crossed her arms. "What's your take? What are we dealing with?"

"We?"

She just looked at him.

He shook his head and glanced away.

"Come on, Duncan. Don't waste my time. Is she like the others?"

He stared at her, and the tight set of his mouth told her exactly what she needed to know.

Leanne closed her eyes and tipped her head back.

"We don't know yet for sure, but she appears to be late teens to early twenties," he said. "Torn clothes. Probable sexual assault."

"Beaten?"

"Yes."

"Right side of her face?"

He frowned. "I didn't get that close. Why?"

She shook her head. "Any idea how long she's been out here?"

"Not long. Maybe a day, tops. Or a couple hours."

"*Hours?*" A chill went through her. "Seriously? You guys should be canvassing this entire place, looking for witnesses! Maybe someone saw something."

"Hey, good idea. Instead, I'm standing here talking to you."

She looked at her feet. "Sorry. I'm just—"

"Stressed. I got that. Me, too."

She glanced up, and the somber look on his face made her feel a surge of dread. This investigation was about to become a circus. She knew it. He knew it. And he wasn't even aware that—as of tonight—Leanne had good reason to believe that not only were all these Jane Doe crimes likely connected, but they might be connected to Hannah Rawls, too.

Duncan looked over the top of her head and nodded. "She's done, I think."

Leanne turned to see petite Izzy amid all the oversize cops. She was standing beside the SUV now and talking to a detective from the sheriff's office.

"Damn, y'all put her with Travis?" She looked at Duncan. Travis Malcom was a condescending prick and one of Leanne's least favorite people.

"He's the lead," Duncan said.

She looked back at Izzy and felt a pang of sympathy that she'd had to sit in that SUV with him, recounting what had to have been a traumatic experience.

Duncan took out his phone. "I need to get this. Talk later?"

"Yeah."

He stepped away to take his call, and Leanne crossed the parking lot.

"Izzy."

She turned around, and the pure relief on her face made Leanne feel good. She didn't have very many girlfriends, but Izzy seemed to have become one of them.

Leanne walked over and gave her a hug. "I got here as fast as I could." She pulled back to look at her. Locks of purple hair had come loose from her ponytail, and a smudge of dirt streaked her cheek. "How are you?"

She shook her head. Her pupils were dilated, and her skin looked pale.

"I feel a little woozy, to be honest."

"Here. Sit." Leanne steered her to a wooden railroad tie at the edge of the parking lot.

Izzy sank onto it.

"Let me get you some water."

"No." She held up her hand. "I've had about a gallon already. I just need to sit down."

Leanne crouched beside her, studying her face. Izzy had worked some ugly crime scenes, including last Sunday. But it was different when you weren't braced for it. Leanne wanted to pelt her with questions but forced herself to wait.

"Do you have any gum?" Izzy asked. "My mouth tastes like puke."

Leanne reached into her jacket and pulled out a pack of orange Tic Tacs. "I've got these."

"Thanks."

She emptied some into Izzy's palm.

"What's with the bandage?" Leanne asked, nodding at her other hand, which was wrapped in white gauze.

"Devil's head cactus. I fell on it."

"Ouch."

Izzy popped the Tic Tacs into her mouth and swished them around. "Sorry."

"Why?"

"I feel stupid. I'm supposed to be a freaking CSI, and I totally lost it. I threw up all over my shoes. So disgusting." She shuddered. "They gave me some flip-flops at the rafting place, but now my toes are freezing."

Leanne watched her, waiting for the anxiety to dissipate. Izzy held out her hand again, and she gave her more Tic Tacs.

"Thank you."

"You can have them."

"No, I mean thanks for coming," Izzy said softly. "I really appreciate it."

"Of course."

"Can I ask a favor?"

"Sure."

"I left my camera and tripod in Justin's truck when he gave me a ride. The sheriff's detective wants to see my pictures."

"You took pictures?"

"Not of the crime scene. But I took shots of the trail and everything. He said he wants to look through them in case there's anything useful."

"Hang on."

Leanne tromped over to the truck and leaned inside the cab. The space behind the seat was filled with wadded clothes and camping gear. A silver tripod sat on top, along with a Nikon camera with a purple strap. A second camera sat off to the side. It was a Canon, and the strap was black.

Leanne grabbed the tripod and the Nikon, holding up the camera for Izzy to see.

"This one's yours?"

Izzy nodded.

Leanne brought them over, and Izzy immediately started scrolling through photographs.

"I don't *think* I got anything useful. But who knows, right? I took hundreds of shots today."

Leanne crouched beside her, studying her face. The color was coming back into her cheeks now, and she looked intent as she frowned down at the screen.

"Leanne."

She turned around to see Duncan waving her over.

"I'll be right back, okay?" She left Izzy to her task and joined Duncan away from the crowd.

"How's she doing?" he asked.

"A little shocky."

He nodded. "The ME's people should be here in five. We've got the scene cordoned off." He paused. "I figured you'd want to see it before they get started."

"I do."

He stared down at her.

"What?"

"Fair warning, Leanne. It's bad."

TWENTY-THREE

Bip slid two packets of sugar across the counter.
"I heard y'all got another one last night," he said.
"Not us this time."
"No?"
"No." Leanne stacked the packets on the lid of her coffee.
"But I heard—"
"Say hi to Mel for me, okay?"
"Will do."

Leanne left the convenience store and drove to the police station, surveying the sidewalks crowded with weekend visitors. The coffee shop on Main was packed, and a line was already forming at the taco truck, where tourists were paying eight dollars for tacos that used to cost two bucks. Leanne reached the police station and pulled around to the back. McBride's Suburban was parked near the door, but no sign of anyone else yet. Leanne had hoped to beat everyone in today, and it looked as though she had.

She tapped in her access code and let herself inside. Booking was empty, which was another stroke of luck. She didn't want her morning getting sidetracked with a bunch of catch-up work from the overnight shift.

She dropped off her coffee at her desk and went straight for the chief's office. The door stood ajar. McBride was seated in front of his computer with a sausage biscuit at his elbow. He wore a flannel shirt and baseball cap, and Leanne would bet money he planned to be on his brother-in-law's fishing boat by lunchtime.

"Morning."

He turned to look at her. "Morning. I thought Josh was on call today."

"He is. You have a minute?"

"Sure."

She took the empty chair as he closed out of an email. Then he swiveled to face her, and his chair squeaked as he leaned back.

"What's up?" he asked.

"You heard about Gold Springs Trail."

He nodded.

"I was out there last night."

He frowned. "Why?"

"Izzy called me."

"Yeah, I heard she found the body." He shook his head. "Bad break."

"Yes."

"She's tough, though."

Leanne cleared her throat. "So, I was talking to Duncan Harper."

"He the lead?"

"Travis Malcom is."

The chief nodded. "He's good."

"Duncan was telling me the MO looks similar to our Jane Doe."

"Similar how?"

"Well, the obvious. Both early twenties female victims, badly beaten, probable sexual assault—"

"We don't know that," he said. "No rape kit results on our Jane Doe yet."

"Right. Well, possible sexual assault, then. Anyway, the other big thing is location. That trailhead is right off Highway 67, not far from where a human jawbone was discovered several years back."

His eyes turned wary. "What are you asking me?"

"I was thinking we should be teaming up on this. Since they're likely related."

He was already shaking his head.

"We could share leads and resources. We could—"

"No way. Not happening."

She pulled back, stung. "Why not?"

"You're suggesting a task force, right? That's what you're saying? The answer is no."

"Sir." She glanced at her lap, trying to tamp down her emotions. "If you compare the two cases, you'll see—"

"You're borrowing trouble again, Everhart. Gold Springs Trail is *not* our jurisdiction. Malcom and his guys can handle it."

She took a deep breath. "What about the other cases? We're up to five now."

"Five? How do you figure?"

"The cold cases from Dr. Sayers, all from this region. Then our recent Jane Doe. And now this new homicide." That wasn't even counting the stray femur and jawbone, only the cases where the victims' sex had been determined. "I was going through the case files, and it's clear there's a pattern here. It would make sense to bring in a canine team at this point."

"A dog team? Why?"

She just looked at him. "Well . . . to see what else we've missed. In the case of the jawbone, there's bound to be more remains to be found out there. And again, that bone was discovered near the same stretch of highway as these others."

McBride tipped his head back and sighed. Then he leaned forward on his elbows.

"Everhart, I put you in charge of the Jane Doe homicide a week ago now. Do you have an ID?"

"Not yet."

"Any possible MP files?"

"No."

"Any leads whatsoever on the vic's identity?"

"No."

"And you're not going to find any, either. You want to know why?"

She just looked at him.

"Because *nobody's looking*. No one cares. You get what I'm saying?"

"No. Respectfully, sir, I'm not seeing your point here. We don't have an ID yet because the victim's prints aren't in the system, and we haven't found a corresponding missing person report—"

"Which we won't. It's like I told you before. These people live and die under the radar. There's no report because there's no one to *file* a report. And I'm not wasting a bunch of valuable taxpayer resources running down bones of every illegal who crosses that desert."

"It's not just the location of the bodies that makes me think the cases are connected," she went on, determined to break through. "There are other similarities. There's the age of the victims. The sex. And the victims were strangled and severely beaten postmortem. Those injuries were all on the *right* side of the victim's face, which suggests a left-handed killer."

Interest flared in his eyes, and she kept going.

"Also, in three of the cases, including our Jane Doe, there was duct tape found near the body or on the body itself. And also—"

"Stop." He held up a hand. "I've heard enough of this."

A hot lump lodged in her throat. She could see by the gleam in his eyes that he was relishing this argument. He liked cutting her off at the knees, putting her in her place, reminding her that she was beneath him in the hierarchy.

Leanne had spent last night tossing and turning in bed, coming up with all the right arguments to persuade him to let her join forces with the sheriff's office to start investigating her Jane Doe case as what it was: part of a pattern. But he wasn't even going to hear her out. He'd already made up his mind about everything.

She felt a sense of déjà vu. She'd experienced this same dynamic with her hardheaded brother, too, and she knew how this would go. The more she pushed him, the more he'd dig in and resist her. She had to come up with another way.

She took a deep breath. "If you don't want to bring in a cadaver dog—"

"That's not happening."

"Then how about—"

"I'll tell you what, though," he said. "The other day you mentioned a tire tread. You've still got that plaster cast?"

"Yes."

"We'll submit it and see what comes back." He checked his watch. "Send it to the lab in El Paso, see if they can ID it. Maybe we'll get a lead on a vehicle."

"Sending it to Austin would probably be faster—"

"El Paso. They know us over there."

He turned to his computer, and that was it. She was being dismissed.

Leanne stood up, and he was already back to his emails, clearly in a hurry to get out of here and enjoy his Saturday.

Leanne stalked into the break room, where she could be alone. She stood by the watercooler, staring at her feet and counting to ten.

She grabbed a paper cone and filled it with water. She drank it down, cooling her throat. She drank another, and another. Then she crunched up the cone and threw it at the trash can.

"That went well."

She turned around. Josh leaned against the doorframe.

"Couldn't help but overhear." He stepped into the room. "Sounds like he didn't buy it. Nice pitch, though."

Frustration festered inside her, but she pretended not to care.

"Aw, come on," he said. "Shake it off."

She filled another cone with water and sipped it.

"You get to send your plaster cast in, right? That's progress."

She glared at him. "Now it's *my* plaster cast? Because I'm the only one who gives a crap about this case, right? Who cares about some murdered girl in the desert?"

Josh sighed. "That's not what I meant. I meant that I know you've been wanting to send in that evidence. Maybe we'll get a lead out of it."

She dropped the cone in the trash. "He's throwing me a bone, hoping I'll shut up, Coop. Everyone knows El Paso is backed up as hell with drug testing. If he really gave a damn, he'd send it to Austin."

Josh stepped closer and frowned down at her. "Do you ever think about how you're making it too hard on yourself?"

"What, by doing my job? Is it supposed to be easy?"

Josh shook his head. "Forget it."

"No. Tell me what you meant."

He sighed again. "Look, Leanne, I know you don't like people telling you what to do."

"Oh, and you do?"

"No, I do not," he said. "But I've been here six years, which is four more than you, and I've learned a few things." He gazed down at her with a look that could only be described as big-brotherly. "I worked with your dad, and I have the utmost respect for him, so would you mind if I give you a little friendly advice?"

She wished she had a dollar for every man she'd dealt with who wanted to give her a little friendly advice.

She took a deep breath. "Fine. Let's hear it."

He glanced at the door behind her, then eased closer and lowered his voice. "You keep butting heads with him, you're gonna derail your career. Permanently."

"Him" obviously meaning the chief.

"That attitude you've got may seem like it's not coming through, but it is," he continued. "He's not stupid."

She swallowed a retort.

"Don't make everything so combative, okay? Yeah, he's throwing you a bone. So fetch it and run with it."

"What's that supposed to mean?"

"It means, *you're* the lead here. So, lead your case how you want and quit trying to win every argument."

She just looked at him. His expression was calm and reasonable, while she was struggling to keep her emotions from boiling over.

Maybe he had a point.

"That's my advice, take it or leave it." He stepped back. "If your dad was here, he'd tell you the same."

TWENTY-FOUR

Izzy agitated the tray, silently counting as she waited for the shapes to emerge from the blank paper.

"Come on, come on..."

Patience had never been her thing. She remembered her mentor standing beside her in the high school darkroom, preaching the wisdom of not rushing the process, giving the chemicals a chance to work.

Finally, it was ready. Using the tongs, she transferred the paper to the tray with the stop bath, then the fixer, then the water bath. After rinsing off the chemicals, she lifted the paper and let the liquid slide off.

Then she clipped the paper to the clothesline above the workbench and stepped back.

Her photo of Devil's Bow had turned out better than she'd hoped two weeks ago when she'd hiked out there to take this roll of film. The details were sharp, and she'd caught a ray of light in the corner of the rock bridge the instant before the sun sank out of view. Too bad the subject matter wouldn't qualify for the *Lone Star Nights* show. She could always go back and get something with the moon in the background. But the idea of hiking such an isolated trail by herself made her anxious now. And she definitely didn't want to go alone at night. Maybe her boyfriend would come along to keep her company and give her a distraction from her paranoia.

Izzy studied her newest prints. She wished she had more nighttime shots. Yesterday's photo of the juniper tree at dusk had a strong composition, but was it strong enough to get her over the line with Zach Olmstead? Insecurity churned inside her. She didn't care about the exhibit so much as the chance to work with a nationally renowned photographer. She'd been reading up on him since their meeting, and he was even more connected than she'd first thought. The fact that he wanted to put her work in front of his influential friends was a huge opportunity, the sort of life-changing chance that could mean the difference between pursuing what she loved and photographing traffic accidents for the next ten years.

A muffled knock sounded at the door.

"*¿Isa? Tienes visita.*"

She stepped closer to the door. "*¿Qué?*"

"*La jefita está aquí.*"

Izzy switched off the red safelight. Kicking aside the towel at the base of the door, she opened it slightly and stepped into the darkened bedroom that she shared with her sister—who had had a chip on her shoulder ever since Izzy came home from New York and converted their shared closet into a photo lab.

Her mother stood in the bedroom.

"*Who's* here?" Izzy asked.

"Leana," she replied, mispronouncing it as always.

Panic zinged through her. Leanne Everhart was *here*?

"*Vamos.*" Her mom clucked her tongue and walked away.

"Shit," Izzy muttered, untying her apron. She tossed it on the unmade bed and hurried down the hallway.

Leanne stood in the center of the stuffy little kitchen, looking unfazed by the chaos. *Family Feud* blared from a mini TV on the counter, and Izzy's nephews sat at the table, eating Cocoa Puffs and playing tug-of-war with an iPad. Her mom thwacked them on the back of the head on her way to the stove, where she was frying onions.

Izzy smiled and tried to look cheerful. "Hey, Leanne, what's up?"

"Hi. You have a minute?"

"Sure."

Leanne moved for the door. "Good to see you, Mrs. Huerta."

"You, too! Come for dinner next time."

Izzy followed Leanne outside and glanced around the porch in dismay. A basket of damp laundry sat waiting to be hung. Izzy leaned back against the railing and faced the house, hoping to distract Leanne from her family's underwear on the clothesline.

"Sorry," she said, tugging off her gloves. "I've been in the darkroom."

"The pictures from yesterday?"

"Those were digital. This was another batch."

Izzy tried to cover her embarrassment as she waited for Leanne to get to the point. Izzy admired Leanne and had been hoping for a chance to get to know her better for months, maybe by meeting up outside of work. But she hadn't ever expected Leanne to show up at her home without warning.

"So, I wanted to check in," Leanne said. "I was worried about you yesterday."

"Oh. Thanks."

"You looked really bad. No offense."

"Just a little rattled. I'm fine now."

Leanne watched her, studying her face with those sharp green eyes that noticed every detail.

"Sure you're okay?"

"Yep."

"Good." She took a deep breath and folded her arms over her

chest. "Another reason I'm here is I wanted to loop you in. McBride gave me the green light on that tire cast."

"That's good news. Wow. What changed his mind?"

"I'm not sure."

"Is it something to do with yesterday?" Izzy asked.

"Honestly, I don't know what it has to do with. But I'm going to run with it. I'm headed to El Paso right now to drop it off before he can change his mind. I'm taking them a copy of your photograph, too, because you were able to enhance so much of the tread detail."

"The El Paso lab is super backed up," Izzy told her. "You know that, right? It'd be faster to send it to the main lab in Austin."

"I'm aware," Leanne said. "But the chief wants El Paso. I think maybe he has some pull over there."

"Well, good, then."

"Listen, I'm sorry for what you went through yesterday. That had to be horrible stumbling on a scene like that."

"It's fine," she said, even though she'd hardly slept last night.

"And I'm sorry you had to give your statement to Travis Malcom. He's the worst."

"Yeah, what's up with that guy?"

"He's kind of . . . full of himself."

"Just a little."

"I hear he's an okay detective, though, so let's hope he makes some progress."

Leanne pulled her phone from her jacket and frowned down at a message. Izzy hadn't heard a sound, so it must have been on vibrate.

"Anyway, that's all." She tucked the phone away. "I wanted to check how you're doing and give you an update."

"I appreciate it."

As awkward as it was for Leanne to show up here out of the

blue, Izzy was glad to be kept in the loop for a change. Leanne was one of the few people at MPD who treated her like an actual investigator instead of some lowly part-timer.

"I'll see you at work, then?" Leanne moved to leave. "Unless something unexpected comes up?"

"Let's hope it's quiet."

"Let's hope."

TWENTY-FIVE

Leanne spotted Sam Carver in an instant. At nearly six feet tall, she stood out in a crowd, especially one made up of backpack-toting students in pj pants and hoodies. It had been Sam's idea to meet at a coffee shop near the UT El Paso campus because she lived nearby.

Sam grabbed a pair of coffee cups and turned around, and her face brightened as Leanne walked over.

"Hey! You're early, too," Sam said. "What's happening to us?"

Sam wasn't a hugger, so Leanne simply smiled as she took one of the coffee cups. "Thanks," Leanne said.

"Black with two sugars, right?"

"Perfect."

A kid got up with his backpack, and Sam rushed over to claim a pair of stools at a bar by the window.

Leanne surveyed the room, enjoying the comforting familiarity of the green signage and big leather chairs. When she lived in Dallas, Starbucks had been part of her routine, but she hadn't set foot in one in more than a year.

"They're packed today," Leanne said, taking one of the seats.

"It's always like this on Saturdays."

Leanne looked her friend over as she peeled off her coffee lid.

Sam had traded her long, honey-blond locks for a platinum pixie cut.

"I love your hair," Leanne said. "Looks good short."

"Thanks. I got sick of dealing with it, so I decided to chop it."

Leanne tore open the sugar packets, amazed that Sam would remember a detail such as how she took her coffee after four years. Leanne hadn't seen Sam since she'd left Dallas PD for the FBI Academy.

"So, what brings you to town?" Sam asked.

"I had some evidence to drop off at the lab here, so I thought I'd give you a call," Leanne said. "How's El Paso treating you?"

"It's okay." She sipped her drink, getting lipstick on the rim. "Not exactly Quantico, though. I miss Virginia."

For as long as Leanne had known Sam, she had had two driving goals: to become an FBI agent and to join the Bureau's Behavioral Analysis Unit. Leanne had been there the night Sam celebrated getting accepted into the FBI Academy.

"You miss it enough to go back?" Leanne asked.

She shrugged. "Miguel loves it here," she said, referring to her special agent husband. "So, I agreed to give it five years. The things we do for love, right?"

Leanne nodded, even though she couldn't relate at all. She had never been in a relationship worth making that kind of sacrifice for. The idea of sharing a five-year plan with a guy was even harder to imagine.

"So, what's up?" Sam set her cup down. "Tell me why you're really here."

"I need to hit you up for a favor."

"I figured."

"I'm leading a homicide investigation," Leanne told her. "I think it might be part of a series."

"How many?"

"Five so far. Possibly more."

She leaned forward. "Shit, Leanne. Why haven't I heard about it?"

"These victims are unidentified."

"All of them?"

"So far. And some of the remains were skeletonized. The cases aren't making a lot of headlines."

Sam tipped her head to the side. "So, what's the link then?"

Leanne took out her phone and tapped open a screenshot of the map she'd made. She slid the phone in front of Sam.

"Those are the recovery sites spread out over three counties."

Sam moved her fingers over the screen to zoom in. "What's this highway?"

"That's the connection. Everything is within a quarter mile of Highway 67 between Fort Stockton and Marfa."

Sam gazed down at the screen, studying the map, and Leanne's pulse quickened. Far from looking skeptical, Sam seemed intrigued.

She glanced up. "So . . . you're looking for a profile, I take it? Your department wants to bring in BAU?"

"Not exactly," Leanne said. "That's the problem. I'm having trouble even convincing my chief that these murders are related, much less that we should consult a profiler. Meanwhile, I've got no IDs. No victimology to work with. These cases are at a standstill unless I can develop some kind of lead."

She lifted an eyebrow. "So, you want *me* to take a look? Like, on the down-low?"

Leanne reached into her jacket and pulled out a thumb drive. "These are the files I have. Crime scene photos, autopsy reports, whatever I've got on each victim. I was hoping you might read through and give me your take."

"They've got me on anti-terror now," Sam said. "I haven't done a criminal profile since I was at Quantico."

"I understand. This would just be, you know, first impressions. Whatever jumps out at you, if anything. And if you don't have time, I thought maybe one of your BAU contacts might be able to look at it."

"No, I've got time." She examined the phone again before sliding it back. "I'll take a crack at it, see if I can come up with anything."

"Really?"

"Sure. It sounds interesting."

"*Thank you.*" Leanne closed her eyes. "You have no idea how much I appreciate this."

"I can tell." She smiled and sipped her coffee. "You know, this isn't at all what I thought you wanted to talk about." She set her cup down and rubbed the lipstick off the edge. "I figured you wanted to hit me up about the Moriarty case."

"You've heard of that?"

"Everyone has. There's a rumor around here that some of our public corruption guys are looking into it."

Leanne blinked at her. "Seriously?"

She nodded.

"But wouldn't that be the Rangers' purview? Their public integrity unit?"

"That I do not know. I'm just telling you the rumor."

Leanne watched Sam's face, and an uneasy feeling settled over her. In law enforcement circles, rumors tended to have at least some basis in fact. But why would the FBI be involved? It would have to be something extremely unusual. And sensitive.

Sam checked her watch. "Damn, I need to get to my meeting." She dropped the thumb drive into her bag. "I should get going."

"Still working weekends?" Leanne asked.

"Always."

They slid off their stools and walked out, and Leanne held the door for a pair of college girls with backpacks. Both wore ripped jeans and had their hair in braids. Leanne was struck by how young they looked—around the same age as her Jane Doe.

"I'll get back to you as soon as I can," Sam said. "It may be a few days, though. My team is swamped right now."

"I understand. Thank you."

Sam pulled a pair of sunglasses from her bag and gave Leanne a worried look. "I'll keep my ear to the ground on that other thing."

The public corruption thing, she meant.

"But you didn't hear about it from me," Sam said.

"Of course. Thanks for the heads-up, though. Maybe it's only a rumor."

"Maybe." Sam slid her sunglasses on. "In the meantime, watch your back."

Leanne walked to her parking space feeling anxious. How was it that whispers about the Sean Moriarty case had reached an FBI field office in El Paso?

Her phone chimed, and she dug it from her pocket. Josh.

"Hey, where are you?"

She caught the excitement in his voice.

"In El Paso, dropping off that evidence. What's up?"

"You need to get back here quick."

She stopped in her tracks. "What happened?"

"We got a hit on those prints finally."

"You mean—"

"We got an ID."

TWENTY-SIX

Leanne studied the two pictures. It was hard to believe they were the same person.

"Is that her?"

She turned around as Will walked over and leaned down to look at her computer screen.

"Valeria Reyes, age nineteen," Leanne said. "She's from Albuquerque. At least, that's what her driver's license says."

"Wow."

There was a lot loaded into that one little word. The driver's license photo showed a smiling eighteen-year-old with shiny dark hair and a sparkle in her eyes. The mug shot of Reyes had been taken less than a year later. In the photo her cheeks looked hollow, and her peroxide-blond hair was limp and dull.

But it was her eyes that really marked the change. They looked empty. And seeing them put an ache in Leanne's chest.

Will shook his head. "Damn. Shows you what drugs can do. I assume that's what's on her rap sheet?"

"No. Just the prostitution charge."

Valeria Reyes had been arrested outside a Fort Stockton truck stop six months ago, one week shy of her nineteenth birthday. Which meant Dr. Korbin had been correct with his age estimate.

Leanne studied the mug shot, then shifted her focus to the driver's license picture.

"Wonder what happened to her," Will murmured.

Leanne didn't know yet, but she could guess. She might have been a runaway. Or maybe her parents kicked her out. Or maybe she'd become homeless after her family hit a rough patch.

He stepped back. "Nothing else on her sheet besides prostitution?"

"That was it."

"Guess we got lucky, then."

"How's that?"

"If not for the arrest, she wouldn't be in the system."

"Well, having an ID is definitely a step forward."

Leanne looked at the mug shot again, hoping Ben never reached a point like that. His last DWI arrest had felt like rock bottom. But at least he'd gone to rehab and gotten a chance to change. Things could have been worse. They could still *get* worse, especially given the people he was spending time with now. Every time her phone lit up at night, Leanne worried it was going to be some horrible news about Ben, that he'd done something to himself or someone else that could never be undone.

Leanne hit print on the two pictures and crossed the bullpen to grab them off the printer.

Izzy walked in and waved her down.

"Glad I caught you." She held out a manila folder. "I got something on that shoe impression."

"From the railroad tracks?"

"Yeah. And I heard we got an ID finally?"

"Valeria Reyes," Leanne told her, taking the file. "Nineteen years old."

Izzy shook her head.

"What about the shoe impression?" Leanne asked.

"According to my research, it's a man's shoe, either a thirteen or a thirteen and a half, depending on the brand."

"He sounds tall," Leanne said.

"That's what I was thinking."

Leanne opened the folder and studied the herringbone-patterned shoeprint. Even though the shoe impression was faint, so far it was the only evidence they had that hinted at a physical description of the killer.

If it even belonged to the killer. As evidence went, this was extremely circumstantial. But it was better than nothing. Who knew what might happen? Maybe they'd find a suspect with a pair of these shoes sitting in his closet.

"This is helpful." She looked at Izzy. "Thanks."

"No problem. I thought you'd want it right away, especially since we have the victim's ID in now. That's two leads in one day. Progress, right?"

"Still more to go."

Leanne reached over to grab the photos off the printer, and Izzy stepped closer.

"Is that the victim?" Izzy asked.

"Yeah. You recognize her?"

"I don't think so." Her tone sounded sad. "She looks so young."

Izzy seemed to be dressed for work, with a zipper pouch clipped at her waist and her Nikon camera looped around her neck.

"You going out on a job?" Leanne asked.

"Just shooting some nature photos."

"Are you going by yourself?"

"Yes, but I'm just going to Town Park and the water tower."

"Be careful."

"I will."

Leanne wasn't used to worrying about safety around here, but the events of the past week had her questioning her assumptions about Madrone. Her hometown was changing in every way imaginable.

"Don't worry, I've got my pepper spray." Izzy patted her bag. "And my phone's charged this time."

"That's good, but pay attention," Leanne said, echoing what her father always told her. "It's all about situational awareness."

"I know."

"Intuition is your friend."

Leanne stretched her quads as the Jeep Cherokee pulled into the lot. Max Scott slid out and slammed the door.

"What's with the boots?" she asked, looking at his feet. "I said sneakers."

"You were serious about that?"

"Absolutely."

He stopped beside her and put his hands on his hips. Besides chunky leather work boots, the reporter had on jeans and a Texas Rangers baseball cap—which she assumed he wore to cover his balding head. As part of her research, Leanne had looked up Max Scott's bio on his newspaper's website. Among other things, she'd learned that he was part of an investigative reporting team that had won numerous awards. Max himself had won none, which told her that he was hungry.

"Guess you're running in boots, then." She zipped her car key into the pocket of her fleece and strode toward the trail. She glanced over her shoulder at him.

"You coming?"

"Hang on."

He opened the cargo hatch and quickly traded his boots for a pair of checkered Vans. He joined her at the trailhead, and she set off jogging at an annoyingly slow pace.

"Why did you want to meet way out here?" he asked.

"It's the most scenic place around. Since you're a tourist, I thought you'd want to see it."

Plus, she didn't want to be spotted in town talking to a reporter. The gossip mill would be on fire.

She glanced back at him. He didn't look happy to be called a tourist. Or maybe it was the steep trail that was putting a scowl on his face.

Leanne pounded up the path with him close on her heels. They passed the big ledge where people liked to take selfies, and by the time they reached the third switchback, he was flush-faced and winded.

"I've been thinking about your offer," she told him.

That seemed to put some spring in his step. "Oh yeah?" he huffed. "I figured it was something like that."

"I'm interested in a trade. But not the one you're thinking."

"What, then?"

"I don't want to be interviewed."

He halted in his tracks. She stopped and turned around.

"That was the deal, though."

"We didn't have a deal. I'm proposing one now." She turned and continued up the trail, race-walking now so he could keep up.

"Okay. Let's hear it."

"I have some questions about this exposé you mentioned." She looked back at him. "You were right—I'm curious about it. In exchange, I'll give you a scoop on something else."

"What?"

"A case that hasn't hit the news yet."

"You mean the dead hiker from last night? I already heard about that."

"That's not the scoop."

They reached an overlook, and the valley stretched out before them. She hadn't been lying about the scenery. This truly was the most beautiful view in the area, especially with the sky clear and the late-day sun giving everything a golden glow. Swaths of yellow stipa grass rippled in the breeze, and a red-tailed hawk swooped over their heads, soaring out over the canyon like a hang glider.

To her right was a madrone tree with twisty limbs and peeling orange bark. Leanne had hiked up here with her dad when she was a kid. The tree had been shorter then, and he'd pointed out the nearby juniper, explaining how it acted as a nurse tree, protecting the smaller tree until it could get established.

The memory put a lump in her throat, and she stepped away to compose herself. For years, she'd noticed how some people would hike to this ledge and tearfully stare out at the setting sun. *Grief.* She'd never recognized it for what it was before her dad died, but now she knew it in a heartbeat.

She glanced at Max. Despite the cold, sweat dripped down his face, and his cheeks were splotchy. But he seemed to be hanging in there. Maybe she shouldn't have brought this guy up here. It was a sacred place to her, and she wasn't sure why she'd decided to share it with a reporter.

"So, I offered you a trade," she said, getting back to the point. "Are you interested or not?"

"I'll need to check with my editor. I can't promise anything."

"Wrong answer. This is an exploding offer. Take it or leave it."

"How do I know you actually have a scoop and you're not stringing me along?"

"You're going to have to trust me. Good thing for you, I'm trustworthy."

He stared at her, seeming to weigh this assertion. Then he turned and muttered something she couldn't hear.

"Make up your mind."

"Fine. All right. Let's hear your scoop."

"I go first," she said. "I want to know the name of your inside source."

"What inside source?"

"The source who tipped you off about this story you're investigating in Chisos County involving prominent county officials."

"I'm not going to tell you that. What kind of journalist do you think I am?"

"The practical kind," she said. "I'll figure it out eventually, anyway. And if you tell me now, that gives you a chance to get a jump on your competition on something else."

"How do I know the 'something else' is worth risking my reputation?"

The fact that he was willing to risk it at all told her that her hunch about him had been right. Whatever ethics he had he was willing to bend if it gave him an edge.

"Again, you'll have to trust me."

His frown deepened.

"But look at it this way," she said. "I have something to lose, too, if I were to mislead you."

"What's that?"

"It's what you told me last time. You're writing an exposé about prominent officials right here in my backyard. I have to assume I work with some of them, so my reputation is on the line potentially. I'm sure you could find a way to make me look bad in your article, if you had an ax to grind."

Leanne watched him, trying to read his expression. What she hadn't said was that he could probably make her father look bad, too. She didn't want to put attention on that particular point, but it was only logical. Everyone knew about her close connection to one of the primary investigators in the Hannah Rawls murder case. The father-daughter link was supposedly the reason various media outlets wanted to interview her—although she'd never really bought into that idea. Leanne believed their real motivation was that they wanted a chance to pump her for information about her dad and her police department. They probably figured they could trip her up in an interview and get her to reveal something damaging.

She stared out at the canyon, acting bored as she waited for him to decide.

"Fine," he said. "I'll tell you in generalities. But I won't give you a name."

She pretended to think about it.

"Deal."

He took a deep breath. "My source is someone in law enforcement."

"PD or sheriff's office?"

"That's it. That's all I can say."

"Law enforcement meaning a badge? Or an officer of the court?"

"I can't say."

It wasn't a name, but it was a starting point. And the information would save her time at a moment when time was running short. With everything that happened yesterday, along with the victim identification this morning, her case was quickly gaining momentum.

"Okay, let's hear it." He crossed his arms. "What's your scoop?"

"This is on background only," she said. "Do not quote me, even anonymously. You understand?"

"Sure. Got it."

"I'm serious about that. If I see my name or anything about me as your source, you will be sorry. Are we clear?"

"I said I got it."

She paused, watching him. "It's about last night's homicide victim."

"I hadn't heard it was officially determined to be a homicide."

"It will be. Local officials have reason to believe that homicide might be part of a pattern."

"A pattern," he repeated. "What, you mean like other victims?"

"Yes."

"As in 'victims' plural?"

"Yes."

"Who?"

"I'm sure you'll have no trouble digging that up," she said. "You seem to have a lot of sources around here."

She watched his face, and clearly this tip had gotten his wheels turning. He had no doubt heard of her Jane Doe case, which hit the news the very same weekend as the Sean Moriarty bombshell. Now he just had to figure out what other cases she was talking about.

This was a calculated risk.

As in almost all risk, almost no calculation. Leanne was fed up with McBride trying to stymie her. If last night proved anything, it was that her theory was right, and his dismissiveness of her work was having dire consequences. She was determined to figure out who was killing these women, and she needed resources to do it. Which meant she had to step up the pressure, but in a way that didn't look like she was doing it.

Max was still watching her closely, maybe deciding whether she was a crackpot or not.

She took out her phone and checked the time. "I have to head back."

"Wait. Just want to be clear here. You're saying there's a pattern of *more* than two homicide victims. Correct me if I'm wrong, but wouldn't that make this a serial killer case?"

She removed her cap and wiped her forehead. "Those are your words. Not mine." She settled the cap back on her head and started down the trail.

"Hold up." He jogged after her. "I'm going to need a lot more information."

"I'm sure you'll find it."

After her less-than-strenuous workout, Leanne swung back by the office, then picked up a veggie taco and headed home. She sped down the highway with the windows rolled down, hoping the cold night air would wake up her brain because she had more work to do tonight.

What was she missing?

She'd been pondering the cases and going through clues in her head during the mind-numbing drive from El Paso.

The El Paso lab is super backed up. You know that, right?

She pictured Izzy on her front porch, telling her to send the evidence to Austin. The backlog at the El Paso crime lab was well-known, particularly their drug section. So why had McBride insisted on sending their evidence there? Was he trying to stall her? Or was it like he claimed, that they had some kind of pull with them? Leanne was skeptical. That was the thing about a small-town police department—they didn't have much pull anywhere.

Lights flashed in her rearview mirror, and she heard the faint whine of a siren. The sound grew louder and louder, and she eased onto the shoulder as a wailing fire truck raced by. She pulled back onto the road, but soon more headlights zoomed up on her. She veered onto the shoulder again and rolled to a stop as an ambulance sped past, siren howling.

She looked over her shoulder for more, then got back onto the highway and reached for her radio. Turning up the volume, she listened to the mix of static and chatter.

The words "Sullivan Ranch" made her heart lurch.

Leanne hit the gas. She grabbed her phone and called her mom. No answer. She tried again, and it went straight to voicemail.

Leanne floored the pedal, racing to catch up to the trucks. She tried calling her brother. No answer. Cursing, she tossed the phone away and punched the gas until her speedometer pushed one hundred.

Finally, the turnoff for Sullivan Ranch came into view. Leanne slowed. Whirring lights bounced off the canyon walls as she jabbed the brakes and swung a left into the driveway. She eased through the gate, bumping over the cattle guard as she strained to see what was happening ahead. Smoke wafted through her windows as she made her way up the narrow dirt road. Approaching the trees surrounding the house, she came upon a row of emergency vehicles.

Beyond the treetops was an orange glow. Her stomach clenched as she neared the house and saw flames licking up from the roof.

"Oh God."

A sheriff's car backed up, and she slammed on the brakes and hit the horn. She pulled into the yard. Shoving her truck into park, she flung open the door and grabbed her phone, hitting redial as she ran toward the house. The commotion was at the end of the driveway. A red fire rig blocked her view of the guesthouse. Leanne's heart skittered as she ran through the haze of smoke.

"Hey!" She rushed up to a firefighter, grabbing his arm. He turned around, and she recognized his sooty face beneath the helmet.

"Rick, what's happening?"

He blinked at her, then seemed to place who she was. "It's the garage." He nodded toward it. "We got it contained."

She ran toward the garage and darted around the fire truck. Her heart was in her throat as she saw the guesthouse through a veil of smoke. No flames, thank God.

A line of firefighters stood near the garage, dousing flames on the roof with a spray of water.

She whirled toward the main house and raced to the front door. It stood open.

"Mom!"

Leanne rushed into the living room. The TV was on. A half-empty drink sat on the table, but both recliners were empty.

"Mom? Boone? *Hello?*"

A firefighter walked out from the bedroom wing.

"They're at the stables," he said.

Leanne ran through the kitchen and out the back door, nearly tripping over a bag of potting soil on the patio. Red-and-white emergency lights reflected off the stable walls as she dashed up the path.

"Leanne!"

She whirled around.

"Over here."

She spied Boone on the patio of the guesthouse. Her mother sat in a chair as a paramedic bent over her.

"What happened?" Leanne rushed over. "Mom?"

Her mother glanced up, wide-eyed, as the paramedic bandaged her arm.

"What's going on?"

Her mom didn't answer, so she turned to Boone. His eyes were wild, and his white hair was sticking out all over the place. "Boone, what happened?"

"That horse damn near killed her!"

"She did *not*," her mom said.

"She sure as hell did!" He looked at Leanne. "Starlight busted down her stall. Then she went crazy and kicked the living hell outta your mom."

"I fell on my butt, that's all. It's just an elbow scrape."

"Where's Ben?" Leanne demanded. "I saw his car back there."

"I sent him out to get the horses," her mother said. "They got loose and ran off. Sandy's helping him."

Sandy's property abutted the ranch's east side. Leanne looked over her shoulder at the three-car garage being doused with water. Thank goodness it was detached from the house.

She turned to Boone. "How did this *happen*?"

He shook his head. "Damned if I know. Nacho started barking. Then we smelled smoke. We called it in, and then your mother ran out there to see about the horses."

Leanne turned to her mom, who looked even more annoyed than the EMT who was trying to treat her injury.

"Not so *tight*," her mom snapped, jerking her arm away.

Leanne took a deep breath. Her heart rate started to come down as she saw that her mom was being her usual bossy self.

"We should go to the hospital and get your head looked at," Boone said.

"I'm *fine*, I told you."

"That damn horse could have killed you."

Leanne left them to their bickering and jogged back to the driveway. They were still hosing down the garage, but the smoke was white now instead of gray. The front door to the guesthouse stood ajar, and Leanne rushed inside, needing to see for herself that the place was empty.

"Ben?"

The one-room cottage was dim, lit only by the glow of the TV. An empty Whataburger bag sat in the middle of the coffee table. She picked her way around the unmade bed and through an obstacle course of shoes and dirty clothes on her way to the bathroom. She switched on the light. The damp air and lingering scent of Axe body wash told her that her brother had showered in here recently. She eyed his medicine cabinet above the sink with a knot in her stomach. Unable to resist, she opened the mirrored door. No pill bottles. Just a can of shaving cream and a pink razor.

Leanne returned to the driveway, where the firefighters seemed to be winding things down at the garage. Steam wafted up from the roof, and she caught a glimpse of blackened rafters that had collapsed on top of Boone's antique cars.

Several firefighters in yellow jackets stood off to the side, swigging from water bottles. Pulling her shirt up over her nose, Leanne tromped over to the nearest truck, where Rick was wiping down his face with a bandana. Besides going to high school together, they knew each other through work.

"Is it under control?" she asked, yelling over the loud hum of the nearby rig.

"Yeah."

"What happened?"

He didn't answer, just wiped his neck and then pulled off his helmet. His short-cropped brown hair was soaked with sweat.

"Don't know," he said.

"Come talk to me."

He looked annoyed, but he followed her to the back of the stables, away from all the commotion and noise. The air was hazy, and her eyes began to sting as she turned to face him.

"How did it start?" she asked.

"Don't know yet. We haven't exactly had time to investigate."

"Yes, but—"

"Smell that?" He nodded at the building behind her.

"No. What?" She sniffed the air.

"Gasoline."

Leanne sniffed again and caught the faint odor of gasoline underneath the smoke smell. Her heart rate kicked up again.

"Stables might have gone up, too," Rick said, "but the homeowner has a sprinkler system there. Good thing he had it installed. And good thing we got here when we did."

The sprinkler system had been her mother's idea, not Boone's. After one of her mom's friends lost her horses in a fire, her mother decided she wanted sprinklers put in.

"Where was all the gasoline?" Leanne asked.

"I don't know." He put his helmet back on his head. "We'll have to investigate, obviously. But you can smell it here and around the garage, too. You guys are lucky it didn't spread."

Leanne's chest tightened as she turned to look at the guesthouse porch. The EMT was gone, but her mom and Boone were still bickering, from the looks of it—probably out of sorts from all the drama.

Beyond the guest cottage was Boone's big ranch house, surrounded by hundred-year-old oak trees. Leanne looked at the darkness to the east of them, where Ben and the neighbor were supposedly rounding up Starlight and Reesie. The horses had to be terrified, and it might take hours to get them back.

She turned to Rick, and he was watching her with bloodshot eyes. He was one of the locals who'd given her the cold shoulder since she'd returned to town. But he seemed normal tonight, maybe because he was in control here. She was the one who felt threatened and panicked.

"Thank you guys for getting here so fast."

"Yeah, y'all are lucky." He nodded toward the house. "This thing could have been deadly."

TWENTY-SEVEN

Warm air and searing guitar chords hit her as she yanked open the door to the Javelina. Leanne scanned the faces and then cut through the crowd of sweaty bodies. Squeezing between a pair of broad-shouldered cowboys, she leaned across the bar.

"Katie!"

The bartender looked up from the taps.

"Where's Duncan? I saw his truck out front."

Katie jerked her head toward the dart board.

Duncan stood in the shadows near a group of off-duty deputies. Everyone was talking and laughing. Except for him. He was several feet apart from the group, staring down at his phone.

Leanne walked over. "Hey."

He glanced up. "Hey, I was about to call you. What's this about your parents' ranch?" He held up his phone. "There's a fire?"

"Was," she said. "It's out now. And it's not my parents'—it's my stepdad's."

"What the hell happened?"

A cheer went up from the dart board. Duncan took her elbow and steered her away from the crowd to an empty high-top table littered with beer bottles.

"I don't know, but I plan to find out," she said. "I need you to talk to Moriarty for me."

He blinked down at her. "Who?"

"*Sean Moriarty.* He's in the back there, playing pool." She nodded at the room behind him.

"Why would you want—"

"He's been harassing my family, and I want you to find out where he was earlier tonight."

"What, like, question him?"

"Yes. I want to know if he has an alibi."

Duncan darted his gaze toward the pool room. "I can tell you right now, he does. He's been in there for the last hour, at least."

"How do you know?"

"Because I got here an hour ago, and he was already there in the middle of a game."

"Fine, I'll do it." She stepped around him, and he caught her arm.

"Wait, Leanne. Don't you think this is a job for the fire investigators?"

"I think it's a job for anyone with a badge." She shook off his hand. "And I think the best time to question a suspect is when something happens. If you won't do it, I will."

She went around him and into the back room. Liam stood in the corner, pool cue in hand, talking to a pair of women in short dresses and cowgirl boots. Sean was at the pool table, plunking balls into a wooden triangle. The spotlight above the table gleamed off his shaved head, and he wore the same stiff new jeans as the other night but with a black hoodie.

Sean's eyes went from Leanne to Duncan and back to Leanne again. He gave the triangle a firm jolt and then lifted it off the table.

"What?" he asked her.

"Didn't I tell you to stay away from my family?"

He gave her a long, cool look before setting the triangle on an empty barstool.

She stepped closer, grabbing the cue ball off the table. Annoyance flared in his eyes.

"Leanne."

Ignoring Duncan, she walked right up to Sean with the ball clutched in her fist.

"Didn't I?"

Sean stared down at her, his gray eyes flat.

"I'll say it again." She leaned closer. "The Sullivan Ranch is private property. Same for the Triple R. Same for my goddamn house."

He didn't react.

"Where were you earlier tonight?" she asked.

The corner of his mouth lifted in a smirk. But he didn't answer.

She glanced at his brother. Liam was watching her now, along with the two young women.

She looked at Sean. "All of those properties have security cameras. Just so you know that."

"Good for them."

She watched his eyes, trying to read them. Then she backed away.

He lifted an eyebrow. "Anything else?"

"No. That's it." She tossed the cue ball, and he caught it in his right hand. "Have a nice game."

Leanne turned and walked out. She felt Duncan behind her as she crossed the bar and pushed through the heavy door into the cold air.

She looked up at the sky, her chest burning with frustration. Tears stung her eyes.

Duncan walked up beside her. "What the fuck, Leanne?"

She blew out a sigh, and her breath turned to frost. She zipped her fleece jacket.

"Hey."

She turned. "What?"

"What was that? What the hell are you doing?"

"Investigating."

"Leave it to the fire department. Jesus." He raked his hand through his hair. "Are you *trying* to piss off a convicted murderer?"

"You don't get it."

"Don't get what?"

She shook her head and looked away. Duncan didn't understand. No one did. Not *one single person* understood what she was up against. She'd been tapped to lead a homicide case, but her department was giving her almost no help solving it. It was like they didn't even care. Forget helping her solve the *multiple cold cases* that were connected to this new one. And now she had to deal with the potentially explosive link between all these cases and Sean Moriarty's overturned conviction. The chief wouldn't even acknowledge a possible link, much less investigate anything.

Which meant she was on her own. Again.

"Leanne?"

She shook her head and strode toward the parking lot.

"Hey, nice seeing you," he called after her. "Glad we could talk."

She waved over her shoulder as she walked away.

TWENTY-EIGHT

The place smelled like a campfire, and Leanne was flooded with memories of cold, dew-covered sleeping bags and burned toast. She trekked up the driveway and surveyed the blackened skeleton that had once been the garage. A shiny black Cadillac was parked beside the guesthouse, and Leanne eyed it warily. Maybe the insurance agent had shown up already.

She glanced around the property. The ranch house looked unscathed. Same for the stables. Leanne looked across the paddock to where the horses stood in the shade of a giant live oak, probably exhausted from last night's adventure.

Sometimes it blew Leanne's mind that her mom actually lived here—and Ben, too. When they were growing up, Leanne and Ben had enough of everything, but nothing like this. They hadn't had horses, or acreage, or fancy cars. Their mom had taught riding lessons and their dad was a cop. Had her mother married Boone for his money? Or did she love him? Leanne honestly didn't know.

Her parents had been in love once—of that she was certain. They'd met at a rodeo in Abilene. As a kid, Leanne had loved hearing her dad tell the story of how he'd fallen for his future wife right away. *A pretty woman on a fast horse, and I was done for*, he'd say.

What attracted her mom was more of a mystery, but Leanne had always figured that her tall dad, with his badge and his quiet confidence, must have represented security. Regina's own father was a cotton farmer whose bad judgment and gambling problems had cost the family their land.

But who knew? The more Leanne learned about her parents, the more she suspected she didn't know either of them at all.

She stepped into the shadow of the burned-out garage. The roof had caved in, and charred shingles dangled down with bright blue patches of sky peeking between the gaps. She stopped beside the Rolls-Royce. The windshield was shattered, the hood smashed by a fallen rafter. She studied the alligator burn pattern on the wood as she picked her way through the sooty debris, following the faint sound of scraping.

"Mom?"

"Back here."

She stepped into the storage closet, where red and green tubs of holiday decorations lay overturned on the floor. Her mother knelt beside a pile of broken Christmas ornaments, sweeping shards of glass with a hand broom.

Leanne's heart squeezed. Her mom wore overalls and muck boots and had her hair back in a scarf that reminded Leanne of her grandmother. Her mother's eyes were bloodshot, and she'd aged ten years overnight.

"What happen here?" Leanne asked.

"The damn roof caved in. What does it look like?"

"Is it safe to be in here?"

"Probably not."

Leanne crouched down to help. "What are they saying?" she asked, dropping chunks of glass into the dustpan.

"The insurance adjuster can't come out till next week."

"Next *week*?"

"They're tied up with the wildfires in New Mexico. They said to take pictures of everything, and we'll use them with the claim. Boone got about a hundred this morning."

Leanne looked around. "Where is he now?"

"On the sun porch, meeting with the car guy."

"What car guy?"

"Some special policy he's got on the antiques."

Leanne grabbed a contractor-grade trash bag by the door and dragged it over. The wooden shelving had collapsed, sending boxes everywhere.

"Anything salvageable?"

Her mom tossed a broken nutcracker into the bag. "No."

Leanne sifted through the pile of shattered snow globes that her mom had collected for decades. Her wooden nutcracker collection was mixed in, too.

"This guy's intact." Leanne picked up a German nutcracker holding two beer steins.

Her mom plucked it from her hand and tossed it in the bag. "Don't bother. What's the point?"

Leanne stood and grabbed the shovel leaning against the charred Sheetrock. The burn pattern made a tall arc, and she wished she knew how to interpret the markings. She wanted to talk to Rick or one of the arson investigators.

Her mom stood as she surveyed everything. "What a mess."

"I'm sorry."

"Why? It's not your fault."

"I know."

Sighing, she looked at Leanne. "Ben came and picked up the records."

"What records?"

"Your dad's LPs. Some of them were melted, but he found a couple boxes that made it. Said he wanted them for keepsakes."

Leanne stared at her. "He actually said that? Keepsakes?"

"Well, I assumed. Why else would he want them?"

Leanne gritted her teeth and looked away. Their dad's collection of classic jazz records was probably worth some money. He'd had hundreds of them.

"What's the problem?"

"Nothing."

"What do you care about the records? You don't listen to jazz."

"Forget it." Leanne crouched down and plucked another nutcracker from the pile, one her father had carved in his shop. It was a cowboy with a lasso made of burlap twine. "Just hope he's not selling them for drug money, that's all."

"He would never."

Leanne glared up at her.

Her mom muttered under her breath and turned around.

Using the shovel, Leanne filled the big black bag until it was nearly too heavy to lift. Broken ornaments and Santa plates and snowflake mugs. The Christmas cookie tins were unscathed, but her mother didn't want them, claimed she was done with all of it.

"This is going to take days," Leanne said. "We should hire someone to help."

"Boone already did. They're coming tomorrow. I just want to get all this personal stuff up first."

Leanne hauled the bag to the front of the garage and deposited it near Boone's pickup truck. Unlike the antiques, it had somehow escaped the falling rafters. She found the charred remnants of what had once been the wooden ladder for the attic. Beside it was a half-burned bankers box. Leanne poked through the singed, soggy carboard and melted vinyl.

She looked up. The plywood floor was gone, and the attic was a crazy network of seared beams.

"Why didn't the sprinklers go off?" Leanne asked.

"They did. That's what Glenn told us, anyway. He said they slowed the burn, but not by a lot."

Glenn Meachum was the fire chief and a longtime friend of Leanne's dad.

"A twenty-thousand-dollar sprinkler system, and what good did it do?" Her mom shook her head. "Damn waste of money."

"Those are designed for kitchen fires. Or maybe a fireplace ember that lands on the roof," Leanne said. "If someone douses the place with accelerant, a residential sprinkler system isn't going to do much."

"Tell that to the sales rep who sold it to us. You know, if they hadn't gotten here when they did, the stables could have burned down, too. Bunch of psychopaths."

"Who?"

"Whoever did this!" She glowered at Leanne. "Starlight and Reesie could have been killed!"

"*All* of you could have been killed."

"They were after the horses, not us. Trust me. These people are sick."

Leanne sighed. Her mom had a long-standing suspicion of animal rights activists, and she seemed to have already made up her mind.

Leanne looked up at the crackled wood with slices of blue sky showing through. "You shouldn't have put his things up there."

"What things?"

"Dad's things. I wish you'd left them with me."

"What do you want with all that junk? It's just a bunch of old baseball magazines and paperbacks."

"And all of his notebooks. His work stuff."

"Like I said, *junk*. What does anyone need with all that?" She turned to look at Leanne. "Oh, don't tell me. The Rawls case? *That's* what you're upset about? Goddamn it, Leanne."

"I'm upset about your house nearly burning down! And with you guys in it! I'm upset about the horses and the cars and, yes, *all of Dad's worldly possessions* that shouldn't have been chucked up in the attic to rot!"

Her mom fisted a hand on her hip. "Now you're being petty."

"How it that petty?"

"I was doing you a favor not saddling you and your brother with all of your father's crap after he died."

"It's not crap to me. I would have gladly taken it, if I'd known you were going to toss it in the attic and never look through it again."

"You had every opportunity to sort through your father's things when we moved. You chose not to."

Leanne's skin flushed with anger. "When *we* moved?"

"Yes."

"You mean when *you* moved. Yes, Mom, when you moved in with Boone a whole *two months* after Dad died, before we'd even picked out a tombstone, I should have come running over here to claim all his stuff."

Leanne glared at her mom. She was tired of holding back her feelings.

"I don't appreciate your tone, Leanne."

"My *tone*?"

"You're being disrespectful."

She snorted.

"You know, Leanne, I've had about enough of your ungrateful attitude."

Leanne shook her head and turned away.

"You have no appreciation for what's been done for you."

She whirled around. "How is that?"

"You think your father was so wonderful to live with? With his black moods and his drinking and his damn whittling projects at all hours of the night? He was *depressed*, Leanne. And he took it out on me for years."

Leanne clenched her teeth and turned away. She'd heard all this before. All the excuses that supposedly made it okay for her mom to start sneaking around with Boone.

"I'm tired of you thinking he was such a hero. You want to know the truth?"

Something in her mother's voice made her turn around.

"He was not."

Leanne's stomach tensed.

"The truth is, I'm glad all that crap is gone." She gestured at the attic. "The boxes, the work stuff, the legal pads. Your dad was obsessed with his job, and it ruined our marriage."

Leanne turned around.

"Fine. Turn away. Turn a blind eye to reality, too."

"What's that mean?"

"It means *open your eyes, Leanne*. You think he had nothing to do with this mess? He was in the room."

A chill swept over her.

"What room?"

"The interview room when they wrung that confession out of Sean Moriarty. How do you think they did it? They tortured him, that's how."

She swallowed. "How would you know?"

"Because I heard the *tape*. He recorded it."

"He—"

"He was there, and he recorded the whole damn thing." Anger sparked in her mother's eyes. "It was a coerced confession, just like they're saying. They held a gun to his head and made him do it. Why do you think your father went and crawled into a bottle for all those years?"

"I don't believe you."

"No?"

"Where's the tape?"

"I got rid of it when he died. Why on earth would I keep such a thing? Unlike him, I know how to let go of the past."

She stared at her mother's tight, angry face. The utter meanness radiating from her was as hot as a furnace, and Leanne knew she'd been wanting to do this for years.

She turned and walked away.

"All right, leave. That's your solution to everything."

Leanne stopped. "What's that supposed to mean?"

"It means I know you, and that's what you do when you don't want to face up to things."

She shook her head and walked away.

"See?" her mom called after her. "There you go again."

Leanne drove.

The highway stretched out in front of her, straight and limitless. She could go to Lubbock or Dallas or anyplace she wanted.

But she didn't want to go anywhere. She just wanted to drive.

Bile rose in her throat. She swallowed it down.

It rose again, and she pulled onto the shoulder. She jabbed the brakes and skidded to a stop. Flinging the door open, she leaned out and stared at the jagged pavement.

Her stomach churned. She let her mouth fall open and waited, but nothing came out. No vomit. No bile. None of this toxic stew that was roiling around inside her.

She slumped back against the seat. Staring through the dusty windshield, she felt numb. Cold.

She wished she'd never gone over there.

She wished she'd never prodded her. She had sensed that she was poking a wasp's nest. But still she'd kept doing it. She'd wanted to make her snap. She'd wanted a confrontation after months and years of keeping her feelings in lockdown.

Leanne leaned forward and rested her head against the steering wheel.

She had to turn around. She had to go back. She had responsibilities, even though all she wanted right now was to crawl into bed and pull the covers over her head.

She took a deep breath, angry now for a whole host of reasons. Less than a day ago, she'd felt sharp. Focused. *Determined.* Her victim had been identified, which was a major step forward. Things had been coming together, finally, and she'd felt such a sense of purpose about what she needed to do. She'd felt like she was up to this case, that she could handle it. That for once in her life she was stepping out of her dad's shadow, doing something completely on her own.

Where had that gone? Leanne wanted it back. She needed it. But instead, her mom's words filled her brain, expanding and swirling, crowding out every other thing.

She stared through the windshield at the infinite highway. She wanted to drive and drive, leaving behind her job, her family, her memories—all of it—leaving everything in the dust.

Open your eyes, Leanne.

She yanked her door shut and pulled onto the road.

TWENTY-NINE

Izzy stepped out of the police station into the cold. She leaned her head back and stared up at the dull black sky. Tonight was cloudy, no stars. Which was just as well because she'd spent the afternoon in front of a computer, and she was way too drained to even think about a nighttime photo shoot.

She zipped her jacket and set off across the parking lot, checking the shadows between cars. She didn't used to even notice things like that here. This was *Madrone*, not New York, but she'd been edgy all week and paranoid about everything. She slipped her hand inside her pocket, closing her fingers around her pepper spray.

"Izzy."

She whirled around, and her heart skipped a beat as a man emerged from the shadows near the building.

Duncan Harper.

"God, you scared me." She breathed a sigh of relief as he walked over.

"Sorry." He stopped in front of her. "Working late?"

"Not really. Sorting through some photo files." She'd been combing through the homicide scene pictures again, hoping to spot some new detail that everyone had missed.

"Glad I caught you." He held up a plastic baggie, and she recognized the memory card from her camera. "Detective Malcom wanted me to drop this off for you."

"Oh. Thanks." She took the baggie with the little gray square in it. Someone had scribbled *I. Huerta* across the front with a Sharpie. "Did he find anything useful?"

"Unfortunately, no."

She looked up at Duncan. Unlike the other night at the trailhead, he wore street clothes now. But even in faded jeans and sneakers, he still looked like a cop. There was something about this man that screamed *law enforcement*, even when he was off duty.

"You think of anything new for us?" he asked.

"New?"

"Since Friday night."

"You mean like—"

"Sometimes witnesses remember things later that they didn't recall in the first round of questioning," he said. "Maybe something from the parking lot where you left your car? Maybe a vehicle or a person? Or maybe even a dog?" He gazed down at her, his look intense. He looked that way a lot, she was learning. Until the other night, she had only known him in passing, mainly through Leanne. "Anything come to you?"

She shook her head. "No."

"Let us know if that changes."

"I will."

He looked over his shoulder at the building. "So, have you seen Leanne today? I've been trying to reach her."

"I haven't seen her." Izzy paused. "You know about the fire, right? At her family's ranch?"

"I heard."

"You might try there." Izzy glanced at the baggie in her hand. "So . . . does the sheriff's office have any new leads in the case?"

"We got an ID on the victim," he said.

"Oh yeah?"

"Her fingerprints were in the system."

The victim must have had a criminal record of some kind. But Duncan didn't explain, and she got the impression he didn't want to share details.

"So . . . are you guys going to team up now?" she asked.

"Who?"

"All of you. Travis Malcom, you, Leanne. Everyone working on these cases. It seems like it makes sense with all the similarities."

He nodded but didn't say anything, and she felt a flare of annoyance. Yet another detective who didn't want to let her into the inner circle. Would she ever break through? She was starting to feel like even in her own hometown she would always be an outsider.

"You guys are thinking they're connected, right? The two murder cases?" She studied his face for clues, but he looked neutral. "There are so many common angles, with the victims' ages and the beatings. Plus, the duct tape they found. Leanne was saying how it would help if everyone investigating joined forces."

He squinted. "Yeah, I doubt that's gonna happen."

"Why not?"

He tipped his head back and forth. "Sheriff Ackley's got a pretty strong personality. So does your chief. They don't usually work together."

"*Demasiados gallos.*"

His eyebrows arched.

"Too many roosters." She waved her hand. "Just something my grandmother used to say."

"Yeah, well. You're probably right about that."

He looked back at the building again, and she knew he'd come here for Leanne and that dropping off her memory card was an excuse to make the drive.

She held up the baggie. "Thanks for bringing this."

He nodded. "If you remember anything new from Friday, be sure to let us know."

Leanne was falling.

She reached for the rope, but it slipped through her hands, faster and faster, and she couldn't get a grip. She waited for her harness to catch and jerk her up.

"Leanne."

She reached for the rope again, but it was too slick. The rock wall disappeared, and there was no rope, no harness, nothing at all. She was in a free fall, being sucked toward the ground.

"*Leanne.*"

She sat up.

It was dark and cold. She was outside on the lounge chair behind her house.

"Hey."

Duncan crouched beside her. She sat forward, feeling dizzy.

"What are you doing out here?" His voice was low and gruff, and she looked at his shadowed profile in the porch light.

"I was just . . ." She closed her eyes. "What time is it?"

"After eleven."

She swung her legs off the chair and grabbed the jacket she'd been using as a blanket. "I fell asleep."

She stood up. Duncan stood, too, reaching for her arm as she swayed.

"Whoa there. You all right?"

"Yeah."

She ran a hand through her hair and looked around. How long had she been asleep out here?

He bent down and picked up her bottle of Jack Daniel's from the ground.

"What are you doing here?" she asked.

He gave a crooked smile. "You don't remember texting me?"

Her cheeks flushed. "Oh. Yeah."

She took the bottle from him and headed for the house. He walked beside her, and she tried to remember exactly what she'd said in her text.

He reached around her and opened the door. "I called and left a couple messages. When you didn't pick up, I got worried."

The kitchen was dark except for the light above the sink. Her phone sat on the counter beside her car keys. She threw her jacket over the chair, then set the bottle down and tapped her phone screen. She'd missed a slew of calls.

"You okay?"

She turned to look at him. He wore jeans and running shoes, and his soft gray T-shirt that had been through the wash a million times. He leaned against the counter, watching her with that intense look of his.

He stepped closer, frowning. "Looks like you've been crying."

She turned away.

"Hey."

"I'm fine," she said.

His arms went around her, heavy and warm, and he eased her against him.

Leanne's stomach knotted. Blinking back tears, she leaned her cheek against his chest. His body felt solid, and he smelled good, like he always did. He planted a kiss on the top of her head, and the tears seeped out.

"Sorry." She pressed her nose against his shirt.

"It's okay."

She squeezed her eyes shut.

"What's wrong?" he asked.

"Nothing."

He eased back. "Tell me what happened."

She tensed. Her mom's face came back to her, angry and contorted as she spewed all those words.

Leanne stepped back. "Nothing."

"Nothing."

"Just forget it." She turned away and wiped her cheeks. "What did you call about? You said you left messages?"

His jaw tightened. She could see she'd ticked him off, but she didn't care. She didn't want to have this conversation.

He leaned back against the counter. "First, we got an ID on the murdered hiker."

"I heard. But she wasn't a hiker. I heard she'd been arrested for prostitution in El Paso."

"That's right. Travis is following up on her background, looking for leads. The other thing is, I wanted to update you on that evidence I sent in last week."

"The duct tape?"

"Yeah. Ackley found out that I submitted it and got pissed."

Dread filled her stomach. The sheriff was known to have a short fuse.

"Did he . . . What did he do?"

"Threatened to suspend me, for one."

"Oh my God. I'm sorry. Did he do it?"

"No." Duncan rubbed the back of his neck. "He was just pissed I went around him, so he called me into his office and reamed me out."

"What about the evidence. Did he pull it?"

"No."

"That's good, at least. And I'm glad you're not suspended."

"Enough about me." He folded his arms over his chest. "I want to know what's going on with *you*."

"I'm fine. I told you."

He stepped closer and stared down at her, his mouth tight. "You're fine."

"Yes."

"You're just . . . hanging out on Sunday night, knocking back bourbon and crying for no reason." He paused. "Is it your dad?"

"Why would you ask that?"

"I don't know. Is it his birthday or something?"

Shame flooded her. She didn't want to talk about this, and especially not with Duncan. She admired him too much. He was a stand-up guy, a good cop.

She'd always believed her father was, too.

Maybe he was, and her mom was simply trying to tear him down out of bitterness. Leanne didn't know anymore. Her thoughts were all muddled, and the bourbon hadn't helped.

"It's complicated," she said. "You wouldn't understand."

"Why not?"

"Because you wouldn't."

"Try me."

Duncan watched her, his eyes determined, as though he was braced for anything. She felt something building between them.

And at the same time, she felt something slipping away.

He sighed. "You know what? I'm sick of this."

"Of what?"

"I risk my neck for you, and you won't even—" He shook his head.

"I won't even what?"

He glared at her. "You don't see it, do you?" He stepped closer, hands on his hips. "You need a favor, you call me. You're feeling lonely, you call me. This is Dallas all over again, and I'm not twenty-five anymore, Leanne. That's it. I'm out."

He moved for the door, and panic spurted through her.

"Wait! Where are you going?"

"Call me when you're ready to have a real conversation."

THIRTY

Sunlight slanted through the blinds, a thousand daggers stabbing into her brain.

Leanne sat up. Someone was at the door.

She kicked off the covers and swung her legs out of bed. She'd slept in her jeans. She grabbed her phone from the nightstand to check the clock.

"*Crap.*"

She rushed through the house. The living room windows faced east, and she squinted at the glare as she went to check the peephole.

Michelle stood on the porch with Gus in her arms. Leanne flipped the lock and opened the door.

"Morning," her neighbor said brightly. "I found this guy pawing at your door."

"Oh. Thanks."

She set him down at Leanne's feet, and he darted inside.

Michelle frowned at her. "Are you sick?"

"No, just . . . no." She combed her hand through her hair. "What's up?"

"I wanted to circle back about the broken steps."

Leanne stared at her, drawing a blank.

"Campsite Four? You said your brother might be able to—"
"Oh. Yes, I'll talk to him."
"You sure?" Michelle tipped her head to the side. "I can call someone else if I need to."
"Let me talk to Ben first. I think he's free this week."
"That'd be great. I need to get it done by Thursday, at the latest. We're booked solid this weekend."
"Got it."
"Thanks."

When Michelle was gone, Leanne took a fast shower. Ignoring her coffee craving, she grabbed a can of Dr Pepper from the fridge and jumped in her truck. She drove to work with the windows down, hoping the cold would numb her headache, but when she reached the station house, her skull was still pounding.

She spotted Marty Krause from the *Sentinel* in the rear parking lot, leaning against his car and smoking a cigarette. The deadlast thing she wanted to do right now was talk to a reporter, so she pulled a U-turn and parked in the front.

Nadine glanced up from her computer as Leanne walked in.
"Good morning," she chirped.
Leanne peeled her sunglasses off. "Morning."
"You don't look too good, hon. You coming down with something?"
"I think I overdid it last night."
She made a face. "Need some aspirin?"
"I'm fine, thank you."
"Well, heads up—the chief's looking for you."
Leanne winced.
"Sorry." Nadine gave her a half smile. "Sure you don't want something?"
"I'm okay."

Leanne smoothed her hair and tucked her sunglasses into her jacket pocket, then pushed through the door into the bullpen.

McBride's office door was open. She leaned her head in, hoping to keep it brief.

"Good morning."

He looked up and frowned. "You're here." He swiveled his chair to face her. "Have a seat. Shut the door behind you."

Leanne's stomach twisted as she stepped into his office and closed the door with a quiet *snick*.

McBride was looking her over, no doubt taking in her less-than-crisp appearance.

"How's your mom doing?"

She relaxed a fraction. "She's all right. Thanks for asking."

He shook his head. "Hell of a thing."

"Yes."

He leaned forward. "Listen, I reached out to Chisos FAR earlier this morning to check in on things."

Something in his tone needled her. She didn't know why McBride would be checking in with county fire and rescue officials.

"What did they say?" she asked.

"They found pour trails. Also, the burn pattern on the walls suggests arson."

Leanne stared at him, waiting for more.

"Now, I talked to Meachum," he continued. "I've deflected him for now to give y'all time to get your house in order."

Leanne frowned. "What's that mean?"

"It means what it sounds like." He leaned back in his chair. "You need to talk to your brother."

A sour ball formed in her stomach. "Why?"

"Come on, Leanne. He's got a record. And everyone knows there's no love lost between him and your stepdad."

"I'm not sure exactly what you're getting at. My brother's an addict—who's been clean for three months, by the way. He's not an arsonist."

"You sure about that? When the insurance adjuster comes out to see about those fancy cars, you think he's going to find out that fire was used to cover a theft?"

"A theft of what?"

"I don't know. All I'm saying is—get your house in order. I tried to buy y'all some time."

Anxiety bubbled up inside her as his implications sank in. He seemed to have made up his mind about Ben. Had Glenn Meachum made up his mind, too? If the police chief *and* the fire chief had decided to look at Ben, did he even have a chance? McBride's logic was weak, and the supposed motive sounded vague, at best. But Leanne didn't like that her brother's name had come up at all in connection with this. She had seen investigations go sideways when people got tunnel vision.

"Next subject." McBride rested his elbows on the desk. "Our Jane Doe case. What's the status?"

She tried to shake off her anxiety and shift gears.

"The status is, the victim's been identified through fingerprints—as you probably heard—so she's no longer a Jane Doe. Her name is Valeria Reyes, age nineteen, from Albuquerque."

He knew this already, but he seemed to want to hang on to his original shorthand, maybe because it made the case easier to deprioritize.

"Reach out to Fort Stockton, where she was booked," he said.

"I was planning to."

"She was arrested for prostitution, right?"

"That's right."

"They should be able to help. Don't be shy about pumping them for information. I want this wrapped up soon. It's already been more than a week."

"Yes, sir."

"I don't want this dragging on, especially with all the reporters we've got camped out around town. Doesn't look good. Not to mention, it's bad for business."

Leanne's temper festered. Bad for his *family's* business, he meant. The chief's cousin ran a bed-and-breakfast in town, and she'd been making a mint with the tourist boom. Leanne suspected that Mc-Bride was an investor, but she couldn't be sure. And the chamber of commerce president was leaning on him, too. Everyone wanted the appearance of law and order, regardless of reality.

"Leanne? You got me?"

"I understand."

"Good. Then you'll understand when I give you a deadline. Two days to get me a name."

"A name?"

"I want a suspect in forty-eight hours, or I'm handing this off to Rodriguez."

"But—"

"That's it, Everhart. Better get moving."

He turned back to his computer as Leanne stood up. She started to say something but then thought better of it.

"Yes, sir."

She walked out, dazed by the rapid-fire turn of events.

Ben was a suspect in the fire at Boone's ranch.

She had forty-eight hours to identify a potential serial killer.

The chief was ready to yank her case away from her. Not only was he ready, he seemed to be looking for an excuse.

Her mind spinning, she went to her cubicle and sank into her chair. Stacks of paperwork covered the desk. Next to her keyboard was a pink message slip with a note from Nadine: *Feel better* ☺ and a pair of aspirin tablets.

"Leanne."

She glanced up as Mark Rodriguez walked over.

"You busy?" he asked, leaning his arm on her cubicle.

She swallowed the pills, then grabbed her mug and washed them down with the dregs of yesterday's coffee.

"I'm slammed," she told him. "Why? What is it?"

"Damn." He looked around the room. "What about Josh? Is he busy?"

"No idea. What's up?"

"I got a callout to that yucca farm out on Lost Mine Road." Mark turned around. "There he is. Hey, Josh."

Leanne shuffled through a stack of papers until she found the arrest report for Valeria Reyes. She'd put in a message to the arresting officer, but she hadn't heard back yet. She had a sneaking suspicion she was going to have to hound the guy.

Josh walked over and leaned on Leanne's cubicle. "I heard about your mom's ranch," he said. "How's she doing?"

"Fine. And it's Boone Sullivan's ranch, not hers."

"Josh, man, I need a favor," Mark told him. "You busy right now?"

"I'm on my way to the motel to see about a couple of car burglaries."

"Mind if I cover that one, and you can take mine? I just got a callout to the yucca farm out on Lost Mine Road."

"Carr Farms," Josh said.

"Yeah, the crazy old guy who owns it claims he saw aliens stealing his crops last night. Said they came in with big white lights and took everything."

Josh frowned. "Aliens like ETs?"

"No, man, like illegals. But this guy's got Alzheimer's or something. He's total batshit and he hates Mexicans. Last time I went out there he aimed a shotgun at me from his porch and started screaming all kinds of shit."

"Poachers," Leanne said. "They were in the park last summer, uprooting yucca plants. They stole a couple truckloads."

"They literally dug up the trees?" Josh sounded skeptical. "That's a lot of work."

"Some of those plants go for hundreds apiece," Leanne said. "You should see the prices in Dallas."

The yearslong drought had created a spike in demand for desert plants as people traded their thirsty green lawns for xeriscaping. Yet another problem for the park rangers to deal with on top of everything else.

"I'm going to get my ass shot off if I go out there," Mark said. "One of you want to trade calls?"

"I'll go," Josh said. "You take the motel burglary. The manager's name is Allison, and it's a couple SUVs in the parking lot that got hit overnight."

"You sure?"

"Yeah, no problem."

"Thanks, man. I owe you one."

Mark walked off, and Leanne turned her attention to her paperwork. She skimmed through the Valeria Reyes arrest report and then added it to her accordion file, which was getting fatter by the day. Grabbing her keys, she stood up.

"Where are you off to?" Josh asked.

Leanne glanced across the bullpen as Mark slid on his sunglasses and walked out. He probably had no idea he was in line to inherit her homicide case.

"Fort Stockton," she said.

"The Reyes case."

"Yeah, I've got a message in to the arresting officer. I'm hoping to track him down today." She paused. "You want to come?"

"Sounds like I'm headed out to the yucca farm to maybe get my ass shot off." He frowned. "So, is your mother really all right? I heard it was a mess out there."

"She's okay. Shaken, mostly." She glanced at the chief's office and lowered her voice. "Listen, I think I'm going to need your help later. McBride gave me forty-eight hours to identify a suspect or he's yanking my case and giving it to Rodriguez."

Josh's eyebrows shot up. "No shit?"

"No shit."

"Forty-eight hours isn't much time. What's the big rush?"

"Hell if I know." She glanced at McBride's door, which was closed now. "What do you think?"

Josh shook his head. "I think you'd better get to work."

THIRTY-ONE

Leanne showed up at Fort Stockton PD and wouldn't take no for an answer. The officer who had arrested Valeria Reyes wasn't on duty today, but Leanne refused to leave until they let her talk to someone who was at least peripherally involved—which was how she ended up behind the Super Suds car wash in the back seat of an undercover police SUV with tinted windows and a broken heater.

"You doing okay back there?" The young detective met her gaze in the rearview mirror.

"I'm fine."

"Sorry about the heater. I put in a request, but you know how that is."

"No worries."

Leanne fisted her hands inside her jacket pockets. She wasn't about to complain, even though her extremities were frozen and she still had a raging hangover. She looked like roadkill today. And just in case she didn't feel crappy enough already, the young detective she was shadowing was not only beautiful and bilingual, she was perfectly made-up, too, from her impossibly long eyelashes to her glossy red fingernails. At a mere twenty-eight years old, Sandra Torres had made detective *and* been placed in charge of her department's vice unit, which was one of the best in the region.

"She should be here soon." Sandra checked her watch. "Any minute now."

Leanne looked out the window at the truck stop across the street. Another eighteen-wheeler pulled into the lot and rolled to a stop with a loud hiss of brakes. The busy compound included two dozen gas pumps, a grocery store, a restaurant, a bar, and a locker room with paid showers. Six months ago, Sandra had participated in a sting operation targeting store clerks who were dealing meth from inside the building. Several young sex workers, including Valeria Reyes, had gotten swept up in the bust. In exchange for leniency, one of those women had become a confidential informant.

"She isn't the only one, you know," Sandra said.

"Who?"

"Valeria. Girls have gone missing before, maybe ended up dead." Sandra sighed. "There was someone last summer. I was trying to talk to her, get her to be a CI for us. Then she disappeared one day."

"Name?"

"Ana Ortiz. Nineteen."

"Any chance she just took off?"

"It's possible. I asked around, but none of her friends knew anything. At least nothing they told me."

Leanne's stomach knotted as she thought of Patty Paulson's words.

If victims had a hierarchy, these women were at rock bottom. Some of them weren't even women—barely older than kids. Leanne watched Sandra in the mirror. She didn't detect any resentment or cynicism—just a flat recognition of reality.

"Did anyone file a report on her?" Leanne asked.

"Doubtful. Not that I heard of, anyway. Girls like that aren't the kind of cases you hear about. They're not some white college student."

"But why—"

"Okay, here she comes," Sandra cut in.

Leanne eyed the side mirror as a young woman approached. Tall, short black skirt, long blond hair that looked like a wig.

"Is she reliable?" Leanne asked.

"It's been a while since she gave us anything useful."

The woman cast a furtive look over her shoulder before reaching for the door. Sandra started the engine as she slid into the front passenger seat.

"I don't have much time," the woman said, glancing back at Leanne. "Who is she?"

"A friend." Sandra reached for the McDonald's bag at the woman's feet and handed it to her. "I got you a Happy Meal."

"Nice." She opened the bag, and the scent of French fries filled the car, making Leanne's stomach growl.

"Jordan, this is Detective Everhart." Sandra glanced back at her. "Detective Everhart, this is Jordan Maleski."

Jordan shot Sandra a sharp look as she grabbed a wad of fries. "You told her my real name?"

"She needs to know it."

Sandra drove around to the car wash entrance and fed a plastic card into the machine. The arm swung up, and she eased through the gate.

"Why does she need to know it?" Jordan asked around a mouthful of fries.

Leanne sat forward. "Jordan, I'm glad to meet you. And I'm hoping you can help me with a case I'm working on."

Jordan shot another hostile look at Sandra.

"Don't worry, she's cool," Sandra said.

Leanne felt grateful that Sandra was willing to vouch for her, even though they'd met barely an hour ago. Leanne definitely owed this detective a favor now.

Sandra entered the car wash tunnel and shifted into neutral. She glanced back at Leanne.

"Okay, I got the deluxe wash, but you need to talk fast." She looked at Jordan. "This detective has some questions for you."

"About what?"

Leanne held up the copy of the driver's license photo she'd printed out. "Jordan, do you know this woman?"

She stopped chewing. Fear filled her eyes. "That's Val."

"Valeria Reyes?"

"Yeah. Why?" She swallowed. "Is she okay?"

"No. I'm sorry to tell you that she was murdered."

"Oh my God." She clapped a hand over her mouth. "What happened?"

"That's what we're trying to figure out."

"Oh my God." She bent forward, hiding her face in her hands. "I can't believe this."

Jordan sat back, and Sandra passed her a napkin. Sniffles filled the car as Jordan held the napkin over her face. After a moment, she dabbed her eyes.

"What happened?" she asked tearfully. "I haven't seen her in a while, and I was getting worried. *Shit.*"

"Do you mind if I record this, Jordan?"

She shook her head.

Leanne activated the recorder on her phone and perched it on the console. Rainbow-colored suds rained down on the windshield as Leanne stated the date and time for the record.

"When was the last time you saw Valeria?" she asked.

Jordan said something into the napkin.

"Sorry?"

"She goes by *Val*. Everyone calls her that." She dabbed the napkin under her nose.

They moved through the car wash, and Leanne watched Jordan wipe her makeup and try to pull herself together as they went through the noisy blowers. Finally, they exited, and Sandra pulled up to a row of vacuum hoses.

"You two talk." Sandra looked at Leanne. "You've got about five more minutes."

"Thanks."

Sandra got out of the car and went to the kiosk to collect a scrub brush for the hubcaps.

Jordan wadded her napkin. "Sorry. I wasn't expecting this." She took a deep breath. "Okay, tell me what happened."

"When was the last time you saw Val?" Leanne asked again.

Another deep breath. "A while ago. Last Thursday or Friday, I think."

Leanne's pulse picked up. According to the ME, the murder likely happened last Friday night.

"Could you pin that down?"

She bit her lip. "It was Friday. I remember because we were busy here. The jackpot had just hit a hundred million, and everyone was stopping in for tickets."

"Lotto tickets?"

"Yeah."

"You know where Val was living?"

"I don't know, really. She got kicked out of her place before Christmas."

"Was that an apartment?"

"I think for a while she was in a trailer with someone? After that, she was just, you know, crashing wherever she could."

"Okay. So, you saw Val last Friday?"

She nodded. "That evening. We usually work nights."

"Walk me through that."

She paused, seeming to collect herself, and Leanne figured she was editing out parts of it.

"We usually hang out between the diner and the bar. Sometimes the grocery store if things are slow. We wait for singles to come in and that's how we meet people."

"Single men?"

"Yeah, you know, guys traveling alone. Some of them come in groups, but we look for the loners. See if they want company. Usually, they buy us a drink."

Leanne could infer the rest. They probably went back to the guy's rig or checked into a cheap motel. There were several nearby, right off the interstate.

"So, do you remember anyone Val talked to that night?" Leanne asked.

"Yeah. It was early." She took a deep breath. "The diner wasn't too busy, so we were mainly hanging out by the front of the store, seeing who walked in." She paused. "I remember this one guy..." A pained look crossed her face. "Oh God. I bet it was him."

"Who?"

She turned in her seat, fully facing Leanne.

"He was weird. I knew it. I even told her, 'Val, *wait*. Don't go with him.'"

"What kind of vehicle was he in?"

"No vehicle. He was on foot."

Leanne's heart sank. She'd been hoping for a vehicle description.

"What did he look like?" Leanne asked.

"I don't remember."

"Was he white? Black? Tall? Short?"

Jordan shook her head. "I don't know. I only really saw him from a distance."

She tried to hide her frustration. "Can you remember his race, at least?"

"He was a white guy. And he was maybe tall, I think."

"What was he wearing? And why did you think he seemed 'weird'?"

She shook her head again. "He just *was*, you know? The way he looked at us. He stood across the street and just *watched us*. For like a hour."

"Across the street where exactly?"

The truck stop had several security cameras, and Leanne could get the footage if she needed to.

"Over there." Jordan turned around. "There by the taco place? He was behind the drive-through line near that dumpster. He just stood there staring at us for a long time, and then he waved her over."

"So . . . you didn't see him up close?"

"No. But still . . . I could tell he was off, and I told her, wait for another one. It's early. But she didn't listen. Oh my God." She covered her eyes.

Leanne watched Jordan, hoping for some additional details, but she simply sat there.

"What was this guy wearing?" Leanne asked. "Do you remember that?"

She rubbed her nose with a wadded napkin and shook her head. "I don't know. Jeans, I think? Maybe a jacket or something?"

"How about his face? Do you think you could describe him to someone, such as maybe a sketch artist?"

Her eyes widened. "A police artist? No. Anyway, I didn't really see him. He was wearing, like, a baseball cap, and his face was in shadow."

"A baseball cap? Are you sure?"

"Yes."

"Do you remember the color or the logo on it?"

She shook her head.

"Did he have any tattoos you could see? Or anything about his clothes you noticed? Or maybe he was smoking?"

Another head shake.

Leanne watched her, silently cursing herself. She'd made a rookie mistake. She should have elicited more detail from this witness before mentioning the sketch artist. Now she didn't know whether Jordan really hadn't seen the guy well, or she wanted to avoid getting mixed up with a police artist.

The driver's-side door opened, and Sandra slid behind the wheel.

"How's it going?" she asked.

"Good. We're making progress."

Leanne watched Jordan, but she could tell she was on her guard now.

"So . . . if you didn't really get a good look at him," Leanne asked, "what was it about him that made you think Val shouldn't go with him?"

Jordan shook her head.

"Was there something about his clothes or his body language?"

"He just had this *look*. He seemed off. The way he watched us all that time from a distance."

"Off how?"

"Just *off*, you know? Like he was into some weird kink. The kind of guy that wants to cut you."

THIRTY-TWO

Leanne shot a look at the clock and gripped the steering wheel. Acid filled her stomach. It was almost nine p.m., so she had thirty-six hours. Thirty-six *hours* to crack the case of a serial predator who had been active for at least a decade, probably more.

She passed the turnoff to Duncan's house and bit her lip, thinking. She wanted his input. He was good at analyzing things, seeing situations from multiple angles. But she couldn't go over there, not after last night. He was obviously pissed at her. For years, Duncan had been her touchstone, her sounding board, her midnight wake-up call, and not once had she thought that he resented the role. But she'd made too many assumptions. Fear nibbled away at her as she imagined their relationship changing. Maybe it already had, and she was just catching on to the fact that their paths were diverging.

Leanne made her way through town, where the sidewalks were Monday-night quiet. As she neared Shooters, she spotted a familiar silver Bronco. Slamming on the brakes, she made a split-second decision and whipped into the lot. They weren't busy tonight—the usual mix of locals, from the looks of it. She found a space near the door and parked.

Leanne flipped her mirror down, then changed her mind and

flipped it up again. Who cared what she looked like? It was only Josh.

She strode into the bar and was relieved to see him alone at the counter with a bottle of Tecate in front of him as he read his phone. She made her way over, passing a high-top table with a pair of off-duty border agents. Leanne gave them a nod.

Josh glanced up as she pulled out the empty stool beside him. "This taken?"

"It's all yours." He flipped his phone over as she claimed the chair.

"You survived the yucca farm, I see."

He shook his head. "Crazy old coot."

"Did he get out his shotgun?"

"Nope." He lifted his beer and took a sip.

A server walked over with a steaming plate of tamales and beans. "Anything else?" she asked him.

"I'm set, thanks."

She turned to Leanne. "Something for you?"

"I'm good."

The woman walked off, and Josh started unwrapping the corn husk.

"So, what's up?" he asked. "I know you didn't drop in just to chat. What do you need?"

Leanne sighed. Evidently, she could stand to work on her soft skills.

"I wanted to run some developments by you."

The corner of his mouth lifted. "No more Lone Ranger now that you're up against a deadline, huh?"

"Ouch."

"Hey, I get it. You like to work solo."

It wasn't so much that she *liked* working solo—although she didn't mind it. But the men in her department talked down to her most of the time, which was beyond infuriating. She'd decided years ago it was easier to work alone and keep everyone at a distance—with the occasional exception of Duncan.

Josh stabbed a jalapeño with his fork. "I'm just giving you crap. Go ahead. Shoot."

"So, I've got an eyewitness at the truck stop where Valeria Reyes was arrested six months ago."

He lifted an eyebrow. "Up in Fort Stockton? I'm impressed. That was fast."

"I had an assist from a vice cop up there."

"Sandra Torres?"

"You know her?"

"Yeah, she's good."

"She put me in touch with one of her CIs there, and this woman was friends with the victim. She saw her leave with a John last Friday night."

His eyebrows lifted. "The timing works."

"I know."

"You get a vehicle?"

"He was on foot. And I'm pretty sure he was aware of the cameras at the truck stop because he parked out of sight. I reviewed the film. He specifically hung out *across* the street, out of view of the security cams, and parked somewhere else."

"So, you're thinking he's the guy," Josh stated.

"Possibly."

"You get a description?"

"Not much of one. She only saw him from a distance."

"You know, a good forensic artist should be able to sit her down and come up with something, even if it was only a brief glimpse. You'd be amazed."

"At the moment, that's not happening. This witness is spooked. Maybe I'll try her again as a last resort."

"Other cameras in the vicinity?" He tipped back his beer.

"There's a gas station down the road, but I checked in with them, and their surveillance cam is out of order."

He shook his head. "Shitty luck. You should try some of the other girls in the area, see if this guy's maybe a regular." He must have read her expression. "Let me guess. You did?"

"Yup."

"Okay, well—"

"Here's the thing. I'm zeroing in on an MO. Hear me out," she said at his skeptical look. "This guy frequents places where sex workers hang out. He's smart. He knows not to pull up in a vehicle, or even get too close on foot. Really, he loiters. He watches. This witness said he was there almost an hour, just observing them, before he lured Reyes over to his side of the street."

"Okay. And then?"

"And then he takes them someplace private in his vehicle, sexually assaults them, kills them, then dumps the body off Highway 67."

"What, like, on his way home?"

"That's what I'm thinking."

"You're saying he's from here." He glanced around and lowered his voice. "You're saying we have a *local* predator killing off women."

"He has to be local. It only makes sense. All seven bodies—"

"Whoa. Seven? Since when is it seven?"

"Four cold cases that the forensic anthropologist at the university told me about. All un-IDed skeletal remains, all dumped near the highway, three of them with crushed skulls and broken limbs. Plus, there's Valeria Reyes, plus the un-IDed femur, and now the homicide at the Gold Springs Trailhead."

Leanne wasn't ready to tell him her suspicions about Hannah Rawls yet. McBride had already balked at the idea, and Leanne wanted to see what Samantha came back with. If an FBI profiler—or at least someone trained by the FBI in behavioral analysis—came back and said her idea wasn't crazy, then Leanne would present her theory to the chief.

Josh turned his beer bottle on the counter. "Okay, well... allow me to poke a hole in your MO."

She tensed.

"Why kill them?" Josh shook his head. "If he's targeting prostitutes, he doesn't need to force them to have sex, and killing them ratchets up his risk. I'm not seeing the logic."

"Who said anything about logic? The guy's sick. *You* saw that body. Clearly, he gets off on pain."

Josh tipped his head to the side, still not looking convinced, and she felt frustrated. Why did she have to explain to other cops that some people simply hated women? Full stop. Misogyny was everywhere, and it didn't need logic or reason to flourish.

"You're saying you think the risk is part of it," Josh said. "Part of the motive."

"Don't you? I mean, look at what he's doing, again and again. I'm no profiler, but it seems like a compulsion."

Josh nodded, but his expression told her he still wasn't persuaded.

He set down his beer. "Damn. Speaking of the Reyes case—I forgot to tell you. I meant to leave you a message."

"What?"

"Duncan Harper stopped in while you were up in Fort Stockton. He dropped off some report."

"He did?"

"Yeah, he put it on your desk. Said to tell you he also emailed you."

Leanne pulled out her phone and checked her inbox, which she'd neglected today. Sure enough, there was a brief email and an attachment.

Leanne read the one-line message with a pit in her stomach. In all the years she'd known Duncan, she didn't think he'd ever sent her an email. Normally, they texted or called, or simply showed up at each other's houses. To anyone else, the five-word message might seem succinct, but to her, it was icy.

She clicked open the attachment. Her pulse picked up as she skimmed through technical jargon. *High performance radial... Ridge Grappler with black sidewalls... shoulder and lateral Z grooves...* The description went on for two paragraphs. Not only had Duncan's contact identified the tire and provided a detailed write-up; he'd also included a generic color photo from a tire catalog. She tried to enlarge the image, but it was difficult to see on her phone screen.

"What is it?" Josh asked.

"The tire tread from the railroad tracks crime scene." She glanced up. "He knows a guy at the state lab who offered to take a look."

Josh shook his head. "Man, that guy knows everyone. Wish I had a network like that."

"Same." She looked at Josh. "You say he left the hard copy?"

"It's on your desk."

She slid off the stool. "I need to go."

"Sounds like two big breaks in one day. You're on a roll."

"I'm on a clock." She rapped on the bar. "Thanks for your help."

"Why? I didn't do shit."

"Thanks for listening."

The Siesta Motel attracted mountain bikers, rock climbers, and other travelers who couldn't afford a pricey inn or a trendy glamping site on their way to Big Bend.

It also attracted budget-conscious reporters, apparently. Leanne knocked on the door and then surveyed the parking lot crammed with SUVs, many plastered with national park stickers. No Ridge Grappler tires in sight, but Max's black Cherokee was squeezed into a space near the ice machine.

The door swung open.

"Hey, you're early."

Max ushered her inside. He wore jeans with ripped knees and a white T-shirt, no shoes.

The place smelled oddly of mildew and marijuana. Leanne glanced at the water stain on the ceiling. Given the arid climate around here, a mildew smell was a sure sign of leaky pipes—not that the motel management seemed to care.

The room was a pigsty. Clothes on the floor. Files and papers strewn across the double bed. An open laptop computer sat in the middle of the bed alongside a half-eaten pizza.

"Am I interrupting your dinner?" she asked.

"Not at all." Max closed the pizza box and dropped it on the dresser beside a crumpled fast-food bag. "Sorry about the mess. I'd planned to clean up before you got here. Want to sit down?"

"I don't have a lot of time." She crossed her arms and stood beside the door. "What did you need to tell me?"

"First of all, thanks for meeting me here."

She didn't respond.

"I figured this was better for you?"

"Better?"

He lifted a shoulder. "You seemed worried about being seen talking to me in Madrone. I figured this would be, you know, more low profile."

"Listen, I've got things I need to do tonight, so—"

"I know, I know." He held up a hand. "I'll get to the point. I uncovered some info I think you'll be *very* interested in."

"Oh?"

"It's about the Sean Moriarty case." The eager look on his face told her he expected her to be salivating over this information.

"Let's hear it," she said. "And then I really need to go."

"Don't you want to know who it's from first?"

She tamped down her irritation. "Who is it from?"

He smiled. "I've developed a major source."

When she didn't ask for a name, he kept going.

"It's Frank Perrine."

"Never heard of him."

"You will," he said. "He's a lawyer out of Houston, and he's about to file a lawsuit against your department on behalf of Sean Moriarty."

She gave a shrug. "And?"

"And aren't you concerned?"

"We expected that."

Max looked annoyed. "I'm surprised you're not more excited. I'm giving you a heads-up here. I'm doing you a favor."

"You bring up a good point," she said. "Why *are* you doing me a favor?"

"Because," he said, "I appreciate the tip-off about this serial killer thing. This looks like potentially a major story. So, you know, I want to return the favor."

Of the various lies he'd told her, this one was possibly the most blatant.

"So, you're giving me info from your amazing new source out of the kindness of your heart."

"Well, yeah. And also, I'd like to keep the lines of communication open."

At least he was being honest now. Or closer to honest. She had no doubt he expected something substantial in return for this tip.

"Okay, let's hear the rest, then," she said. "What's the big scoop from Moriarty's lawyer?"

"First off—like I said—he's about to file a lawsuit on behalf of Sean Moriarty, seeking millions of dollars in damages."

"Tell me something I don't know."

"*And* I got him to reveal to me what they've got. At least some of it."

"What 'they've got'?"

"Yeah, you know, their strategy. How they're planning to go after the department." Max stepped closer, invading her personal space, and she eased back. This guy was oblivious to boundaries.

"See, everyone thinks it's all about the coerced confession," he said. "And it *is* about that, at least according to the filings we've been able to see. Turns out, part of the judge's decision was based on sealed testimony of someone who was *inside the room* when Moriarty confessed."

Leanne's shoulders tightened.

"He got it on audiotape, apparently," Max went on.

"Got what on audiotape?"

"The *coerced confession*. Sounds like they literally put a gun to this kid's head and threatened him within an inch of his life if he didn't admit on video to murdering Hannah Rawls."

Leanne watched his face. She felt a cold sweat coming on. Had that really happened? And had her father really been in the room?

He recorded the whole damn thing.

Her mother's words came back to her, and she tried to keep her reaction in check.

"I don't know what all you've read about Moriarty's trial," Max went on, "but the case basically rested on three pillars. First—and what got a lot of attention—was his confession." He leaned against the dresser, relaxing into his story now. "But there were two other key elements that the jury focused on. One, Hannah's blood was in his car. How did it get there? The defense never explained it. And two, there was a credible eyewitness, an off-duty firefighter, who *saw* Sean Moriarty's car turning off Long Canyon Road around midnight on the night Hannah went missing. So, when her body was discovered in an abandoned well not far from that road, this witness contradicted Moriarty's story that he wasn't anywhere *near* there that night."

Leanne's pulse was racing now, but she tried to look bored. "So, what's your point?"

"My point is, this attorney plans to show that investigators *withheld* evidence from the prosecution about one of those three pillars of the case—the blood."

"How's that?"

He nodded. "Turns out, they interviewed one of Hannah's friends who said they'd been out drinking that night right after the fireworks, and they were drinking at the Dairy Queen where people were hanging out together. This friend saw Hannah trip and cut open her hand. So, according to this friend, that might explain the blood in Sean Moriarty's car, since he admitted to giving Hannah a ride after she left the Dairy Queen." He paused for emphasis. "So, the blood is explained, and the confession is explained, and that knocks out two of the three main pillars of the case. The only thing left is the eyewitness, but you know how those are. Eyewitness testimony is notoriously unreliable. He could have gotten the cars mixed up."

Leanne watched the reporter, reviewing the series of events in her mind. Nothing she'd read said anything about this interview with Hannah's friend, or about Hannah tripping and cutting herself on the night of her disappearance. So, had someone removed the interview from the case file? Kept it out of sight of Moriarty's defense lawyer?

Had her father done that?

Max smiled. "Interesting, isn't it?"

She nodded.

"Knew you'd agree."

Leanne waited for the ask. What did this reporter want, and why had he invited her out here to dump all this info on her about the lawsuit against her department?

"So, back to our quid pro quo," he said, right on time. "I've been looking into this thing about the Highway Killer, and—"

"'Highway Killer'?"

"It's just a name I've been throwing around," he said. "We might come up with something better. But, you know, it's potentially a major story, so it needs a moniker. We're talking about *three* women's bodies discovered near Highway 67 in the past four years. I can't believe no one's writing about it." He paused, searching her face for a reaction.

"I agree. It's pretty unbelievable."

"Anything else you want to tell me?" He watched her expectantly, but she didn't respond. "Such as . . . are there any more I should know about?"

"More?"

"More victims. Besides the three? I'm thinking there could be others that haven't gotten any notice in the local papers or anything."

"Sounds like you're asking me to do your job for you." She took out her phone and made a show of looking at the clock. "Like I said, I have things to do tonight."

"Wait." He stepped closer, and this time she held up her hand.

"You mind?"

He eased back. "Sorry. I just want to make sure I'm getting everything relevant. My paper is very interested in this story. We're planning to do a spread on it after the exposé comes out. Or maybe before. The timing's loose, at the moment."

"Welp. Good luck with that."

"Yeah, and on the subject—any chance I can get a picture of you to go with the article? Not where you're identifiable or anything. I'm thinking maybe a black silhouette in front of a window or something along those lines."

Leanne moved for the door. "Not happening."

"Your identity would be completely protected," he said. "This would just be for visual interest. Something to run with the story."

"That's a hard no."

THIRTY-THREE

"You got a minute?"

Izzy glanced up to see Leanne standing over her desk. The detective's nose was sunburned, and her hair was a wild mane.

"Sure." Izzy plucked out her earbuds. "Outdoor crime scene?"

Leanne rolled her eyes. "I've been running around to tire places all morning." She dragged a chair from a neighboring cubicle and sank onto it. "Then I made the rounds at used car lots. I'm trying to track down this." She pulled a phone from her jacket pocket and set it on the desk near the keyboard. "Any ideas?"

Izzy slid the phone closer, and her pulse picked up as she examined the picture.

"This is the tire from our crime scene, I take it?"

"Duncan's tire expert in Austin IDed it for us."

Izzy studied the generic photo, which looked like it came off a website.

"Does it look familiar?"

She glanced at Leanne.

"I was hoping there was a chance you might recognize it from an accident scene or a skid mark you may have photographed," Leanne said. "Anything strike you at all?"

Izzy shook her head.

"A total long shot, I know." Leanne tipped her head back. "*Damn* it. I was counting on this lead panning out."

"So, the tire places aren't familiar with it?"

"The ones I talked to know about the brand, yeah. But no one I've talked to has a record of putting these tires on any vehicles around here. At least, they couldn't find any records."

"What about manufacturers? Do these come standard on anything?"

"No. That's the thing." Leanne sighed. "These are specialty tires. Which—originally—I had *thought* was a huge break for us because they're unusual. But turns out, that's making them harder to find."

Izzy studied the picture and handed the phone back. "Sorry, I don't recognize it from any cases I've worked. And you tried used car lots?"

"Yeah, I was thinking maybe a dealership got a souped-up truck in, and these were a selling point. But that didn't go anywhere, either."

"What about lift places? One of my uncles has one of those kits on his truck and you practically need a stepladder to get into it."

"That's a good idea."

"There's a place in Alpine, I think. It's right on the highway."

"I'll look into it."

Leanne leaned back and scrubbed her hands over her face. Then she glanced at Izzy's computer and frowned. "What are *you* working on?"

"That string of car burglaries. We got some fingerprints this time. The motel manager heard a car alarm and chased someone off. They dropped a vape cartridge, and I was able to lift a few partials."

"Nice work. Are they in the system?"

"Don't know yet. I'm working on it."

Leanne stood up and checked her watch. "Well, I'm starving. I missed lunch."

"If you'd like to grab dinner, I'm free after this."

The instant the words were out, Izzy wanted to take them back. In all the months they'd been working together, she and Leanne had never once done anything social. Izzy had been hoping to change that, but now she felt awkward.

"I don't have time tonight. Sorry. Maybe another time?"

"Sure." At least she sounded open to it.

Leanne looked at her watch again. "I'm up against a clock. McBride wants a murder suspect by tomorrow morning."

"He actually gave you a deadline?"

"Nine a.m.," Leanne told her. "Or he's yanking my case."

The silver Airstream glinted like a mirror as Leanne pulled up. She got out and looked around, shielding her eyes from the glare as she surveyed the campground. Most of the Airstreams looked occupied, and many of the vehicles beside them had out-of-state plates.

The woman she had come to see was in the center of the grounds rearranging turquoise-colored Adirondack chairs around a firepit.

Leanne walked over. "Hey, Selma."

She glanced up. "Hey there. Haven't seen you in a while."

With her long blond braid and hemp overalls, Selma looked like a hippie version of her mother.

"We've got two parties checking in at four," Selma said. "So, I can only do twenty minutes today. Sorry."

"That's fine. Thanks for squeezing me in. Looks like you're busy."

Nadine's daughter managed the most popular glamp site in town, but she didn't own it. The Hideaway belonged to a hotelier from Austin. One of the bitter ironies of Madrone's transformation into a tourist hub was that outside investors were reaping some of the biggest profits while the locals got stuck with higher prices.

"We're always busy," Selma said. "Not that I'm complaining." She grabbed a crumpled Hershey wrapper off the ground. "I swear, people are such litterbugs. Come on, let's get some shade."

Leanne followed her across the campground, which consisted of twelve Airstreams centered around a giant stone firepit where people would hang out and roast s'mores each night. Instead of a yurt, like Michelle had, the Hideaway used a patio with a corrugated metal roof as a dining area.

Selma claimed a red picnic table beside a food counter. "You want a latte or anything?"

"I'm good." Really, Leanne could have used some caffeine, but she didn't want to cut into their interview time.

"So, what can I do for you? You said something about an investigation?"

Leanne took the bench seat across from her. "It's about Hannah Rawls."

By Selma's expression, Leanne could tell this didn't come as a surprise.

"Given everything that's happened, I'm just taking a look at some things about the case," Leanne told her. "We're retracing our steps a bit."

She blew out a sigh and looked away. "Damn. It's been so long. Hard to believe."

Interesting that Selma didn't immediately start talking about what a travesty it was that Sean Moriarty had been released. Maybe she was one of the handful of locals who harbored doubts about the conviction.

"I'm checking in with some of Hannah's friends," Leanne said. "You two were close that summer she died, right? I saw your name in the files, along with some of the friends that were interviewed."

Selma nodded her head side to side. "We were and we weren't. I'd say we were more frenemies than friends."

"Oh yeah?" This was news to Leanne.

"I mean, we were on the volleyball team together and hung out with the same group. But we were pretty different. And we had a falling-out over a guy once, so . . . you know how that goes."

"Who was the guy?"

Selma raised an eyebrow.

"Was it Sean Moriarty?"

"You know, you're the first cop to ask that."

"Really?"

She nodded. "I always thought it was weird that it never came up." She shrugged. "But, whatever. I've got nothing to hide. Sean and I were together the winter of my senior year."

Leanne had the urge to get out her notebook, but she wanted to keep the conversation flowing. "He graduated the year before you and Hannah did, right?"

"Yeah, and Hannah always had a thing for him. He was a big football badass, along with her brother. So once him and Jake graduated, I think she just decided to, you know, make her move."

"So, she and Sean dated after you two did?"

She rolled her eyes. "I wouldn't say 'dated.' More like hooked up. Hannah wasn't really public about it because she didn't want her parents finding out. But I knew."

"How did you find out?"

She lifted a shoulder. "I don't remember. I just knew Sean was lying to me, and I figured it out."

"This was in the winter? Do you recall when, exactly?"

"I think January or February? So going into that summer, me and Sean were over and me and Hannah were no longer on speaking terms."

Leanne studied Selma's eyes. She was being surprisingly forthcoming, so Leanne decided to ask the question that had been percolating in her head.

"Do *you* think Sean killed her?"

Selma gave her a long, steady look. Another sigh, and she looked away. "You know, no one ever asked me that, either. At least, none of the cops did."

"Well, what do you think?"

She looked at Leanne. "I never could see it."

"No?"

She shook her head. "I mean, yeah, Sean could be a hothead sometimes. And he was aggressive. But that was more on the football field. He never raised a hand to me."

"What about fights with other guys?"

"I never saw that side of him. I know he had his share of discipline issues, but I never saw the kind of explosive temper they talked about during his trial. And we had some arguments, too. It wasn't like we never pissed each other off." She scoffed. "Hannah definitely *wasn't* the first thing we ever fought about."

"Okay, what about after your breakup? Do you know if there was friction between Hannah and Sean?"

"I don't know. After he dumped me, I steered clear of them."

"So, you weren't with Hannah the night of July Fourth?" Leanne asked.

"No."

"Any idea, maybe something you heard, about what they might have been fighting about at that time? It came out at trial that they'd been arguing at the Dairy Queen after the fireworks."

"No idea. But knowing Hannah? I wouldn't be surprised if it was another guy."

"You say that because . . . ?"

"Because that's how she was. And, yes, I know it's not cool to say this about someone who's dead, but she was kind of a bitch that way. She didn't have any loyalty."

Leanne watched her, hoping she'd elaborate. "Do you have any idea who she might have been seeing that summer?"

Selma tipped her head back and seemed to think about it. "Nothing concrete, no. And police *did* ask me that at the time. I remember that question."

Leanne waited, sensing she had something she wanted to add.

"She may have had a boyfriend in Marfa."

Leanne's pulse picked up. "Why do you say that?"

"I don't know. Just conjecture, really." She shrugged. "I remember she drove down there a few times to go to stuff. I told one of the detectives that, too, back at the time."

"Stuff? Like, what, you mean parties?"

"Parties, live music. They had a lot more going on there back then. You remember how dead it was here. God, we didn't even have a coffee shop. It wasn't like now where there's actual nightlife in town."

"So, Hannah would go to Marfa?"

"I remember her going to see a film there or something. And an art opening. She talked about it, just to make sure we all knew. I think she thought it made her sound sophisticated. Which, I mean, it did, right? We were all out here eating Blizzards and drag racing. She's down there hanging out with these people from Los Angeles or wherever."

"So . . . you think she may have met a man at one of these parties?"

"I don't know. Maybe? It wouldn't surprise me. Guys were always coming on to her." Selma sighed again and looked wistful now. "That was *Hannah*."

"How do you mean?"

"There was just something about her. They were like flies to honey."

THIRTY-FOUR

Leanne was down to twelve hours. After interviewing Selma, she'd hit the one remaining auto shop on her list, but no new lead on the Ridge Grappler tires.

None of the lab work had come back yet—not the rape kit the ME had submitted and not the duct tape from Duncan. Leanne had tried to set up another conversation with Jordan, but Sandra said the CI was ignoring her messages. Jordan was spooked, which meant Leanne had a long night ahead of her poring over paperwork in search of a fresh lead.

Leanne looked out over the moon-drenched valley as she headed home. You could drive for miles out here and not see a single porch light. This place was remote, and it wasn't just the landscape. The people could be remote, too. They treated newcomers with skepticism, and for good reason. So many people moved out here thinking they wanted to get away from the city and the congestion and the frantic pace of modern life. But they brought their computers and cell phone culture with them. Other people came out here and genuinely tried to give it a fair shot, only to discover that wide-open spaces made them feel claustrophobic, even suffocated. So after a while they picked up and left.

Leanne herself had had some problems with reentry when

she'd first moved home after her dad's death. People kept her at arm's length, as though expecting her to leave again, and she knew they'd taken her departure as a sort of rejection, which it was. So she'd been working to build back trust.

But the truth was, even after almost two years back, she still had mixed feelings about being here. She still hadn't fully unpacked yet. Maybe she needed to. Maybe it would do her good. It was hard to build trust with people when they sensed your ambivalence. Maybe they also sensed how much she resented being pulled away from the independent life she'd built for herself to deal with her family's dysfunction. Was that why she hadn't made more friends here, or dated, or spent more time at bars? Possibly.

It was also possible that she was who she was, and no matter where she lived, she was destined to be a loner. Talking to Duncan was the closest she'd ever had to therapy. She didn't need a psychologist to tell her she was the way she was because of her hypercritical mother and her silent father who'd withheld approval all her life. But she didn't mind being alone. At least, she didn't *usually* mind it. And when she did, she got by.

A sign loomed ahead for Lost Mine Road. Leanne looked out the window as she passed the yucca farm that had been targeted by poachers the other night. Rows and rows of succulents raced by, their spiky tops bathed silver in the moonlight. All seemed quiet at the moment—no trucks or spotlights or any other indication of thieves digging up plants.

She thought of Mark Rodriguez asking her or Josh to trade assignments. He'd been so matter-of-fact about how they worked in a place where some people's open racism put his life at risk. Anyone who wore a badge accepted a certain amount of danger as part of the job, but for Mark it was more. She'd never really considered it before. All her career, she'd felt alienated from the good-old-boy cop culture that surrounded her. Maybe Mark felt that, too, but for different reasons.

Leanne drove over a rise, and then she was coasting downward toward the smattering of lights that marked the town. A blinking red dot on the hillside indicated the area's only cell phone tower.

She neared Duncan's neighborhood, a cluster of low brick homes. His house was on the far end, and she spotted a light on. She shouldn't stop.

Or maybe she should.

"Screw it," she muttered, tapping the brake.

She drove down Duncan's street and was relieved to see his truck in the driveway, which told her he hadn't gone to bed yet because he always kept it in the garage overnight. She parked in front of the house, and a chorus of barks went up from the neighbor's yard as she approached his door.

She took a deep breath and knocked. Nerves flitted through her stomach as she waited and waited. Finally, the door swung open.

"Hi," he said evenly. He wore jeans, no shirt, and had a can of shaving cream in his hand.

"I have a quick update. You headed out somewhere?"

He pulled the door back. "Yeah."

She stepped inside, and for a moment they stood there in the dim foyer.

"I'm working tonight." He led her down the hallway to the guest bathroom, which was across from the spare bedroom that he'd converted into a closet for all his gear. The faucet was running, and a roll of electrical tape was perched beside the sink alongside a tiny microphone. A half-eaten grilled cheese sandwich sat beside a can of Red Bull.

"What's all this?" she asked.

"I'm undercover." He sprayed a dollop of cream on his fingers and spread it over his chest. "So, what's up?" he asked, leaning toward the mirror.

She watched, holding her breath, as he shaved his sternum.

"Where is this op?" she asked.

"Odessa." He rinsed the razor and tapped it on the sink. "Why?"

"And you have to wear a wire?"

"Yeah."

"Aren't you worried you'll be recognized?"

"No."

Well, *she* was worried. She tensed as she watched him make another swipe at his chest. Then he set down the razor and grabbed a towel.

"What's up, Leanne?" He eyed her in the mirror as he wiped down his torso. "If you're wondering about that duct tape, there's nothing back yet. I called to check in, but there's some kind of delay at the lab."

"Not surprising. But that's not what I wanted to talk about." She met his gaze in the mirror. "I wanted to thank you for dropping off that report. It was helpful. Your contact is really good at his job."

"I know."

She cleared her throat. "Also, I want to apologize."

He lifted an eyebrow.

"I was kind of a jerk the other night. I was upset."

He grabbed a black T-shirt from the counter and pulled it over his head, then rested his hands on his hips.

"You weren't a jerk."

"I didn't feel like talking." She bit her lip. That wasn't exactly true. "Actually, I was embarrassed."

"Why?"

She stared up at him as her heart thrummed.

"My mom told me some stuff about my dad, and I think he may have coerced a confession from Sean Moriarty."

Duncan stared down at her, no reaction at all.

Her breath whooshed out.

"You *knew*."

"I heard a rumor," he said.

She turned away. Her stomach clenched, and her cheeks burned.

"Hey."

She turned to look at him.

"It's just a rumor, Leanne. It doesn't prove anything."

"It's on tape. She *heard* it."

"Who heard it?"

"My mom."

He frowned down at her. "What tape?"

"What does it matter? She heard it herself, and she said he was in the room, which means it happened." Leanne shook her head. "This whole thing is a disaster. He destroyed a man's *life*."

She turned away, and he caught her sleeve.

"Hey. Listen. *If* it's true—which you don't really know, if you haven't heard the tape yourself—then I doubt he did it alone."

She gaped at him. "So what?"

He folded his arms over his chest. "Where is this audiotape?"

"Why does it matter?"

"If it exists, then it matters a lot." He gazed down at her, his eyes intent, and Leanne knew what he was thinking, because she'd thought it, too.

If her mom had listened to the tape and knew her dad was in the room for that confession, then she knew who else was in the room with him.

"Is she safe?" Duncan asked.

"I think so."

"You think?"

"She told me she got rid of it years ago."

He just stared at her, thinking God only knew what about her entire family.

She shook her head. "This is going to be . . . I can't even think of a word bad enough."

"It's not on you."

She glared at him.

"What? It's not," he said. "You and your father are two different people."

Leanne's chest squeezed, and she almost laughed at the irony. Throughout her life, people had told her the opposite.

You're so much like your dad...

Following in your father's footsteps...

Your dad is so proud of you...

And even worse—*Your father's a legend in this town. You must be so proud...*

Yes, her father had his flaws, but she'd never doubted his integrity before now. This was the man who'd drilled into her the importance of honesty. Of telling the truth. When she was six years old, he'd caught her with a pack of gum she'd stolen from the drugstore. He'd turned the car around and made her go back, cheeks flaming, to return the pack and apologize to the clerk. She'd never forget the disappointed look on his face as he'd watched her do it. It was something she'd carried around for years. But the more she learned, the more she believed her dad had caved in to pressure to produce an arrest. He'd *caved in to pressure*, and now a man's life had been derailed and a killer had been allowed to roam free. That coerced confession had spawned loss and heartache for years to come.

"Leanne?"

"Sorry," she said, shifting her focus to the surveillance gear spread across the counter. "I know you have to go."

He didn't argue, and she turned to leave.

"Hey, you never gave me the update," he said, following her down the hall.

"We IDed our victim. Her name is Valeria Reyes, originally from Albuquerque."

"Josh told me about that."

She stopped at the door. "Did he also tell you McBride gave me forty-eight hours to come up with a suspect, or he's yanking my case? That was Monday morning." She opened the door and stepped out. "And the only witness I've been able to locate who knows anything is now ghosting me."

He leaned against the doorframe and looked at her. "What are you going to do?"

She shook her head.

"I know you have a plan. What is it?"

"My plan is to go home, load up on coffee. And then comb through those case files until I figure something out."

THIRTY-FIVE

"What's wrong? You look terrible." Sam handed her a cup with two sugars stacked on top.

"Hey, it's my turn to pay," Leanne said.

"Don't worry about it. Let's sit on the patio. I'm not the only agent who stops in here, and people are nosy as hell."

Sam was right. Glancing around the coffee shop, Leanne saw that it was laughably easy to spot the FBI agents amid all the college students in ripped jeans and hoodies. She led Sam outside to a table on the patio's edge, away from eavesdroppers.

"Thanks for letting me hijack your morning," Leanne said.

"No problem." Sam scooted in her chair. Today she wore a very agenty-looking black pantsuit and white blouse. "Are you going to tell me what's wrong?"

"I got about two hours of sleep last night." Leanne peeled the lid off her coffee and dumped in the sugar. "And as of an hour ago, I've probably been pulled off my case. But, hey, other than that, I'm great."

Sam's brow furrowed. "'Probably' pulled off?"

"My chief threatened to yank my case if I didn't come up with a suspect by this morning. Right now, your profile is my Hail Mary. No pressure or anything."

"I work best under pressure," Sam said, pulling a file folder from her tote bag.

"Well, thanks again for squeezing me in. I owe you." Leanne sipped her coffee. It was scalding hot, but she was too sleep-deprived to care. "First, some key updates. The most recent victim has been identified through fingerprints. Her name is Elena Saldivar."

"The Gold Springs Trail victim?"

"Yeah, the one the papers were calling a 'hiker.'"

"Let me guess," Sam said. "She's not a hiker."

"Not at all. And we knew that from the beginning, even though the media didn't," Leanne said. "She's in the system. Two arrests last year, both in El Paso."

"Prostitution?"

"And drugs."

"That tracks, too." Sam opened her file and jotted some notes. "Okay, let's dive in. Based on everything you gave me—which was a lot, by the way. It took me hours to wade through."

"I may have overloaded you, but I wanted you to see everything I had."

"No, it was fascinating. The more facts I have to look at, the better. Anyway, based on what you gave me, I put together a basic analysis. That's what, why, and who. Let's start with *what*. The question is, What do these crimes have in common? And the answer is: a lot."

Leanne felt a surge of relief. "So, I'm not crazy, then. You think these murders could all be connected?"

"I'd bet money on it."

She stared at Sam, one of the smartest investigators she knew and someone she'd admired for years, as both a cop and a friend.

"To hear you say that..." Leanne shook her head. "There have been so many moments when I've thought I was crazy. Or paranoid. Or that it was all a bizarre hunch, with no basis in reality."

"I don't think you're crazy at all. I believe at least six of these crimes were committed by the same UNSUB, or unidentified subject." Sam flipped a few pages and skimmed her notes. "Let's start with Hannah Rawls." She looked up. "And, *yes*, I believe she's part of the series."

Leanne closed her eyes as a fresh wave of emotions swamped her. Vindication. Disbelief. Disgust.

But underneath all that was sadness, not just for Sean Moriarty but for her entire community. This was going to come as a shock to so many people. More than that—a betrayal. How would their town ever recover from it? And how would they trust the police again?

"You okay?" Sam asked.

"Yeah." She shuddered. "I'm just thinking. This is going to be a nightmare."

"Focus on the investigation. That's where your head needs to be right now."

"I know."

Sam took a deep breath. "So, *including* Hannah Rawls, we've got eight known victims whose remains were recovered within a quarter mile of Highway 67 between Fort Stockton and Marfa. In two cases, the remains consist of a single bone—a femur and a jawbone. Let's put those two cases aside for now, since we don't have much info to go on. Besides those, we've got *six* victims who were brutally bludgeoned. In several cases, the pathologist believes the weapon was a smooth, blunt object. So not, for example, a rock, but more likely the butt of a pistol or something similar."

Leanne's stomach knotted as she pictured the disfigured face of Valeria Reyes.

"And something interesting about all those victims? Based on the pattern of their injuries"—Sam paused—"I can tell you know where I'm going with this."

"He's left-handed."

"Exactly." Sam leaned closer. "Which could be an advantage, from your perspective, if you zero in on a suspect."

"When, not if. I'm determined to be optimistic."

"In addition," Sam continued, "*all* of those victims were women in their late teens to early twenties, according to the autopsy reports. *Four* of those were strangled, as evidenced by the broken hyoid bone. In at least three cases, the victims are Latinas. You following so far?"

She nodded.

"In three cases, duct tape was recovered from the crime scenes. And, of course, duct tape is good because it's sticky. It might be possible to recover the perp's DNA if he handled the roll of tape any time before or during the crime, and he might not have been wearing gloves every time he handled it."

"Good point."

"We broke a case wide open based on DNA from duct tape once, so for me, it jumped out," Sam said. "What else? Oh. Also in two cases, he cut a chunk of hair from the victim."

"Why?" Leanne asked.

"It's a souvenir. A trophy. Something he can use to help him relive the event."

Leanne winced.

"Disturbing, I know, but it's more common than you might think. Serial killers like souvenirs. It's a big enough chunk of hair to be noticeable to the examining pathologist, and it looks like he uses scissors."

"Meaning he comes prepared. These aren't spur-of-the-moment crimes."

"Right." Sam glanced down at her notes. "After going through all this, I believe Hannah was his first victim, which is both good and bad for you. Good, because it was his first kill and he made mistakes. Bad because someone *else* was convicted of that crime, which enabled this UNSUB to fly under the radar for years."

The knot in Leanne's stomach tightened. So many years wasted. It cut to the heart of what most disturbed her, what had been keeping her awake at night. Sean Moriarty's wrongful conviction had set off a terrible domino effect, and so many innocent lives had been affected in the ensuing years. And—maybe worst of all—people in local leadership positions seemed more worried about lawsuits and bad publicity than figuring out what actually happened.

"So, that's the *what*," Sam said. "Now let's talk about the *why*."

"He hates women."

"Not to be overly simplistic, but, yes, that's the crux of it," Sam said. "These are all cases of overkill. Take Valeria Reyes and several of the others. They were strangled to death and then savagely beaten postmortem. That shows a deep-seated rage that goes beyond a simple homicidal impulse."

Leanne visualized Valeria in her driver's license photo, with her sparkling brown eyes and beautiful smile. When Leanne had seen her in that culvert, she'd been beaten beyond recognition and left to be feasted on by animals.

"That level of overkill," Leanne asked. "What is that about?"

Sam leaned her head to the side. "There are always multiple factors contributing. Almost all of these guys were victims of abuse, at some point. With this sort of female-focused aggression you might have either a mother who was abusive herself or who abandoned the child to an abusive caregiver. The causes vary, but the result is a deeply ingrained contempt toward women, not to mention poor self-esteem and inability to control violent urges."

"Violence begets violence," Leanne said softly.

"That's heartbreakingly true." Sam paused for a moment, looking down at her notes.

"What about the *who*?" Leanne asked. "We're desperate for actionable information, at this point. He's killed two women that we know about in the past two weeks, and I feel like he's escalating."

"He is." Sam closed the folder and looked her in the eye. "So, for the profile, some things are clear and virtually certain with this UNSUB. Other things are an educated guess given the evidence."

Leanne held her breath as Sam seemed to be collecting her thoughts.

"I believe he's midthirties to midforties," Sam said. "That's based on the date of Hannah Rawls's murder, which was sixteen years ago. I believe he's highly intelligent *and* capable of learning from mistakes and modifying his behavior. Not all intelligent criminals can do this."

"That's based on what?"

"His evolving MO," Sam told her. "Like I said, I think he started with Hannah Rawls, and he made multiple mistakes. First and foremost, his victim selection. Actually, I don't think he selected Hannah so much as *she* was the moment when he first lost control and gave into his overwhelming urge. He killed her in a fit of rage, probably when she resisted him in some way, such as refusing to have sex with him."

"Hannah's rape kit came back negative," Leanne said.

"That could make sense, if he went overboard and killed her in reaction to something that happened between them. But, like I said, he learned from his mistakes; he altered his MO. He saw what happened after Hannah died. The response was big and immediate."

"She disappeared, and there was a search launched within a day," Leanne said. "She missed her curfew, and by the following day, we had people from everywhere converging on the town to help look for her. Hannah's from a prominent family. At the time, her dad was a big contributor to political campaigns—the sheriff's, judges'. He had pull with everyone, and he used it."

"So, that's key. That likely freaked this UNSUB out," Sam said. "Next time around, what does he do? He picks a victim he thinks no one is going to miss, or at least not file a formal police report right away. Someone on the fringes."

"Two of the victims have been positively identified as sex workers," Leanne said. "The others, we don't know. But based on the fact that they don't match up with missing person reports, we can infer these women were people on the margins of the community, who tend to avoid interfacing with police."

She thought about Ana Ortiz, who had mysteriously disappeared last summer, according to the vice detective. *Girls like that aren't the kind of cases you hear about on the news.*

"Could be undocumented migrants, or runaways, or drug addicts," Sam said. "Vulnerable groups that don't want to mix with authorities for whatever reason."

"You're saying he's choosing his victims that way."

"Right," Sam replied. "I'm saying he saw what happened with Hannah—how all hell rained down, and someone was arrested and tried and went to prison—and he knew he needed to adapt his method, because he wouldn't get that lucky twice."

"All right." Leanne reread her notes so far. "What else about him?"

"Besides being smart, he's detail oriented and meticulous. He comes prepared. I think he uses a murder kit. He's got the duct tape, the scissors, and the pistol or whatever blunt object he uses to beat them—those are all part of the tool kit he brings with him. It might have condoms, too, so he doesn't leave DNA behind. He's too smart for that."

"So, an intelligent and organized killer." Leanne took a deep breath. "Anything else? Anything physical?"

Sam nodded. "Well, based on the size thirteen shoe, he's likely taller than average. And he's strong enough to maneuver his victims' bodies around, dragging them and lifting them in and out of a vehicle. Also, most importantly, the left-handed thing. Only ten percent of people are left-handed, so that is potentially a huge factor for you."

"It's also a factor in exonerating Sean Moriarty," Leanne told her. "Sean's right-handed. I checked."

"I didn't see anything in the file."

"I ran into him at a bar the other night. I tossed something at him, and his reflex was to catch it with his right hand."

Sam's eyebrows tipped up. "You seriously did that?"

"I needed to know."

"Okay, then. I'll add that to the rest. And the last piece of the profile? I believe this guy's local."

"You think he's from around here? Or that he lives here?"

"Both," Sam said. "It goes back to the locations where he's disposing of his victims, starting sixteen years ago with Hannah Rawls. That abandoned well where he dumped her? That's on private property. It's someone's ranch, and I saw the crime scene photos—the area is *near* the highway, yes, but it's surrounded by brush. A search dog discovered it, but otherwise it might have remained hidden for years. Anyone who knew that old well was there and was able to find it within hours of Hannah's death, that person is familiar with this area in more than just a casual way."

"And you think he lives here?" Leanne asked.

Sam nodded. "Absolutely."

"That's what I think, too."

"He's picking up victims at population hubs—truck stops, gas stations, towns like Fort Stockton and El Paso that are bigger than Madrone, where it's much easier to go unnoticed and blend in. Then he's carrying out his crimes and depositing the victims on the highway, on his way home."

Leanne paused, letting Sam's words sink in. The feeling of dread that had been lurking inside her since that very first morning by the railroad tracks was back now, stronger than ever. This predator was *local*.

Which meant he was someone she knew.

"You believe he still lives here," Leanne stated.

"Yes." Sam paused. "Don't you?"

"I've thought that from the beginning," Leanne said. "I think he lives and works in Chisos County. I think he knows the area. I think it's become his hunting ground."

Leanne felt numb as she left the coffee shop.

He was local.

He'd been killing for years, without attention or consequence, right in her backyard.

And he was still doing it.

Again, she thought of the missing woman from Fort Stockton. Sandra had sent over what little she had on her from when she'd been trying to recruit her for CI work last summer. Leanne now had a mug shot and fingerprints, but neither would be much help if all that was left of her was skeletonized bones.

She slid behind the wheel of her pickup and stared through the windshield as a combination of guilt and anger roiled inside her.

A murderer was at large and had been for sixteen years.

And her father was partially responsible because he had looked the other way.

At least six women *dead* and one man's youth forfeited due to the actions and inaction of people Leanne had looked up to all her life.

The anger was like a hot glob of acid in her throat. Her dad was part of this, part of the unforgivable act that would have a devastating effect for decades to come. It would destroy people's trust in the very cause that he'd devoted his life to, the cause she'd committed *her* life to. That was his legacy now.

Her phone chimed, snapping her from her daze. She dug it from her pocket. Ben. She stared down at the screen, deciding whether to answer.

Look out for your brother. Her father's words came back, like they always did when she had this debate with herself. Ben's crap was the last thing she wanted to deal with at this moment. But it might be an emergency.

She picked up.

"Where are you? I've been calling for days," she said.

"I had my ringer off. What's up?"

His blissful nonchalance irked her.

"Did you listen to my messages?"

"What about them?"

That was a no, then.

She took a deep breath, blocking out her irritation. "I need to talk to you. It's important. Are you at home?"

"I'm in Austin."

"What? Why?"

"I sold some of Dad's LPs to a private collector here."

"You . . . what? What the hell, Ben?"

"Relax. You'll get a cut of the money."

"I don't *want* a cut of the money. I can't believe—"

"You should be thanking me," he said. "This is a good buyer—a music producer, and he's willing to pay top dollar. I found him through Roland."

"Roland Rivas, the drug dealer?"

"He's not a drug dealer, he's a musician. You don't know what you're talking about as usual—"

"You know what? Just *stop*, okay? I don't want to hear it," she said. "I need you to listen to me."

Silence.

"Ben? Are you there?"

"Yeah. What?"

"Someone from the fire department wants to interview you. Possibly Glenn Meachum, the fire chief. You need to be prepared."

"Interview me about what?"

"Boone's ranch," she said as she backed out of her parking space. "They're saying it's arson, and they're looking for suspects. They're going to want to know where you were right before the fire started."

"I was home."

Leanne turned out of the parking lot. "Were you alone?"

"None of your business. And they can interview me all day long because I didn't do shit."

"Okay. But you can't just—"

"And Glenn Meachum can fuck off."

"Ben . . . would you just listen a minute? Ben?"

He'd hung up.

"Shit!"

She tossed her phone aside. Now what? Her brother was going to walk right into a buzz saw, and he didn't even seem to care.

Her phone chimed again, and she grabbed it.

"Ben?"

Nothing.

"Hello?"

"Uh, I'm trying to reach a Detective Everhart?"

The voice wasn't familiar. She checked the screen, but she didn't recognize the number.

"This is Leanne Everhart."

"I'm calling from the El Paso crime lab," he said. "I have a note about a rush request?"

Her pulse picked up. "Yes?"

"I wanted to let you know, the evidence you submitted has been processed, and the report is available."

"Thank you." She glanced at the clock. She had already blown through her deadline, so what would another detour matter?

"By 'available,' you mean it's ready right now?" she asked.

"That's correct. Would you like me to send—"

"No, I'll be right over," she told him. "I'm on my way."

THIRTY-SIX

The lobby of the crime lab was buzzing with cops from an alphabet soup of agencies, and the twentysomething front-desk clerk looked utterly overwhelmed. Leanne stepped away from the traffic snarl and listened to her missed phone messages as she waited for the crowd to subside. After the last paunchy detective walked out, Leanne approached the counter.

"Hi."

The clerk glanced up, wide-eyed. She had wispy blond hair and a smattering of freckles on her nose, and she looked even younger up close.

"I got a call about some evidence ready for pickup. I'm Detective Everhart."

She dropped her gaze to the heap of paper in front of her. "Everhart... Everhart..."

"With Madrone PD. I just spoke to someone on the phone?"

"Everhart, you said?" She reached for a file tray and thumbed through a stack of thick manila envelopes.

"Yes, with Madrone PD. The evidence was expedited."

"Must have been one of our technicians who called. Did they give a name?"

"No. This was something bulky, though. It was in a flat cardboard box"—Leanne held up her hands—"about this big?"

Her face brightened. "That's probably in the intake room, then. That's where we keep bulk items. Sorry, I should have asked. This is my first week."

"No problem. Can you direct me—"

"One moment, I'll get it." She stood up and rushed through the door behind her desk.

Leanne checked the clock on the wall, then stepped over to the empty seating area and listened to another missed message, this one from Josh.

"Hey, just a heads-up. The chief's looking for you. You're probably on your way in, so . . . if you are, ignore this."

Then a message from Mark.

"Leanne, hi. I was at the station house, and McBride was asking where you are. Just FYI. Later."

And then Nadine.

"Hey, hon. What's your twenty? The chief wants to talk to you, and he's in a foul mood. Gimme a call."

Leanne stared out the lobby window, fuming. Her deadline had come and gone hours ago. Did she have a suspect? No. What she *did* have was a criminal profile based on a boatload of facts, all supporting the idea that not only had her department completely botched the investigation of Hannah Rawls's murder sixteen years ago, but they'd mishandled multiple others since. She pictured McBride leaning back in his chair as he spouted his platitudes.

The desert's a cruel place.

Dehumanize and deprioritize, that was his motto. Who cared if a serial killer was out there preying on women, so long as he didn't target any more ranchers' daughters?

Was Alma Cruz's missing daughter a victim, too? After going

out drinking with friends, Marisol Cruz had disappeared from a parking lot in Fort Stockton not far from where Valeria Reyes and Ana Ortiz were last seen. A high school girl with her whole life ahead of her, suddenly gone. Each one of these young women was somebody's child, somebody's sister, somebody's friend, and yet their cases had attracted little attention. In Marisol's case, almost none at all. Six years after her daughter's disappearance, and Alma Cruz was still suffering through day after day with no answers.

Frustration smoldered inside her. Was Leanne the only one who saw these victims as people? She pinched the bridge of her nose. No, she was not. There was Sandra Torres. And Jen Sayers. And Patty Paulson. They cared, even if the chief didn't. But he was an obstacle, and she needed to figure out a way around him.

"Detective?"

She turned.

The clerk was back with a cardboard box. "Found it," she said, setting it on the counter. "It's not as heavy as it looks."

Leanne walked over. "Yeah, it's made of plaster."

"I just need you to sign this," the clerk said, passing her a clipboard.

"Thanks." Leanne signed and handed it back.

"One of the envelopes was wedged behind the shelf in there, so sorry it's all dusty." She set a pair of manila envelopes on the box.

"No problem. Thanks again. And good luck with your first week."

Leanne tucked the envelopes under her arm and returned to her car, replaying her flood of missed phone messages. Obviously, the chief wanted a meeting ASAP, probably so he could yank her case, if he hadn't already. Now she either had to wrestle control away from Mark Rodriguez or work behind the scenes to get him to use the profile she'd just obtained as a road map for his investigation. But Rodriguez was a junior detective and not likely to rock the boat. Maybe she'd be better off working through Duncan and the sheriff's office. Duncan might listen to her, but Travis Malcom was the lead detective, and she and Travis had a history of butting heads. No matter how insightful the criminal profile was, Travis would almost certainly reject it if he knew it came from her.

No, he *would* reject it. No question. Because he had a fragile ego, and he was in charge. Which meant she had to find a way around him, too—yet another obstacle to deal with before she could get down to the business of *solving this case*, which was the only goal that mattered, and yet here she was, wasting her energy navigating self-important men and their bullshit.

She hated the politics of it all.

Leanne slid behind the wheel and set the box on the passenger seat. The return address on the top envelope consisted of a scrawled name, *Robert Goldberg*. The envelope flap was bradded closed, not sealed. She opened it and tugged out the paperwork.

The three-page report included a large photo of the Ridge Grappler tire with black sidewalls, the very same shot Duncan's tire expert had used with his write-up. Goldberg's typewritten notes were practically identical to Duncan's guy's, but the Austin expert had included a few key details, such as a note about a nicked tread, which—according to the Austin expert—had likely resulted from running over a hard metal object. If and *when* Leanne zeroed in on a suspect with these tires on his vehicle, that one tiny detail might prove critical for linking the suspect to the crime scene.

Leanne moved on to the second envelope, which was thinner. No technician's name on the outside, and the flap was sealed. She tore open the envelope and slid out a one-page form with the heading, "EP Crime Laboratory." The form was filled out by hand, but she didn't see a technician's name at the top. She flipped the envelope over again, but the only writing on the back said: *L. Everhart, Madrone Police Dept.*

A cold feeling settled over her.

She studied the form again. "Chemical Testing, unknown substance." It was different from any form she'd seen previously from a regional forensic lab. She turned it over. Beneath a few more lines of handwritten notes was a signature, plus the name WAYNE OLDHAM written in messy block letters. She flipped the form over and noticed the date at the top.

The form had been filled out *sixteen years ago*. October fifth, to be precise, the same year Hannah Rawls was murdered.

This report was meant for Lee Everhart.

He'd never picked it up. Why? Maybe because it fell behind a shelf or got misplaced or forgotten. Meanwhile, police had plunged ahead with their investigation, closing the net around an innocent man.

October fifth. By the time this report came into existence, Sean Moriarty was sitting in jail awaiting trial for Hannah's murder.

Leanne's heart thrummed as she read the report again, trying to make sense of all the jargon. Maybe this was something inconsequential and routine—some evidence her dad had submitted that didn't really matter.

Madrone evidence used to be sent to the El Paso lab routinely. It was the closest place. But the lab there had become notoriously backlogged with drug cases in recent years. Why did McBride still use it? Did he really have an in there, or was he trying to stymie her progress?

Leanne read on. *Sample tested for the following: amphetamines, barbiturates, cocaine* . . . The list continued.

None of the chemicals was marked, and at the bottom someone had circled "None of the Above."

The second half of the report was labeled "Further Analysis, Mass Spectrometer."

Handwritten notes included reference to phenidone, and a chemical formula, $C_9H_{10}N_2O$.

Leanne sat back and stared through the windshield. She pictured her dad's legal pads filled with to-do lists from the early days of the Rawls investigation. He'd mentioned something about going to the lab. And something about white powder on the victim's clothes. Leanne had assumed that powder was drugs, and maybe he had, too.

But was *this* that unknown substance? Had her dad sent it in for testing?

Holding the report in her hand, she felt a sudden connection to her father. An odd dizziness came over her as his words echoed through her brain. *Intuition is your friend.*

It was one of her dad's favorite sayings. And right now, her intuition was telling her this clue was important.

A ringtone broke the silence. She grabbed her phone. It was Nadine again, but Leanne ignored the call as she tapped open the browser and looked up the word.

"Phenidone: organic compound, common developing agent used in BxW film developers."

Darkroom chemicals. Of course. He was a photographer. From the very beginning, this clue had been right there in front of her, but she hadn't understood it for what it was.

Leanne's heart thudded as she looked around the busy parking lot, so many cops and border agents and detectives, all streaming back and forth, going about their routines. But nothing about today was routine anymore. Today was a watershed.

She had to do something. Now. This minute. Before anything else happened. She didn't have time for diplomacy or politics or another round of pointless arguments with the chief.

With trembling fingers, Leanne tapped out a text to Duncan. Thoughts racing, she got on the road.

THIRTY-SEVEN

After four separate tries, Izzy finally answered the phone.
"Hey, what's up?"

Leanne whipped into a parking space in front of the Marfa Chamber of Commerce.

"Where are you?" Leanne asked.

"Uh, in my car. Why?"

"Listen, you work in a darkroom, right? I mean, I know you do digital photography, but I assume you've used a darkroom, at some point?"

"Well, yeah," Izzy said. "I worked almost exclusively in a darkroom when I was at school. Now I mostly do digital photos. Except when it comes to nature shots. Lately, I've been experimenting with—"

"So, you know the chemicals, then, right? Darkroom chemicals?"

"Yes. Why?"

"I'll explain later. I just need—" Leanne glanced at the sign in front of her. NO UNAUTHORIZED PARKING. She fished the police hang tag from her glove box and hooked it onto the mirror. She should have picked up an official car at the police station earlier, but when she had set out for El Paso this morning, she'd been determined to avoid crossing paths with the chief.

"Leanne? You there?"

"Yeah. Listen, Izzy, I need your input. I just got a report from a crime lab that says something about phenidone. You ever heard of it?"

"Sure. It's a developing agent."

"Do people still use that now? Or is it obsolete?"

"Depends," Izzy said. "Personally, I don't care for it for high contrasts. But some people like it because it's less toxic to skin so less likely to cause dermatitis. I haven't used it since I learned to develop film in the yearbook office, way back in high school. Why? What's this about?"

Leanne turned to look back over her shoulder at Dark Sky Gallery. The afternoon sun slanted through the windows, reflecting off the abstract metal sculpture in the center of the room. Was Zach Olmstead there? Based on her previous legwork, she knew he drove a black Range Rover. She didn't see one parked on the street, but maybe he'd parked around back.

"Leanne?"

"Sorry, I'm just—" She closed her eyes and took a deep breath. She needed to calm down. She needed to settle. She couldn't go in there looking manic. "I'm a little scattered right now. This day's been insane."

"Is there any way I can help?"

"Maybe in a bit. I mostly wanted to know if that chemical was commonly used or if it was something rare," Leanne said. "Will you be around later? At the station house?"

"I'm off this afternoon unless something comes up. I'm working on some personal stuff. But call me if you need anything."

"Thanks. I will."

Leanne slipped her phone into her pocket. She smoothed her

hair and slid from her truck. Traffic was light on Highland Street, so she crossed without going to the light and strode straight up to the gallery's front door.

A wall of cold air hit her as she stepped inside. What was it with this place? It was always freezing.

No instrumental music today, only silence. A giant wooden crate sat near the back, Styrofoam peanuts scattered on the floor around it. A crowbar sat atop the crate, and it looked like someone was unpacking a shipment.

Leanne did a slow 360, once again taking in the enormous floor-to-ceiling nature photographs, all taken at night. Snippets of the criminal profile came back to her, and her stomach felt queasy.

He's detail oriented and meticulous.

And what was it Zach had told her?

I've been out here eighteen years. . . . Before that, I moved around.

The timing fit. Ditto his height, his build.

A faint gurgling noise came from the back of the gallery. Leanne followed the sound to the break room, where she found Zach's slender blond assistant standing in front of a shiny red cappuccino machine.

"Freya?"

She whirled around, and her eyes widened. Once again, she looked like a runway model, this time in a white cashmere sweater with camel-colored pants and boots.

"I'm Detective Everhart," Leanne reminded her. "We met last week?"

"Yes, of course. May I help you?"

"I need to talk to Zach. Is he here?"

"No." She stepped closer, and her body language indicated that she didn't care for random members of the public popping into her break room. "He's not in today."

"Has he *been* in?"

Her perfect eyebrows arched, like she didn't get the question.

"Have you seen him at all?" Leanne asked.

"No."

Clearly, Freya was in gatekeeper mode, and Leanne realized she needed to lighten things up.

"Well, shoot." Leanne put her hand on her hip. "I was hoping to catch him. I had something I wanted to ask him about. I guess I'll try him at home."

"He'll be in later," Freya rushed to add, and Leanne got the distinct impression she didn't like the idea of another woman visiting Zach at his house—which confirmed Leanne's take that not only did Freya and her boss have a personal relationship, but she didn't trust him.

"May I give him a message for you?" Freya asked.

"No, thanks." Leanne smiled. "But you can answer one quick question. . . . Do you know where he keeps his studio?"

"Studio?"

"His workspace. His darkroom. Where does he do his photography work?"

She stepped closer, looking puzzled by this new line of questioning.

"His darkroom is there." She nodded across the hall at a closed door.

"Right here, on-site?" Leanne stepped toward the door and tried the knob before Freya could object. It was locked.

"That is his *private* workspace." Freya folded her arms. "No one goes in there. Not even me."

"I got it. Thanks." Leanne nodded. "Anyway, I'll try back later, see if I can catch him."

Leanne started to leave and then paused beside the wooden crate, thinking about the sort of damage that crowbar could do to a human skull.

She glanced up, and Freya was staring at her, clearly perturbed.

"One last question, and then I'll get out of your way," Leanne said. "Do you know if Zach is right-handed or left-handed?"

She leaned forward. "Pardon?"

"Right-handed." Leanne lifted hers. "Or left-handed?"

Freya said something that sounded like Swedish.

Leanne picked up a pen from the table. "Which hand does he use to *write*?" she asked, scribbling in the air.

"Which is his dominant hand, you ask?"

"Exactly."

"He is right-handed."

"Are you sure?"

Now she looked annoyed. And maybe a little smug.

"I know him quite *well*," Freya told her. "Yes, I am sure."

THIRTY-EIGHT

Leanne raced toward Madrone, manipulating the puzzle pieces in her mind and trying to make them fit together.

Hannah Rawls was his first victim, and phenidone was recovered from her clothes.

Phenidone was used in darkrooms, by photographers.

Leanne's father had had the business card for a gallery owned by a renowned photographer clipped to his notes about the case. And that photographer, whose phone number was written on the back of the card, had been living and working in the area at the time of Hannah's murder.

And he still was.

Leanne had assumed her dad had picked up that business card when he'd been to visit the gallery. But maybe he'd found it among Hannah's possessions. Detectives had gone through her room and her car after her disappearance, searching for clues.

Zach Olmstead fit the profile well. He was tall. And strong. And could easily have a size thirteen shoe. At forty-one, he was the right age. Most important, he was local. He worked outdoors—often at night—and knew the parks and canyons around here probably better than half the rock climbers and river guides who'd made this area their personal playground for years.

Also important—Zach was attractive and had the sort of smooth, low-key charm that might lure a woman in and put her at ease.

But he *wasn't* left-handed, at least according to Freya. Should Leanne take her at her word? Or find a way to confirm for herself?

Or should she stop wasting time on Zach Olmstead and move on to other area photographers, who might be a better match? Just the idea was daunting. This region was a gateway to several popular parks. So many photographers passed through here, it was impossible to keep track.

But which of them were permanent residents and had also lived here sixteen years ago? That requirement significantly shrank the suspect pool.

Leanne clenched the steering wheel, brimming with frustration. If only she could comb back through her dad's legal pads, looking for more clues with this new profile in mind. But his legal pads, along with most of his other possessions, had gone up in smoke.

She envisioned the cardboard box with all her dad's notes from the Rawls case. She pictured the copies of the *Madrone Sentinel* he'd had sitting on top. She had assumed he'd saved those newspapers because of the articles about the murder. But maybe it was something else.

On impulse, she grabbed her phone and scrolled through her messages. She found the string of missed calls from Marty Krause at the paper.

"Hello, Mr. Krause? Leanne Everhart here."

"Well, well, well." His voice was gravelly from decades of smoking. "It's about damn time."

"I've been meaning to get back to you, but everything's been so hectic."

"Better late than never. I been trying to set up"—hoarse coughing—"an interview. How about tomorrow—"

"Possibly. I'll have to see how the rest of today goes. Listen, I have a question for you about the Hannah Rawls case."

"You have a question for *me*?" Now he sounded amused.

"You covered the story, right? I think I remember your byline in the *Sentinel*?"

"It was a shared byline. Me and old Dave Westinghouse. He was the editor back when—"

"Right, I remember. Listen, who was your photographer at the time?"

Leanne waited, gripping the steering wheel. As the seconds ticked by, she realized this was a complete long shot.

"You mean our staff photographer? On the paper?"

"Yes."

"That'd be me."

"You?" She couldn't keep the surprise out of her voice.

"Yeah, back then I wore multiple hats."

Leanne's mind raced as she tried to force-fit what she knew about Marty Krause with the criminal profile. Besides the fact that he was older than dirt, Krause was a short, wiry man, and she couldn't picture him hauling a woman in and out of his car and stuffing her into an abandoned well, even sixteen years ago.

"Ya there?"

"Yes, sorry. So, besides yourself, was there anyone else taking photographs for the *Sentinel* back then?"

"Well, sure. We had a lot of folks. The stringers we got from the high school took photos."

"The stringers?"

"Yeah, the yearbook teacher would send them over each year. Some of them came to work for us for a while after they graduated."

"Stringers, as in—"

"Part-timers. They covered some of the small stuff. You know, Friday night football games and whatnot. Sometimes community events."

"Like, you mean, maybe picnics and Fourth of July parades?"

"Sure. Whatever was going on. We've got a shoestring budget, and we've been using cheap labor forever."

"Thank you. You've been a big help."

"Now, about that interview. What say—"

"Let me get back to you on that. I'll call you."

Another day off wasted.

Izzy slid into her car and unlooped the camera from around her neck. She set it on the seat beside her and pulled out her phone.

Nothing good today, she told her boyfriend. **The light's all wrong.**

A gray bubble appeared as he responded.

You headed back then?

Yeah. You? she answered.

I'm leaving now.

She slid her phone into the pocket of her fleece jacket and started the car. She had time to not only shower and change but pick up something for dinner. They could spend the evening on the sofa together binge-watching a show. She'd been exhausted lately. Her energy was drained again, and the only thing she felt up for tonight was some mindless TV.

Izzy pulled out of the lot, surveying the cars parked near the trailhead. Ever since her interview with Detective Malcom, she'd been noticing all sorts of details she'd never picked up on before.

Things that had previously escaped her interest—everything from faces to cars to bumper stickers, even people's *pets*—now stuck in her head and refused to go away. Anything suspicious caught her attention, and she'd even started taking notes on her phone. Why? She wasn't sure. It wasn't logical, really. What were the odds that she would stumble over another dead body while she was out hiking with her camera? It was a freak thing, completely unlikely to happen again, ever. And yet, the possibility haunted her wherever she went.

A man emerged from the trail, and Izzy tensed. Tall, heavyset. He wore a camo baseball cap and a black sweatshirt with jeans. As he crossed the lot, the taillights of a pickup truck flashed.

Izzy jabbed her door locks. The man glanced over at her, and she held her breath as he slid behind the wheel of his truck. Every muscle in her body tightened as he reversed from the parking space and pulled out of the lot.

Calm down. Don't be paranoid.

But paranoid was her default state right now, and she couldn't help it. She couldn't sleep or eat or focus on work. Images of those dead girls kept running through her mind. She couldn't escape them, no matter what she tried to distract herself.

The pickup's taillights receded down the highway, getting smaller and smaller until they faded to nothing. Izzy pulled out of the parking lot—the same lot that had been jammed with emergency vehicles the last time she was here just a couple of days ago.

Why had she come back? She wasn't sure. Was it morbid curiosity? Partly. But part of it was the idea that by coming here and retracing her steps, maybe she could replace the ugly visions in her mind with something else, something beautiful. Or—if not beautiful, then at least something not grotesque and disturbing, like what she'd seen last time.

But it hadn't worked. She was just as messed up now as before, and she'd wasted another one of her days off snapping an endless blur of mediocre photos. Not one of them was strong enough to add to her portfolio, much less put in front of Zach Olmstead or any of his influential friends.

Tears filled her eyes as she sped down the highway.

Time was closing in on her. With each day that went by, she felt every goal she'd set for herself slipping farther away. If she didn't make something happen soon, she was going to end up like her mom and her aunts and her two sisters, stuck in this do-nothing town, drowning in unpaid bills and babies and other people's laundry. Years ago, she promised herself she'd find a different path, and she thought she had, but now she was back here getting sucked in by the same forces that had trapped her aunts and her mother and her sisters, too.

Sunlight glinted over the mesa, and she flipped down the visor. Glancing to her right, she watched rows of yucca trees rush by, mesmerizing lines that stretched toward a distant vanishing point. She passed the sign for Lost Mine Road. The old mining cabin came into view, a jumbled pile of rocks that only vaguely resembled the shape of a house.

Izzy tapped the brakes. Pulling onto the shoulder, she parked and dipped her head to look through the passenger-side window. She stared at the crumbling house for a moment, then grabbed her camera and slid from the car. Keeping her attention on the run-down structure, she walked around the back of her car and looped the camera strap over her head.

This old mining cabin was at the far edge of the yucca field near the base of a canyon. The abandoned mercury mine was somewhere around here, too, if she remembered her local history right.

Izzy glanced around, lifting her hand to shield her face from the late-day sun. Quicksilver Canyon, she was pretty sure this was called. She slid the phone from her fleece and consulted a mapping app. Yes, Quicksilver Canyon, which cut through the west side of the yucca farm.

She glanced up and spotted the distant sign for the farm that she'd driven past so many times. But she'd never stopped before, or even really noticed this place. Her boots crunched over the gravel as she crossed the shoulder and approached the barbed-wire fence that separated her from the property. A pair of metal NO TRESPASSING signs dangled from the rusty wire. One of the signs included an AR-15 graphic to drive home the point.

Izzy looked past the fence, and her pulse picked up as she studied the old ruins. No roof, no doors, just crumbling walls and a chimney surrounded by creosote and cactus bushes. Time and weather had sculpted the flat stones, and they looked like stacked pancakes, golden and glowing in the evening sun.

Izzy ducked through the fence. Her fleece snagged on a barb, and she jerked it free. Glancing around, she looked for the farmer or landowner, but no one was in sight. In the distance beyond the yucca crop was a low white farmhouse and a gray trailer home tucked beneath a cluster of oak trees. Beside them was an arched hut that looked like maybe a nursery for plants.

Izzy adjusted the settings on her camera as she approached the old ruins. The evening light was perfect now, creating crisp shadows, and the golden prairie grass rippled in the breeze. Picking her way through, she circled the crumbling house, searching for the perfect vantage point. Nothing felt quite right, so she just began shooting.

At the paneless window, she crouched down to get a more dramatic angle. The stones made a frame around a rectangle of pink sky streaked with feathery clouds. It was a striking sunset view, and she could only imagine how the same scene would look when the stars came out. The composition reminded her of La Ventana, the rock formation she'd photographed back at Gold Springs

Trail. If she could capture the Milky Way through this window, the two rock windows could be a pair—one man-made and one created by nature. The idea of it brought a rush of adrenaline.

Izzy rounded the building, getting more and more excited as she captured shot after shot in the fading light. Why had she never been out here before? This place was a gem. But unlike the landmarks within the park boundaries, this spot hadn't been photographed repeatedly to the point of being overdone.

She crouched down and captured another shot through the window, and her energy picked up again. She felt giddy with excitement. This subject was original. She needed to come back after dark and really nail this.

Izzy stood and looked at the farmhouse again. Normally, her philosophy about private property was to snap away and hope no one noticed. And if they did, she would politely explain that she was a nature photographer and something on their land had caught her eye. But she should probably get permission this time. For one thing, she wanted to come back again after dark. But for another thing, the AR sign.

She slung her camera around to her side and started trekking toward the house, following a narrow path that linked up with the dirt road coming off the highway. She studied the rows of yucca and agave plants as she walked. This whole place was worth photographing. She imagined what the crop rows would look like from a high vantage point, such as the top of the stone bluff to the west.

For the first time in months, she felt a genuine spring in her step. The confidence was back, a tangible *thing* that she had once taken for granted but that had been replaced by fear and exhaustion. Lately, her confidence had seemed to shrink, and she'd been overwhelmed by feelings of defeat, a dark sense that no matter how hard she tried to carve a path for herself, her choices were predetermined, and her dreams were destined to fall by the wayside.

Right now, though, in *this* exact moment, at the close of *this* exact day, she suddenly felt different. Like herself again. And hopeful—*hopeful*—so much so that the whiplash of it made her smile.

Her shoe caught on a rut, and she stumbled forward, catching herself. Deep tire marks were carved into the road, and she looked at the pattern as she neared the farmhouse.

Izzy halted.

She studied the tire impressions. Then she glanced up at the trailer near the house, where a dusty truck was parked. The old white pickup looked like hundreds of others around here. Except for the tires. They weren't the standard size, but bigger.

Her pulse picked up and her mind started racing. Approaching the trailer, she thought back to the photo Leanne had shown her. Coincidence? Maybe. But something in her gut told her no.

About ten yards from the truck, Izzy stopped and stared at the Ridge Grappler tires. Her pulse was racing a mile a minute now. Before she could talk herself out of it, she lifted her camera and took a photo.

"Hey!"

She whirled around to see a man on the front porch pointing a shotgun straight at her.

Leanne whipped into her driveway and rushed to her door. Fumbling with her keys, she ignored Gus's high-pitched mewing. She hurried inside, and Gus darted in behind her.

Leanne went straight to the spare bedroom, where cardboard moving boxes were stacked against the wall. She hadn't touched a single one of them in months.

She lifted several boxes off the top and heaved them onto the floor as she read the labels. Then she grabbed another box and moved it atop the first two.

The large bottom box was labeled "Books/Misc."

Leanne retrieved a metal nail file from the bathroom, sliced through the packing tape, and opened the flaps. The box smelled musty and neglected, like so much of her personal life since she'd moved home to Madrone. She rummaged through a layer of paperbacks until she reached the hardcover books at the bottom. Culling through the piles, she spied her yearbooks. She grabbed the oldest one, from her freshman year, and set it on the tower of boxes. Hannah Rawls would have been a senior, and Sean Moriarty would have graduated the spring before.

"Come on, come on," she muttered, flying through the glossy pages until she reached the section for after-school activities.

Yearbook Staff.

The photo beneath the heading showed a group of high school kids slouched in chairs around a row of computers. Some kids had their feet propped on desks and some had cameras around their necks. Leanne skimmed the faces, trying to conjure names to go with them.

Her attention caught on a familiar smile.

"Oh. My. God."

Izzy's heart was in her throat.

"I . . . please," she stammered. "I was just—"

"Enough!"

Her stomach seized. She wanted to throw up. The man glared at her down the barrel of the shotgun.

A screen door squeaked open somewhere behind her.

"Whoa, whoa, whoa, Dad, *no*!"

The door smacked shut. Someone ran up behind her, but

she had tunnel vision, and all she could see was that black gun barrel.

The old man looked over her head. "You know this one?"

"She's fine, okay? Put that thing away."

Scowling, the man lowered the gun and gave her a long, hateful look. Then he spat on the dirt and walked inside. The screen door slammed behind him, and Izzy's shoulders slumped.

Slowly, she turned around.

"Sorry about that."

THIRTY-NINE

Duncan called her as she sped down the highway.

"Where have you been?" Leanne asked. "I tried—"

"Big development," he cut in. "Where are you?"

"Driving."

"Okay, I just got off the phone with a buddy of mine in the FBI field office in El Paso. You know how I told you there was something screwy with the lab, and my DNA results got put on hold?"

"You're talking about the DNA test on the duct tape?"

"Right. Well, I found out what the holdup was," Duncan said. "Turns out, the sample I submitted got a cold hit."

"A cold hit. You mean—"

"It matched a sample from *another* crime scene. A cold case," he said. "And get this—that cold case is one of the ones on your list."

"You're kidding."

"I'm dead serious."

Leanne veered around an eighteen-wheeler doing a sluggish sixty miles per hour.

"Which case is it?" she asked.

"One of the ones the forensic anthropologist told you about.

This case was eight years ago down in Presidio County, near Marfa."

Leanne's pulse picked up. "The woman with the duct tape in her hair."

"Exactly. But it wasn't duct tape that was submitted. This was from a DNA sample from under the victim's fingernails."

Leanne knew the case immediately. "The side of her face was bashed in, too, and she had a broken wrist. Did Jen Sayers submit this? Why didn't she tell me?"

"Because she's not the one who sent it," he said. "That's the other thing. This evidence was submitted by the FBI as part of an investigation."

It took a moment for his words to sink in.

"Since when does the FBI investigate murders in Presidio County?" she asked.

"*That's* what I'm getting at. They're involved in this somehow, but I'm still not sure why and to what extent. I'm trying to get answers. But in the meantime, my friend gave me a huge tip. After this original profile didn't get any matches in CODIS, the FBI sent it to a genetic genealogist, who was able to develop a family tree based on links between this perpetrator's DNA and DNA samples that have been uploaded to those commercial ancestry sites. You know what I'm talking about?"

"Forensic genealogy."

"Right," he said. "So, this genetic profile traces back to a family right here in Chisos County."

"Justin Carr."

A beat passed.

"How the *hell* did you know that?" Duncan asked.

"Because five minutes ago he became my prime suspect," she told him. "I'm on my way to interview him now."

"What?"

"I need to talk to him, feel him out. And I want him on his guard in case he's thinking about doing anything."

"Are you fucking kidding me? You can't just show up at this guy's door, Leanne."

"Why not?"

Silence.

"You know damn well that's what you would do if you got a suspect in your sights," she said.

"*No*, I wouldn't. First, I'd get my shit together and confirm it's him."

"I know it's him."

"How?" he demanded. "According to this genealogist, there are *three* male relatives in this family who could have done it. Justin and his brother, Joel, and also his dad, Harlow. All three resided in Chisos County eight years ago at the time of the murder, and any one of them could have—"

"It's Justin. I've got corroborating evidence, and I don't have time to explain everything now, but I can tell you he fits my criminal profile."

"Since when do you have a criminal profile?"

"Since this morning."

"Just . . . wait, okay? Think this through a minute. What are you going to gain by charging over there and banging on his door before we're ready?"

"I *am* ready. Now! Today! If he's our guy, then he's killed *two* women in the past two weeks alone. He's escalating, Duncan. I'm going to go over there and talk to him and take a look at his tires and hopefully get probable cause for an arrest warrant so we can—"

"All right, all right. I hear you. At least wait for me and I can meet you over there."

Leanne didn't want to wait. It was dusk already. What if he was planning to go out tonight, trolling for his next victim? What if she missed her chance to intercept him?

"If it's really your guy, then he's been active for twelve years, Leanne."

"Longer than that."

She still hadn't told him her controversial theory about Hannah Rawls. She'd been too ashamed of her dad's involvement to bring it up, but there was no avoiding it now. Everything was going to come out—the wrongful conviction, the cover-up. The subsequent murders that had been virtually ignored.

"Don't blow this whole case by being impatient," Duncan said. "Wait for me, all right? Where are you?"

"West edge of town. Justin lives in a trailer on his dad's yucca farm."

"What if he's not home? He could be at work or—"

"He's a river guide with Big Bend Outfitters, and I called over there to check," she said. "He's off work today. I've already made a plan, and you're not talking me out of this."

"I'll meet you there in ten minutes. We'll talk to him together."

"I don't need—"

"You're better off with two people, Leanne. Don't be stubborn and sabotage all your hard work."

She bit back an argument because she knew he was right. And she also knew that if she had a better relationship with her police chief, she would have called him to fill him in and obtain backup from her own department.

But the bottom line was, she flat-out didn't trust him, and she'd rather risk going alone than let McBride in on her plan.

"You know I'm right," Duncan said.

"Fine. Be there in ten, or I'm going without you."

They disconnected, and she cursed to herself as she stared at the highway ahead. If it had been Duncan rushing off to interview a murder suspect, she could be damn sure he wouldn't have called her for help.

But it wasn't a bad idea to have backup. She could admit that.

Still, she hated waiting, especially when she desperately wanted to take a look around and get some sort of evidence that she could use as probable cause for an arrest warrant. Maybe she could get Justin to give her a DNA sample somehow, maybe by getting him to touch something or by picking up some of his trash, such as a drinking straw. She'd have to figure it out on the fly, because what she *wasn't* going to do was let him slip through her fingers and go out hunting for his next victim. Delays and inaction had already resulted in unspeakable tragedy.

Justin Carr.

Justin.

She'd known him for years. For her entire *life.*

Going into this whole thing, Leanne had realized that when she finally homed in on a suspect, it might be someone she knew. As soon as it became clear the UNSUB was someone local, she'd braced herself for that outcome.

Or at least, she thought she had. But she'd never imagined this.

It was a gut punch.

Justin. Someone she'd gone to school with and had beers with and even had sex with years ago on a booze-soaked New Year's Eve when she'd been home visiting. They'd met up at a friend's party, and now just the memory of his hands on her body made her want to hurl.

Leanne shuddered, wishing she could erase the memory. She felt nauseated. Justin Carr was a predator. A monster. She pictured him back at the Javelina Cantina, hanging out with Liam Moriarty on the weekend of Sean's release. She remembered how his words had cut her.

Your dad ruined his brother's life.

Fury burned inside her. No, *he* had ruined Sean Moriarty's life—Sean's life and so many others. So many decimated families, including her own, all because of him. He'd cut a path of destruction through their lives, and he'd done it silently, stealthily, without anyone even knowing it, including every last cop who'd sworn a duty to protect this community.

And every last one of them had failed.

The sign for Carr Farms came into view, and Leanne slowed. A silver Honda Civic was pulled over on the side of the road. Leanne's heart skipped a beat.

Izzy's car.

What the hell? She pulled a U-turn and parked behind the Honda. It looked empty. Leanne jumped out, glancing around as she approached the vehicle.

"Izzy?" she called.

She cupped her hand over the glass and peered inside. A set of keys sat in one of the cup holders. In the other was a water bottle.

With a sinking feeling, Leanne opened the door and examined the seat and the steering wheel, looking for blood. She touched the water bottle, and it was still cool.

"Damn it!" Leanne looked around. "*Izzy?*"

Leanne circled the car but didn't see any sign of a flat tire or engine trouble or a dented bumper. Why had she pulled over?

Leanne called Duncan but it went straight to voicemail.

"New plan," she told him. "I'm going now."

Izzy stared at Justin across the cab of his truck. He didn't look at her. Didn't talk. But that silver handgun on his dashboard said a lot. He'd offered her a ride back to her car, and she'd tried to refuse, but he had insisted. And in the moment, she'd thought it was better to act normal than let on that she was afraid of him.

But when he got behind the wheel and put that gun there, it was obvious she'd made a terrible mistake.

She looked out the window now as they bumped over the ruts

in the road, moving farther and farther away from the highway where she'd parked. Heart racing, she glanced down at her door handle, but it was locked.

She cleared her throat. "Thanks for the ride."

Her voice sounded thin and raspy. Had he heard the fear in it?

She looked at him. "Where are we going?"

He didn't answer. Just kept driving.

She looked away again. Her heart was pounding so fast she was lightheaded. Bile welled in the back of her throat.

Justin Carr. *He's the one.*

Her brain felt numb from it. She'd known him for so long, she couldn't even remember meeting him. They hadn't gone to school together or shared the same friends. But somehow, they'd always known each other's names. Like she'd always known Nadine and Bip and Father Walter. Justin was someone who was just *around*, like everyone else, part of her scenery.

Izzy's stomach churned as they bumped along, and she tried to think of what she knew about him, frantic to come up with some kind of leverage she could use. But what she knew didn't amount to much. Justin was a river rat, a rafting guide. He rode mountain bikes, too, and he was an amateur photographer. She'd seen his pictures here and there, and he did social media posts for his company, Big Bend Outfitters.

An icy realization washed over her.

He'd been right there at the trailhead the other night. He must have just—

"Saw you checking out my tires," he said.

Izzy's stomach knotted.

"Why'd you take that picture?"

"What picture?"

He shot her a look. "Don't play dumb, Izzy. I saw you."

Her mind went blank. She opened her mouth, but nothing came out. She couldn't think of a single excuse.

He looked at the road again, shaking his head. "You should have minded your own business."

"I wasn't—"

"*Shut up!*"

His outburst shattered the fake calm. She looked ahead, heart thundering.

There was no pretending now.

She knew.

He *knew* she knew.

And that gun on that dashboard—within easy reach for him—was an undeniable signal that she'd made a bad mistake.

Izzy's heart pounded as she tried to come up with a plan. What little she knew about him seemed like nothing compared to what she *didn't* know. Where was his family? Besides his crazy father who'd threatened her with a shotgun, who were they? Did anyone else live here on this farm with them? Standing on that porch, Justin's dad had looked wild-eyed. By contrast, Justin seemed calmer.

But she sensed the hot *anger* coming off him in waves.

Justin felt trapped. Because of her.

She'd cornered him—without meaning to, but she had. And now she was going to pay the price.

This man sitting inches away from her had killed women and beaten them to a pulp. She pictured the victim by the train tracks, and suddenly the bile was back again, making her want to throw up.

Don't do it. Don't! Think of a plan . . .

She looked out the window at the rows and rows of spiky desert plants. Her palms were sweaty. Her back, her neck. And her heart was beating so fast, it felt like it might burst right out of her chest.

What had she been thinking, coming here? How had she let her guard down? She'd been so caught up in the moment, she'd let go of the paranoia she'd carried with her for days. And she'd walked right into this.

Would anyone see her car on the side of the highway? She thought of the phone in her pocket. Slowly, she eased her hand toward it, praying he wouldn't notice.

The truck pitched forward. She bit her tongue and caught her hand on the dash as Justin skidded to a stop.

"We're here." He grabbed the gun and pointed it at her, then used his other hand to shove the gearshift into park.

"Get out."

"But I—"

"Get the fuck out!"

Out was good. She could make a run for it. Panic spurted through her as she looked around at the desolate landscape. She reached for the door handle.

FORTY

Leanne jogged up to the farmhouse, scanning the dusky shadows. It was nightfall, and the last of the day's light had nearly faded. She spied a truck up ahead, near the tree by the trailer.

Liam Moriarty's truck.

The screen door of the farmhouse slapped open, and Leanne halted, reaching for her weapon. A shadowy figure sprinted down the steps.

"Stop!"

He turned toward her voice, and Leanne strode forward, aiming her gun.

Sean Moriarty. She'd know those wide shoulders and that shaved head anywhere.

He rested his hands on his hips and watched her approach him.

"He's got Izzy."

She halted. "What? Who does?"

"Justin. He took her off in his truck." Sean nodded at the house. "I just talked to Harlow Carr."

"But why would—"

"I know where they went." Sean moved for his pickup.

"*Stop.*"

Leanne stepped closer, still pointing her weapon at him.

"I know where they are," he growled. "Don't waste time."

Leanne stopped in front of him, studying his lean face in the dim light. His gray eyes looked intense, and the tendons of his neck bulged.

"Hands against the truck."

"Are you fucking kidding? We don't have *time*."

"Hands against the truck!"

Shaking his head, he turned and put his hands on the roof of the pickup.

Leanne did a quick pat down and came up with a pistol tucked in the back of his jeans beneath his shirt. She didn't know what Sean was up to, coming over here armed, but it couldn't be good.

He glared over his shoulder. "You done?"

She tucked the gun into the back of her own jeans and then holstered her service weapon. "Let's go."

Sean jogged around the front of the pickup, and Leanne swung open the passenger door with a creak. As she got inside, she glanced around the truck cab for any other weapons. Fast-food cups littered the floor and the truck smelled of tobacco spit.

"What are you doing out here?" she asked him.

He didn't answer, just fired up the engine and shot. He shoved it into drive and lurched forward on the bumpy road.

"Where's he taking her?" she asked. "Did you see him?"

"No."

Leanne pulled out her phone and called dispatch. She relayed her name and location and urgently requested assistance. Then she hung up and called Duncan. No answer.

"God*damn* it!"

She tapped out a text and sent it, then turned to Sean.

"Where is he taking her?" she asked again.

"I don't know."

"What do you mean you don't know? You said you—"

"I don't know for sure," he told her. "But I think the mine."

Leanne's stomach plummeted. "The *mine*? Like, the abandoned mercury mine?"

"Yeah."

"Where is that?" She whipped out her phone and pulled up a satellite map. "Why would he take her there?"

Sean sent her a sideways glance, and Leanne's blood turned to ice.

Did he think Izzy was dead?

Sweet Lord, was he dumping a *body*?

Leanne's phone chimed. Duncan.

"Why did you—"

"Get to Carr Farms, ASAP!" she told him. "He's got Izzy."

"*What?*"

"Did you listen to my message? Izzy's car is out here, and she's not in it. I'm with Sean Moriarty, and he thinks he knows where Justin's taking her."

Silence as Duncan absorbed this.

"We're moving west, I repeat *west*, on an interior road"—she twisted in her seat and looked out the back window—"heading away from the house that's on the property. You copy?"

"Did you say you're with Sean Moriarty?"

"Yes." She glanced at him. "He's familiar with the area. Call it in, all right? I already did, but it'll help to hear from both of us."

Nothing.

"Duncan?"

"Roger that. Be careful."

Leanne hung up and looked at Sean behind the wheel. The glow from the dashboard lights reflected off his shaved head. He looked intense. Focused. The vein at his temple pulsed.

He looked enraged.

Leanne gazed ahead as the twin headlight beams bounced over rocks and cacti. They weren't even on a road now. They were driving through a field, mowing down plants.

"Why are we—"

"Shortcut," he snapped, seeming to read her mind.

Leanne stared ahead as fear settled over her. She closed her eyes and thought of that cold water bottle in Izzy's car. If only she'd gotten here ten minutes sooner.

The truck bounced as they curved left, making an arc around a weathered wooden windmill. Sean seemed to know his way around here.

What else did he know?

She studied his profile in the dimness, the angle of his nose and the hard set of his jaw. A prison tattoo peeked up from his collar, another reminder of all the years he'd spent behind bars, time he would never get back.

"Justin did it," Leanne said.

She watched his face, needing to see how he'd react.

Nothing at all. Which told her he knew.

"When did you figure it out?"

"I had fifteen years." He glanced at her. "That's a lot of hours to fill."

She looked ahead as they bounced and pitched over the rugged terrain. Fifteen years, stolen from him. Did he blame Justin? Her father? Cops in general?

And did he want revenge?

"Why'd you come out here with a gun?" she asked.

No answer. He just stared ahead.

"Why would you risk your freedom after all this time?"

Still nothing.

"You need to let the police handle it," she told him. "Don't do something stupid. You need to stay out of the way."

Again, nothing, but the air between them was electric with tension.

Leanne rested her hand on her holster and at the same time felt the weight of Sean's pistol against the small of her back. It was surreal that she was here, in a truck with a man she had demonized for her entire adult life. How many times had she wanted to confront him, to yell and scream and vent all her hatred at the person whose heinous act had caused so much suffering for so many people she knew?

That long-ago summer had been an earthquake. A bomb blast. Pick your disaster. It had marked the beginning of the end for her family. The murder of Hannah Rawls was the moment everything fell apart. It was the moment her parents' marriage started to crack and her little brother went into a tailspin. It was the moment Leanne's life was upended, the moment she lost her innocence and her footing and her faith.

Did she want it back again? No. Those things were bound to go sometime. Anything resembling optimism was a liability for someone on her chosen career path. But still, she'd been angry. Bitter. Furious at Sean Moriarty and everything that his one fateful act had cost them all.

For all these years, she'd blamed him. Part of her still did, even though logic told her she was wrong, and she needed to trust him.

Trust him.

Trust *Sean Moriarty*.

The thought alone made her eye start to twitch. In this pivotal moment, she was putting her trust in a man she'd hated for years, who no doubt hated her right back.

He glanced at her. "What?"

She looked out the window. "I hope to hell you know where you're going." She shook her head. "You better not be driving us off a cliff."

Izzy glanced around, trying to get her bearings. It was dark now, and the only light came from the headlight beams, which stretched across an endless field of scrub brush. Where were they?

"Come on."

"Where are we—"

"*Move.*" He shoved her shoulder blade, and she tripped to the ground, then scrambled to her feet.

"*Faster.*"

Izzy's heart squeezed as she stumbled forward into the darkness. In her path were weeds and cactus plants, and she stepped around them as she tried to come up with a plan. Then the truck's headlights went off, and everything became pitch dark. She slid her hand into her pocket and tapped at her phone, hoping she could maybe call someone.

Behind her, a flashlight switched on.

"Hey," he said, wrenching her arm back. He pried the phone from her fingers and stared at it a moment before swiping at the screen, powering it off.

Killing her last hope of calling for help.

"Justin, please. Could you just—"

"Go! Now!"

She turned around and moved forward, picking her way through the field. The beam of his flashlight lit up weeds and plants, casting haphazard shadows across the dirt. She glanced up at the sky. It was dark, not even a moon yet to see by. And never in her life had she felt the vastness of the land until right this moment. It was huge. And *empty*. She could run and scream, and no one would hear her, way out here. They probably wouldn't even hear a gunshot.

"Stop."

She halted, glancing around. There was nothing and no one, just shadows and scrub trees.

She was isolated. She turned to face him, shielding her eyes against the glare of the flashlight.

"Please. Justin." She stepped toward him. "Let me go. I promise I won't tell anyone—"

"Shut the fuck up." The light jerked sideways. "Over there. Go." The light jerked again. "*Go.*"

She turned. But all she saw was a big black hole, like a cave.

"I don't understand. What—"

"*Now!*"

Pain jolted through her as he kicked her hip, sending her into the abyss.

FORTY-ONE

Sean rolled to a stop beside a huge boulder. He shoved the truck into park, killed the headlights, and jumped out.

Leanne checked her phone, but no word from anyone. She jumped out, too, and slammed the door.

"Where are we?"

Sean was already tromping off into the darkness.

"Hey!" She jogged after him. "Where are we?"

"He took her out here."

"Where? What is this?"

Sean grabbed her arm and dropped into a crouch, pulling her along with him. "Keep your voice down," he said.

She rested her knee on the ground, and the cold seeped through the fabric of her jeans. "How do you know about this place?" she whispered.

"It's the only thing out here. We used to come here and smoke weed."

"Who did?"

"Me and Justin and my brother. This is where he'd take her, trust me."

The interior light of the truck went off, plunging them into total darkness. She couldn't see a damn thing. She crouched there beside him, squinting into the gloom and letting her eyes adjust.

"You were friends with Justin?" she asked quietly.

He grunted. "Liam was. This was back in high school. Justin had a thing for Hannah then, too. Everyone did."

"You think he—"

"Shh!"

They fell silent. Leanne couldn't hear anything, not even traffic on the distant highway. As her eyes acclimated, she became aware of a tall black canyon wall rising to their west, sheltering them from sounds and lights of the surrounding area.

"Where the hell are we?" she whispered.

"The mine entrance."

The mercury mine. The cinnabar ore that made these canyons red contained mercury, also known as quicksilver, and the remnants of mining operations were scattered around the area. This mine had been abandoned for half a century.

Leanne's chest hurt as she thought about why Justin might bring Izzy out here, either alive or dead. She gripped Sean's arm in the darkness.

"Where is it?"

He leaned closer, and she felt his warm breath on her ear. "The entrance is about ten yards that way."

Leanne got to her feet and squinted into the blackness. She couldn't see anything at all.

Sean stood up.

"*Show me*," she whispered. "We have to get to her!"

Instead of answering, he grabbed her sleeve and pulled her forward. She rested her hand on his back, following him through the darkness that he was somehow able to navigate fine. Meanwhile, she may as well have been blindfolded.

He came to a stop, and she bumped into him.

Snick.

His hand lit up with the flame of a Zippo lighter. Using it as a torch, he crept around a massive boulder that Leanne hadn't even realized was there.

He stopped.

"There," he whispered.

"Where?"

Peering around his wide shoulders, she saw nothing. Then the earthy smell of bat guano reached her. Squinting into the shadows, she made out a black-on-black rectangle.

"Is that—"

"The mine entrance."

Her stomach clenched. "You think they're in there?"

"Definitely. I saw his truck parked back behind that tree."

"What tree?"

"Come on," he said, tugging her forward.

Sliding her weapon from its holster, Leanne followed him from what now seemed like semidarkness into a tunnel of complete and utter *black*. Even the glow of his lighter barely penetrated.

The temperature dropped as they crept through what felt like a spacious tunnel. The guano smell wafted around them, and she heard a faint, faraway squeak.

Bats.

How many thousands or millions might be in here? She stifled a shudder as she crept along, listening to their distant squeals.

And something else. Something human.

She grabbed Sean's arm. "Hear that?"

"Yeah."

He quickened his pace as they moved through the cold blackness, closing in on the sound. It was a low voice. A woman. And the tone was unmistakable.

Leanne's heart convulsed. It was Izzy, and she was pleading for her life.

The Zippo lighter disappeared, and they were in total blackness, but still moving forward. They seemed to veer right, and Leanne made out the texture of wood planks along the walls as the tunnel curved, getting brighter and brighter, until there they were.

Justin. And Izzy, kneeling before him, hands in the air, pleading tearfully as he pointed a gun at her chest. Beside Izzy on the ground was a flashlight that cast both of them in a ghostly white light.

Sean yanked Leanne back, out of view, but it was too late, and Izzy stopped pleading midsentence.

"Hey!" Justin called. "Who's there?"

Silence.

Then a scream pierced the air. Leanne ducked around Sean and lifted her gun.

"Police! Drop your weapon!"

Justin had Izzy in front of him, holding a gun to her throat.

"Don't do it. Don't fucking do it or I'll blow her head off!"

Izzy whimpered and closed her eyes.

Leanne's heart squeezed. *How* had she let this happen? She stepped closer, keeping her arms steady as she took aim at the edge of Justin's head.

Which was right behind Izzy's. He was ducking behind her, using her as a shield. Meanwhile, his left hand pressed the gun to Izzy's neck.

"Justin, man," Sean said. "Don't be stupid."

"Hey." Leanne didn't take her eyes off Justin as she spoke to Sean. "You stay out of it."

Justin's eyes jumped from Leanne to Sean. "What the fuck are you doing here? Why'd you bring her?"

"She's looking for her friend."

"*Hey*." Leanne shot Sean a glare. "Not another word."

"Put the gun down!" Justin hooked an arm around Izzy's waist and yanked her closer. "Put it down or she's dead!"

"Let's calm down, Justin," Leanne said. "Okay? Let's all relax."

"I said put it down!"

Izzy yelped as Justin jabbed the gun at her throat. She squeezed her eyes shut, and the wet tracks of tears glinted on her face. Another whimper as he shoved the gun at her jaw.

Leanne's thoughts raced. She'd trained for this. Back at the academy, years and years ago. But the hostage then had been another cadet playing a role, and nothing about that situation seemed relevant now as she looked into Justin's frantic eyes and saw the stark terror on Izzy's face. Her chest heaved up and down as Justin squeezed her against him.

He lifted the gun to Izzy's temple. "I said . . . Put. The fucking. Gun. Down."

"Do it," Sean murmured.

Leanne's throat went dry. She felt the hard press of Sean's confiscated pistol tucked into the back of her jeans. Slowly, she raised her left hand in the air, keeping her right hand steady as she gripped her weapon.

"Okay, Justin, I hear you. All right? Let's talk through this."

"We'll talk when you put the gun down."

"Putting it down now, okay?" She slowly bent her knees, lowering her weapon to the ground. How fast could she pull Sean's pistol out? She couldn't even remember what kind it was. She didn't know if it had a safety, or if it was even loaded.

Justin lurched forward, thrusting Izzy ahead of him, still pressing that gun to her head.

"Kick it," he ordered.

"What?" Izzy squeaked.

"Kick it!"

Bug-eyed with fear, Izzy glanced back at Justin, and then looked down at Leanne's pistol, lying useless in the dirt. She met Leanne's gaze for an instant before kicking the gun away. It skittered past Leanne and careened into the tunnel wall, well out of reach.

"Justin, man, you don't want to do this, trust me."

"*You*, shut up!"

"What are you going to do? Kill all of us?" Sean snorted. "You think you're going to get away with that? Come on, man. They're onto you."

"Justin, tell me what you want," Leanne said.

"Shut up!" He backed away, pulling Izzy with him, and then glanced over his shoulder at something behind him.

For the first time, Leanne noticed the ledge.

A big black . . . nothing . . . a few feet behind Justin. Panic spurted through her. Was it the mine shaft? It had to be hundreds of feet deep.

She stared at Justin. Even if she could pull out Sean's pistol in time, and take aim, she didn't have a clear shot with Izzy blocking most of his body mass. It would have to be a head shot.

"Man, think this through," Sean said. He'd inched away from her at some point, creating distance between them. "Let her go, and you can walk right out of here."

"Fuck you, Moriarty. I know what you're doing."

"What?" Sean took another step sideways.

What *was* he doing? He was moving farther away from both of their guns. Maybe he was trying to create a distraction so that she could whip out his pistol and get a shot off.

Leanne focused on Justin again, but he had Izzy plastered against him so close, it was an impossible angle. She glanced around, grasping for a plan.

And then she saw it. The glint of something in Sean's back pocket. In a heartbeat, she realized what was about to happen.

Sean darted a glance in her direction, signaling her, and she tried to signal back—*Don't do it!*

But Sean reached for the blade, and everything seemed to slow, like moving through water.

Light caught the blade as it cartwheeled through the air with a *swoosh*.

Leanne lunged forward.

An ear-piercing shriek echoed around them as Justin fell.

Leanne grabbed Izzy's wrist, yanking her to the ground.

And then Sean leaped on Justin, and everything became a tangle of arms and legs and dust.

"Hey!" Leanne lurched into the fray. "Sean! Get off him!"

Blood streamed down Justin's face as he twisted on the ground, dodging Sean's blows, the knife handle protruding from his cheek.

"Stop!"

Leanne flipped Justin onto his front and dropped a knee onto his back.

"I got him," Sean said, pinning Justin's arms.

Leanne whipped out a pair of handcuffs and reached for his wrist.

Sean did a double take. "What the fuck? Shoot him!"

She glared at him. "No." She reached for Justin's other hand and wrestled it behind his back as he bucked beneath her, bellowing like a stuck pig.

Sean leaned down and yanked the knife from Justin's cheek. Blood gushed from the wound.

Amid the chaos, a fleece-covered arm reached in, and Leanne glanced up to see Izzy digging something from Justin's back pocket. A cell phone.

"Are you okay?" Leanne asked her.

Izzy looked shell-shocked as she backed away from the howling, bleeding man, clutching the phone in her hand.

"Go outside," Leanne ordered. "Call 911."

Izzy blinked at her, as though the words didn't compute.

"Izzy, listen to me! Call 911."

She turned and ran.

Searing pain flashed across Leanne's face as she took a blow to the eye.

"Hey!" she yelled. She grabbed Justin's flailing elbow and pinned it to the ground with her knee.

"Fucking cunt! Get off me!"

She pressed his bleeding face into the dirt. "You're under arrest."

FORTY-TWO

Leanne's eye was killing her.

She shifted the ice pack on her face and squinted at the crowd gathered in front of the gray trailer. Police vehicles and ambulances and even fire trucks lined the road. The scene, which was lit up by portable klieg lights, was crawling with cops and first responders, and she didn't even know them all.

But she recognized the blurry form approaching her.

"Hey," Mark said, stopping in front of her. For the past ten minutes, she'd been perched on the tailgate of a Chisos Fire and Rescue truck, icing her face as she waited for McBride. "How's it going?"

"Fine," she said, pulling the ice pack away.

Mark winced. "That looks bad."

"How's the chief?" she asked, nodding toward the huddle of law enforcement brass where McBride seemed to be giving a briefing.

"He's pissed," Mark told her. "What exactly did you do, anyway?"

"No idea," she lied. "You'd think he'd be happy we cracked the case finally."

Leanne knew part of what had gotten under McBride's skin

was the "we." He didn't like sharing the spotlight—or the credit—with the sheriff's office, which included Duncan. And he sure as hell didn't like sharing credit with the FBI, which had provided the critical DNA lead that broke the case and ultimately implicated Justin Carr in the string of murders.

"Well, at least he got to have his perp walk," Leanne said.

After showing up at the scene, the chief had ordered Leanne to stay here for a debriefing while he personally escorted Justin in for booking, which no doubt included parading him in front of any reporters who were there.

"So, what's *he* doing here?" Mark said, nodding toward the farmhouse.

Leanne turned around. Sean Moriarty leaned against the front porch, his arms folded over his chest as he watched the scene play out in front of him. He had refused to talk to investigators until his lawyer showed up, and Leanne didn't blame him. He wasn't under arrest for anything, but he'd been instructed not to leave, and every cop here was treating him like he was radioactive.

"He and Justin Carr have a beef about something," Leanne told Mark.

"About what?"

She shook her head. "It goes back a long time."

Mark frowned down at her, clearly picking up on the fact that she knew more than she was saying. But she didn't plan to reveal anything else. The story would come out at some point, but right now there was still no proof that Justin Carr killed Hannah Rawls.

Leanne believed it.

Sean Moriarty believed it.

But without more evidence, the case was circumstantial, and being left-handed wasn't a capital offense.

Mark glanced around at the emergency personnel. "Hey, you haven't seen Josh anywhere, have you?"

"Last I saw, he was in the house." Leanne nodded toward it. "He and Akers are helping with the search warrant."

Duncan trudged over, and Leanne braced herself for a confrontation. He had arrived along with the first wave of sirens, and they still hadn't had a moment alone together.

"Leanne?"

She looked at Mark. "Sorry. What's that?"

"I said, do you need anything here?"

"No. Thanks, but I'm good."

Mark nodded. "I'm going to go see if Josh wants a hand."

He walked off as Duncan reached her.

"Hi," she said.

He towered over her, hands on hips, his sheriff's badge dangling from a lanyard around his neck. "You get your head checked out?"

"Not yet."

"That shiner looks bad, Leanne."

"It's not." She rested the ice pack in her lap. "What's up?"

"Thought you'd want to know—the FBI is on the way down here."

"Good for them."

"This is going to turn into a turf war."

"It already is." Leanne surveyed the scene. She'd counted four separate law enforcement agencies so far, and those were just the ones she could see from her vantage point. "What'd you expect? Everyone wants a piece of the action."

Duncan's jaw tensed as he stared down at her. He was still unhappy that she'd gone in without him—not to mention that she'd gone in with Sean Moriarty—and she didn't plan to defend her decision.

"I offered to drive Izzy home," Duncan said now.

"Izzy? I thought she left already." Leanne slid off the tailgate and looked around.

"The paramedic was checking her out. He gave her the all clear."

"You sure? She seemed like she was in shock to me. I think she should go to the clinic."

"She says she wants to get home."

Leanne spied Izzy near a fence post talking to Travis Malcom. She wore an oversize Chisos County Sheriff's jacket that practically swallowed her. Leanne's heart went out to her.

"Thanks for driving her," Leanne said. "Tell her I'll give her a call later."

"Will do."

Duncan stared down at her for a long moment.

"What?"

"Nothing."

"*What?*"

He shook his head and walked away.

Leanne watched him go with a lump in her throat. She didn't know why, really, just that her emotions were raw tonight.

"Leanne."

She glanced around and spotted Josh beside the door of Justin Carr's trailer. The quickie search warrant they'd secured had included both buildings on the property.

Leanne left her ice pack on the tailgate and walked over, aware of Sean Moriarty watching her every move.

"What's up?" she asked Josh.

"You need to see this," he said in a low voice.

Leanne searched his face. Something in his eyes put her nerves on edge. She mounted the warped wooden stairs and stepped into the trailer.

A familiar *click click click* came from the back as a forensic photographer snapped pictures. But it wasn't Izzy this time. Leanne surveyed the cramped living room. CSIs had set up a spotlight in the corner to illuminate the scene. A stained green futon was shoved in the corner opposite a TV, and a woven Mexican blanket lay wadded on the floor beside an empty pizza box.

"Here." Josh handed Leanne a pair of paper booties to cover her shoes. Leanne pulled them on and then followed him through the galley kitchen, where a sink overflowed with sour-smelling dishes. A pair of county CSIs in white Tyvek suits stood in the doorway of the minuscule bathroom lifting fingerprints from the mirror.

"Fellas? You mind?" Josh squeezed past them, and Leanne followed.

Most of the bedroom space was taken up by an unmade bed and a nightstand overflowing with beer bottles. Leanne stared at the rumpled bedding, which would be bagged up and sent to the lab for analysis. Had he brought any victims here? Or was his truck the primary crime scene?

Between the bed and the wall, the forensic photographer knelt on the linoleum floor. Mark—also in paper shoe covers—stood beside the man, peering over his shoulder.

A vent cover had been unscrewed from the floor, and the CSI was photographing a cigar box filled with miscellaneous items.

Leanne's skin went cold.

"This box was stashed in here," Josh said.

"What is that?" Mark leaned down. "That leather tube thingie?"

"A lipstick case," Leanne said.

Mark's eyebrows arched.

She crouched down for a better look as the CSI used a pair of tongs to sift through the items.

"Is that *hair*?" Mark asked.

"It is."

The chunk of dark hair was tied with fishing twine, and the CSI shifted it aside to reveal something beneath—what looked like a white leather wallet.

"What's that jewelry?" Josh said from behind her. "Go back to that."

The CSI used the tongs to nudge the wallet aside. A delicate chain caught the light. On it was a silver pendant shaped like a letter *A*.

Leanne looked over her shoulder at Josh.

"You know any A's?" he asked.

"I'll have to check the MP files." She looked at the box again. "There's something else tangled in there. Is that a bracelet?"

Beneath the wallet was yet another chain, this one with oval-shaped links.

"A charm bracelet," Leanne said. Her chest tightened with dread as she leaned closer. She glanced up at Mark. "You mind moving over? You're in the light."

He stepped aside, and Leanne got a better look at the silver bracelet. It had several charms on it—a heart, a volleyball, a horseshoe.

Leanne gasped.

"What is it?" Josh asked.

"Oh my God." She leaned closer to study the silver horseshoe, which had an *R* inside it.

"Leanne? What is it?"

"The bracelet." She looked up at Josh. "It belonged to Hannah Rawls."

FORTY-THREE

Leanne was late.
She yanked open the door of her truck and sloshed coffee all over her jeans.

"Crap!"

Dropping her duffel bag onto the driveway, she grabbed a napkin from the console to blot the spill.

Leanne glanced up as her brother's blue Kia clattered up the driveway, blocking her in. She checked the time as Ben slid from his car. She was due in El Paso at eleven, and this was the worst possible morning for her to sleep through her alarm.

"Hey," he said.

"Hey."

He walked over, cigarette in hand, and she shielded her face from the bright morning sun. It was one of those crisp blue days, perfect for speeding down the open highway and making good time. But now she was going to be too late even for that.

Ben stopped in front of her and leaned his hand on the truck. "That's a sick bruise."

"Thanks."

Her three-day-old shiner had turned a putrid shade of purple.

Ben didn't ask where it came from, but she figured he'd heard about it from their mom.

She tossed her duffel into the passenger seat.

"You headed out of town?" he asked.

"Yeah."

"Where?"

"El Paso."

He took a drag. "Why?"

"Work stuff."

He looked only mildly curious as she leaned in and tucked her insulated mug into the cup holder.

"What's up, Ben? I'm running really late, so—"

"Here." He pulled an envelope from his back pocket and handed it over.

"What's this?"

"Your money."

"I don't want it."

"Yeah, you do." He gave her a crooked smile that reminded her of ten-year-old Ben, and she felt a nostalgic pinch in her chest.

Leanne opened the envelope and thumbed through a stack of bills. Twelve hundreds.

"Jesus. What is this?"

"I told you. I found a good buyer." He tossed his cigarette away and folded his arms over his skinny body. He was in a T-shirt today, even though it was barely forty degrees.

Leanne looked at the cash, and a hot wave of resentment washed over her.

Her dad's LPs were gone. She didn't even like jazz, but she wanted the records more than she wanted any money. She probably would have tried to buy them herself if Ben had bothered to ask.

She looked at her brother. He was watching her reaction closely, as though he suddenly cared about what she thought.

"I'm leaving," he said.

"What do you mean?"

"I'm going to Austin with Izzy."

"Izzy who?"

"Huerta."

She blinked at him. "*My* Izzy?"

"She's not *your* anything."

Leanne stared at him. She had to have misunderstood, but his steady gaze told her that she hadn't.

Leanne's mind reeled. Ben and Izzy, a couple? She couldn't picture it. And, good God, he was going to screw up her life.

"What's in Austin?" she blurted.

"A job. It's full time with the PD there."

"You mean like—"

"She interviewed last fall, and they just now called her back." He tucked his hands into his front pockets. "She's excited about it. It's got full benefits, too, which is good because she's pregnant."

Leanne's mouth dropped open.

"Izzy and you . . ."

He crossed his arms and stuck his chin out defiantly. This was teenage Ben. Rebel Ben. The Ben who ditched school all the time and lied to their dad's face about it.

"I'm going to start looking for something there, too," he said. "We're getting a place together. That's what I needed the money for."

A choked laugh burst out.

"You're going to need a lot more than twelve hundred dollars! Are you out of your mind? You can't be a *parent*. You're barely out of rehab."

He muttered something and walked away.

Panic spurted through her.

"Wait!"

Ben was leaving. Izzy was leaving. Next, the ground would open up and suck her right under.

"Ben, *wait*."

He turned around and glared at her with those clear blue eyes.

Her father's eyes. They were exactly the same, and she felt another jolt of panic.

She stepped toward him. "You're really moving?"

"We need to get a fresh start." His bony shoulder lifted in a shrug. "She really wants this. And I want her to be happy, so . . ."

He trailed off, and Leanne stared at him. Her throat felt tight. For the last two years she'd battled this festering resentment over being dragged home after her father's death and all the sacrifices she'd made to work on the Madrone police force. She'd left her life behind to move back here for her family and help handle everyone's problems. It hadn't occurred to her that *they* might leave *her*.

"What is it?" Ben asked.

"I feel . . ." She coughed out a laugh. "God, some detective I am. She's really pregnant?"

He sighed. "She didn't want everyone to know, so . . ." He looked away uncomfortably. "Listen, I need to get going."

"Here." She shoved the envelope at him.

"That's yours."

"No. Take it. Are you kidding? Y'all are going to need it."

He took the envelope and tucked it into his pocket. Then he walked to his car, and she trailed behind him, watching numbly as her little brother slid behind the wheel. A pang of love pierced her heart.

She rested her hand on the door and gazed down at him. "You and Izzy. Wow."

He smiled shyly. "She's amazing," he said, and the look on his face put a lump in her throat. He was in love.

"What can I do for you?" she asked.

"We're good."

"I want to help. Please?"

He shook his head. "I'm not sure yet." He glanced up at her, looking wary and young and completely in over his head. "I'll let you know."

The adobe building sat between a laundromat and a resale shop on the west side of town. From the road it didn't look like much, and that was how people liked it. Most of the tourists drove right past it on their way to Shooters or the Javelina.

Leanne parked in the gravel lot out front and took a moment to take everything in. Paco's Pub. Her dad had frequented this place, which was why she didn't. She had only set foot inside once, to attend a going-away party for a Madrone EMT who had moved to Midland. It was a cop hangout, and she recognized more than a few of the pickups parked in the front row.

Leanne got out and crossed the gravel lot, mentally rehearsing what she wanted to say. She rubbed her palms on her jeans before opening the carved wood door.

Inside was warm and dim, and a couple of guys at the bar glanced over their shoulders as she stepped inside. She spotted several border agents she recognized, along with Glenn Meachum and Jim McBride. They occupied a corner of the bar, along with a third man in a camo puffer vest.

Leanne walked over, acutely aware of the curious looks she was getting from the regulars who had never seen her in here.

Meachum noticed her first and stopped talking.

She nodded at him, then looked at McBride, who clearly was surprised to see her at her dad's old watering hole.

"Sorry to interrupt, Chief. Could I talk to you a moment?"

McBride traded looks with the others. Then he grabbed his beer glass and glanced past her at some empty tables. "Sure."

"Thanks."

He slid from his stool.

"Mind if we sit outside?" she asked, nodding toward the back.

He arched his brows. "Fine by me." He grabbed the wooden bowl of peanuts on the bar. "This way," he said, leading her down a narrow hallway that smelled of stale beer.

The courtyard in back was nothing more than a patch of concrete underneath a few swags of lights, but most of the picnic tables were filled with people smoking and vaping. McBride led her to a table tucked against the cedar-slat fence.

"Sorry to bother you after hours," she said, taking a seat opposite McBride as he swung a leg over the bench.

"No problem." He dumped the peanuts on the ground and set the bowl on the table, then dug into his camo jacket for a pack of Marlboro Reds. He lit his cigarette and took a deep drag.

"What's up?" he asked contentedly through a stream of smoke.

"We've got a situation."

He lifted an eyebrow and ashed his cigarette into the bowl.

"I had a meeting with Frank Perrine," she said.

"The lawyer out of Houston." His brow furrowed as he took another drag. "Why were you talking to him?"

"I was hoping to get ahead of some things, sir. Specifically, what all he plans to put in his filing. I heard from a reporter that Perrine is filing his lawsuit tomorrow, and turns out that's true."

"So what? We expected that."

"Well, after talking to this attorney I'm pretty concerned about what's in the lawsuit."

He didn't say anything, just watched her through the haze of smoke.

"It sounds like Sean Moriarty plans to say my dad and you

coerced a confession from him during his questioning about Hannah Rawls. That you did it at gunpoint."

McBride reached over and ashed his cigarette again. "And?"

"And . . . doesn't that . . . alarm you, sir?"

"Not really. We knew this was coming."

"Well, what's the plan, if you don't mind my asking? See, *I'm* concerned that as soon as the press gets wind of this, it's going to destroy my father's reputation. Not to mention damage our credibility as a department."

McBride didn't look at her.

"Aren't you worried about the same?"

"I talked to our lawyer," he said, leveling a look at her across the table. "He thinks we can beat this thing. The guy's a known piece of shit, and it's his word against mine."

"You mean Sean Moriarty," she said.

He nodded.

"Well, I think the media scrutiny is going to be intense," she said. "They're going to put our whole department under a microscope."

He rolled his eyes. "That's already happened. What's your point?"

"I just wanted to get your assurance, sir, that you won't throw my dad to the wolves." She watched the chief's face. "I don't want to see his legacy ruined."

He took a long drag, then blew out a stream of smoke. "You know, if I were you, I wouldn't be worried about my dad's legacy right now. I'd be worried about my job."

She drew back. "How's that?"

He shook his head as he stubbed out his cigarette. "Insubordination. Ignoring orders from your superiors—"

"When did I—"

"*Stealing* property from the evidence room." He leaned forward. "You think I don't know you've been feeding evidence to your lover boy? You think I don't talk to the sheriff? That I don't know what's going on in my own department?"

"I didn't—"

"You're on thin ice, Everhart. If I were you, I'd be thinking about finding a way to keep from getting fired."

She leaned back. "So, are you planning to scapegoat him?"

His face flushed. "Evidently, you're not listening. So let me spell it out. I spent the last sixteen years *protecting* your father from his own mistakes. I've done all I can do, and this thing is bigger than me now."

She nodded. "So, that's it. You're going to scapegoat him. Say it was all him, that he acted alone."

"There's nothing more I can do now."

She watched the chief's cold gray eyes as a swarm of butterflies gathered in her stomach. She felt queasy. Sick over what she was about to do. Her throat went dry.

"I have the tape."

His eyebrows arched. "What tape?"

"It didn't burn up in the fire, if that was your intention."

He leaned closer, close enough for her to see the pink gin blossoms on his nose. "Just what do you think you're playing at?"

"I'm not playing," she said, and her voice sounded wobbly. "If you try to pin this thing on my father, I plan to go to the FBI."

His eyes drilled a hole in her, and she tried not to move or even blink. He eased back.

"You're not going to do that," he said.

"No?"

"No."

"Why not?"

The side of his mouth curled up, and he shook his head. "You forget that I watched you grow up. I watched you worship your daddy. I watched you spend your whole damn life trying to win his approval. You're not going to ruin his name now. It's *your* name. *Your* reputation, too. And going to the feds would be career suicide." He paused, watching her eyes closely, like he was trying to read her soul. "You know I'm right."

She swallowed.

"Come on, Everhart. Use your head. You've worked your whole life for a seat at the poker table. Now you've got a chip in the big-boy game, and you're going to play it."

She stayed stock-still, forcing herself to maintain eye contact. She didn't want to look away first. But she blinked. And in that instant, he knew that he had her.

He took a sip of beer and set the glass down. "Where's the tape?"

"Somewhere safe." She cleared her throat. "Not at my mom's."

He looked away for a long moment. Then he shook his head. "You know how old I am?"

The question surprised her. "Fifty-eight."

"Fifty-nine next month." He rubbed the white stubble on his chin. "I'm retiring next year. I'll be recommending Josh Cooper as my backfill. The town council listens to me, so it's going to go through." He paused. "I can recommend you for deputy chief."

She stared at him. "We don't have a deputy chief."

"We could. And it could be you." He nodded. "Think about that."

She watched his eyes, trying to gauge whether he was serious.

He drained his beer and plunked the glass on the table. Then he swung his legs over the bench and stood.

She looked up at him as he loomed over her like the giant he'd once been in her mind.

"I want that tape on my desk in the morning," he said. "And then we won't talk about this again."

"No."

His eyebrows arched.

"I don't want to wait a whole year," she said. "I want a promotion now."

Annoyance flashed in his eyes.

"Agree, and you can have the tape now." She pulled it from her jacket pocket and placed it on the table. It was an old-school cassette from a mini tape recorder. The word *Moriarty* was scrawled across the yellowed label.

She looked at McBride, and she could tell he itched to grab it. "Fine."

He picked up the tape and tucked it into his pocket. He gave her a long, cold look and then walked off.

She watched him go inside.

Then she followed, keeping her eyes straight ahead as she made her way down the narrow hallway and through the pub, watching from the corner of her eye as McBride reclaimed his place at the bar. She stepped outside again and strode to her truck.

She got behind the wheel, and a cold numbness overtook her as she pulled out of the parking lot and got on the highway.

Holy holy holy *shit*. What had she just done?

Up ahead, the DQ sign glowed. She pulled in and drove around back. She whipped into a space near the outdoor tables.

The same tables where Hannah Rawls had hung out with her friends on that long-ago summer night. She'd spent some of the last moments of her too-short life here.

The passenger door opened, and Sam slid inside. She wore jeans and hiking boots and a brown leather bomber jacket that Leanne remembered from their Dallas days.

Leanne backed out of the space.

"You okay?" Sam asked.

"No."

Leanne exited the parking lot. A Jeep loaded with teenagers swerved in front of her, and she jabbed the brakes and laid on the horn.

"Jesus!"

The Jeep peeled off with a squeal of tires.

She glanced at Sam as she tucked a tall cup into the console.

"I got you a Coke," Sam said. "Figured you'd need the caffeine."

Leanne got back on the highway and trained her gaze on the yellow lines. She glanced at her clock and did a double take.

Fifteen minutes.

That was how long it had taken to tear down the career she'd spent more than a decade building. The career she loved.

"Did you get all that?" She looked at Sam.

"Miguel said the audio was crystal clear."

Leanne pinched the bridge of her nose. She tried to focus on next steps, not on the thing she had just done. Next stop was the Madrone Motor Lodge, where the FBI had rented two adjoining rooms to use as a staging area. More than a dozen members of the Bureau's public integrity section were in on tonight's operation.

Sam's phone buzzed, and she picked it up. "Hi."

Leanne heard a male voice on the other end, presumably Miguel, Sam's husband.

"Yeah, we're on our way," she said.

Leanne grabbed the drink from the cupholder and took a long sip to cool her parched throat. Her leather jacket felt heavy, and the T-shirt underneath was plastered to her skin with sweat. She took a deep breath and tried to calm down.

She had broken the unspoken oath to protect her fellow officers, betraying her department. Even though she'd done the right thing, the result was going to be painful and permanent.

"Okay, got it." Sam hung up and looked at her. "We're all good. Our agents are leaving the bar now."

Leanne nodded.

"You all right? You look a little pale."

"I'm just . . . kind of in disbelief."

"I get it."

Anger flared inside her. Sam didn't get it. She couldn't because she had a job to wake up to tomorrow.

Leanne glanced at her. "I'll never work again. Not as a cop, anyway. And definitely not here. They'll circle the wagons, like they did with Uvalde. I've seen it before."

Sam sighed and looked ahead. "I know. But look at it this way. You can—"

The phone buzzed again, and Sam grabbed it. "Yeah?"

The voice sounded urgent now, and Leanne glanced at her.

"What do you mean?" Sam paused. Then she looked at Leanne. "Who was he with?"

"McBride? You mean back at the bar?"

"Yeah."

"He was with Glenn Meachum, the fire chief," Leanne said. "And Glenn's brother-in-law. Why?"

Sam relayed the info and then looked at Leanne.

"All of them left, but McBride's vehicle is still in the lot." Sam got back on the phone. "Did they check inside? What about the bathrooms?"

A black pickup passed them on the highway, and Leanne glanced at the rearview mirror.

"That's him. Sam, *that's him.*"

"What?"

"We just passed McBride. He's in Meachum's black F-150, right back there."

FORTY-FOUR

Sam turned in her seat to look back. "Are you sure?"

"Yes!"

"Was he alone?"

"I think so. I only saw one person in the front seat."

"Miguel, listen, we just passed McBride on the highway in his friend's truck." She glanced around. "Where the hell are we?"

"Tell him we're on Route 12." Leanne watched the rearview mirror, waiting for the truck to disappear over a rise in the highway. When it did, she hit the brakes. "And tell him we're now southbound."

Leanne pulled a U-turn, slinging them around, as Sam braced her hand on the dashboard.

"Slow down! He'll see you," Sam said.

"No, he won't."

Leanne sped over the rise. Meachum's truck was miles ahead, a distant pair of red taillights.

"Don't let him notice you," Sam said.

"I won't."

Sam went back and forth with Miguel and his team, but Leanne wasn't listening. She was trying to figure out what McBride's plan was.

Sam got off the phone. "He must have made one of the undercover agents in the bar and realized it was a setup."

"I think it was me."

Sam frowned at her. "Why? You were perfect."

"I should have resisted more. Made him talk me into it." She pounded her fist on the wheel. "*Damn*, I blew it."

"Not yet."

The F-150 made a sharp right turn, and Leanne fought the urge to tap the brakes. She maintained her speed as she watched the truck stop at a gate.

"Where's he going?" Sam asked.

"I don't know."

Sam texted on her phone, and Leanne watched, not slowing, as the truck rolled through the gate. Leanne kept going, watching in the rearview mirror until the black pickup disappeared out of sight.

"Hold on," Leanne muttered.

She pulled another U-turn, hoping McBride hadn't noticed he was being followed.

"I'm looking at a map, but where are we? Nothing's labeled," Sam said.

"We're at the back of a nature preserve." Leanne neared the turnoff and slowed. "It used to be a cattle ranch, but now it's public land. Forty-two hundred acres. This is the northernmost access road."

"How do you know all that?"

"I just do."

Leanne made a sharp turn and pulled up to the gate, which had a sign posted: AUTHORIZED VEHICLES ONLY. No padlock, but there was a keypad mounted on a metal pole with a solar panel.

"Perfect," Sam said. "Any chance you know the code, too?"

Leanne threw it in reverse and looked over her shoulder.

"What are you doing?"

"Hold on."

"Leanne, what the—holy *crap*!"

She punched the gas and burst through the gate, sending it flying off its hinges with a loud *pop!*

"Are you crazy?"

She slowed and took a moment to get her bearings. It was a narrow dirt road, and there weren't any lights or buildings visible at all, just flat scrub brush.

"Tell Miguel to hurry, okay? I think I know what he's doing."

Sam sent a message on her phone. "They're on their way," she said. "About ten minutes out."

"They need to come faster."

"What—"

"This property abuts Highway 67. From there it's a straight shot to the Presidio border crossing."

Sam gaped at her. "You really think he'd—"

"If he thinks he's about to be arrested by the FBI? Hell, yes."

Sam got on her phone as Leanne scanned the surrounding area. No hint of headlights anywhere, and she tried to remember the topography of the place. The east side sloped down to a dried-up creek bed, and there was a low-water bridge somewhere out here. But Leanne hadn't been here since the fall, when she'd helped a game warden with a poaching bust.

Leanne stopped and pulled up a map on her phone. She stared down at it, heart pounding, as she tried to put herself in McBride's head.

He had to be desperate to try this. Which meant he'd figured out just how much trouble he was in.

Leanne switched off the headlights, then turned on just the yellow running lights. It was barely enough to see by, but she'd have to go with it.

She veered off the dirt road, and they bounced over the uneven terrain.

"Leanne, you're scaring me."

"Relax, we're okay," she said, trying to project confidence she didn't feel. This meticulously planned operation was falling apart, all because of her.

Leanne's palms felt slick on the steering wheel. This was a bad situation, and rapidly getting worse. McBride was armed and dangerous. And he knew that if he didn't escape now, his life was about to becoming a living hell.

The truck pitched forward as they hit a dip, and Sam braced her hand on the dash again.

"Sorry." Leanne looked at her. "Better hold on."

Leanne drove as fast as she could without being able to see more than ten feet past the hood.

"Miguel's texting for an update," Sam said. "They're five minutes out."

"Tell him we're cutting across the park, hoping to intercept him before he reaches the western access gate. Hold on!"

The truck lurched down, then back up again as they hit a ravine. Leanne focused on driving. Sweat slid down her neck. They bounced along over ruts and ridges as Leanne's teeth clattered and Sam made little yelps from the passenger seat. Leanne consulted her phone, and the blue beacon told her they were nearing the western edge of the property.

"Careful!"

Leanne swerved around a giant boulder that would have taken out her truck. "Sorry!"

She hit another rut, and then plowed over a few prickly pears. She swung around and slammed to a stop.

Leanne buzzed the windows down and switched off the running lights.

"Where are we?" Sam asked.

"Blocking the gate. Put your phone away."

"But—"

"It's making a glow. Put it away!"

Sam stuffed the phone into her pocket, and they sat still in the quiet hum of the idling truck engine.

"Should I—"

"Shh!" Leanne looked over her shoulder. "You hear that?"

"No."

"Listen."

A low rumble neared them, gradually getting louder.

"Where the hell is he? Why don't I see any lights?"

"*Crap!*"

"What is it?" Sam asked.

"He's running dark. I think he knows he was followed."

The noise got louder and louder, until it was almost a roar. Still no lights.

"We have to get out," Leanne yelled. "Now! Now! Now!"

They flung the doors open and dove from the pickup. Leanne hit the ground hard and log-rolled into something sharp.

A horn blared, then an earsplitting crash of metal on metal. The deafening screech echoed through her head as she tried to make out the wreckage in the darkness.

An interior light went on as McBride shoved open his door. He swatted away an airbag and stumbled out, cursing. The F-150 had T-boned her pickup.

McBride looked around, dazed, and Leanne could barely see him in the light spilling from the truck cab. He took a few staggering steps, then reached for the holster at his waist.

"FBI! Drop your weapon!" Sam's voice came from the other side of the wreckage.

Leanne tripped to her feet, then went down on one knee as her ankle turned. "Shit!"

McBride took off running.

Leanne scrambled after him, yanking her gun from the holster as she tore through the brush. She grabbed the mini Maglite from her pocket and switched it on. The narrow beam barely penetrated the darkness, but she followed it, gasping for breath as she plowed through the scrub trees.

"Stop! FBI!"

Another beam lit up the dirt beside her, and she heard Sam rustling through the brush nearby.

Leanne tripped over a cactus and kept going. Something snagged her jacket, and she yanked it free.

The two white beams bobbled unevenly as they stumbled through the bushes. Leanne clutched her flashlight in one hand and her weapon in the other as she tried to navigate. Up ahead, she heard rhythmic panting, like a coyote loping through the woods. They were gaining on him.

A flash of blue caught her eye. Leanne sprinted ahead and made a leaping tackle.

They landed hard together. Her flashlight was knocked loose, but she managed to hang on to her gun. Her shoulder was on fire as she wrestled one-handed with the man beneath her.

"FBI! You're under arrest!"

Suddenly it was two on one, wrestling in the dark, with Sam's flashlight beam shining into the grass nearby. Sam managed to flip McBride onto his belly, and Leanne scrambled up and stomped on his wrist. He yowled in pain as she grabbed his loose pistol.

"Cover me," Sam yelled, yanking out a pair of handcuffs.

Leanne stepped back and aimed her weapon at McBride as he squinted up at her with his face in the dirt.

"What the *fuck* do you think you're doing?"

Sam slapped on the handcuffs. "You're under arrest."

"You crazy bitch! Do you know who I am?"

Leanne stared down at the dusty, spitting man. The sleeve of his jacket was torn, and the ear of a prickly pear cactus clung to his back.

Sirens sounded faintly in the distance. Leanne lowered her gun and stepped back, gasping for breath.

She'd just arrested the chief of police.

He rolled onto his side, away from her, cursing and squirming as the sirens drew nearer. Still panting, Leanne holstered her pistol and stepped back, eyes glued to McBride as the sirens wailed and the diesel engines got closer. Then lights were everywhere, making everything bright white as SUVs thundered up to the scene.

Agents jumped out, weapons drawn, and rushed over.

Leanne unhooked her badge and lifted it into the air as agents swarmed around her. Over the chaos, Sam made eye contact.

"Leanne!"

She turned around to see Miguel striding toward her, radio in hand.

"You're bleeding," he said.

Leanne looked herself over. Something warm trickled down her cheek and she touched her chin.

"You okay?" Miguel beamed a flashlight into her face, and she blinked down at her bloody fingers.

"I have no idea."

FORTY-FIVE

Leanne followed the croon of Linda Ronstadt to the tack room, which smelled of wood chips and leather cleaner. Bridles and harnesses hung from a pegboard. Her mother's phone sat in the center of the desk beside a vase of pink tulips.

"Mom?"

Leanne grabbed an apple from a basket and walked to the farthest stall, where she found her mother with Starlight. She leaned her head against the mare's nose and spoke in the soothing voice she reserved for horses and babies.

"Mom."

She turned around. "Hi. I didn't hear you come in. What in *God's* name happened to your face?"

Leanne touched her forehead. "I conked my head during an arrest last night."

Her mom stepped closer, frowning as she studied the gash.

"How many stitches is that?"

"Ten. It's no big deal."

"No big *deal*? It looks horrible."

Leanne approached the horse and held the apple flat in her hand. Starlight's lips tickled her palm as she chomped the fruit.

"Are the flowers from Boone?" she asked.

"From Ben." Her mother beamed. "He sent them for my birthday."

Leanne couldn't remember the last time her brother had remembered anyone's birthday. Maybe he was maturing. Or maybe he needed something. Either way it was progress.

"So, what brings you here?" Her mom grabbed the curry brush from the wooden ledge. "Sounds like you've been busy."

"I have a few updates."

Her mom made circular strokes over the horse's chestnut coat, moving from shoulder to flank. She glanced up. "I'm listening."

"Jim McBride is being arraigned this morning."

She stopped. "You're kidding."

"He was implicated in a bribe-taking scheme, along with some others."

"Who?"

"I can't say yet."

One of the others was Ron Hausmann, a current judge and former Chisos County district attorney.

The day after Justin Carr's arrest at the yucca farm, a pair of FBI agents had shown up at Leanne's house to debrief her about the case. They had also informed her that Hausmann was under investigation for bribery. As part of a plea agreement, he had implicated Jim McBride in numerous illegal incidents, including the time when he used a loaded gun and death threats to coerce a false confession from nineteen-year-old Sean Moriarty. As the then county prosecutor, Hausmann had been in the room during the interrogation.

So had Leanne's dad.

"You don't look surprised," Leanne said.

Her mom traded the curry brush for a soft brush and started on Starlight's legs. "I'm not."

"So, I have a question." Leanne folded her arms. "Did you know Dad went to the Texas Rangers with his tape?"

She stopped. "What tape?"

"The original of the one you had, the tape of Sean Moriarty being interrogated."

"When was this?"

Leanne studied her mom's expression. She looked genuinely surprised. She must have believed the cassette she'd discovered after her husband's death had been the only one. But it had been a copy.

"The year after the trial," Leanne said. "Dad took it to the Rangers' Public Integrity Unit."

This, Leanne had learned from the FBI agent who'd been leading an investigation of high-ranking local officials for the past ten months.

"I didn't know." Her mom rubbed her forearm over her brow. "Can't say I'm surprised, though. He probably couldn't live with the guilt of it. What happened?"

"Someone over there buried the report," Leanne said. She didn't know who, but she could tell the FBI did. "Nothing came out until they were investigating another public official, and this person offered to give up what he knew about the Moriarty thing as part of a plea deal."

Her mom tipped her head to the side. "'Another public official'? Let me guess. Ron Hausmann?"

Leanne lifted an eyebrow.

"That man always was a weasel. McBride, too."

Her mom scooted around her and started brushing Starlight's neck.

The wrongful conviction of Sean Moriarty very easily could have stayed secret forever. For sixteen long years, McBride had buried it. Hausmann had buried it. The Rangers had buried it. Every step of the way, people in power had protected one another and run from accountability. If it weren't for Sean and his enterprising lawyer, there would have been no reckoning. Sean would have spent the rest of his life rotting in prison and a serial murderer might still be free.

"You need to be prepared," Leanne said. "There's a story running in a major newspaper tomorrow, and when all this comes out, there'll be reporters sniffing around."

Her mom scoffed. "What? More than now? They're all over town. You can't hardly go to the gas station."

"Probably even more."

"How do you know all this, anyway?"

"I've heard."

And she had talked to the reporter personally. Max Scott's two-page spread was set to run in the morning. Even without Leanne's help, the reporter had managed to dig up most of the salient facts, and the rest were sure to come out eventually.

"You'd better be careful who you talk to." Her mother gave her a sharp look. "Someone could come after you."

"I'm careful."

She shook her head. "I swear, Leanne."

"What?"

She shot her a glare. "What do you mean, 'what'? Look at your face! You're all beat up. You walk around every day looking *dead* tired. You have no man. No personal life. I truly wonder why you do this job." She paused. "Why do you?"

"I'm good at it."

Her mom blew out a sigh. Starlight nudged her with her nose, and she stroked the white star on her forehead.

"So much like your father." Her mom turned to face her. "He was so damn stubborn, wouldn't ever let anything go."

"Could you not bad-mouth him right now, please? I've heard enough disappointing shit about him lately."

"I'm sure some of it's true," her mom said. "But . . . I will *also* tell you that he tried to do right. That whole thing with that confession wasn't his doing. He just witnessed it. Your father had flaws, but he also had a good heart."

"Tell that to Sean Moriarty."

She set the brush down and gave Leanne a long, pensive look. "You sound cynical."

"I am."

"It's like I said, that job of yours is a hell on good people. It chews you up and spits you out." She paused. "Sure you don't want to change careers?"

"What do you hear from Ben?" Leanne asked, switching the subject.

"Talked to him last night." Her mom grabbed another brush from the ledge. "He wanted me to cosign the lease for his apartment with Isabella."

Leanne looked through the door at the sloping ranchland, aglow with the morning sun. It was so quiet out here that you could walk for miles without seeing another person. She thought of Ben showing up in traffic-choked Austin with no job and a head full of dreams.

"I can't believe he's going to be a father," her mom mused. "He's barely been out of rehab three months."

"One hundred and four days."

She looked up. "You're counting?"

Leanne shrugged. "I worry about him. And I worry he's not ready."

Her mom laughed.

"What? Do *you* think he's ready?"

She smiled. "Of course he isn't! You think *I* was ready? Or your father? Hell no." She walked over and softly patted Leanne's cheek. "No one ever is."

FORTY-SIX

Leanne parked and looked out at the canyon. She didn't really have time for this, but she'd promised herself and she'd broken enough commitments lately.

"So, that's today's bombshell," Sam told her over the phone.

There had been so many bombshells lately, Leanne could barely keep track. The latest news involved the fire chief.

"Okay, well, if you hear about anything happening at the sheriff's office, give me a heads-up," Leanne said. "Our work overlaps with them, and I don't want to step on any land mines."

"You got it," Sam said. "Talk to you soon."

Clicking off, Leanne slid from the shiny new pickup she'd rented while hers was in the shop. She guzzled some water down and tossed the bottle into the passenger seat. Then she bent over and plucked sticker burrs from the laces of her running shoes.

Tires on gravel made her look up as a black Silverado rumbled up the road. Leanne's pulse quickened. She leaned against her door and folded her leg back, stretching her quads.

Duncan parked by the trailhead sign and got out.

"Hey," she said.

He slammed the door and tromped over. He wore a T-shirt and brown tactical pants, and his boots were coated with dust.

"You coming or going?" he asked.

"Just got here." She switched legs, stretching the other one behind her. "Want to join me?"

"No."

He rested his hands on his hips and looked her over.

"I got your message," he said.

"I was going to come by your house later."

"Saw you here and thought I'd save you the trip." He stepped closer. "We can get it over with."

"Get what over with?"

He paused a beat. "You're leaving, right?"

Her chest squeezed. "Where'd you hear that?"

"Come on, Leanne."

She clicked the locks with a *chirp* and zipped the key fob into her belt bag.

She looked up, and Duncan was watching her with that steely gaze. He was spoiling for a fight, and she didn't blame him. She'd been dodging him for days now.

"Things have gotten bad at work," she told him.

Bad was an understatement. In the six days since Jim McBride's arrest, the FBI had shown up and raided his office. Same for the fire chief's. As of this morning, McBride was sitting in jail, after being denied bail, and according to the phone call Leanne had just had with Sam, Glenn Meachum had been charged with three counts of bribery. That didn't even count the other potential charges related to him testifying falsely against Sean Moriarty. Evidently, Meachum had been the "off-duty firefighter" who claimed to have seen Sean's car leaving the scene where Hannah Rawls's body was found.

The whole thing was a debacle that implicated multiple local officials from multiple agencies. The Chisos County Sheriff's Office hadn't been hit yet, but there were rumors flying that they could be next.

Some people blamed Ron Hausmann for ratting out his lifelong friends. Some people blamed McBride—the bad apple that had spoiled the bunch.

Others blamed Leanne. As a relative newcomer *and* someone whose father was involved, she made a fair target.

"I'm not leaving," she said.

Duncan squinted. "No?"

"No. That's not why I called."

"Oh." His shoulders relaxed a fraction. "What is it, then? It sounded important."

She tightened her ponytail and crossed her arms over her chest. "I wanted to see if you wanted to go to dinner with me."

"*Go* to dinner." He leaned forward. "What, like a date?"

"Yeah."

"In public?"

"Yeah."

He looked blank.

"If you don't want to be seen with—"

"No, no," he said. "I'm just—I thought you wanted to keep it casual. No strings, no gossip, and all that."

"Yeah, well." She shrugged. "I've decided I don't care what people say anymore."

"You don't care," he stated, and the side of his mouth curved up.

"That's right."

He stepped closer and slid his hand around her waist. "It's about fucking time."

"So, you're in?"

"I'm in. You mean like tonight?"

"Sure."

"Name the place. I'm *all* in." He pulled her against him. "Or we could just stay home."

"I want dinner first. I'll be hungry." She eased back, and he released her. "Give me two hours. I have some stuff to do."

He looked skeptical again. "Something's up. What is it?"
"What do you mean?"
"I know you."
She held his gaze for a long moment. "We'll talk about it later."
She went up on tiptoes and kissed him, then set off on the trail. Gravel crunched behind her as he drove out of the lot.

As of today, Duncan was one of the few cops who was still talking to her. Josh Cooper was, too. And Mark Rodriguez. Yes, plenty of people hated her—including Nadine, who hadn't spoken to her all week. Leanne was getting the cold shoulder from half the uniforms in her department and even some of the fire and EMT guys. Last night she'd come home to find the word *BITCH* graffitied in fluorescent orange across her front door.

This morning she'd borrowed a can of paint from Michelle and painted over it. Then she'd gone to work, where she'd gotten another surprise when Josh, who had been appointed acting police chief, pulled her into his new office and offered her a promotion. Deputy chief of police. And Leanne would get a chance to help hire her backfill. The job was hers if she wanted it. After overcoming her initial speechless shock, she told him she'd think about it.

That was nine this morning, and she'd thought of almost nothing else since.

Leanne focused on the trail and picking her footing on the uneven rocks. She hadn't been out here all week, and she felt it in the way her lungs started to burn before she made it to the third switchback. She increased her pace, punishing herself, as the trail sloped up. A cramp bit into her side, but she ignored it, focusing instead on the steep terrain. After pushing and pushing, she made it to the overlook.

Leanne stopped, gasping for breath. To her left was a huge boulder—Eagle Rock. And to her right was the peeling orange madrone with its twisty limbs. Her heart squeezed as she thought of her dad bringing her up here when she was a child.

Still catching her breath, she looked out. The sun was sinking over the bluffs, coloring the cliffs pink and lavender. A purple shadow to the south marked the deep gorge where water had cut through layers and layers of rock.

Tears burned her eyes as she thought of him again. What would he have said to the Rawls family now? And to Alma Cruz, who was still waiting for news of her missing daughter? Leanne had talked to Alma repeatedly in recent days as word spread about the serial killer in Chisos County who had been hiding in plain sight all this time. Leanne could tell from Alma's eyes that she understood. She knew that when the forensic evidence came together, the hope she'd been keeping alive for years likely would be snuffed out forever.

How many other families would get word soon that their missing daughter or sister was never coming home? The question haunted Leanne. With the recent advances in DNA, it was only a matter of time before all those unidentified remains Jen Sayers had processed in her laboratory could be given a name.

The question that haunted her most, though—the one that jolted her awake in the middle of the night—was a different one: How many of those victims would be alive right now if someone had acted sooner? If only someone had done the right thing, instead of the easy thing, way back in the beginning.

Wiping her eyes, Leanne stared out over the vast canyon. The beauty of this place always got to her. The ruthlessness, too. She followed the ribbon of highway where years ago she'd set out on her long trip north, so determined to escape this place and the ties that were strangling her.

She'd been so focused back then. She'd had a goal, a mission. Things had looked so clear in the beginning. Leave it to her hometown to muddle everything up. In some ways, Madrone was just like her family—conflicted, flawed, dysfunctional. But they were stuck with one another, for better or for worse, swept up in the same strong current and forced to swim together.

She thought of Jim McBride leaning back in that chair in his office. He and others had told her justice was complicated. But it wasn't. On this *one* thing at least, Leanne agreed with Max Scott and the reporters who'd been covering their story with thinly veiled outrage.

There was right and wrong. It was that simple. There were lines, and people had crossed them.

Her father had.

And the fallout from what had happened on that hot July day in that stuffy interview room was still going on sixteen years later.

People felt betrayed. Their trust was broken. And working without trust—not to mention basic cooperation—made her job infinitely harder. It wasn't just Leanne's problem now—it was Josh's, too, and Mark's, and Duncan's, and everyone who wore a badge. Every cop out here was facing blowback now, and the news just kept coming. Local law enforcement was strained enough already, dealing with immigration and the pressures of tourism and the messy politics of it all. And now they had shattered trust to deal with on top of everything. Restoring people's faith was going to be a long, hard slog, if it could even be done at all. Sometimes things were lost, and there was no getting them back.

Leanne unzipped her pack and took out her phone. She paused for a moment, giving herself one last chance to reach a different conclusion. She took a deep breath and made the call.

"Yeah."

"Hey, Coop, it's me."

"I know."

She pictured Josh at the chief's old desk, neck-deep in problems and paperwork, drowning in his new role and desperate for a lifeline.

"About our conversation earlier—" She cleared her throat. "I'd like to accept."

No response. Leanne waited, holding her breath as the seconds ticked by.

And then finally: "Good."

Good. So much relief, and confidence, packed into that one little word.

She smiled. "Okay, then."

"Thanks, Everhart. I'll see you at work."

She ended the call and tipped her head back to look at the sky as emotions washed over her. She looked out at the canyon again. On the far horizon, feathery gray clouds gave way to a burgeoning thunderhead.

Leanne got back on the trail, picking up her pace. She needed to finish before the cloudburst.

ACKNOWLEDGMENTS

Each book is a labor of love, and I'm so grateful to the many people who helped bring this one to life. Thank you to the incredible team at Berkley, especially Kerry Donovan, for her brilliant editing, and Claire Zion, for her vision and insights. Also, thank you to my first reader and trusted agent, Kevan Lyon. A heartfelt thanks to the knowledgeable and patient rangers at Big Bend National Park, who answered my questions, along with all the dedicated NPS workers who keep our parks running. You are a national treasure. Thank you to my dear friends Laurie and Lynn, for the many (mostly) fun campouts and adventures. A special thanks to my longtime friends Melva and Dina for the West Texas research help, along with my author friend Julia London, who is always up for brainstorming plot ideas over pancakes.

I'm so thankful for the booksellers, librarians, and reviewers who help connect books and readers. And thank you to the readers, who inspire me with their messages. You keep me digging deeper with every story.

And finally, a special thanks to my big, wonderful family, for giving me so much encouragement over the years. Last, but certainly not least, to Doug, Meg, and Em—I love you beyond words.